FULL CIRCLE

The American Civil War was a bloody conflict which cost more lives in four years than the two World Wars, Korea, and Vietnam added together. Approximately one hundred and eighty six thousand black soldiers served valiantly in the conflict, but no black person was allowed to rise above the rank of Sergeant. This is black slave Joshua D's story. He tells of his escape from slavery on John Franklyn's estate in North Carolina and how he became a soldier and, later, a Sergeant, in the Union Army.

Books by Clifford H. Fry
Published by The House of Ulverscroft:

NORTH TO ABILENE
OUTLAWED!
AND A WOLF WAS BORN

CLIFFORD H. FRY

---◆---

FULL CIRCLE

Complete and Unabridged

ULVERSCROFT
Leicester

First published in Great Britain in 2001

First Large Print Edition
published 2006

The moral right of the author has been asserted

British Library CIP Data

Fry, Clifford H. (Clifford Henry), *1927 –*
Full circle.—Large print ed.—
Ulverscroft large print series: general fiction
1. Fugitive slaves—United States—Fiction
2. United States—History—Civil War, *1861 – 1865*
—African Americans—Fiction 3. Large type books
I. Title
823.9′14 [F]

ISBN 1–84617–135–0

Published by
F. A. Thorpe (Publishing)
Anstey, Leicestershire

Set by Words & Graphics Ltd.
Anstey, Leicestershire
Printed and bound in Great Britain by
T. J. International Ltd., Padstow, Cornwall

This book is printed on acid-free paper

Acknowledgements

I could not have written this book without the aid of the following excellent books.

With grateful thanks to Octopus Publishing Group Ltd for their kind permission to use the map from page 115 of Phillips New World Atlas (7th edition).

Douglas Welsh's Complete Military History of the American Civil War. Philip Haythornthwaite's Uniforms of the Civil War, which also includes the battles, types of weapons and a host of other useful information. Books One to Twenty-four of Collier's Encyclopedia, and some very helpful librarians.
    To you all I offer my grateful thanks.

In addition, I offer my very special thanks to Elizabeth Roberts and Audrey Harvey, who read everything, offered a wealth of advice, and help of every kind.

And finally:
To my dear wife, Enid, who had to read every word at least three times. My sincere and most grateful thanks my darling.
Clifford H. Fry

Grant's seige
of Richmond
a   ⊕ Richmond

...rsburg

...tte

North Carolina

Carolina

...harleston

ATLANTIC OCEAN

NOTES

This map is for information only and the author cannot guarantee its correctness regarding size, scale etc; it is only included so that the purist can follow the fictional travels of Joshua D. It also indicates part of the reason for the title:

FULL CIRCLE.

Other Notes:

1/ West Virginia was not so named until 1863 so it is shown in the story as Virginia.

2/ At the time of the Civil War Winston and Salem were two towns.

The factual 'March Through Georgia' is indicated by the heavy black line. The route travelled by the fictional character of Joshua D is shown by the hatched line.

Although this story is set within the American Civil War period, it is not essentially a war story, but a fictional tale within a factual war.

SOME HISTORICAL FACTS.

The bloodiest war ever!

A conflict that cost more lives in its four bloody years than the two World Wars, Korea, and Vietnam added together.

We can only thank God that the Gatling Gun was not given serious consideration by the North, simply because the inventor was a Southerner, which made the North deeply suspicious of his motives.

The estimated terrible toll of the dead and wounded on both sides is given as over 1,200,000 The 'March through Georgia' was notorious because of its 'Scorched Earth Policy'. A policy that split the Southern States in two, laying waste by burning a sixty mile wide swath through the country.

However, my tale is about the progress of one black slave who became a soldier and, later, a Sergeant, in the Union Army. His name: Joshua D.

Many people are completely unaware that approximately 186,000 black soldiers served valiantly and well in the conflict, but no black person was allowed to rise above the rank of Sergeant. All ranks above were white.

It was intended that I should write this story from a third person's point of view, but Joshua D had other ideas, so I thought: To hell with it! It's his Goddamned story so let him write it.

Yeah. Right! It's my story. OK? So let's cut the palaver and get down to business. Maybe my use of the American language ain't so hot, but I'll get there, and you can bet a stack on that.

Now, let me take you back to when I first broke away from my days of slavery, on Mister John Franklyn's estate in North Carolina . . .

1

I was running. Man, how I was running! The rain was beating down something awful. I was bone cold and as hungry as a bear coming out'a hibernation.

Somewhere behind me, there were men with dogs. They wanted me real bad, and it showed how my safe little world had changed over the past three years.

The small creek I'd been running in for the last half hour or so, to put the dogs off my track, petered out as I cut into the timbered country. My thin shirt and pants had given up on the idea of keeping out the rain within the first two minutes. I needed somewhere warm and dry, where those damned dogs wouldn't find me, to rest my aching body for a while.

A jumble of rocks led me into a small valley of scrub oak and cottonwood. Pushing aside a big bunch of choke-weed, I found my haven. A tiny cave in the hillside. So small a man had to belly-crawl into it.

Hoping to God there were no varmints using it, I pushed my way inside. There was a lump of rock in my hand, just in case, but I'd stand no chance against a cottonmouth.

Luck was on my side. No one was at home except little old me, so I curled up into as small a ball as possible, steaming like a turkey gobbler in a stewpot as my body began to feel the benefit of being out of that icy downpour. My dry throat started to ease a little and the sobbing gasps began to cut back to something easier to handle without choking.

The smoky tiredness of exhaustion gradually took over my aching limbs. Guess I must have dozed off because my mind started to carry me back ... back to the cotton plantation where my life had begun some seventeen summers ago. It had seemed so good back then in North Carolina ...

2

They called me Joshua D. My daddy was proud of the fact that he could cipher. He'd been named Joshua, by Mister Franklyn, and when his first son was born, he'd asked Mister John — that's what my daddy called him — if he could name his sons Joshua also. Well, he'd just laughed and said, 'Sure thing, but make sure we can tell the difference between 'em, like A, or B, OK?' So, my daddy called us all Joshua.

Joshua A was the eldest. I never knew him; he was sold to a passing wagoner heading towards Texas. My second brother, Joshua B, died of the fever, and Joshua C was snake-bit. I missed him for quite a while after he died.

But my daddy! Now there was a man! I remember looking up at him from where I was playing in the dirt one time. Tall as the tallest tree, that's what he seemed to be to me in his gray colored shorts. He never wore anything else come rain or shine. He looked as solid an' hard as black oak, with a kind'a gloss to his skin like it'd been burnished with steel chain. His legs were thicker around than my whole body, and shoulders so wide you wouldn't believe! He had a solid, clean-looking face, like it was carved out of rock, and when he lifted me so high in the air that the breath near caught in my throat, I could see the close-cut black curly hair with a sprinkling of white, like frost on a winter's morning.

Yeah, a strong, stern-looking man was my daddy, but then he'd smile, and it seemed like the sun had come out from behind a cloud. His face would soften and two big dents would show up on his cheeks. I was told they were called dimples or some-such thing and, as time went by, I learned that those dents sure made the womenfolk go all a-twittery an' no mistake.

You could say we were lucky to be slaves on Mister John Franklyn's cotton plantation, as lucky as slaves were ever likely to be. He wasn't like some owners who kept their people in terrible conditions and beat them, sometimes just for the fun of it.

Mister Franklyn treated us like real folks. We never went short on grub, and he'd often come out with my daddy in the buggy and chat to one or two of us as they made their way around the estate.

Our family was rather special because my daddy was in charge of the whole shebang. Mister Franklyn didn't believe in overseers with whips n' stuff. He was always laughing and joking with us like we was a proper family.

My special friend was young Master Luke. He was a year younger than me, but I was big for my age so Mister Franklyn was happy to let us play together as we grew up. Luke was kind'a small and spindly. I felt quite proud when Mister Franklyn took me aside one day and said that he relied on lil' ol' me to keep Master Luke safe from harm. And I did too!

One time his brother, Matthew, who was always a bit of a bully, threw Luke into the pond and ran off. Luke's head had hit a rock, leaving him out cold, so I'd dived in and dragged him out of there, picked him up like a baby and ran all the way back to the big house with him over my shoulder. It was only then I realized that I was creeping up on Pa. Near up to his shoulder, and me only thirteen or so at the time.

I was a real hero that day all right. At least I thought I was when they took me right into the big house. I didn't realize then how saving Master Luke's life that day was gonna change my own.

Man! That house was big! Biggest I'd ever seen in all my born days. Mind you, it had to be, from what I'd seen of the outside, but if anyone had told me just how big I'd have called 'em a liar, straight out.

I'd never been close up to Mistress Emily Franklyn before, or her daughter Norah either, though I'd seen them both from the bottom of the garden lots of times and Mistress Emily seemed to drift up and down the flowerbeds as if she was floating on air. Always dressed in white she was, and so slight my daddy could have put his two hands around her waist and touched his fingers together with no trouble at all. Close up, the smell of gardenias from the garden seemed to be all around her. So dainty and fluffy. She made me think of one of them dandelion seeds when they're floating around looking for some place to settle.

Well she bustled me off to her bedroom like a mother hen with a chick although I towered over her. She was tut-tutting about my wet clothes 'n' stuff all the while. Couldn't see why she was so all fired het up about it myself, I was mostly wet all the time in winter anyway, but she put her tiny arm around me and I was already on my way before I could tell her anything. Miss Norah was following close behind, carrying a big towel and a pair of shorts she'd gotten from somewhere. Made me kind'a worried about her, she being about seventeen an' all. Well, a fella does get his feelings.

Anyway, they stripped me off in no time at all, and Mistress Emily began rubbing my back down in this warm towel while Miss Norah was standing in front eyeing me up and down. She seemed to be having a bit of trouble, breathing all gusty-like she was. Then her ma came around the front, beginning to wipe me there too! And God help me. I felt a stirring in my loins as she knelt down and began to wipe my legs. It was a feeling I'd been getting of late if a young woman happened to be bending over picking cotton in the fields. Well like I said, my body was growing fast for my age.

I was scared of what was happening to me. Scared Mistress Emily would screech out for Mister John to have me flogged for my impertinence, as white folks called it. But she didn't, and when I plucked up enough courage to look down she just smiled up at me and let the hand holding the towel drift right up between my legs. There was a sudden heat running up my body as my mind cottoned on to what she was doing, and when Miss Norah reached forward and took the towel from her mama. The sweat of fear began to run out'a me. Miss Norah was breathing kind'a fast, like she'd been running or something.

'Let me do it, Mama, please.' It seemed

7

like she could hardly speak.

'Lan-sakes gal, if your daddy comes in he'll whip all three of us,' Mistress Emily hissed at her.

'You watch the door Mama,' urged Norah. 'Aw please, Mama, I can't stop now and he won't talk to anyone about this . . . Will you?' She looked like a she-wolf as she stared into my face and I shook my head like a big dumb ox. Who'd believe me anyway?

In less time than it takes to tell, it was all over. I was too young and inexperienced. No woman had ever touched me there before, 'cept my ma, and that was years ago.

It only took the soft white hand a few seconds before Miss Norah sighed and pressed the towel against me.

'It's all right now, Mama. It's over,' she called in a trembly kind'a voice as she stood up and passed me the dry shorts. 'Get those on at once, and if you ever tell anyone you'll get a good whipping for telling such awful lies, d'you understand, boy?'

Her voice wasn't trembly now. It was sharp and demanding. She stared into my face, hands on hips, head to one side. 'Mama was here all the time, she'll swear nothing ever happened and no one would ever believe you anyway.' She pushed the flat of her hand against my chest. 'Answer me, damn you.'

'Yes'm,' I stammered, backing away towards the door.

They both smiled at me, softly and sweetly, but for those few moments I'd seen the other side of those two fluffy, sweet-smelling ladies. Vicious as she-wolves guarding their young they were, not light an' dainty now. No sir!

'If you're very good we'll let you be our driver,' Mistress Emily murmured as we walked towards the stairs. 'After all, you're a hero now, it's fittin' that you should be the one to drive us around.' She looked into my face; hers was real hard an' pinched. 'Remember. Keep your stupid mouth shut!' she hissed without moving her lips.

Then she changed completely as she smiled an' allowed her eyes to flicker open and shut real fast like women do sometimes. 'Here's the hero, John dear. All clean and dry. I think he should be promoted to become our driver, don't you?' she called as we came down the stairs into that great room.

My knees was trembling so bad I figured they'd never hold me, but nobody seemed to notice.

'That's a good idea honey. We'll get you a nice new uniform, Joshua D,' called Mister John cheerfully, as I backed towards the front door, bowing slightly as I had been told to do by my daddy.

'Yes sir, thank you, Mister John,' I muttered as I reached behind me, opened the door and slipped out into the sunlight. Mistress Emily's tinkling laugh beat against my skull as I leaned against the wall to try to stop my legs from trembling.

'Glory be, y'all should have seen the poor dear lamb, honey.' Her voice was high and scratchy. 'He was so embarrassed! When I started to dry his shoulders I just had to leave him in the bedroom all on his own, would you believe? And me old enough to be his mother, God forbid of course. But so innocent, bless him.'

That tinkling laugh came again. I stared at the big lawns where I had played for hours with young Master Luke and his daft Labrador dog, barking and jumping on us enjoying the fun, and I realized those times had gone forever.

Or had it? Somehow, I could still seem to hear that great lollopy old dog of Master Luke's barking somewhere in the distance . . .

3

My eyes sprang open in fear. Sleep must have held me for quite a while, because stiffness had seeped into my bones through lying in such a cramped position. My ears were strained to catch the slightest sound of the barking I'd heard in my sleep. Then it came, the distant baying of dogs floating on the wind. Bloodhounds! And they were still out there.

I pushed myself back out of the hole. The rain was coming down like it was gonna flood the world. My clothes were soaked in seconds. In one way the rain was good. The dogs were acting up; that meant they'd lost my trail because of it, but it was so damned cold that my body was already trembling as the chill bit into me. My stomach was screaming for something to eat. I either had to stay in my little shelter till I was past caring, or climb onto my hind legs and start running again. Well, giving in was just no use at all so, pushing myself up, I set to running.

It was full dark, but the sickle moon showed itself once in a while, glinting through the scudding rain clouds. It told me which way to go. Last thing I wanted was to run in the wrong direction. My mind was closed to what would happen if the men ever caught me. A runaway slave stood no chance, but a runaway slave who had also raped a white woman! The blame wasn't mine, but if they said it was, everyone would believe 'em. I shook my head to get rid of the thought and stared into the rain, putting one foot in front of the other from memory alone. Hungry? Yeah, but the way that rain was coming down thirst was gonna be no problem at all.

North was my course, which according to my daddy put me on the closest heading for a place called Ohio. Luck, and lots of it, was what this black fella needed because it seemed there was one helluva long way to go. Getting across the Northern tip of Virginia alone was gonna be bad enough; I didn't even know there was such a place until my daddy had told me about it. 'Keep the sun or moon coming up over your right shoulder and setting over your left, son,' my daddy had said, and that was it. My grumbling stomach had to be ignored, food always gonna be scarce and my hope of meeting up with somebody going North to join the Union Army, or to happen upon a blue-coated patrol, seemed kind'a slim in this God-forsaken country; but it could happen! Men were out there somewhere fighting this here war to free slaves like me, or so I was told by a drummer who had visited our little town last year before he'd been tarred and feathered and driven out of town, tied belly down on his hoss.

As my bare feet thumped into the sodden earth, they seemed to beat out the slow boom boom of tom-toms, dragging me into some sort of trance, driving my memory back once more into the past . . .

The war was being talked about everywhere. Men were running around in strange uniforms, arguing about something they called 'secession', and some General name of Beauregard who was going to attack a place called Fort Sumter.

Then Mister Franklyn and Master Matthew came home wearing uniforms, and said they were going off to war. That's when things really began to change on the plantation, because soon after that my good friend Master Luke went off for something called 'Officer training', leaving the whole place in the hands of Mistress Emily and her daughter.

I still wore a smart driver's tunic, but bigger now. I'd busted out of two, growing and spreading. I'd been driving Mistress Emily and her daughter around for nigh on three years before Mister John and Master Matthew left for the war.

Almost as soon as the men were gone, Mistress Emily and Miss Norah started their shenanigans again. Like I said, I'd growed some in that time, and making out to be almost as big as my daddy; and it wasn't long before the two women began telling me to take their parcels right into the big house. Then it got so's I had to carry 'em on up to the bedroom.

A little while later they said to bring my latest uniform over to the big house and leave it there for cleaning. Them two females were eyeing me the way a pair of vultures would look at a dying animal, and when I went over to collect the uniform, they told me to change into it in the big house from now on and change out of it there too, once my driving work was finished. It didn't take much guessing to know what was coming and my knees was trembling something awful that first day.

It started pretty much where it left off that last time. But it got worse as one week followed the next, till they were almost quarrelling over whose turn it was. Spitting and snarling at each other like a pair of she-cats and each time they were getting nearer and nearer to taking what they really wanted.

Man! I was so scared, even sleeping was becoming a problem to me; I'd worry and fret so. Then one night I poured out my worries to my daddy. He didn't say anything for a long time afterwards. Thinking real deep on it, he was. Then he looked at me. The worry lines showing in his face and that's when he started telling me where this 'Ohio' place was and how I should run for it if trouble ever came to me.

'I'll send you out to the North Fields, son,' he told me. 'If the ladies at the house asks for y'all I'll tell 'em you're too far away to fetch, an' offer 'em old Tom as a driver. It may keep you out'a their hands for a while, but they might send for you anyway.'

Well it worked for a few days, but then old Tom came riding out on the buggy and fetched me. Told me that the mistress was roaring mad at my daddy, and for me to come straight up to the big house at once.

When I got there, they were both waiting for me. They looked untidy and out of breath, but somehow excited as well. There was a blood-covered rawhide whip on the floor and a big smear of blood on that good rich carpet.

They stared at me like a pair of vultures. 'Any time your daddy ever sends you out to the North Fields he'll feel that whip again,' Mistress Emily snarled. Her face was screwed up tight, but her eyes was filled with some kind'a joy.

She'd beat my daddy with a whip . . . and enjoyed doing it!

I dragged my eyes away and looked at Miss Norah. She had a splash of my daddy's blood on her cheek and a wide, mad smile on her face. It looked as if they had both found a new way of making their life exciting. There was no denying what they wanted to do as they hustled me up the stairs, only this time they were already half mad with the excitement of beating my daddy.

Between them, they did everything they could to me . . . except the one thing I hoped they'd never do. They seemed almost out of their minds, rubbing their naked bodies up and down against mine. Closer and closer they came until Mistress Emily seemed to lose all her control. She suddenly forced herself down on me, real hard, wrapping her legs around me tight, as I slipped deep inside her.

Miss Norah started trying to drag her off, telling her to stop, but Mistress Emily clung to me and nothing could move her. It was like a dream. Nothing else seemed to matter as my seed poured out. I felt her go limp, and she rolled off me like she was dead.

Miss Norah was staring at us. She was

shaking her head and backing away. 'Oh lan-sakes, Mama, what's gotten into you? You've spoiled it all!' Her voice started in a wailing whisper but it was getting louder an' louder all the time. 'You stupid, stupid woman Mama, you've let him rape you!' That last bit came out as a shout.

Mistress Emily pushed herself up from the floor where she'd fallen, staring around as if she was coming out of a deep sleep, but she was still panting from the excitement of it all. 'I, I, had to do it, Norah,' she said, all whispery and faint. 'Lordy, Lordy, I just couldn't stop myself.' Then her eyes seemed to clear as she stared at me. 'That's right!' she said quietly. 'You raped me!' Then she began shouting louder and louder. 'He's raped me! Oh God, he raped me. Help me, my darling girl. Get some men in here. Hang the dirty son-of-a-bitch.' She was screaming it at the top of her voice now and Miss Norah was helping her.

Grabbing up my pants and shirt, I ran out of the bedroom and down the stairs, dragging my clothes on the best way I could. It was lucky there was no one else in the house. The two women must have sent the servants out so's they wouldn't know what the mistresses were up to.

Running out into the yard where the buggy

was still hitched up, I jumped into the driving seat and set the horse off at a fast gallop. Out to see my daddy; but his place was empty, so maybe they had him chained up somewhere in the big house. Perhaps he was dying in some cellar! There was no time to waste; they'd be after me as soon as Miss Norah could raise the alarm. The buggy was my only hope.

I climbed into it and headed towards the North Fields. Daddy had said North, so this had to be the right direction. A man was running towards me carrying a bullwhip. He was gonna try to bar my way so I drove straight at him. He jumped to the left, missing the horse but the side of the buggy caught him in the chest. The big steel-rimmed wheel thumped over him. I glanced back but he wasn't moving! The panic gripped me even more. I stood up and whipped the horse into a mad gallop. The fields were flashing by me. I had no clear idea of what to do, only to get as far away as possible.

The horse left the track and began to cut through the field. It couldn't last. The horse put its foot into a gopher hole, the leg cracked like a pistol shot and the animal let out one Godawful scream as it pitched over, the buggy crashed into it, and I flew over its head, landing face down in the mud. I was stunned for a few minutes, but climbed to my feet and staggered back to take a look at the horse. The animal was dead, so I started running and the rain started pouring down. Just like it was right now —

★   ★   ★

— My thoughts dragged me back to the present, to the slap, slap, of my bare feet in the muck, and feeling the solid punch of the pain travelling up the back of my legs, along my spine and into my head, with that tom-tom still pounding away each time my feet slammed into the soggy mess. There was a darker patch on the ground ahead, pr'aps it was the shadow of a tree or something. A warning flashed into my brain but I paid it no mind. I should have known better, you don't get black shadows in the darkness, especially not on a flat level field with no moon to speak of.

My mind scrambled when my running feet didn't slap into the wet earth but kept on going, down, down into nothing. I started going ass over tit. My head hit something awful hard, and then there was just blackness . . . Until I groaned with the pain.

My head was ringing like the start-work

bell my daddy used to beat with a club at dawn to get the men out of their beds. Things began to crowd back on me then. For a while the thoughts of the plantation was very real to me and I lay there, trying to give my situation some thought. I was in a wagon of some kind and it was travelling along at a good clip, so maybe the men with the dogs had caught up with me!

It didn't seem likely; I wasn't tied and no one was in the wagon with me as far as I could tell. There was a blanket over me and I felt real warm for the first time since I'd started running. There was some wrapping around my aching head. Man! It was thumping somethin' awful, so I eased up off the bed; everything slipped out of kilter. Would have been as sick as a pig then, if I'd had anything in my stomach to be sick with. A loud groan pushed past my lips with the feeling of it.

'Hey! You in there! Back in the land of the living are you?'

The voice sounded too damned cheerful for a guy in my state of mind, but I managed to grunt, 'Yeah, who's asking?' Which was pretty miserable of me seeing as how he'd gone to the bother of the bandaging and loading me into his wagon an' all. But then, I was feeling miserable and I had no idea where we were going. Could be he was taking me right back where I'd come from. Panic gripped my gut at the thought.

'You hungry, fella?' asked the voice.

I was liking this guy better by the minute. 'Hungry ain't exactly the word I'd use, mister. Plumb starving's nearer.'

'Some cold deer meat and soda cakes in the bucket by the bed; help yourself,' he shouted.

I scuffed around some in the darkness an' soon found the bucket. Man! I was on that meat like a chicken on a bug. With all this grub to hand, the guy had every right to be cheerful.

'Find it?'

'Sure did, thanks mister,' I spluttered around a mouthful of meat 'n' stuff.

'There's a bottle of root beer close to the bucket. Help the meat to go down a treat.'

Grubbing around some more I found the bottle. Was beginning to figure I'd died and gone to that 'heaven' place the white folks was always talking about. The beer felt real good on my raspy throat and made the meat slip down a treat.

'I'll pay you back, mister,' I shouted; my head had almost stopped banging, and all this good luck was beginning to get too much to handle.

'What are y'all running from?'

My head began to thump again and my guts churned up a bit. Felt like all that good food was about to go to waste. I'd hate like hell to have to kill a man who'd helped me, but there was no way I was going back.

'Ain't none of my business, you understand,' shouted the man, interrupting my scrambled thoughts. 'I don't hardly want to be taking y'all the wrong way do I? Mind you, I get the feeling that we're leaving them dogs behind. That suit you?'

My face split into a smile of relief. This guy was one understanding fella. 'If I never hear them dogs again it'll still be too soon, mister. I'll pay you back though. I'm a real hard worker, you'll see,' I shouted

'You just feed yourself. Then get some shut-eye. I'll keep moving along till I've lost 'em. We'll have a good long talk later. OK?'

'That suits me just fine, mister,' I answered, wiping greasy fingers on my shirt before snuggling back down in the blanket. Man! At last Lady Luck was smiling or, as my daddy would have put it, 'She ain't just smiling son, she's grinning from ear to ear'. Why even my head had let up playing the drums, so I closed my eyes and thought about those two women back there. I'd never worried too much about slavery in the past, but now I was beginning to realize what this here war was all about.

Those two women had caused all my problems, yet I would get the blame . . . Be hung if I was caught. Freedom! That was the key . . . my mind kind'a drifted, and the rocking of the wagon soon set me to sleeping once more, only it was a different kind of sleep this time, the kind that relaxes a man, leaves him feeling fitter and stronger. That sure was what this tired and aching body needed.

4

I came awake as the first gray streaks of dawn showed in the sky. I couldn't see them from the inside of course, but habit is sure one hard thing to break. The wagon was stopped, and there was the most mouth-watering smell of sowbelly frying. I was stiff and sore from my long run but that smell dragged me out of the wagon in no time at all. It overcame my fear of the man who'd found me. Yeah, and even those men with the dogs too.

I didn't have to put clothes on; I was still wearing my pants and shirt. It was all there was anyway so I padded to the back of the wagon, pushed aside the tarp an' climbed down. The smell kind'a dragged me around to the front . . . by the nose if you get my meaning. At the first corner I stopped and peeked around it. The glow of the fire showed me the figure of a man in a wide-brimmed hat stooping over the fire tending to a spitting skillet.

He didn't look up so I figured that maybe he couldn't see me in the dark. That notion went haywire when he said, 'You gonna stay there all day fella or do y'all fancy some sowbelly and eggs? Because I ain't gonna fetch em over that's for sure!'

He had the same broad 'Down-home' way of talking I'd always been used to, and that made me kind'a shy and fearful as I eased away from the corner, ready to run if that's what it took. But that smell sure kept me a' coming. It's funny how the rumblings of a man's belly kind'a ride roughshod over his common sense, especially when he smells ham an' eggs sizzling in a hot skillet.

The false dawn was lightening the sky and as the man stood up, I could see that he weren't overly tall, but kind'a stocky with it. He was wearing one of them heavy 'coach driver' coats that reached almost to the ground and had a big collar that kind'a draped right over the shoulders to help keep the rain out. The coat had two slits in it, so's you could push your arms out for the driving. Edging slowly towards that lovely smell I could see he was holding the skillet and looking me over at the same time.

'Goddamn! No wonder y'all were so heavy! You sure are one big son-of-a-bitch ain't yuh? Getting you into the wagon was like lifting lumps of lead covered in grease. Pull up a stone an' set. Grab that there tin plate while you're at it fella.'

The words came out all in one long stream

like he wanted to get it over with, so I dragged up the flat stone and squatted without saying anything at all.

Man! Did that grub taste good! The fella kept right on cooking and I kept eating. His coffee wasn't up to much but I wasn't about to grumble. I'd tasted worse. Finally, my stomach was as full as it'd ever been in my whole life. I kind'a slid off the stone and lay against it staring at the man with dull-eyed contentment, like a puppy in the sun, burping now and then, to let out the gas.

'Guess I ate y'all plumb out of groceries, mister, but I'll work real hard to make it up to you. You're the kindest man I ever met in my whole life, 'cept for my daddy that is.'

The man lit up a long black cigar with a piece of wood from the fire and leaned back against the edge of the wagon wheel. 'Tell me all about it, fella, I reckon you owe me that much,' he said quietly.

So I told him. Slowly at first, not sure how he'd take it about the women an' all, but in the end it came out in a rush and to hell with it. Weren't no use me trying to run away, I couldn't run ten paces, my cheating stomach was that full. But I didn't have to. He just kept puffing away at that thin cigar, nodding his head every so often like he understood I was telling him the pure truth.

It was hard to know if he was angry or not because he had this short pointy beard and a moustache that was curled to points at each end, but he seemed calm enough to me.

He threw the stub into the fire and wiped his hand across his mouth. 'What d'you intend to do now?' he asked. 'They'll have a notice posted on you as fast as the coach can deliver it. You can leave when you're ready, son . . . if you want to, that is.'

'I sure don't wanna cause you any trouble, mister, but I'd like to stay with you for a spell, to pay you back for all your kindness.'

'But where are you heading, man, that's the question.'

'Was heading for a place my daddy told me about, it's called Ohio. I could maybe join up with the army there.'

'That's one hell of a way to go on foot. You'd never make it.'

This guy was getting my dander up, nice as he was. 'I got no other place to go, mister, so I just gotta make it.' I told him as patiently as I could.

Well he thought on that for a spell, then he said, 'How'd it be if I made up some papers showing that you belonged to me and that I'd bought you from somewhere down South? In Georgia say? Then you could travel with me

27

as my helper. I'm heading for Ohio too, as it happens.'

'I'd be your slave you mean?' The tone of my voice said the idea didn't set too well with me.

'To everybody else, yes.' he explained. 'Between you and me, we'd just be helping each other and once we get to Ohio I'd sign another paper setting you free so's y'all could join the Army with a clear sheet if that's what you want.' He stuck out his hand. 'Is it a deal?'

Well there wasn't but one way to go. This was a real stroke of luck for me, so gripping his hand in both of mine I gave it a real good shake.

'What do I call you, mister?' There was a lump in my throat big as a fist.

'When we're among white folks you'd best call me Mister Jess. My name's Jesse Turnball, the magic maker and healer of all ills.'

He was kind'a wincing a little and there was the beginning of a tear in the corner of his eye but I couldn't figure why.

'D'you reckon y'all could let me have my damned fingers back?' he grunted, and I realized that I'd bin squashing them flat in my two-handed grip.

'Gee I'm sorry, Mister Jess, Sir,' I mumbled

leaving go of his fingers like they were hot.

'Just keep the sir bit for the customers huh,' he said, rubbing his hand like I'd broke it or something.

'Yes sir, Mister Jess,' I said, real smart. 'You'll have no call to be regretting taking me along with you and that's a promise.'

'What's your name, fella?' he asked, still rubbing his hand.

'Joshua, Mister Jess; that's Joshua D, sir.'

'Joshua D huh? Can you read, Josh?

'Well sir, I kin cipher some; right from A, clear through to Zee. Git kind'a mixed up picking out the different ones to turn 'em into real words though.'

'But you can read?'

'Some . . . maybe.'

'OK, Josh, let's load up the wagon and get moving, I hope to be riding down the mainstreet of the next town in a few hours. Maybe we can earn a few dollars and buy some more groceries, huh?'

'Yes sir.' I was feeling kind'a guilty about all the food I'd eaten. 'Guess you're right out of eggs with me eating so many.'

Then he did the darndest thing. He just reached over to my ear and rubbed it. 'I always got plenty of eggs, Josh,' he laughed. Then, damn me for a liar if he didn't pull one clean out of my earhole. 'You ate one too many, Josh,' he chuckled, 'nice of you to let me have it back.' He handed it to me. 'Put it with the rest, son an' let's be moving on,' he said, then walked around the side of the wagon still laughing.

Well I stared at that egg for a good long time before I put it with the others. It was real right enough. My hand drifted up to my ear in case another one had popped back out, but there was nothing there, and all the time Mister Jess was laughing away fit to bust a gut. This guy seemed one all right fella to me.

The covered wagon was fair to middling in size, pulled by two horses, and the big canvas sheet covering it was painted and daubed to look like a sunset, with Mister Jess's name on it; and underneath his name it said, 'Elixir of Youth cures all ills'.

'Course I didn't really read it my own self. Mister Jess kept giving my brain a nudge or two as I spelled out the letters, but together we sorted 'em out after a while. Though what Elixir was supposed to be was beyond my figuring, but there was a whole pile of bottles stacked inside the wagon so I suppose this elixir thing was something to do with those.

Once I'd loaded the pots and pans we climbed up onto the driving seat and sat, him in one corner, me in the other. I picked up the lines and got us moving while Mister Jess lit up one of his thin cigars.

'I'll buy you some decent duds when we get to town, son. Can't have you looking like some damned scarecrow now, can we?' he said with a small grin.

I looked down at my torn, muddy shirt and shorts, then took a long look at him. His heavy coat was undone, spread out to let the morning sun in, and as he leaned back into the corner of the wagon seat I could see his smart black suit with the thin white stripes running down it. Where the suit coat was also open, there was a heavy looking watch chain dangling across his smart checkered vest. This fella was fairly short and thickset but there didn't seem to be a bit of spare meat on him anywhere. He had a heavy belt strapped around his waist with an army holster fixed to it, like the one Mister Franklyn wore with his uniform, only it didn't have a top flap. It looked as if it had been cut off, because the handle of a pistol was sticking out of the top, kind'a back to front, making it real easy to reach with his left hand, even sitting on the wagon seat. The black Stetson was tilted over one eye, and together with the moustache and beard he looked one fearsome fella.

'Seen enough, Josh?' he asked me, still without looking in my direction.

Should have figured that he knew I was

watching him out've the corner of my eye. This guy didn't miss a damned thing so I had best keep my own wits about me.

He took the thin cigar out of his mouth and pointed ahead with it. 'Town coming up, son, be there by nightfall. We'll stop a couple of miles short of it and camp overnight then ride in first thing in the morning.' He turned an' grinned at me. 'We'll fit you out real good there, OK?'

I grinned back at him kind'a doubtful, then stared ahead once more. I'm beginning to think this fella is seeing things that just ain't there; my eyes were hurting from staring real hard into the sunlight but I couldn't see anything that looked like a town, not even a shack. It took another hour or so before the first sign of a house showed itself.

I glanced at Jesse Turnball again and he winked at me. 'Didn't believe me huh? Wa'al you'll learn,' he grunted. Right off, I made up my mind to watch this fella . . . and learn. Seemed like he was always one step ahead of the game.

Then he proved it all over again. I didn't see the jackrabbit scudding through the brush beside the trail, or the gun come out. Fact is I damned near jumped clear over the horses' back when Mister Jesse fired it. Don't reckon the jackrabbit even knew it was dead before it skidded nose first into the dirt. It was that quick!

By the time I'd sorted my stomach out and pulled my eyes back into their holes, he'd nipped off the wagon seat, collected the jackrabbit, and was climbing back on to the wagon again. 'That's supper taken care of old son,' he grunted, as he dropped it at my feet and sat back in the corner again, like he'd never even moved.

I swallowed a few times to git my stomach back in place. 'Jesus, Mister Jesse that was awful sudden.' My voice was kind'a trembly-like.

He gave a sort of belly chuckle. 'There's times to set and times to move, son and that rabbit wasn't about to wait around for us to make up our minds about him now, was he?'

'Guess not, but Mister Jess, I didn't even see the varmint.'

'That's right, Josh, you keep your eyes on the trail.' He laughed some more. 'I'll fill the pot, you do the chores, OK?'

Which suited me just fine because the noise that gun made right beside me damn near made me get rid of my breakfast, and I don't mean I felt sick neither! It's been a damned long time since my mammy had to clean a messy pair of pants, but man! Oh man! How close can a body come?

'Teach you to shoot like that if you stick around with me all the way to Ohio, Joshua,' Mister Jesse offered. 'After all, if y'all want to join the army you'll have to get used to guns.'

'That's as maybe, Mister Jess. Be a good idea if I kind'a snuck up on it a bit at a time though, huh? That bang damn-near frightened the . . .'

'Yeah I know it did, son,' he interrupted, close to laughing some more. 'But you're gonna have to get used to it, mark my words.' That belly laugh was still rumbling deep in his gut.

Along about then we saw a dust cloud some two or three miles away. 'Get in the back, quickly Josh,' Jesse said, kind'a sharp. 'Looks as if we might have trouble coming up. That's a posse or I miss my guess.'

How the hell he knew that is beyond me. All I could see was a small cloud of dust, but after that business with the jackrabbit, I was more than willing to take his word for it. So, slicker than spit on a greased rail, I passed the lines to him and slipped over the seat and into the cover of the wagon.

'There's a piece of chain on the floor, Josh, bind it around one leg and fix it around the bar of the seat, then put this lock on it so's you're chained to the seat.' The lock thumped down by my side and the chain was easy to find, but when it came to locking myself up to the wagon bar, well, that was a hoss of a different color. It wasn't that I didn't trust Mister Jess you understand, well not exactly, but we'd only met a short time ago, and this lock business was something else. I'd be trapped!

'If you don't want to do it, son you'd best start running,' growled Mister Jess, interrupting my wandering thoughts, his voice kind'a touchy. 'You have about two minutes to make up your mind. It's spit or close the window time, Josh.'

His voice was harsh, like he was real worried. My mind was spinning around getting nowhere. Hell, there was no chance for me out there anyway, suppose they had the dogs? They'd tear me to bits for sure. That thought made up my mind for me! I pulled the lock together and wound down the key, hesitating again before passing it back to Mister Jesse.

'Just trust me, son,' he said, kind'a quiet like. 'Say nothing, do nothing. Just act like I might give you a good whupping if you so much as open your mouth. They'll like that. Savvy?'

'You're the boss-man, I'm in your hands now like it or not, Mister Jesse. If I die, don't take no blame on yourself. No-sir, no blame at all.'

The posse came up in a clatter of hooves and a few shouted war-whoops, with me crouching in the corner of the wagon trembling and chained like an animal. So scared clear through, that the chain was rattling something awful and my ears were straining against the noise, trying to find out what was going on.

The blood chilled inside me as I heard one man talking about a runaway slave, making me close to crying like a babe from the fear of it. A dreadful gut-wrenching fear that was close to souring my stomach leaving me, a big man of over six feet four, as broad and as strong as my daddy ever was, like a trembling frightened baby. Because those men and their damned dogs would tear me to pieces and enjoy it if they ever caught me; I believed I could hear them dogs snuffling around outside even now, or was it my imagination? A man could maybe stand a hanging without screaming for mercy if it had to be, getting a whupping too perhaps. But the thought of them damned dogs snarling and snapping, with men acting like animals also, just turns my good blood to water. My breath kind'a clogged in my throat as Mister Jesse asked about the runaway. Telling them just what he'd do if his slave ever tried it.

My body set to shaking even more when

the man said the runaway was no-but a boy, and a puny one at that. There was a damp burning warmth on my legs as my bladder gave way to the relief.

There was sorrow in my heart for the runaway, sure, but it wasn't me they were looking for and that was my blessing. 'Praise the Lord,' I muttered in my mind. It was what my daddy always used to say if something good happened, and if it was good enough for him, well I'd say it also.

My eyes were screwed up against the sudden sunlight when the men pulled back the tarp and stood in a bunch staring in at me like they wanted to make sure I was tied up good and tight. They were impressed with the chain about my leg, but opined that I ought to have one on my arms as well. That was when they noticed my wet shorts. The smell helped me 'cos it made 'em want to leave and that couldn't be too soon for me; they made some nasty remarks about my habits, then spat in the dirt before dropping the tarp back into place. The men hung around for a while, confabbing with Mister Jesse, then they mounted up and rode away. I felt the weakness of a newborn babe wash over me and the trembling still hadn't let up.

My heart seemed to have been torn out've my body and squeezed in a big vice, like the one they have in the blacksmith's place on the plantation. My hand felt sore an' I realized that I'd been chewing on it all along and the blood was running down my chin.

Standing on my trembling legs was just no good, so I sat there and shivered. There were tears running down my cheeks for the shame of it. Mister Jesse must have known how it was with me 'cos he didn't look in or say anything. Just climbed back onto the seat and soon the wagon started moving along towards the town somewhere up ahead.

After some little time had gone by, Mister Jess pushed the tarp aside and gave me the key to the lock. He still didn't say anything at all while I freed myself, put the lock and chain away and settled back on the wooden floor well away from my bed, I didn't want that stink in my blanket. No sir!

A long time later the wagon stopped and I crept out the back of it like a cur-dog in trouble. I felt sore ashamed of my wet pants and the stink coming from me, but Mister Jess must have known all those things without saying anything about it.

'I figure it's about time you gave those muddy clothes a damn good wash son,' he called out, before I could walk around the front. 'Yonder stream is just the place to do that, wouldn't you say? I'll get this jackrabbit in the pot. Wash 'em good now, we don't want you all muddied up for the customers when we hit town, do we fella?'

Goddamn, but I was grateful to Mister Jess. I ran down that bank and hit the water full tilt, swimming and splashing like a fish in the sunshine, scrubbing my body so hard to get the mud and stink off me that I was sore by the time I'd finished but I was pleased too. Pleased to scramble up the bank of the stream, cleansed of my shame. To stretch out on the grass in the hot sunshine drying off and letting my pride come back.

Mister Jess didn't ever speak of it. He knew my shame and said not a word, for which I was truly grateful. He just went off for a wash of his own, giving me the chance to fetch a bucket of water or two and scrub that there wagon till the stink was gone out of it. Yes sir, Mister Jess was one understanding fella.

Time I'd finished the cleaning and Jess had done with washing, that old jackrabbit was smelling something prime. We chopped up a whole load of vegetables and piled 'em all into the pot. There was enough food in it to feed three healthy men, let alone just the two of us.

Then I'll be double damned if Mister Jess didn't up and surprise me all over again.

Without turning around he called quietly,

'Best come out of the hay box, son. That posse is chasing all over the place by this time. They'd never think of you climbing into my hay box and riding back to where you came from.'

Well there was a rustling of hay, then the door to the haybox was kicked open and the most skinny looking kid I ever did see came tumbling out. Shaking like an aspen leaf in the wind he was, and naked as a Jaybird. Well! My mouth was open so wide! Mister Jess told me to close it up or I might get a bee in it.

I jumped to my feet and hurried over to the boy, gathering him in my arms like a babe. He was trembling so's, he was like to shake to pieces, and thin! Man, his legs weren't much thicker than a whupping stick. I put him down by the fire and hurried into the wagon to fetch the blanket I'd slept on, then I wrapped it around him to cover his nakedness.

Mister Jess seemed pleased about this and patted the boy's head before he said 'Let's eat,' in a kind'a funny choky voice.

Man oh man! Could that younker eat! I swear that for all the grub he put away he just couldn't have any innards at all. Took me all my time to keep up with him, and that's a fact!

Both Mister Jess and I had seen the cuts on

the kid's back and shoulders. His legs had taken a beating also. It looked as if a cane or bullwhip had been used on him, maybe both. I was gonna ask the kid about it myself but Mister Jess caught my eye and shook his head, saying nothing.

A little bit at a time, Jess drew the lad out, just like he'd done with me. Two grown men had beaten the boy, just for talking on the job. Then they'd thrown him into a barn, more dead than alive, but he'd surprised them all by escaping in the night. He'd climbed into the hay box while I was sleeping. Jesse had seen him do it but he didn't let on to the posse when they came a-calling.

I was learning more and more about this slave thing all the time, and it made me more sure than ever that I'd join the Army.

5

Mister Jess drove us into town early next morning. I was in the wagon with the chain around my leg — the way a slave should be kept according to most white folk — but in one way it was different, because I had the key. The boy was back in the haybox; Mister Jess had a special section in the back of it. The piece of board fitted just so and when a body took all the hay out you'd swear you were seeing all of the box, but when the piece of board was pulled out there was plenty of room behind it. I don't rightly know why he had his hay box made that way, but that's where Hector was right enough. Yeah, that was his name all right. Hell of a name to saddle a fella with, huh?

I was peeking out between the joins in the tarp, watching the people going by; there didn't seem to be many young men about, so I figured they'd gone off to join the army like Mister Franklyn an' his sons had done.

By 'n' by Mister Jess pulled up outside a General Store and the wagon seat creaked as he stepped down into the street.

'I'm gonna get you those clothes I spoke

about, Joshua,' he muttered. 'Then we'll get some stores. Don't be making a noise now, y'hear.'

'Yes sir, Mister Jess and thank you kindly,' I answered, kind'a quiet-like my own-self. Wouldn't do for white folks to hear us talking so friendly like. The timbers creaked as he climbed up onto the boardwalk then things seemed to settle down some.

A little time later I felt a tingle at the back of my neck and the hairs felt as if they were lifting. My nerve-ends were warning me that something was happening outside the wagon, it was the same feeling as when them damned dogs set up their baying back there a'ways. Then the tarp was pulled to one side, smart-like, an' three white boys were staring into the wagon. They couldn't see me, what with the sunlight outside, and the gloom inside the wagon. They were all on the big side, and one of 'em had a pistol in his hand. They were up to no good that was for sure.

They took a quick look around to see if anyone was watching, then the one with the pistol grabbed the side bar and started to heave himself up into the wagon. He still couldn't see me but I dassent attack no white boy. I had to do something but what?

Then it struck me! I could always do a good job of copying that lollopy old dog of

Master Luke's, and the chain would also come in handy. So quiet as a mouse, I wound back the key in the lock and slipped the chain from around my leg, then rattling it like mad I set to barking and bouncing around, making the wagon fair rock about an' it made that white boy jump out've the wagon like Old Nick was about to bite his pecker off. Man! Did he move! Mind you, I don't know what would have happened if Mister Jesse hadn't come along just then, but I was damned glad to stop jumping and howling when I heard him giving 'em a good old tongue lashing.

After a bit Mister Jess climbed back into the driving seat, pulled the tarp aside and gave me the duds he'd bought, all wrapped up in a parcel they was.

'Get them on, Josh,' he said, and I could hear that belly laugh beginning to rumble. 'Never seen a Labrador dog all dressed up in a shirt and pants before. That should bring the crowds in tonight. Fancy a bone, fella?' Then the belly laugh really broke out. He must have been smoking one of those thin cigars of his at the time, 'cos he started choking as well, which was just what he deserved I figured, as I unwrapped the bundle and stared at the brand new shirt and shorts. Man! I couldn't believe it! Brand spanking new! I'd never had anything new in my whole life. There was a lump in my throat as big as my fist as I threw off my old stuff and put on these new duds.

'I'll bark for you any old time you like, Mister Jesse,' I muttered, trying to hawk the lump out, but getting nowhere with it.

'You sure are a good friend to have around, Joshua D,' he laughed. 'We're gonna get on well together, you and me.'

Friend! That clicked in my mind. Mister Jesse had just called me his friend! The only other white man ever to call me that was Master Luke, and all the while Mister Jesse was still laughing and choking at the thought of me, dressed in my new duds and chewing on a bone. There was a big daft grin on my own face also, because this was how friends ought to be with each other, and how I wanted to be with my good white friend, Mister Jesse Turnball. Man! Was I one lucky fella or what?

Jesse stopped the wagon just a little bit up the road. 'Right, Joshua,' he called. 'You all dressed up proper? If you are, open up the back and let's get set up for trade.'

The wagon gave a jolt as he jumped down from the driving seat and I let down the back flap like he'd showed me, before pushing the tarp to one side. Then I dragged out the trestle table ready for him to go to work.

Man! Could he talk up a storm! Seems like this elixir was good for just about everything from toe rot to the measles. Cure cows, calves and sheep of anything they might have wrong with 'em. He even told one fella it would cure his bandy legs, and if a man was having trouble making babies, well damn me if it weren't good for that also.

As fast as I was passing down the bottles of this here elixir, Mister Jesse was selling it. The crowd of folks grew and grew. They couldn't pay their fifty cents fast enough. Then, when they'd all been seen to, some more than once, he began to show 'em how he could make a dollar vanish right in front of their eyes. He also pulled some eggs out of their ears, just like he did with me.

I ain't got any idea just what that elixir stuff is made of, but after two bottles or so most of the men, and some of the females too, was going kind'a cross-eyed and laughing fit to bust.

Then Mister Jesse pulled a pack of playing cards out of the air and started a game called 'Find the Lady'. Well, I thought Mister Jesse was a clever man, but even I could see where he dropped the lady every time, and most everybody else could also. The men wanted Mister Jesse to bet money on where the lady was, and he did a few times, but he just kept losing so he called a halt to the betting.

One or two of the men started getting kind'a upset and told Mister Jess that he'd better go on with the betting, or else! So he told 'em that if they was so set on it, OK, but that nobody could bet less than a five-spot. Funny thing though. Once they started betting again, nobody could find that damned lady. Time and again I thought I knew just where she was — but she was gone by the time he turned the card over — and if anybody grumbled about losing Mister Jesse would just shrug his shoulders and remind 'em that he hadn't wanted to bet in the first place. It was them who'd forced him to bet, and all the time Mister Jess kept talking, sometimes selling his elixir, or making what he called 'magic' things happen; he also had some dice, which never seemed to lose.

There were three men in the crowd who always seemed to be grumbling; they crowded around when Mister Jess pulled the cards out of the air again. They watched real careful as he took the three cards out of the pack an' flicked 'em together. Then right under their noses, Mister Jess dropped the cards in a line.

The men grinned at each other as they dropped a ten-spot each on the middle card and waited patiently until Jesse reached forward to turn the card over. There was a big wide smile on their faces as they let Mister Jess see the pistols in their hands.

'Don't touch them cards, mister card-sharp,' the leader of the three said, kind'a mean like. The man pointed to a woman in the crowd. 'Let her turn it over, and there had better be a lady under that money.'

Seemed like they had Mister Jesse cold, but he just shrugged his shoulders. 'As you wish gents, if the lady is willing,' he told 'em in his Sunday-go-to-meeting voice.

Well the lady stepped up; all twittery and shy, like women do, and turned the card over. It was the Deuce of Spades.

The crowd let out a kind'a sigh, things was looking bad for my good friend, but he just stared at the men with a sad sort of smile on his face.

'Looks as if you lose, gents,' he said quietly.

But the men weren't about to let things go at that. 'OK lady. Just turn over the other two cards,' growled the leader, real savage. 'Let's see who really won.'

The woman was getting kind'a frightened now, going all shaky like she wasn't sure if she should touch the cards.

'Don't worry, Ma'am,' Mister Jesse told her. 'Just do like the man says.'

I was standing on the back of the wagon, making up my mind that if I had to, I'd jump clear over Mister Jesse and into those three men, pistols or no.

The lady turned over the second card; it was the Three of Clubs.

I took a good deep breath, ready to jump as she reached for the last card, and I heard three clicks as the men eared back the hammers on their pistols. The lady turned the card over . . . It was the Queen of Diamonds!

There was a bigger sigh from the crowd this time and a little cheer as well.

'Like I said, gents, you lose,' Mister Jesse said quietly. 'I don't cheat, so y'all can keep your dollars as you're such sore losers, but don't play at my stall ever again.'

The men just didn't know what to say, they'd been so sure that the queen would not be there. I don't know just how Mister Jesse did it, but I'm blamed sure he must'a done something!

Right after the men had snatched up their money and pushed their way out've the crowd, Mister Jesse told me to put all the things away and close up the wagon. Which was maybe just as well because I do declare, those three white men looked mad enough to chew iron and spit nails. They sure didn't look the forgiving types to me. No sir!

'We'll ride on out to the edge of town, Joshua,' Mister Jess said quietly. 'The

49

youngster will be starving and I could do with some food myself. If we travel through a good part of the night the lad can sleep in the wagon, be more comfortable than in the hay box.'

I was kind'a worried about Hector myself. If that posse backtracked an' found him with us we'd all find ourselves strung up to the nearest tree. Maybe I shouldn't be thinking this way but that's how it is. I ain't one to be a joy-killer you understand, but if somebody's ass is gonna be on the line I'd just as soon it was the other fella's . . . if y'all get my drift' . . .

. . . It was full dark when we pulled into a small clearing near a stand of trees. I busied myself setting up a fire an' getting the cooking pot out, while Jesse pulled the hay out've the box an' let young Hector out. You should have seen that kid's face when Mister Jess gave him some new duds just like mine. Grateful ain't the word! That boy marched up and down in front of the fire like one of them Generals I saw back there in Carolina. Sure did look chipper and no mistake.

We were about halfway through feeding our faces, when three men stepped out've the darkness. It was the same three who'd argued about the card game; they had a sort of mask over their faces, but I knew who they were right enough an' so did Jesse.

We got to our feet kind'a slow 'n' easy. I took a quick glance to where the kid had been sitting but he'd faded at the first sign, probably under the wagon, out of sight.

One of the men already had a pistol in his hand. He waved it at me. 'Stay out of this,' he said kind'a nasty like. 'We're gonna teach your owner a lesson. Try anything and I'll blow a hole in you big enough to back the wagon through.'

Me an' Mister Jess stared at each other. It was my way of telling him I'd pitch in to help, although I'd get hung for hitting a white man. He understood my meaning right enough, because he shook his head just enough to tell me to stay out of it, then he took off his heavy driving coat and hat, took his gun out of its holster and laid the whole lot on the ground.

'Well which of you is going to try first? Just step right up gents.' There was a little bitty smile on his face; it should have warned 'em that Mister Jess weren't about to crawl.

The other two men stepped up like geese at a pecking session. 'We're both gonna take you apart, mister smart-ass,' they said, as they came in swinging.

I thought Mister Jess was gonna take a real hammering and I was fair quivering, like a hound dog waiting for a rabbit to run, but that damned gun was showing dead center on me. If I moved one foot I'd be dead before t'other started working. Now I dunno what Mister Jess did exactly, but one minute they was taking a swing at him, and the next they seemed to be fighting each other, all arms an' legs they were, tangled up together like you'd never believe. Then Mister Jess really started taking 'em apart. I never did see the like of it.

My daddy learned me to fight with my fists, and I was real good at it, but this was different, Man, how it was different! He just chopped 'em to pieces, like a scythe through wheat and the man pointing the gun at me was getting kinda scared, he could see this weren't going the way they wanted, so he ran towards Jesse and was gonna pistol-whip my friend.

While he was making for Mister Jess he yelled out something, and I saw three black men come out of the night with some two-by-fours in their hands. Well maybe a black man dassent hit a white man, but by damn, I sure could take my spite out on my own kind, so giving a real banshee yell to warm Mister Jess, my head went down and I charged full tilt into those three black men, hitting out left and right. I turned some corn into chaff my own-self that night and took real spiteful pleasure in it too. A two-by-four cracked across my shoulder but it didn't make one damn bit of difference. I landed him a blow that left him spitting teeth, and as he bent over to do it, I planted my bare foot real hard between his legs, figured he wouldn't be using his pecker for many a day to come.

One guy was smaller than the other two; he came at me, squawking like a banty rooster on heat, swinging his timber club. Batting it away like it was nothing I picked him up and threw him at his mate. They went down in a tangle of arms and legs, then I moved among 'em. My daddy would have been real proud of me. Fists a-pounding and feet a-kicking like mad, those fellas soon had enough of my kind of punishment and took off on the run while the white folks staggered off, looking like they'd been caught up in something real nasty, like a twister or something.

There was a cut on my head, and one fist was bleeding from taking out those teeth, but man! I'd enjoyed getting my pride back. And there was Mister Jess, lighting up one of his cigars, cool as you please. Then he let go with that big belly laugh of his. 'Told you, Joshua,' he shouted. 'We make a damned good team, you and I.'

'We sure enough do, Mister Jesse,' I said,

grinning like a kid. 'We sure do and that's a fact.'

It wasn't until we started looking for young Hector that we realized he'd run off. We both made a quick search of the place, calling and shouting that it was all over, but he was nowhere around; then we spread further out and spent a long time second searching for the lad, before Mister Jesse decided to move on.

'Guess he was scared half to death when he saw those other three coming towards the wagon as well, Josh,' he said, as we climbed aboard the wagon. 'He could be miles away by this time, and we can't hang around. Those three jailbirds could get real spiteful and bring a whole slew of trouble down around our necks if we aren't careful. Get the horses moving, son, we might get lucky and find him up ahead.'

We plodded on for an hour or more before Mister Jesse reached out an' touched my arm.

'Something going on up ahead,' he muttered, close to my ear. 'Ground hitch the horses and follow me, but not too close, OK?'

Slipping from my seat with the ground-hitch leather and weight in my hand I hooked it to the horse's bit and turned to follow him.

I could hear the scuffling up ahead myself now, and I recognized the voices! Those same three men who attacked us were laughing and chuckling about something, and you can bet it wasn't anything good.

There was a little bitty fire in the clearing and the three men were standing, looking up at a whippy sapling that was swaying backwards and forwards in the wind . . . only there weren't no wind, so it took me a minute to realize what was happening.

The bundle hauled up into the branches was a body . . . The body of a boy, real skinny he was, and the men were holding onto a rope which was tied to the top of the sapling. They'd haul it down near to the ground, then let it go like a real big slingshot. They'd laugh fit to bust a gut as the body was thrown way up into the air until it reached the end of the rope, then it would whirl around like crazy. They thought that was real funny.

Mister Jesse sucked in his breath real hard. 'Keep out of my way, Joshua,' he whispered. Real quiet it was, but I ain't ever heard such raw anger in a man in my whole life.

I didn't know exactly what Mister Jess had in mind, but it surely was gonna be bad. I crouched low to the ground, ready to shoot forward real fast if need be because I'd recognized that poor skinny body jerking backwards and forwards up there and tried to draw back the selfish thoughts I'd had about him, but it was too late. Bad thoughts or bad words can't be un-thought nor un-said neither. My daddy taught me that a long time ago an' it was too late for poor skinny Hector also. The way his neck had been stretched said it all.

Mister Jesse had been slowly pacing towards the three men. Now he stopped and leaned forward, kind'a crouched, like he was leaning into a wind. His voice was still quiet, but deadly sounding. 'You've bin hankering to use those guns, you scum, so now's your chance, turn around and die.'

Seems like he spat them last words out.

The men spun around, startled, but going for their hardware just the same.

Man they was fast! But Mister Jesse had the fire in front of him, with them beside it, so their first shots were wild.

As Mister Jess fired his first shot, I saw one man stagger backwards. An' that's when I started running up the side, but staying in the darkness and out of the line of fire till I was level with the men. The bullets were flying fast now. A second and third shot came from my friend and the second man stumbled. Then there was a shot from the third man and he yelled. 'I've hit the bastard!'

I was real worried for Mister Jess. I'd never even thought of hitting a white man before this, but my dander was up good and proper.

Tearing across the ground in front of that bitty fire and to hell with the bullets, I dived straight at the third man as he was setting himself for another shot at my friend.

My head hit his with one God-awful whump. Damn near knocked me out I can tell you, and my head was thumping something awful but I was on my feet again and charging towards one of the men on the ground who was also about to fire. I was just about there when he seemed to jerk a couple of times as Mister Jess's bullets took him. The last one of the three was half in and half out of the fire, he wasn't moving although his clothes were burning so I figured that if the fire didn't move him he was past caring about anything.

I looked towards Mister Jess, he was down on one knee, cussing in a quiet level voice, like he was mad at himself for getting shot, and by the time I'd gotten to him he'd pushed himself to his feet, still cussing a blue streak.

'You all right, Mister Jess?' I panted, still out of breath from all that charging about.

'All right be damned! Of course I'm all right man, just a flesh wound is all,' he growled, kind'a sharp. 'Damned stupid of me to get tagged like that, I knew he was the one to watch but let my temper get the better of me, ruined my trousers though. Hey, that was one helluva head butt you gave him. You OK, Josh?'

'Damned old noggin is thumping up a storm,' I told him. 'Maybe we'd best go and take a look-see at him, in case he wakes up and wants to shoot everybody, huh?'

Mister Jess was limping as we went over, but I kept my mouth shut in case I hurt his feelings.

'Your head must be solid rock,' Jess told me when he'd taken a look at the man. 'You've spilt his skull clean open like a rotten melon.'

'Y'all mean he's dead!' I was shocked! For me to kill a white man was the worst thing, they'd hang me for sure. Mister Jess would be reporting me at the next town. After all, he was white also.

'Don't look so worried, Joshua.' he kind'a grunted as he stared at the dead man, like his mind was on something else entirely.

'I done got every right to be worried,' I said. 'You're gonna have to report me for this Mister Jesse.'

'Like hell I do.' he snapped back.

'Y'all mean you ain't?

'Damn right I ain't. Those men were animals, Josh. Even if they weren't you saved my life, they all deserved to die, son, and don't you forget it' Mister Jess pointed up into the tree. 'What harm do you think that skinny kid ever did to them, Joshua? None! So, they're better off dead. Wipe it from your mind, old son. Let's get poor Hector down from that sapling and give the boy a decent burial. OK?'

Man, was I relieved; Mister Jesse was one hell of a man and no mistake, I thought, as I hurried off to fetch the wagon. Guess we knew it wouldn't make no difference at all to Hector, to hang there for a little while longer; we needed the wagon anyway, to pull the sapling down so's we could reach to cut the lad free.

My mind kept slipping back to those unkind thoughts I'd had about Hector as I dug a good deep hole, deep enough to keep the wild critters from digging him up; but it was no use, my thoughts still bothered me. So after we'd laid him to rest I told Mister Jess all about my worries as he was bandaging his leg where the bullet had passed clear through.

'Don't you worry your head about such things, Joshua,' he told me. 'There's gonna be many times in your life when you'll say, or think, things you'll regret later. Put 'em aside, son. Life goes on. Just think that you've paid for those thoughts by giving the boy a decent burial, and you saved my life today to boot, so those thoughts are cancelled out. Right!'

Well it was a fair long speech, but it surely helped me to set my mind at rest, because deep down I didn't wish poor old Hector any real harm. Seemed that my friend knew an awful lot about everything, and I was learning something new from him every single day.

Mister Jess said a short prayer over the place where we laid the boy, but when I asked him what we were gonna to do about those others he said, 'Leave 'em for the coyotes, it's all they deserve.' I ain't never heard of a white man burying a black one, then leaving whites for the wild critters to eat up, but if that's what Mister Jesse wanted then I sure as hell wanted it also.

Soon after that, we climbed into the wagon and set out for the next stop on our way to Ohio. We both knew that somewhere back there were those hunters, with bloodhounds, so hanging around was not a good idea.

6

Week by week Mister Jesse taught me to read and write. I was a quick learner, he said. I needed to be. There was so much to know and being able to read was like opening a big barn door . . . from the inside, if you catch my drift, and looking out into the wide blue yonder.

He taught me to use a gun too. I learned that he carried an Army Colt .44 caliber pistol. He even found me an old holster so's I could practice whipping it out real fast. He told me I had an aptitude for it, whatever the hell that was.

Then he showed me some long guns he kept in a special box under the driving seat of the wagon. One was a Spencer rifle and I soon got the hang of it. The seven copper rimmed cartridges slipped off their carrier and into the butt smooth as silk. It was real neat how the trigger guard dropped the breechblock and pulled out the spent case while it also pushed in a new cartridge.

But the gun I really liked was the Henry rifle. Man oh man, you could flick a cartridge into the barrel slicker than spit on a greased pole. And if a body followed Mister Jesse's teaching, like holding your breath just before y'all squeeze the trigger, and I mean squeeze gentle like, well there was no missing the target I can tell y'all. Fifteen shots she held in that there magazine, and I could bang 'em off in nothing flat. Mind you, I ain't saying how well I'd do pointing it at another fella. Mister Jess tells me it's some different looking down the sights and seeing a real live man at the other end, but jackrabbits or coyotes, why I could take 'em out without half trying.

We had already seen signs of the war about us, and from what Jesse told me, the Confederates were pushing the Union armies around a bit. Quantrill's raiders were causing all sorts of trouble raiding and looting along the Virginia borders.

I learned that we were travelling somewhere along the Cumberland Plateau, on the borders, between Virginia and Kentucky. I was learning fast. Jesse had some maps 'n' things and we'd spend many a night going over 'em, in the wagon, by lamplight. Jesse never left the maps lying around though; he said it could get us into trouble if anybody noticed 'em.

Some things was kind'a hard for me to figure. Like how come the state of Virginia had seceded to the South, yet the Western part of Virginia still sided with the Union? It didn't seem to make sense, but Mister Jess said that's just the way it was in a Civil War. Brother would be shooting at brother and father killing son, all over slavery! I couldn't see my daddy killing me and I sure wouldn't be killing him, not for anything on God's good earth.

What with one thing an' another, I was getting there fast. Reading every paper Jesse brought to the wagon, looking over those maps of his for hours and hours, and with him picking me up on what he called my slovenly speech, I was getting quite an education

I mind one time when Mister Jess told me to stop the wagon. Just before sundown, it was; we were perched on the top of a slope leading into a long narrow valley.

'Look at that, Joshua,' he said, kind'a quiet, like people do when they're in a church or something.

Well I looked but there was nothing to see. 'Look at what?' I asked. In my mind, I was looking for a town or riders.

'That! In the sky. Look at those colors, son. What a beautiful land this is!'

So I looked, and after a while a sort of peacefulness seemed to wash over me. Sure was good to look at. This was something else I'd been missing.

'What d'you think Josh?' he asked, still kind'a quiet.

'Yeah, sure is purty, Jesse. Guess I just never noticed it before'.

'The word's pretty, not purty, Josh' he said quietly. 'Haven't you ever noticed the mornings either? Just before the sun lifts itself over the horizon?'

'Nope, can't say I have, Mister Jess.'

'Well son, for what we're looking at right now, the word 'pretty' just ain't good enough. Fantastic, is getting nearer the mark. See how the colors of the setting sun are flickering through all them clouds and how the dust in the air is picking up the light and changing the colors? It's just stupendous, Joshua, it's the only word to describe it.'

'If you say so Mister Jesse, but I'm gonna take some time to git my tongue around that one. No mistake about that.'

'Just you keep looking and learning Josh, you've got a good head on your shoulders. You'll soon get the hang of it.'

'Oh I'll keep trying you kin bet on that. Sure is a real nice word, what was it again? Stupin — ?'

'Stupendous. Just keep at it, son,' he interrupted.

After that, it became a habit of mine to enjoy looking at the sunrise and sunset.

Funny how I never noticed it before though.

Mister Jesse reckoned I'd be a sergeant in no time at all. My daddy would be plumb startled to hear me going on about the different states, the war an' all that stuff, but I had to know everything there was. Why Mister Jesse was even teaching me to string words together, like one of them Goddamned preacher fellas. 'Not 'we was', Josh,' he'd say, it's 'we were', which managed to get me more confused than ever.

Another thing that set me to wondering, was why Mister Jesse would always wander off for a day or so in each town we stopped at, while I had to stay in the wagon with that damned chain around my ankle till he came back again. It was just a little thing, but it made me wonder just the same.

We were still heading along the border between Virginia and Kentucky, going North towards Ohio. What I couldn't figure was, if Kentucky was mostly in favor of the North, and that seemed to be true, because the newspapers said the Union had won a battle at a place called Mill Springs along about January, then why ain't we heading that a way? Toward the Union soldiers, not away from 'em. Yet, Mister Jesse still keeps easing across the border into Virginia, where Jackson and his marauding Confederates were getting folks all stirred up.

That Jackson fella had hit Virginia really hard earlier in the year, and there were Johnny Rebs traipsing about every which way. Yet here I sit, in another small town close to the border, waiting for Mister Jesse to come back. I'd been in my chain for two days this time and was beginning to get worried about Mister Jesse. Two days was about the longest time he'd ever been away.

Each day I'd turn myself loose and drive the wagon to another spot, just like Mister Jess had told me. There were so many wagons moving around, what with the troops 'n' all, that nobody took much notice of one extra wagon, lessen it stayed in one place too long. The third day came and went, and still he didn't show. I was getting real worried by this time. I knew Jess was good at taking care of himself, but there was something awful funny about him mixing with all those Southern officers and such. 'Specially when he was so strong against slavery.

On the fourth day he still hadn't showed, so I figured it stood to reason that something bad had happened, and he just weren't coming back lessen I go out and find him. It was no use me just going out and strolling along the streets, no black fella worth his salt would do that. Somebody would want to know who my owner was, quick smart, and going without something to defend myself was no use either, and that gave me something else to ponder on.

A black man wandering around on his own was a bad idea, but with a gun! Man, it just didn't bear thinking about, but that's just what I had to do . . . Think on it.

Like I said, Mister Jesse taught me real good so first I took off my good duds and put on my old uns; they'd hardly fit me I'd growed so much over the past few months, but I struggled into 'em. Then using water and the dust from the floor of the wagon, I dirtied myself up some.

It was still real early when I slipped out of the wagon and shuffled along in the dirt close to the boardwalk; it didn't do for a slave to walk on the boardwalk. That was for white folks.

The way I saw it, my first job was to find out where Mister Jesse was, so by acting as his slave I could scuff in the dirt, bow and scrape, asking the storeowners where I could find my master. Everybody liked a good slave who would worry about his master and take the trouble to hunt for him but this time it didn't work very well. Everybody was too busy to even talk to me, and in the end, I squatted in the dirt outside a saloon, keeping well away from the boardwalk in case a swamper saw me and slung the dirty water from his mopping of the floors over me.

The constable came along and gave me a bit of a kick. 'What y'all lazin' there for boy?' he growled, in that old 'down home' way I knew so well. Except he said it like he was in a bad temper or something

I put my voice into the kind'a singsong voice they all expected from black people. 'Ah sure is sorry to be a sittin' heah, Mista Constable Suh, an' I surely hope I ain't in your way, but my Massa, he said, y'all sit there out'a the white folk's way, boy. Ah is goin into that there saloon, an if y'all move one tiny inch I'll fetch the hosswhip to y'all, so that's why ah is a'sittin heah, Suh.'

He laughed at that an' gave me another small kick. Then he bent right down, so's his face was close to mine. 'Y'all ain't a spy now are you, boy?' he shouted into my face. 'Not like that Southern gent the army picked up a few days ago?'

He must have thought the idea of me being a spy was funny because he laughed again as he began to stroll away. 'That'll teach the bastard to try to make a good Southern cavalry captain look stupid. Pulling an egg out of his ear indeed.' He laughed again. Then he stopped and stared at me, I could see he was wondering if I was worth another kick, but then he spat in my direction and walked away.

I'd pricked up my ears when the man talked about a spy. But when he said about the egg, it told me that Mister Jesse was in deep trouble, and as soon as the constable was out of sight I hurried back to the wagon. It had to mean that Mister Jesse had been captured by the army, and it needed some thought. I started looking through the things in the wagon, hoping some sort of notion would spring to mind.

His long driving coat started me off. Jesse wasn't near as tall as me, but he was very thick in the chest, and he always bought 'em long enough to cover his ankles, almost dragging the ground. I pulled it on, it was a bit tight across the shoulders and didn't drop much below my knees, but it covered an awful lot of me. I searched some more; he always had plenty of clothes 'n' stuff. One of his Stetsons pulled well down covered a good part of my face and a bandanna tucked into the coat collar and pulled up close almost hid the other part. My legs sticking below the coat was bare and I'd never worn boots in my whole life.

Something would have to be done about that. Mister Jesse's high-sided boots was too small for me, so I had to do some more figurin'. Although I could drive the wagon around the town without causing a ruckus, if I started to drive it out of town, on my own, the white folks would think I was stealing it and I'd be strung up to the nearest tree in nothing flat.

My sleeping blanket would cover my legs 'n' feet while I was in the driving seat, but my black arms and hands had to stick out through the slits in the coat. I tried on one of Mister Jesse's suit coats but the arms were much too short, and besides, the driving coat wouldn't close over it.

Tossing some thoughts around in my head, I came up with the idea of cutting off the sleeves of the coat and pulling 'em up my arms till they looked like they fitted, then I put the driving coat on again and pushed my arms through the slits. It worked! Anybody looking from the street would think I was wearing a Sunday go-to-meetin' coat, underneath the driving coat.

I rubbed some flour into my face so that when the hat was pulled right down and the bandanna was tucked up high, nobody from the road would see much of me.

Mister Jesse's white gloves, the ones he used for his magic, was big 'n' loose on him so's he could hide a card, or a silver dollar. They were his trick gloves and I knew about a lot of those tricks by this time. I stared at the small still in the corner of the wagon, and the bags of corn he used to make his elixir as I pulled on the gloves. They just about fitted me a treat, so now was the time to put my ideas to the test.

The street wasn't busy yet, so I climbed through the front tarp straight into the driving seat, covered my legs and bare feet with the blanket, then set off, driving slowly out of town. Nobody gave me a second look! The white gloves made the people think of white, so they thought they saw a white man, muffled up against the morning's cold.

I knew the army camp was about seven miles out of town and the more I thought on it, the more it drove home to me, that I'd only done the easy bit so far. If Mister Jesse was still alive, he'd be somewhere in the encampment, with a guard watching over him.

It called for some more deep thinking, but I'd wait until the camp was in sight, then I'd hide the wagon and set my mind to the problem. All the while I'm hoping that no one will stop me for a harmless chat, or want directions. The minute I opened my mouth they'd realize I was black and they wouldn't wait for any tale of mine.

7

I breathed a big sigh of relief when I drove the wagon into a stand of timber and found myself moving into a small coulee. Night was settling in but there was no time to stare at the sunset.

I'd been moving the horses along real slow so's no one would take much notice of us, and was pleased that my plans had worked out so well. I didn't hardly want to come upon the army camp in broad daylight, but had to be in time to take a quiet look-see around and get the lay of the land. Mister Jesse had a spyglass in a leather case, with a strap so's a body could slip it over a shoulder for easy carrying. Real pretty it was; a man only had to stretch it out, twist the end and y'all could see a bug, eating his dinner, half a mile away.

After setting the horses to graze 'twixt the trees, with a long rope on 'em so they didn't wander off, I slipped the leather case over my shoulder and set off towards the edge of the trees, but keeping well away from the wide trail.

Big I might be, but I'd give a raccoon a

race up a tree any old day, so picking the tallest one, I loped on up and was soon sitting snug in the top branches. The ground was free of trees from here on and was sloping gently down into a valley. There was some bushes meandering through the bottom which had to be following a stream, and the army tents was staggered alongside the bushes, but there weren't as many as I thought there'd be.

Darkness was beginning to close in and wisps of mist was spreading along the bottomland down there, which kind'a proved to me that I was right about there being a creek or stream down there.

I un-shipped the glass and set it to working. Man! It seemed like them tents were right here in the tree with me. Fires were being lit in front of the tents and men were bending over them making their suppers.

My stomach gave a rumble, telling me to get the same idea, but I ignored it and set to counting tents. There were some places where tents had been, which told me that the troop was on the move and had probably split up. My count was twelve, but there had been around thirty or so. These men would probably be on their way at first light tomorrow, to catch up with the rest of the troop.

The glass picked up a line of three field-pieces. This was something else Mister Jesse had told me about. The things I'd learned from that fella don't bear thinking about. They were Napoleon six pounders with their caissons resting beside them. Quiet now, at peace, but they still looked cold, black and deadly. Mister Jesse once told me that when they let rip the noise would wake the dead and set 'em to galloping. There was a soldier at each end of the line, guarding them: something to take note of if I ever managed to find Mister Jesse.

As the dusk turned into night I passed the glass over the line of tents one more time. The fires were sparking bright in the gloom, with the darker shadows of men moving closer around them as the chill set in. Then I noticed that all the tents had fires except one, and that odd one had two men standing guard by the flap, which was closed tight, and I didn't need Mister Jesse to tell me why that was. No sir! That was a prisoner tent sure enough. Tent number seven, the number would stay set in my mind. Closing the glass and setting it in its case, I shinned down the tree and made my way back to the wagon.

Munching on some soda cakes and drinking cold beer was not the best thing in the world for a grumbling stomach, but the idea of drinking Mister Jesse's 'white lightnin' — the stuff he made his elixir from — made me shudder.

I'd been lucky to choose today to search out Jesse. If I'd come before, there would have been a full troop of eighty to a hundred men in that valley, if I'd come tomorrow, it would have been too late. So it had to be tonight! There was no doubt in my mind that I was gonna try to get into that camp and free Mister Jesse. No sir!

The Army Colt was loaded and the Le Mat, always kept in a little box built into the floor, now lay beside me. It was a weapon to scare the daylights out of anyone. It had nine shots in the upper chamber, but slung underneath the bullet barrel was a shotgun barrel to take 20 gauge shot; it was also fully loaded.

Packing a supply of ammunition with the pistols, I wrapped them into a parcel of old newspapers and cloth, then rolled the whole thing in some soft doe-skin with an extra pad at the bottom so's it would sit nicely on my head. Then I used two leather belts to strap the whole thing together, making it into a nice tight parcel

My mind was set. Using the creek would be the best way to slip past all the other tents in the line. The bundle would stay dry if I used two more straps to fix it to my head, and if the water was too deep for wading, why I'd just let the water take me with it and still keep the parcel dry. I had two Bowie knives strapped around my waist, under my pants and shirt in case they were needed. Stowing everything else away in the wagon, I took a last look around before climbing out and padding away into the night, knowing full well that if things went bad on me I would be dead before sunrise.

Pushing those thoughts out've my mind I trotted along beside the dirt roadway that led around the top of the shallow valley. Keeping off the road meant that the soldiers down there couldn't see me against the lighter background of the sky. Yes sir, I'd sure learned a thing or two since Mister Jesse started teaching me. My pride made my chin go up.

The stars seemed brighter and clearer somehow, till that old sickle moon started pushing its way into the sky. The night was chilling out quite a bit, but that made the mist weaving over the water thicken some. You'd think a good captain would have men posted above the mist line . . . My mind clicked to a stop and I dropped into a crouch.

What was it Mister Jess was always saying? 'Pride goeth before a fall' or something like that. Why should I be smarter than the captain of that group of men down there . . . Maybe, just maybe he'd already set pickets! Crouching low my eyes searched the darkness; my ears began the search also, waiting for sounds. The insect an' animal noises had stopped because of my approach. My body was resting close to the ground. Still and silent I waited for the night sounds to come back. The time dragged by but there was nothing! Nary frog nor cricket.

A cough and a hawking spit to my right, and just below, warned me that I'd have run right into the man in a few strides. The sweat of fear sprang out on my forehead, but I swallowed the fear and eased gently forward. It suited me in a way that he was there. The man would believe that he was stopping the animal noises . . . if he thought about it at all.

The mist was curling around my feet now. The man was a few yards away, but level with me. The water was close, but getting into it without him knowing would be a neat trick if I could do it. There was a swirl of mist directly in front of me. The hair on the back of my neck began to tingle, warning me of danger, there was a belch in the darkness, as he let out the gas from his supper, and I drew one of the Bowie knives.

I'd never deliberately set out to kill in my

life, but no one was gonna stop me from trying to save Mister Jesse. My lips was pulled back from my teeth, like an animal waiting to pounce on a new-born calf, then I breathed a quiet sigh of relief and my body relaxed. There was the hiss of running water as he relieved himself; I could hear it splashing against the side of a tree.

This was my chance! Easing my way down to the water's edge, I slid into it without a ripple . . . Goddamn! But it was cold; it was hell's own work to keep my teeth from clacking together like walnut shells on a tin sheet. Pins and needles started running up and down my legs like fleas in a warm bed. The water was deep. If I tried to wade through it the man on the bank would hear me.

Slipping the knife back into its sheath, I strapped the bundle to my head, good and tight, then lowered myself into the water till just my nose was clear of it. The creek was running real fast, so lifting my feet I let myself drift with it, the bundle on my head was well out of the water but the mist was covering it fine. Oh man! But it was so damned cold!

There was a dark blob on the bank; it had to be a tent so I began to count down. It seemed such a long time before the next one showed that by the time I'd counted to seven my body was chilled to the bone and I could hardly move my arms. Maybe it was seven, maybe eight. My time was up; this water was killing me. A low branch was leaning out into the creek so I took it. My hand was so cold my fingers could hardly grip it, but hand over hand I pulled to the bank and dragged myself ashore.

For a short while it was good, but then the cold pinched at me more than ever. Forcing myself up I began to work my legs and arms to send some feeling back into them. I didn't give a good Goddamn whether anybody heard me or not, but I was lucky. Then the pins and needles came back. Man they were everywhere! I could have screamed with the pain of it, but my mind was set on my task.

A scream of warning shot through my body like a lightning flash, but it was only some damn-fool of a Johnny Reb playing 'Taps' about two feet in front of me. If there'd been a tree handy I'd have been sitting in the top branches by this time, and I don't dare say what I'd like to have done with that fella's bugle if I could get a hold of it.

One by one the lights in the tents were put out; the fires had been douched with water and the blackness was that thick you could cut it with a knife. Somewhere along the line, that old sicklemoon had slipped behind a cloud. The mist clung to me like smoke, but it helped to damp down any noise my clumsy feet might make. The bugler had finished playing 'Taps'. He pushed his way into the tent in front of me; the one I'd counted at number seven.

The Bowie knife had jumped into my hand at the first sound of the bugle, and I still held it. If that bugler was in there with Mister Jesse, he'd have to die. Sneaking up close to the tent my mind closed up, so that I could hear what was going on. There was a lot of muttering and swearing so it had to be the wrong tent!

So, which was the right one? My night vision was coming into play, but even so, three feet was about my lot, and there were those sentries to worry about out there somewhere panic was gnawing at my gut like a dog on a bone. I took a chance, moving around to the front of the tent — and put my bare foot slap dab in the hot place where the fire had been. Man oh man! The skin on my feet is thick, but that would be the second time I'd have run clear up a tree this night — if there'd been one handy.

It gave me an idea though. The prison tent didn't have a fire in front of it, but it did have two guards outside and those guards would have to change. Now if I was outside the tent where the bugler slept, then it fair stood to reason that it was the guard tent. I'd just have to bide my time, but as it turned out, I didn't have long to wait before the tent flap was lifted and two soldiers marched out. They turned left, which just goes to show that my idea of where Mister Jesse was being kept was way out of kilter.

While they were marching along the front of the tents, I was skittering along at the back. Man! I was way out! We passed three tents before they stopped marching. As I settled down behind the tent to wait, it came to me that I weren't no great shakes at this here spying business, but after only a short time, the other two guards came out and headed towards their sleeping quarters.

The Bowie was in my hand; it was now or never, before the new guards had time to get settled into their guarding. I don't mind admitting my heart was in my throat as I pressed the knife into the canvas but there was no need to worry; the knife was real sharp, slicing into the heavy canvas without a sound. It would be a waste of time making a small slit; it was so dark that I wouldn't be able to see inside anyway. So hanging my hat on Lady Luck, I made a good long cut and slid through. Barely able to see, I eased across the ground on my belly, toward a darker bundle in the middle of the floor.

It was Mister Jesse, tied up tighter'n a roasting pig at thanksgiving. He had a lump on his head that must'a been real hurtful when he was awake, which he weren't just then. Now I had me a real problem, getting Mister Jesse out awake and healthy was one thing, but this was a hoss of a different color. It's what I had to do though. Him being tied up was a help in a way, because the rope gave me something to pull on as I dragged him, bit by bit, towards the slit in the tent and by the time we got there I was beginning to wish he weren't so Goddamned heavy. Any minute I expected one of the guards to pop their heads into the tent, but after some sweating and finangling we were through the hole and into the cold night air.

Now that I could do without it the old sickle moon was up there, shining away like a light from heaven, which is not where it would have gone if I'd had my wish, that's for sure.

The mist was still heavy over the water, but clearing a little at ground level and as I lowered Mister Jess down the bank, he let out a deep hollow groan, which was something else we didn't need.

Untying the bundle of guns and ammunition from around my waist I strapped it around his, so that it was resting in the small of his back. That way I could carry him across my shoulders and still keep my powder dry. This idea didn't work too good either because when that cold water hit Mister Jesse he came awake wriggling, struggling and cursing worse'n a man who'd hit his thumb with a hammer.

Man was I scared? You'd better believe it! Only way to shut him up was to dunk his head real deep into the water, he shut up quick enough then, you kin bet on that! Just then there was some scuffling and shouting up by the tents so I dragged Mister Jesse under some big roots which were sticking out into the water, and by this time my friend had come round enough to realize who I was.

'Good man, Josh,' he spluttered. 'Never thought to see you again.'

'Me neither,' I answered, cutting the ropes that bound him.

'How'd you find me?'

'Ne'mind that, Mister Jess,' I muttered. The package I'd tied on his back was almost under the water, but the Bowie soon made short work of the strings.

'What's that?' he asked.

I grinned in the darkness, pushing the Le Mat into his hands. 'Know what that is Mister Jess?'

He tapped my shoulder. 'Good man,' he said again. 'Let's move out.'

It was quiet up on the bank now so we drifted together, downstream. No way we could go back up, the water was running too fast, and after a few minutes, I could hear his teeth starting to chatter.

'Damned cold,' he muttered.

'Nothin' like a nice swim on a cool night, Massa.' I whispered in my old 'down home' voice; we'd drifted past the last of the tents now so I figured I could get sassy, but he was still one ahead.

'Like you said,' he replied, quick smart. 'This is nothing like a nice swim young Josh.'

Somebody back there by the tents spoiled it all by yelling that the prisoner had gone. Then some other fella shouted to search the water. A rifle banged, they were coming our way right enough. Jess headed for the bank with me close behind. We heard two more shots, those boys were getting closer all the time, I thought, as we dragged ourselves out of the water and started to belly-crawl across the field. Men were out in force now, carrying lighted faggots to help them search.

Close to the ground like we were, I could see the dark bulk of the field-pieces over on my left. Then I remembered the guards, and that old sickle moon was just about bright enough for me to tell Mister Jess, by sign, what was worrying me.

He nodded and we moved on. Then it came to me. The horses! Grabbing his arm, I pulled him the way I wanted to go. Over a slight rise we went and down a long shallow slope. The horses were chomping grass right behind the caissons.

Mister Jess patted my arm again, only this time his hand lifted and stayed in front of my face. He made a stabbing movement with his hand. I understood, and unbuckled one of the knife belts. He strapped it on, and was gone like a ghost in the night.

Man! But he near frightened the living daylights out've me when he tapped my shoulder again, to signal me to go forward.

'What happened to the guards?' I whispered as we moved among the horses

'They died,' he replied.

'Just like that?'

'Them or us, Josh. You OK bareback?'

'Is there any other way?'

'Nope.'

'Bridles still on?'

'Yeah, we were lucky.'

'So let's go, Mister Jess,' I muttered, slipping easily onto the horse's back and leaning well over, so's not to show an outline. Jess was right there beside me as we rode away from that hollow.

The blast of the shotgun part of the Le Mat damn near deafened me. Didn't do much for the rest of the horses neither; they were already skittish from the different noises. That gun going off so close, and the whine of the 20 gauge shot buzzing along over their ears, did nothing to calm them down. Fact is it scattered them all to Hell.

It wouldn't take long for them to settle again, but any time gained would be helpful to us, so, heads down and asses up, we rode like the devil was on our tails. There were a few shots from the soldiers, but they only helped to scare the loose horses even more.

'Which way?' shouted Jesse as we rode knee to knee.

My daddy's teachings came in handy again. That old sickle moon was above us, moving right along, and the slope away from those cannon felt about right also. 'Just keep going Mister Jess, we're right in line for the wagon.' Maybe I sounded a damn sight more sure than I really was, but. Hell! A fella has to do some guessing sometime, don't he?

Seemed no time at all before we reined in alongside the wagon, and then we were up and away, heading fast across the border and into Kentucky. The Johnny Rebs would think twice about following us while we were heading in that direction. Like I said, there weren't many of them back there. Guess they had to catch up with the rest of the troop, probably under orders, so I figured we were home free.

After about an hour or so we stopped for some food. This here spying business sure made a fella hungry and no mistake.

I reckoned Mister Jesse had learned a hard lesson back there, but had he? Hell no, man! In no time at all he was telling me to swing around in a big loop and there we were, heading for the border again. I tell the world, this guy is gonna get us both killed iffen I don't watch him real careful. Seems like I'd be a damn sight safer in the army.

8

We were still travelling backwards and forwards along the border between Kentucky and Virginia, when 1862 came to a close. It kind'a looked as if I'd never get to where I wanted to be. We'd been heading towards a small town near the Ohio River, but still in Virginia, and Jesse Turnball was still up to his tricks, while I was left to sweat blood every time he left me alone in the wagon. He'd had quite a few close calls over the months but it didn't seem to faze him none.

We still had the horses we'd stolen from the Johnny Rebs that time. They didn't have any brands on them, so Jesse said we'd earned them, and I figured maybe he was right at that. Jesse had ridden on into the town, while I was cooking up some vittles. I was getting real good at putting a meal together; guess Jesse was pleased about that too. It was a chore he didn't cotton to, and I kind'a liked doing it.

I was busy stirring the pot when I saw dust heading my way. It was always the same! My gut began to churn and I eased back close to the wagon seat, where the Le Mat was kept under a horse blanket while Jesse was away. It was different in one way, because now I'd use the gun, and I didn't give a good Goddamn who it was, but still that old churning nagged away at me.

I watched the dust coming closer till I could recognize Mister Jesse. He was sure in one hell of a hurry though, so I figured it must be trouble of some kind. He came up in a swirl of dust; real close to my pot of vittles.

'Hey!' I hollered, 'all that dust is going in my good broth!'

'Don't worry about that, Joshua,' he shouted, like he was real excited, 'it'll help to thicken it. Your damned stew is always too thin anyway. Here, take a look at this.' He came over waving a scrap of paper. I was right! He was excited. 'Look Josh, Abe Lincoln has made an Emancipation Proclamation.' He shoved the paper into my hand like it was pure gold.

Well I could read some, but not real fast, and he just couldn't wait.

'Emancipation!' he shouted at me, like I was deaf or something. 'Emancipation, Joshua old son!' He banged the flat of his hand on my back till I figured he was gonna do me a mischief.

I couldn't see what the blazes he was getting so all fired het up about.

'You don't figure it do you?' he hollered. 'It means that any black man who wants to be free — is!'

'You mean the war's over?'

'No, Josh, but it means that any slave within the United States is free!'

'Is my daddy free?'

'Not yet, my old son, but soon, real soon. Once we've won this war there won't be any slaves.'

I read the piece of paper two or three times before it really got home to me. The date on the paper was January the first 1863; it was nigh on eight weeks old; there was a well of excitement building inside my body and I knew that date would stay in my mind forever.

'But we're still at war with the Johnny Rebs, Mister Jesse. What happens to the slaves in their territory?' I asked.

'When we've won this damned war they'll be free, too,' Mister Jesse said, still excited.

'You mean, if!'

'No, Joshua. When! We have to win it and we need every man we can muster.'

I stared at my good friend for a long time. 'Every man counts,' I said, real serious, 'it's time I joined the army. My daddy is down there in Carolina, if he's still alive. It wouldn't set right with me iffen I didn't do my damnedest to free him from those women.'

Jesse had a kind'a lost look on his face, when I'd finished speaking.

'Parting of the ways then, is it, Joshua?' He asked quietly. 'You know I have my job to do, and it's very important. I'd like you to stay with me, to help, if you would.'

I was already shaking my head. 'Like you said, Mister Jesse. This spying thing is your way and I know what you do is downright dangerous, but I ain't up to that sort of work. Y'all unerstan' suh?' My emotion made me revert to my 'Down Home' way of talking; a way I'd almost forgotten.

'Sure, I understand, Joshua, you always were going to join the army,' he said, kind'a sad, 'but we'll stay together until we get you back into Ohio, then we'll make a run for the first decent town and get you signed in before we part company.'

Our stew was eaten mostly in silence; we were both kind'a moody. Inside me, my stomach kept bubbling with the excitement of it all. My good friend was going his own way and so was I; we might never see each other again. And as much as I might try to shrug it off, this man was both a brother and a sort of father to me; and it didn't seem right somehow, that I could have such deep feelings for a white man. Even Master Luke, who would always be my very good friend, didn't near fill the gap Mister Jesse would leave inside me, and I could feel that he was as sad about it as me.

Neither one of us could enjoy our supper, and as the sun started to settle, I looked up at the sky, marveling at the different colors, as they changed from the hard brightness to softer pinkish colors, then deeper reds and blues as the night drew in.

'Looks grand, huh, Josh?' Makes a man feel kind of small somehow.' His voice was soft and low.

'Uh-huh, Mister Jess. Sure is a big Old World ain't it? Don't seem possible that I never even noticed all those colors till you pointed 'em out to me. Like you said, makes a man feel real small.'

We sat there till long after dark, like we didn't want the mood to end, but bed was calling and clear-up time, too, so I climbed to my feet and broke the spell that held us . . .

We were up at first light, doing our chores as usual, but we both knew that the change was going to happen.

The new sun was pushing the dawn from the sky as I set the horses to their task. Mister Jess sat in his corner, quietly drawing deep on his cigar and staring ahead; no words were passing between us, but I figured his thoughts was on the parting, just like mine.

'We should make good time, now we don't have those Johnny Rebs to worry about.' He said it like he was just trying to make conversation.

'Reckon we've left 'em behind right enough, Mister Jess,' I replied.

'Y'all will have to stop doing that Josh,' he snapped, sounding kind'a irritable.

'Stop what?'

'That mister bit,' he replied. 'Do I call you mister?'

That made me laugh. 'Why the blue blazes should you call me mister?'

'Now just you listen to me, Josh. You may be going to join the Army of the North, but there'll be people, even there, who'll try to treat you just as bad as some Southern men would.'

'That so?'

'Yeah, that's so! And you have to stand up to 'em. Be your own man, Josh. Get it into your head, that you are as good as any man breathing. Give every man his proper title and treat every man with respect, but if they try to hooraw you, then give as good as you get. You understand me Josh?'

'You mean white men, Jesse?'

'Any man Josh, because if you don't, this war just won't mean a damned thing.'

I just shook my head and said nothing. I ain't never heard of such a fool thing in all my life. Me! Talking back to a white man? 'It just don't bear thinking about, Mist — Jesse.' I just about managed to stop myself saying 'mister' because of that scowly frown.

'OK, if you say so,' I said; just to keep the peace. 'Man! But it sure is gonna be a hard thing to do.'

'So get some practice,' he grumped. 'From here on I'm Jess, or Jesse. No mister! Savvy?'

'Yes sir M — Jess,' I said, watching him out of the corner of my eye.

There was a lopsided grin on his face. He knew I'd done that last bit on purpose and things seemed to perk up a bit after that, because we both knew I had to do this.

Jess told me, that in about three days we'd be fording the Ohio River and heading for a place called Cincinnati. I don't rightly know how Mister Jesse knew just where the troops would be, but I wasn't about to argue with him.

I realized that we were in safe country, because Mister Jesse didn't hang around for anything; almost seemed like he'd be glad when we reached where we were heading, and it didn't seem no time at all before we saw the first real soldier's camp in the distance. I ain't seen so many horses and field-pieces in all my born days. Men! They was just about everywhere, all in uniforms of one sort or another. All kinds of men, black and white, yellow skinned men and Indians to boot! I reckon if a man tried to count 'em, he'd be there forever.

Tents, all in neat lines, and smart as all-get-out. There was some real nice smells rising from the cook-fires also, and my stomach told me we should be cooking our own supper.

A soldier on a fine horse was riding towards us. As he passed each tent, the men all jumped up and saluted him. I'd heard all about this saluting thing from Jesse — he'd taken a deal of trouble with me, to make sure I did it just right, so I knew that the man on the horse was some kind of an officer fella.

Figured Jesse would get down from the wagon and we'd do some of this saluting stuff, also, but damn me if the officer didn't sit all stiff on his horse and salute Jesse! Then he turned, and led our wagon right up to the biggest tent of all, where men in real smart uniforms were standing around a table set outside the tent, with all sorts of papers, maps and such on it.

'Stay here, Josh,' Jesse told me, as he climbed down from the wagon, 'I have some business to take care of.'

Well he strolled up to the table lighting one of his long thin cigars, and men were saluting him left and right. Reckon my eyes needed fixing. Jesse weren't even in a uniform, yet those men were jumping around like fleas with the itch.

After about ten minutes or so, Jesse climbed back into the wagon and there was another whole slew of this saluting thing, before Jesse told me to drive off.

'Y'know, Jesse,' I said out of the corner of my mouth, 'some vittles would sure hit the spot about now, watching all those men jumping around fair worked up a hunger in me.'

'Me too, Joshua,' he laughed, 'but it'll be ready time we get there, don't you fret.'

It was too! We just stopped at a tent and there it was. Man! Did that stew smell good. I don't know who'd cooked it, but Jesse said it was ours, and if he said so, that was good enough for me; so I was out of that wagon quick-smart, and in no time at all we were filling up on that good stew.

Sleep didn't come easy that night. My mind was telling me to go with Jess. But in my heart I knew that I wanted to hit back hard; for me, my daddy, yeah and Hector too, along with every other black man who'd ever suffered beatings and such. So, it didn't seem like any time at all before the blaring of bugles drove me out of my blankets and getting to work at making breakfast.

Last night's melancholy was back again and it lasted clear through the morning, till the wagon was loaded with food 'n' stuff for Jesse's next trip.

At last, he was ready to go. Man! My gut was set to churning something awful. 'All loaded and set then, Mister Jess?' I mumbled, more for something to say than anything else.

'Yeah, all set, Joshua old son,' he replied, his face set real serious, 'and remember. No more mister! OK?'

I just nodded. The lump in my craw was just about choking me as he took my hand in both of his. Firm and strong that grip was.

'You watch yourself, son,' he muttered, as he pulled me real close. 'We're good friends, you and me. Hope to see you after this war is over, and if you ever need me, just call Josh, and I'll come a-running.'

I was beginning to think I'd seen a tear in his eye, but then again, maybe it wasn't, because he said something about the damned keen wind hereabouts as he turned away from me and climbed aboard.

Just when I thought Mister Jess would never be able to surprise me again; he reached down into the wagon and passed me a brand spanking new Henry rifle and a belt holster with a new Army Colt pistol in it.

Before I rightly knew what he was at, he'd flicked the reins, and the wagon was moving off . . . I can't explain how lonesome I felt. Standing there, with the Henry in one hand and the holstered pistol in the other, watching that old covered wagon moving steadily down between the rows of tents. Goddamn, but I figured Jesse was right. That wind must be real keen; it was making my own eyes run something awful. The urge was in me to run after him, but it was not to be, so I watched the wagon get smaller and smaller till the heat-haze and distance gobbled it up.

9

I soon settled into the army routine. I had my troubles, sure, but like Jesse said, you stand on your two hind legs and let people know you ain't gonna be messed around.

In no time at all, I was fitted out with a brand new dark blue uniform; they had some trouble with my size but it all came out right in the end. I'd been looking forward to getting some boots for the first time in my life. Man, was that a mistake! They are the most uncomfortable things I ever did wear. My name was a bit of a problem also. The officer told me he couldn't put Joshua D on the form for some Goddamned silly reason, so he changed it to Joshua Dee! Still can't figure why, it sounds the same to me.

I was attached to the black section of the Army of the Ohio. We had orders to move, the tents were being taken down and loaded on the wagons. All hurry and bustle it was, but three months is a long time in the army, and a man soon learns when it's time to move out, and how fast it can be done. He also gets to know who his friends are. We'd bin in a few skirmishes, an' I knew the difference between the ones who'd stick and the ones who wouldn't when the going was tough.

There were some who'd like to have had my guns; they were far better than the old flintlocks most of the men were using. I just followed Jesse's advice and more than one fella was left holding a sore jaw.

I had two stripes on my arm already, and it looked as if Jess was right when he said I'd soon be a sergeant. Learned to smoke too, and take things a lot more calmly than I used to. The big guns didn't scare me now and my good Henry rifle had turned more than one healthy man into an invalid. Or worse! Kind'a surprising how quickly a body can get used to seeing people maimed, injured, or just plain blown to bits.

It was early September, and rumor had it that we were preparing to move on Major General Bragg's Confederate Army. We were also hoping that things would be better for us than at Gettysburg.

The scrap of newspaper I'd seen — which was over eight weeks old — put our losses at over 23,000! It's kind'a hard to imagine that if the rebels lost about the same number, it meant that around 46,000 men were lost in just one battle, between June 9th and July 4th! Man! It just don't bear thinking about, so I closed my mind to such thoughts as I began to load the next wagon; it ain't good to dwell on things that can't be altered.

Before full dark, we were on the move towards Chattanooga, heading for my first really big battle. The fieldpieces had gone ahead with their escort. We could hear them beginning to open up, and as we moved rapidly up to the monsters, the awful noise of the explosions, together with the scream of canister and shot, smashed into our brains, leaving each man in a terrible, brain-numbing world of his own.

Barely heard above the din was the dreadful screams of the wounded and dying, and within it all, the frightened, screaming neigh of the horses, as we charged forward into the man-made hell, with twelve pounder Howitzers, trying to outdo the noise of the twenty pounder Parrot fieldpieces.

My legs were like jelly, but they pounded forward anyway, the mind scrambled into a thoughtless mass by the noise, and a throat caked with the awful taste of powder fumes. A bullet or musket ball tore at the shoulder of my coat. I ran on, the unheard scream of 'charge' was still tearing at my throat as a wraith-like figure appeared through the dust and smoke just a few yards in front of me. My finger squeezed the trigger of the Henry Rifle and the man fell away. Moments later, I leapt across his dead body, charging onward into the smoke.

Spitting the bitter taste of gunpowder from my lips, I paused, frantically sucking the filthy air into my lungs, almost choking on it as I did so. A soldier charged out of the gloom, the bayonet glinting red in the flickering fires around us, gobs of blood still dripping from it. My rifle lashed down hard, deflecting the bayonet from my gut. Even in all that noise, I heard the scraping slap of the old flintlock hammer, as it dropped past the striker and into the pan. It was a misfire!

I saw the instant look of shock, hate and stark horror pass across his face, as the man realized he was going to die. My gun jerked from the recoil and the man was thrown away from me, as if a giant hand had smashed into his chest.

I started to run again, another one was sprawled on his back in front of me. He began to raise himself as I approached; at the last second I saw the pistol in his hand. The butt of the Henry smashed into his face as his gun exploded and I felt the heat burn along my leg. It had been close, but luck was with me. The sudden rush of blood inside my body made me feel unstoppable, but I knew it couldn't last. The noise of battle was already dimming and that awful deadness, that always seems to follow the clamor of heavy guns settled in my skull.

I could hear the cries of the wounded and dying now. The scream of a horse in torment echoed across the battlefield as the trembling returned to my knees, and a body sickness tore at my guts. It would not do for anyone to see me this way, so I slunk into the doorway of a burnt-out building until my sickness left me.

Men were no longer running forward in a mad charge. They were standing around in small groups, or wandering aimlessly about, their minds numbed, first by the deafening noise and then by the lack of it. No one could understand why the battle was so suddenly over.

This would not do, I told myself. I was a corporal, and should be helping to bring these men into line. Ignoring my stomach cramps and trembling legs, I called the nearest group of men to me. 'Snap it up,' I said sharply. 'D'you want the Rebs to drop canister or shot in on you while you're mooning around. Straighten up there! Let's move through these buildings like soldiers. Look out for snipers!'

In next to no time at all, I had quite a detail of men, all obeying my commands; collecting the wounded of both armies, laying them in orderly rows and attending to their injuries. Some had also been foraging for food and ammunition. By the time the officers arrived on the scene, my small section was really organized.

The officers were very impressed, and I knew Jesse had been right when he said, 'Look after number one.' I could see that third stripe coming any time now.

It wasn't until next morning that we were told the Rebel Army had pulled back from Chattanooga. They'd only left a small delaying unit behind while the main army had moved into the dense wooded area of Chickamauga. So, it looked as if the real battle hadn't even started and we had to do the whole thing over again.

The mass of troops around Chattanooga was like an anthill, as the men sorted themselves out, ready for the march on Chickamauga. It was heavily wooded country so it would be rough going, and I, like everyone else, was charging about sorting out my platoon, ready for the sergeant and lieutenant's inspection.

Sergeant McBain was a nasty, loud-mouthed, son-of-a-bitch. Sheer spite oozed from every pore of his huge body. I'd already had a few run-ins with him; he'd made a couple of attempts to take my Henry rifle and belt gun — being white he figured he might get away with it. He made a few threats about what could happen to me, but gave up when he found I made tough chewing.

Lieutenant Sutton, on the other hand, was real nice. It was easy to see that he didn't like McBain any more than I did, but his hands were tied; because, although this was a black unit, most of the sergeants and all of the officers were white. It kind'a made me wonder why some of them were fighting for the Union at all when they'd be more at home with the Johnny Rebs, judging by their attitudes.

We had some real young lads in our unit and I'd taken it upon myself to watch over them, so as the duty corporal started the roll call I listened to the replies of 'Yo'.

It seemed that our platoon had managed to come through without losing anyone, until the corporal yelled 'Ervine!' There was no reply. The corporal waited a moment, then called a second time, before passing on down the roll.

Ervine was missing! It didn't seem possible! I was sure I'd seen Daniel's cheeky face around since the battle. He was the kind of lad you noticed, he always had a big wide smile on his face and an air of truthfulness, even when he told the lieutenant he was eighteen when no one in their right mind would believe he was no-but fourteen summers.

Once the roll call was over I stepped to the front and called, 'Anyone seen young Danny Ervine?'

There was some shuffling of feet, but no one said anything. I stared hard at the group of lads on the end of the line and slowly walked towards them. They were looking everywhere except at me, and my slow pace was deliberately intimidating them.

Six foot three and as broad as a barn door, my kepi tilted over the right eye, and the stub of a cigar stuck in the corner of a mouth covered with a three-day stubble, I looked tough, and I was.

One boy seemed more agitated than the rest, so I poked the barrel of my rifle into his gut and his breath came out in a whoosh.

'You!' I snapped at him, like I was about to bite his head off, 'where did you see him last?'

He hummed an' hawed, staring at the friends standing each side of him. 'I, um we, that is me an' Tommy seed him bein' carted off by Sergeant McBain, Corporal,' he stuttered.

'How d'you mean, carted off?' I growled.

'He, that is, Sergeant McBain, had Daniel by the ear, twistin' it somethin' rotten he was,' muttered the lad.

I felt the anger building inside me and it must have showed on my face, because the three youngsters were getting more frightened by the minute.

'Please don't tell Sergeant McBain we told you, Corporal,' murmured Tommy, 'he'll give us hell if he finds out.'

'Where's he taken young Daniel?' I snapped, making a good guess why McBain had dragged the boy off.

'In one of the houses, down there,' replied Tommy, pointing vaguely along the empty street. 'We all hid away when we heard he was on the rampage, but Daniel, well he just weren't quick enough.'

My temper felt like it was about to blow my kepi clean off my head. 'You carry on, Corporal,' I snapped, damned near biting my cigar through in my temper. I shoved my rifle towards him. 'Hang on to that till I get back, and if you lose it I'll have you for dinner. Understand?'

Corporal Bellamy was mostly not the type to argue, but he knew what would happen if he gave up my Henry rifle to anybody. I needed to find McBain and young Daniel Ervine. Fast! There were rumors floating around the black units that McBain was rather fond of young boys. I'd heard of it, but

I was a black corporal, while he was a white sergeant. I could get shot for what I was thinking of doing to Sergeant McBain, but Mister Jesse's words were buzzing through my head. 'Stand up and look 'em straight in the eye, Josh', he'd said, and that's just what I was gonna do if I died doing it.

I moved rapidly from house to house, knowing there couldn't be much time left. The boy might put up a bit of a fight, but McBain was a real big man and he wouldn't hesitate to beat up on the boy if he gave him any trouble, maybe even kill him if there was no other way.

The thought was with me that the search was going to take forever, when I heard a boyish yell from what must have been a livery; the place was partly burned down, but there was one timber shed that had somehow survived. There was no door on the barn-like place, and another squeal of pain set me running towards it.

Stopping just inside the opening, I saw McBain holding the boy, face down, over a saddle fence. The lad had put up a struggle, but he was no match for the sergeant, who had just finished tying young Daniel to the fence, and was pulling the pants off him.

McBain must have become aware of the loss of light in the barn as my body blocked the doorway. He turned his head, worried, until he realized who I was, then he grinned. 'Git back to your business, Corporal,' he sneered, 'an' let me git on with mine.'

He started to unbuckle his belt, but paused when he saw I wasn't moving. 'You goin', Corporal? or do you like to watch. Is that it eh?'

He chuckled deep in his throat, but it was cut off as I slowly crossed the floor of the barn. He pulled the belt tight up and flexed his huge arms. 'We-ell now,' he gloated, 'looks as if I'm gonna take a corporal apart first. That'll suit me just fine, I always did hate your damned guts.'

As he was talking, McBain was moving towards me, balanced on the balls of his feet, with his hands weaving in front of him. He moved the fingers on both hands, coaxing me to come to him. I could see he knew what to do, but I'd been in a few fights myself, and, now that the inbred fear of tackling a white man had left me, I was more than ready for McBain . . . but I wasn't about to take him lightly. No sir!

He started to move around me, to get the light at his own back, but I wasn't having any. I moved towards him and stuck a straight left into his face. He hadn't been ready for that and he stepped back a pace, so I followed it with two more lefts and a right cross. They all landed, but it didn't seem to make any difference.

Suddenly he jumped forward and wrapped his beefy arms around me, pinning my own arms at my side. It felt like being held in a giant vice, as he lifted me clear off the floor, and began to really squeeze.

His eyes were wild as he stared into my face. 'I'll bust every Goddamned rib in your black body, you bastard,' he snarled, as spittle drooled from his mouth. 'Then I'll tear your filthy black head off an' feed it to the dogs.'

I had to hand it to him, he was one strong fella, but he shouldn't have reminded me about my hard black head. It was the one thing left to me, and I struck him right across the bridge of the nose with it. Man! The blood really pumped out. He let go of me and I got down to business, with short chopping punches that really cut to the bone. Left right, left right, those punches really socked home, and as he sagged down the wall my fists drove him back up, I could feel the shock of 'em clear to my shoulder. My mind was a blank, with just one small window in it, the window framed the bloody face in front of me, and I just kept hitting.

The voice of Lieutenant George Sutton washed over me like iced water, bringing back all the old fears of hitting a white person.

'I say! Would you mind letting the poor fellow fall now, Joshua Dee? After all, there seems less life in our good sergeant, than in some steaks I've eaten.'

My fists fell to my sides, and the red mist that had blinded me to everything except the hated face of Sergeant McBain, slowly cleared.

The lieutenant was making tut-tutting noises. 'Bad business this, Corporal Dee,' he muttered, 'A Corporal hitting a Sergeant? Not done you know, court-martial and all that, could be shot. Good job I brought you your promotion stripe isn't it?'

The lieutenant dangled the stripe in front of my eyes and I took it without speaking, as I stood to attention.

McBain groaned and attempted to struggle to his feet. 'I wan' 'im charged thir,' he mumbled through thick and bleeding lips, 'I'm white an' he attacked me. I'll 'ave 'im shot.'

'And I shall spread the word about your nasty little games, Private McBain,' replied the lieutenant suavely. 'You cannot remain in a black unit as a private but, unfortunately, we do not have the time to have you transferred. So, for the forthcoming action you will keep your chevrons. After that, you will be transferred. Understood? Get yourself cleaned up and be on parade ready for the march. Now get out!'

How McBain ever managed to stand, never mind stagger out of that barn, I don't know, but he did. Meanwhile, I untied young Ervine and sent him scampering on his way, with a caution on keeping his mouth shut about what had happened in the barn.

'He won't you know,' the lieutenant murmured, 'and you can't expect him to. You're his hero and a real tough one too, if I may say so. Major Jesse Turnball was right about you, Joshua Dee.'

'You know him sir?'

'Very well! Better than you think, I'm his brother-in-law. A very brave man is the Major. Now you cut along and get cleaned up. Sew that extra stripe on as soon as you get the chance, you're the senior N.C.O. now. You've got a good head on your shoulders and I'm going to have to rely on you in the battles to come.'

'Yes sir. Thank you sir,' I muttered, still unable to believe my good luck. I threw a smart salute and walked out of the barn feeling more than ever that my luck was still riding on the shoulders of Mister Jess.

10

As day followed day, more and more of our troops arrived and by the 18th of September, we were set to defend Chickamauga creek, by guarding all the fords and bridges, with a skirmish line clear along the riverside

We kept them at bay during the daylight hours, but once darkness closed in, the Confederates managed to get most of their army across, and we were suddenly called upon to help support the left flank, which was under pressure.

Our troop ran into heavy artillery fire as we jogged towards the men of the left flank, and once again, the noise of canister and shot screamed in the air, sending men running every which way. Slowly but surely we'd be pushed back, re-group and hold again, while the mind-numbing hell continued to crash and explode around us, as we stopped charge after charge. It seemed as if all the rebels in creation were trying to ram their bayonets down our throats, and frightened boys, like young Daniel Ervine, were loading their single shot muskets time after time, without firing a shot in their terror.

The rain was teeming down. Huge gobbets of muck, mixed with chain and shot, flew through the air, as once again we dropped back to a new defense line.

I saw one boy break open a cartridge, pour the powder into the muzzle of his musket and attempt to ram down the pad. He'd forgotten all about the ball still between his lips, or priming the pan. There was madness in his eyes as he raised the musket and pulled the trigger. Nothing happened, but his mind was beyond knowing. He snatched another paper cartridge from his belt, hands shaking as he started to load the gun again.

There was a huge explosion and a great gaping hole appeared where the boy had been standing. I felt blood and muck splash across my face and body, the shock of it forced me out of my dreamlike state and sent me diving for cover, as even more shot screamed overhead and exploded behind me.

Men were running back towards Chatta-nooga as frantic screaming men in gray were overrunning our position.

We'd helped to stem the tide for more than twenty-four mind bending hours, but now it was time to go so crouching low, to make as small a target as possible, I zigzagged through the shattered and burning trees.

Ahead of me were two boys and one taller

figure; I started to gain on them, my heavy boots pounding in the mud and slime underfoot.

One of the boys must have heard me above the din because he turned and dropped into a crouch. I had time to realize that the gun lining up on me was a modern type rifle, not an outdated musket. My face dug into the soft earth as I sprawled flat on my stomach, as a bullet whipped the kepi from my head, spinning it away like something alive. I rolled frantically to one side, as another bullet gouged the earth where I had been lying.

The kid was not about to give up, I saw him flick the lever and raise the gun again. I yelled my name as loud as I could. The gun butt dropped from the boy's shoulder as he stared at me through the smoke and gloom. 'Joshua? Is that you, fella?' he shouted, above the noise of battle.

In spite of the shrill pitch of fear in his voice, I recognized Danny Ervine. 'Move Danny,' I yelled, 'they're right behind me, son.'

I was on my feet almost as soon as I started shouting. Those insane screams were awful close now and I could hear the swish and slush of their feet in the mud. The heavy guns had packed up, which meant that they couldn't tell friend from foe, so the foot soldiers had to be real close.

We were some of the last to make it back to Chattanooga, where officers and men were lining up to make a stand. We'd lost the battle of Chickamauga, and if they hit us now we'd stand no chance at all.

I put my hand on young Daniel's shoulder. 'Thanks for not blowing my stupid brains out, pardner.' I wiped a muddy sleeve across my filthy face and spat out the iron taste of blood, 'You behaved like a real trooper out there, son.'

'Sure am sorry, Sergeant Joshua,' he muttered, 'figured I was done for that time, you bein' so close an' all.'

'Forget it, Danny, who was that with you?'

'Corporal Bellamy an' Tommy. There they are leanin' agin that big gun.'

Lieutenant Sutton came striding over just then; the saber in his hand still dripped blood. 'Get your men together, Sergeant, and help manhandle some of the guns into position. Move it man, they could be upon us in minutes!'

'Sah!' I shouted, but the Lieutenant was already on his way down the line.

Grabbing young Daniel's shoulder, I pushed him towards Corporal Bellamy. 'Go, tell the corporal to round up as many of our platoon as he can find, lad, and get 'em back here, quick-smart.'

The boy scurried off, pleased to do my bidding, while I called the men close to hand. In no time at all we had a good squad of men, both black and white, levering and pushing the heavy guns through the mud and rain to form a defense, and as a miserable, smoky wet dawn broke over Chattanooga, we were about as ready as we'd ever be. Tired and worn out, I stared out at the war-torn ground. In the distance, trees poked their scorched and broken branches towards the sky, like accusing fingers, still smoldering in spite of the rain. The sharp curve of Moccasin Bend, which cut the town in two and carried the Mississippi River, was swollen and dark brown from mud and rain as it twisted and turned, as if in sullen agreement with the accusing trees. At least there were no charging soldiers in gray, or the pounding of heavy guns to break the stillness of the miserable, God-forsaken morning, that smelled only of death, smoke and gunpowder.

I was wondering if this land would ever look the same again, when a bugle sounded calling us to parade, and as we lined up, small sections were detailed off to carry out various chores.

Lieutenant Sutton began to call out names. He reeled off Danny Ervine, his mate,

Tommy Malleck, Corporals Bellamy and Jackson, myself and Sergeant McBain. 'Search detail. Sergeant!' he snapped. 'Seems that the Johnny Rebs are going to leave us alone for a spell. Let's get out there and see if any of our brave lads are lying in the mud, waiting to be rescued.'

Having delivered the order, he hurried on past the big gun I'd been leaning against and marched towards the beginning of the wooded area. I saluted and ordered the men to follow me as I hurried after him.

There was pain in my heart as we came across one twisted, broken body after the other. Boys in their early teens; older men, probably leaving wives and children with no man to care for them; wounded men almost dead for the want of food and warmth. We struggled to move them together, for whatever comfort they could find just by being with each other until they could be taken back to Chattanooga in the carts that were following us.

McBain kept glaring at me as if I was personally responsible for every death. 'You know, black man,' he gritted between clenched teeth. 'Just because your officer friends learned y'all to talk proper, it don't make yuh any different.'

'Don't make more trouble for yourself,

man,' I told him. 'You've already lost your stripes.'

'They ain't gone yet boy!' he snarled. 'Don't count your chickens.'

I shook my head as he stumbled away, following the Lieutenant into the timber. It was beyond my understanding why he was dressed in blue, instead of gray. The man hated the very thing he was fighting for, yet it was eating away at his guts like a tapeworm.

Shrugging my shoulders, I turned to help an old-timer who'd almost had his arm shot off. He groaned as I started to move him. 'Painful huh?' I asked, more for something to say than anything else.

'Naw,' he husked, ''taint the arm, son, it's me rhumatiz, damned old knee hates the wet, arm's nothin', long's I've still got one to hold me pecker I'll make it OK.' He spat blood. 'Could do with a chaw of baccy though.'

'Don't have a chaw, fella, got me a cigar though.' I laid him down with the rest of the wounded, pulled a broken cigar out of my pocket and gave him half, pushing the other piece into the corner of my own mouth. Rubbing a stinker into flame against my pants leg, I lit the stub and sucked gratefully on the smoke, allowing the acrid tang of the tobacco to kill the iron-blood taste in my mouth. The old man didn't need the match; he was chewing the other half like it was a piece of steak.

The old-timer wouldn't last much longer; he'd lost too much blood and his body felt cold as ice. When I left him he was still muttering about his rheumatics, but his voice had become kind'a whispery and far away.

The men were spreading out too much and I was just about to warn them not to get too far apart, when there was a gunshot up ahead, closely followed by a second one.

We heard McBain cursing and swearing about 'dirty sneakin' Rebs' as we raced forward. Lying half in and half out of some bushes was the lieutenant; a bullet had taken half his face away. It didn't need a doctor to tell us that the war was over for Lieutenant Sutton.

'What happened here, McBain?'

'D'you need someone to tell yuh?' flared McBain, 'Christ, you must be stupid or somethin'.'

'Answer the question!' I snapped.

'Don't you come that tone with me, boy!' he snarled. 'I'm the senior sergeant in this bailiwick an' don't you be forgettin' it.'

'You've bin moved down to private, McBain, the lieutenant demoted you.'

'Is it on the record, sonny?'

'No, but you and I know that the lieutenant

was putting you on report, as soon as the company re-organized.'

McBain hawked and spat. 'Don't remember no such thing, black boy, now move along, afore I kick your no-good ass.'

The realization was late coming to me. 'You damn well killed him, you sneaky bastard.'

'Hope you kin prove that, mister, y'all start talkin' like that an' I'll have those pretty stripes off you quicker'n spit. Court martial too I shouldn't wonder, bad mouthin' a white senior sergeant with a first class war record is a dangerous business — for a black man. Now, take the poor lieutenant back, an' lay him in the pile with the rest of the cadavers.'

As the two corporals carried the lieutenant away, McBain pushed himself close to me. 'Y'all watch your back you black bastard. First chance I git you're dead, an' there'll be lots of chances between now an' then. Try pushin' me off my perch an' I'll 'ave you, sonny, leave me alone an' you just might live to a ripe old age.'

We made our way back to the camp in somber silence. Lieutenant Sutton had been well thought of by the black troops, and to make matters worse it was McBain, in his role of senior sergeant, who reported that the lieutenant had been killed while hunting for wounded troops . . .

★ ★ ★

. . . It seemed that the rebels were going to be satisfied with trying to starve us out, by keeping us under siege. They'd set their big guns on Lookout Mountain, which gave them a commanding view of the river at Moccasin bend, so no food or ammunition could be brought in that way. They also put troops on Missionary Ridge, which overlooked the Southeastern side of Chattanooga, leaving us in a valley between the two high points. Nothing could move in or out of Chattanooga without the Johnny Rebs knowing about it.

Day followed miserable day, and with little or nothing to do, Sergeant McBain was making life pure misery for the younger men; boys really, but it was hard to think of them that way when they had fought so well.

'Sergeant Dee!' McBain's raucous voice shook me out of my dreaming. I instinctively stiffened my body. 'Latrine duty,' he snapped. 'Collect Corporals Jackson an' Bellamy, then grab those two kids you're so fond of. It's time we had some new latrines dug . . . '

122

'But we already dug 'em only two days ago.'

'Don't but me, Dee, just get to it, NOW! At the double, mister! Collect shovels from the quartermaster; I'll show you where to dig. Come on! Come on! Move it!'

Temper was making my head spin; I knew just where he'd chosen for us to dig, I'd seen him marking the place out. He'd deliberately picked an old latrine ditch that would be useless, but by the time we'd finished, no one would want to be within half a mile of us, especially not downwind.

September was past and we were pushing our way into October, seemed like there was more rain in the sky than I ever thought possible. Sunrise and sunset was the same: cloudy, overcast and rain, rain, rain.

We squelched near knee-deep in the mud as we tramped over to the spot. The shovels sank easily into the soft surface, but when the boys tried to lift them the mud slurped and gurgled but held on like glue, and even the two corporals could hardly move them.

'Git in an' show 'em how it's done, Sergeant Dee,' bawled McBain, giving me a hefty shove in the kidneys, 'show 'em how to shovel shit.' He must have thought it was funny because he brayed with laughter.

My temper was getting to fever pitch and

there was a great temptation in me to swing the shovel around and re-arrange his stupid face, but I knew he'd just love that; so somehow I did my best to control myself, but it sure wasn't easy.

'Why don't you take a swipe at me, black fella? You know damned well you want to. Give me a chance to bury your stupid head in the muck where it belongs.' His laughter brayed out again, tempting me even further.

While I was still thinking on it, the replacement officer for the dead lieutenant walked past; he'd been a good friend of Mr. Sutton and had no time for Sergeant McBain at all, so perhaps he also knew of McBain's habits. Maybe he even suspected McBain of killing his friend.

'Sergeant Dee! Get your men out of that damned muck at once! I need you men for more important duties. Clean up and fall in outside the command post in thirty minutes.'

He strode off, completely ignoring McBain, who stared after the officer muttering foul curses, as we thankfully eased ourselves out of the mire.

McBain marched us up to the command post although he had not been included in the order. Our 'cleaning up' could only consist of washing off our boots and trouser bottoms. We had no other gear to change into, and by the time we had marched through the deep mud to the command tent, no one would know if we'd cleaned up or not.

I had found a kepi, to replace the one young Danny had lifted from my head with his bullet back there in the woods, and we carried a full pack each. My Henry rifle and the Colt .44 tucked into my holster made up my firepower. I'd cut away the flap on the holster to allow for a faster draw if I should need the gun in a hurry.

Young Daniel Ervine was carrying a Spencer. God only knows where he had 'acquired' it because it was a very new item, but he was always 'acquiring' something from somewhere. He was probably the only black private to have such a good rifle. Now all he needed was the cartridges for it; he'd find them, I was sure of that, if McBain didn't manage to steal the weapon from the boy first. He'd already tried to get the gun several times, but so far, young Daniel had managed to hang on to it.

The two corporals carried Maynard breach-loading carbines, while young Tommy had a rather worn-out 1842 musket. McBain carried a Starr breach-loading carbine, with a Starr percussion pistol in his holster. The carbine fired a massive .58 charge. A real man-stopper.

Lieutenant Savage stepped from the tent as we marched up. 'This is a reconnoiter job, Sergeant McBain,' he said, lifting one very bushy eyebrow. 'I rather wonder if I should allow two of my sergeants to go on such a trip together.'

McBain said nothing and Lieutenant Savage shrugged a careless shoulder as he flicked ash from his cigar. He was a bit of a dandy and liked posing before his men, but other than that, he was a real nice fella.

'Step inside men,' he offered, waving his hand with the invitation, 'don't want to get the maps all wet, do we, eh?'

There were three senior officers in the big tent and I believed one to be our commander, Major General Thomas, but I could not be certain, because he remained very much in the background, allowing the lieutenant to lay out the plan.

The Lieutenant explained that we were to use the damp, misty weather to discover the possible strength of the rebels on Lookout Mountain. We were also told that three other groups had set off before us in relays, but that no one had yet reported in. If we could link up with any one of them, we should pool our information and send one of our number back to report. The lieutenant made a great point of telling us how important our mission was, before we were dismissed.

We waited in a small broken down cabin on the edge of town, for the evening shadows to close in, and I was staring out of the glassless window frame at the wavering curtain of rain.

No beautiful colors painted the dark lowering sky this night. I allowed my mind to drift back over the times Jesse and I had watched the evening colors work their magic in the sky. My hand drifted into my pocket and selected a silver dollar from the change; I'd never even owned a dollar until I'd joined the army, I thought, remote in my nostalgia. The coin turned over and over, backwards and forwards along the backs of my fingers, the way Jesse had taught me, and as it reached my thumb I flipped the coin high, caught it, and brushed my other hand over the one with the coin in it. My hand opened and the coin was gone. I hadn't realized that young Daniel had been watching me do the small conjuring trick until I heard his gasp of amazement. I turned and grinned at him.

'How the cotton pickin' hell did you do that, Sergeant Josh?' he asked.

So, I completed the trick by reaching forward and taking the coin out of his ear, chuckling at his gasp of shock. I could remember how surprised I'd been when Jesse had pulled the same stunt on me with the egg.

'Man, that's real magic!' he murmured, his eyes round.

'Easy trickery is what that is,' sneered McBain, his voice full of derision. 'A kid's game anybody kin play.'

On impulse, I flipped the coin at him. 'Show him how it's done, big mouth!' I knew I shouldn't have done it, because we were both waiting for the opportunity to be at each other's throats and this was no time, or place, to pick a fight. Shortly we'd be depending on each other as we made our way into — and hopefully out of — enemy territory, but I just couldn't help myself; my blood still boiled at the thought of him deliberately shooting Lieutenant Sutton.

The confident smile became strained as he caught the coin. 'We don't have time for this foolishness,' he muttered, as he prepared to throw the coin back to me.

'We've got nothing but time till it's dark enough to move out,' I replied without heat, 'so go on, show the lads how it's done, smart-ass!' The word hissed through my teeth.

He threw the coin at me, real hard, hoping I'd miss, and lose it in the rubbish of the cabin, or perhaps he hoped that it would hit me in the face. Either way it didn't work, my hand flicked out in automatic reflex and plucked the coin out of the air, I passed my other hand over my clenched fist and the coin had vanished once again, much to everyone's surprise.

'Think that's clever do you?' sneered McBain, 'wait till you try to catch a bullet in your teeth, Sergeant Dee, then we'll see who's clever. Come on, let's go!'

It was still too early to go, but he was in charge, so we all filed out into the thickening gloom of the night and jog-trotted towards Lookout Mountain.

11

We moved swiftly over the valley floor and, although the two lads were very young, they moved in complete silence as we trotted up the first slopes and into the woods. Lined out in single file we climbed steadily. The place smelled of death and cordite, burned and charred branches were everywhere as we climbed higher and higher. The mist was thicker now, wrapping itself around us making it almost impossible to see even a few feet ahead.

McBain was beside me as he reached for a lever to pull himself up on to a ledge. He grabbed what seemed to be a tree root in the darkness. The root was in fact, a man's leg; it must have been blown from some poor soul's body and landed beside the base of the tree and McBain fell backwards with a snarled curse, followed by a hoarse shout from higher up the mountain.

'Whut th' hell was that, Concho?' a plummy 'back home' type voice called in a hoarse whisper, 'Y'all down there Joe?'

We all crouched, still and silent prepared to explode into action at a second's notice.

'Hot damn,' another plummy voice grumbled, 'Y'all don't think some more of them God-damned Yankees are creepin' up here agin do yuh, Mort?'

We heard the clear sound of a 'hawk and spit' obviously from a tobacco chewer. 'Naw Concho,' the first voice replied, keeping up the hoarse whisper, 'them damn Yankees ain't gotten the guts tuh come up here any more, we'uns'l slaughter 'em iffen they try.'

'You betcha,' muttered another voice, mere feet above us, and we crouched even lower.

'That you Joe?' the hoarse whisper asked a second time.

'Yup, now shadup. Iffen there was Yankees in these here hills you'd let 'em know right where we are, you Goddammed blabber-mouth!'

'Kind'a tetchy ain't he,' whispered the voice I now recognized as Concho's.

Touching Tommy on the shoulder, I signaled for him to inform the man next to him that we were moving out. I put my finger on my lips, but he didn't need me to tell him to keep quiet. The timber slopes were alive with Johnny Rebs, but we had to get a lot higher to assess the true strength of the men around us. There could be a whole slew of them up here.

We moved slowly, inch by careful inch away

131

from the men. They sounded like real hill countrymen to me, and if they were, they'd be the hardest to get past. Wooded hills was home country to them, they could move through the brush slicker than spit on a greased pole and twice as quiet.

We were over an hour, easing ourselves out of danger and climbing above Concho and his pals. On our mettle now, because every shadow spelled danger, every movement suspect.

No matter which way we moved, up down or sideways, we spotted, and passed, many small independent groups of men bivouacking, regardless of the fine rain and icy cold mist. Sleeping out in pouring rain was not a problem to these hardy people, so they would not give a second's thought to the cold, or the misting rain.

As sharpshooters, they had no equal. A dab of spit on the end of the foresight, to reflect the slightest glimmer of light, was all they needed to turn an age-old musket into a deadly killing weapon. The further we climbed, the more there seemed to be. I reckoned there was a full strength army scattered around and — for a change — McBain was of the same opinion, when we eventually crouched in the lea of some boulders to assess the situation.

Lookout Mountain rose some 1,500 feet from the valley floor, so we could not even cover a small portion of the total area. Camping on the mountain, with so many troops around, didn't bear thinking about. How those mountain-men could be so cheerful when it was so damned cold and wet beat me all to hell.

McBain was attempting to do some quick calculating and I have to admit, much as I hated him, he was good at it.

'Reckon you're right, fella,' he muttered. 'There must be at least full Army strength up here, an' that's what I'm gonna report. Agreed?'

I nodded. 'If we're lucky enough to get back down, I'll back you.'

'I'm so pleased black sergeant, sir.' The sarcasm fairly dripped from his mouth, like liquid acid. 'C'mon, let's get started,' he growled, 'we wanna be off this damned hill before daybreak.'

As we started to move away from our protection, there was the faintest of rustles behind me. I dropped to one knee and turned, all in one fluid motion, my bayoneted rifle stabbing upwards as the heavy body plummeted towards me.

★   ★   ★

Then they were upon us. No sound, no shouting, just bayonets glinting dully in the rain. I dragged my bayonet from the fallen man and turned to defend myself as young Tommy Malleck was smashed to the ground with a blow from the butt of a musket; a second later the boy's attacker had turned the musket and skewered Tommy to the floor. The man stepped away, withdrawing the bloody bayonet as my bullet took him through the throat. Corporal Jackson was giving a good account of himself, as he and Corporal Bellamy fought back to back. Apart from my one shot, the fight was taking place in almost total silence, the swirling mist and curtains of sweeping fine rain dampening out the smaller sounds of the struggle.

As quickly as it had started, the fight was over; leaving five men sprawled on the ground, our only casualty being young Tommy.

Looking around, I happened to glance towards a jumble of small rocks and brush; Sergeant McBain was leveling his rifle in my direction. Dropping to the ground, I rolled towards a small cairn of stones as the noise of the gun crashed in the silence.

Corporal Jackson had just stepped into McBain's line of fire as the distinctive hollow sound of the Starr shattered the stillness. The heavy caliber ball lifted the poor man and slammed him into a huge boulder. He was dead before he hit the ground.

We were all stunned by the suddenness of it; though, but for McBain's treachery, we could have been running free. As it was, we had lost a damned fine corporal, and worse, we could hear a scurry of movement somewhere above us. I swung my rifle towards the place where McBain had been, but he had lost himself in the darkness and there was no time to spare for hunting him. Jumping to my feet, I silently urged Corporal Bellamy and the boy to follow me. I twisted and turned between rocks and bushes, to put the men behind us off the scent, at the same time hoping to be lucky enough to avoid the many scattered groups of Confederate soldiers below.

We heard the heavy boom of the Starr a second time, far below us, just before Corporal Bellamy fell to a volley of shots, fired from the trees. Veering away from the danger, with young Daniel close behind me, I had a fleeting thought that told me our headlong run could not last, when something slapped across my skull. A white-hot searing pain flashed along the side of my head, and then there was nothing . . .

. . . My eyes opened slowly, the pain making me squint; sunlight was blazing down between the branches of the trees. I was lying on my back, in a small natural hollow, made deeper by a fallen log lying across the lip of the depression. I could not see the trail because the log was almost covering me; ivy and long grass had also helped to give me shelter. My head was much lower than my feet and staring up into the sunlight was more punishment than I could stand.

My mind raced back over what had happened. How long had I been lying here. Where was young Daniel? My clothes were bone dry, except where my back had been resting in the grass; there my clothes were very warm and damp and my head was pounding like there was a battle royal going on inside it.

I lifted a hand, which felt like a ton weight, to touch my head. Numb fingers explored the gash, increasing the tempo of the battle within. Crusted blood, sticking to the side of my face like a red frost, would have made my wound look far more serious than it actually was, if anyone had bothered to inspect it in the rain and mist of last night. There was no sign of my beloved rifle around me, so perhaps it was still up there on the trail, or more likely some Confederate soldier was congratulating himself on a lucky find. My searching hand discovered the pistol still in its holster so at least I was armed.

Easing my body into a more comfortable position and covering my face with leaves, damp and musty from a mixture of rain, fire and gunpowder, I decided to rest right where I was until full dark. I was hungry, sure, but I'd been hungry before and survived. Night-time was my best bet and rest was called for, hunger would have to wait its turn.

The day passed on leaden feet. There was a time when men and horses, towing some heavy artillery, passed by on the track above me, followed later, by the heavy crunch of foot soldiers on the march; but unless someone was actually looking, they'd pass me by. I dozed for some of the time, and I must have passed out too, because when I awakened it was full dark but my mind was still fixed on getting off this damned mountain and back to my own troop. There was a burning hatred in me for McBain. He was responsible for the deaths of three good men, because I had to believe now that young Danny had either been captured, or shot.

There was the remote possibility that he'd outrun the soldiers, being light and nimble;

he might even have managed to hide, but it was unlikely. It would take me all my time and a lot of luck to get out of the mess I was in, so a mere boy making it seemed almost out of the question.

My thoughts settled on McBain. That guy had more twists in his tail than a sidewinder; I had to get back, if only to make sure he'd go before a court martial. If McBain made it back alone he'd be a damned hero, probably even be made up to officer rank.

My musings were interrupted as I moved further along the shallow slit in the ground and my hand hit something soft. I pulled the bundle towards me: it was my pack. The two shoulder braces must have busted when I fell, but the buckles had held, so I figured Lady Luck was still on my side, even if she was a bit unreliable at times. The water bottle fixed to the side of the pack had split, but there was grub in that bundle. Hell, who needed water? I thought, stuffing food into my mouth. I'd seen enough water falling out of the skies lately to last me for quite a spell.

The meager fare took the cutting edge off my hunger. So making a quick repair of the straps, by tying the two broken pieces together to make a longer sling, I threw the bundle over my shoulder. Checking the percussion caps were set ready for use in my

Colt, I eased my aching body out of the slit and up to the track.

The moon was just off full and the sky had cleared, so I had no trouble setting my course for Chattanooga. The problem was going to be getting past the troops swarming over the mountain. Man, that was gonna be some chore. I had to figure that if one Company carried 97 men, and it took ten companies just to make up a Regiment . . . and that was only the beginning!

My mind stopped trying. It wasn't all that long ago I was proud to be able to cipher. Now I was trying to figure how many men made up a whole Goddamned Army!

Moving downward, my mind began to hone in on the sounds of the night. The chill was beginning to bite and snow was dusting the floor, just tiny flurries now, but it could turn nasty. Although the surrounding trees cut down the light of the moon quite a bit, I could still see my frosting breath puffing out in front of me.

I stopped! My nose keening the slight breeze. My taste buds began playing up. Someone close was brewing coffee. Water I could do without coffee, that was a hoss of a different color. Easing slowly forward into a small clump of bushes and brushwood, I slipped the pack from my shoulders and pushed it into cover.

Inch by careful inch I moved downward. There was the clink of tinware against stone. I was crouched low keeping my body close to the ground, feeling, with hands almost frozen, for anything my feet might stumble into that would give me away; moving the odd stone, dead branch or twig as I progressed. Then my searching hands found the edge of a small depression; it was covered in brush but fell away steeply under the covering. Only my method of approach had saved me from tumbling into the small coulee below, where the merest glimmer of light, barely flickering in the intense blackness of the coulee, sent out its warning.

The smell of coffee was real strong, up here on the ledge where I was resting, trying to ease the cramps in my legs. The sizzle of meat being laid on a hot stone, the sound being subdued by the distance, came to my ears, closely followed by that 'Just cookin'' smell, that made taste buds drool in anticipation. I waited a real long time to make sure how many men was down there, but the lack of any kind of conversation eventually convinced me that it was a one man camp.

Easing my way into the slope without making a sound was quite a chore, but that smell was just like Momma, calling me home.

My Colt was set easy in my hand, I had no intention of firing it, but a sharp tap on the old think box would be just as effective and less disturbing to the neighbors . . . If you get my drift. The moon was not shining into the small coulee, for which I was very grateful, because it allowed me to get real close to the man sitting on a large flat rock.

It seemed a real careless way for a man on his own to behave, I thought, as I rose behind him like a ghost in the night. Still, that was his hard luck; it was his head on the block, not mine. My Colt was raised high, ready to part his hair, when there was a deep growl and a rush of displaced air behind me.

My mind said 'Sheeitt!' as a dog, big as a Timber Wolf, hit into my back and sent me spinning towards the fire. The dog followed me and I finished flat out, staring up into the face of the biggest damned curdog, all set to take my throat out in one easy bite.

'Stay Toby!' The voice was soft, yet firm, and thank the Lord the dog knew when it was spoken to. I didn't much like him, slavering that close to my windpipe, but anything was better than him going ahead the way he'd intended.

'Y'all made enough damned noise comin' over that ridge to waken the dead, fella. Figured you'd never git here, and even old

141

Toby was about fed up with waitin' on yuh.'

'D'you reckon you could call him off, mister?'

'Know of a reason why I should?' he asked; reasonably enough, I thought.

'Nope, sure don't.'

'Was y'all lookin' tuh steal my supper young fella?'

'Yep.'

'Made one helluva mess of that chore, huh?'

'Yep. D'you think you could let me up now? I ain't gonna hurt you none.'

'You do surprise me. Reckoned you'd about figured to bust my head with that there gun of yours.'

'Figured to. Hunger gets to a man.'

'Sojer boy, huh?'

'Yep. You?'

'Nope.'

'So what are you doing on this mountain with all these Rebs?'

'I alus bin here, they're new. Me, I can't see the reason fer this here war.'

'It's so's slaves can be free. Don't you care about that, mister?

'Dunno, never had me a slave. You want some of my supper?'

'Be mighty obliged.'

'Toby ain't gonna like it, he's waited quite

a while to git a taste of you.' He leaned forward and turned the meat. 'Maybe you could drink some Arbuckle also, shouldn't wonder?'

'Maybe just a taste, old-timer.'

'I ain't old. Don't seem right I should disappoint old Toby, he'd be entitled to git upset, 'cos not only is he gonna miss out on takin' a piece out of you, but he's gonna have tuh share his grub with you also.'

I was gettin fed up with the backchat, and that dog looked too eager for my liking. 'Hell look old-timer,' I snapped, 'you gonna let me up or . . . ' My voice tailed off, as that big old dog growled deep in his throat. He eased forward, so that I could feel his hot breath on my face, and I kind'a jerked a bit when a big blob of saliva plopped on my chin: he was drooling like he thought I'd be real tasty.

'Easy now, Toby,' the old man said quietly.

He pointed a pronged stick at me; the one he'd bin turning the meat with. 'Y'all git uppity with me, young fella, an' you'll make Toby real eager to get his chore done. Put the gun on the ground an' Toby'll let yuh get up.'

Until he mentioned it, I'd forgotten the gun was still in my hand. I let it go like it was hot, and the damned dog sat back and wagged his tail, like he was the most pally critter on earth, which didn't make me change my mind about him one little bit. So I stood up slow and easy, then started to pick up my gun.

'Leave it lay,' grunted the old man, as he poured some Arbuckle and offered it to me. 'You surely don't want old Toby to git upset with y'all a second time.'

'No sir! I surely don't,' I replied, as I took the mug and sat on the stone beside him and offered my hand.

'Name's Joshua D. Sergeant in the Union Army.'

'Well now, that sure comes as a big surprise tuh me young fella,' he replied, dryly, 'seein' as how you'm dressed in a blue uniform and have three bars on your arm.' He slurped some coffee. 'Yes sir, real surprisin'. Help yourself to some meat an' tell me about this slave thing.'

I did both, and I guess my temper showed some in the telling.

'You mean to tell me that y'all couldn't go where you like, when you wanted to? That you worked all day an' every day, fer just grub? That these people actually owned you! Like you was a hoss or somethin'?'

I nodded. 'That's just the way it was, fella'.

'Hell! No wonder y'all is runnin' around killin' people. The name's Zeke, by the way, 'old-timer' sticks in my craw. What y'all doin' up here anyhow?'

'Supposed to be trying to find out what's going on, ain't bin too successful so far. Six of us started off, only me left an' I still don't know from diddley what the strength of the opposition is.'

'You should have said. What d'you wanna know?'

'D'you know anything, Zeke?'

'Ain't much I don't know about this here mountain, son.

'Fer instance, I know there was a big movement of troops over the last couple of days, moved a whole slew of men. Cannon and ammunition too, clear offen the mountain. Heard talk of General Longstreet takin' his men to Knoxville.'

The memory came back to me, listening to all that movement on the track above me yesterday, or was it the day before? I disremembered. 'All of his men, Zeke? You sure about that?'

'It's what I heard, an' like I said, there was a lot of big guns movin' offer the mountain agin last night.'

'Is this Knoxville place far from here, Zeke?' My mind was in a whirl; this was just the kind of information we needed.

'Too far to come back an' help out here, if that's what you're thinkin', son. It's way up the valley at the headwaters of the Tennessee

River. Y'all understand, it ain't none of my business who wipes who out in this here war, an' normally I'd tell yuh to git to hell out've my camp, but this slave thing. That's different! Don't cotton to that at all.'

'You got my word on it, Zeke,' I told him, 'and what's more, this information could save a lot of lives on both sides. Believe me, mister! If I ever get off this damned mountain you'll be real glad you told me about this.'

'Take you off if you like,' he offered.

'What about all these troops?'

'Pshaw,' he grunted, 'done told yuh. I know this here mountain. Take a couple of days, lessen y'all wanna take a real chance an' make a dash fer it. Don't advise that at all, fella, there's some real good mountain men up here an' they kin shoot like nobody you ever saw. Pick a fly offen a turd without damagin' the crust.'

There was real excitement in me about all the information I'd gathered, and without half trying too! It would make a real fool of McBain and I was just human enough to enjoy doing that.

'I'll leave it all up to you, Zeke,' I grinned. 'You tell me what to do an' I'll do it.'

'You don't have much choice do you, young Joshua?' he replied dryly, 'you was even headed in the wrong direction. Another few miles an' you'd have run straight into Braxton Bragg's main camp. Try tappin' that lot over the head with your little pistol an' see how far you'd git.'

I guess old Zeke had forgotten more about mountains than I was ever likely to know, so I kept my lips tight shut. Except when I had to open them to take another bite of meat an' I weren't too pushy about doin' that neither, because I kind'a got the feeling that old Toby was beginning to wonder just how much of his share I was eating. I noticed because he pulled over close to me and stared up, like he was saying, the next bit's mine, fella! Mind you, he wasn't any bother but I felt the need to take a quick count of my fingers every time he snatched a few pieces of meat from me.

12

We both slept all the next day, confident that Toby would keep watch over us, and it was the best sleep I'd had in a while; it sure helped the drums in my head to settle an' no mistake.

Once the blood and muck had been washed from the side of my face, Zeke said that the musket ball had hardly scratched me. The old man reckoned he'd cut himself worse shaving, which was probably why he'd grown a beard in the first place. Toby didn't seem too keen on me to begin with, I reckon he remembered he'd had to share his meal with me and didn't like the idea; dogs can be funny that way.

We moved off at full dark, after I'd collected my pack from under the brush where I'd hidden it. I could see what Zeke meant by the noise I'd made stalking his camp. He was like a ghost drifting between the trees; a puff of smoke was noisy against that old fella. A man would swear that there wasn't a rotten branch or twig lying anywhere in those woods, nor a loose rock or crackly leaf neither, and what's more, that damned

Toby slipped through quieter than any mouse I ever heard of, in spite of his size. So, what I'd like to know is, how come I found every Goddamned rotten branch in creation, and every blamed loose rock to boot? Man! I still had a lot of learning to do.

We bivouacked in darkness, just before the false dawn. Zeke sai. 'No coffee!' and I remembered how I'd first located him by the smell. The cold food, with nothing to swill it down, hit my stomach like a lead ball and filled me with gas, so sleeping didn't come easy. The cold didn't help either, yet that old mountain goat ate his meal sweet as pie, then stretched out and was asleep in nothing flat, while the dog moved off, out of sight, without needing to be told.

I lay awake a long time watching the sun poke its way through the trees. The wind shifted the branches to and fro, sending dappling shafts of light flickering across the tiny clearing, as if they were alive. Along about midday, the wind picked up a bit and big flakes of snow began to weave through the trees, like it was getting ready to be serious. Then the rain started again, cold and hard; but through it all, that old man just kept on sleeping and the dog didn't show itself once.

I must have dozed off sometime after that, because the next thing I knew it was full dark and Zeke was shaking me awake. He was holding one hand over my mouth. So I knew enough to keep it shut. Anyway, his hand was so Goddamned dirty, that if I'd opened my mouth I might have caught something nasty; and that big old dog was crouched close to me, staring off into the night, ears pointing forward. Something out there was making him kind'a restless.

I tapped my hand on Zeke's, to let him know I was awake. He took his hand from my mouth and slid down; so close that the smell of him made me stop breathing for as long as possible.

'Lots of movement up there,' he muttered in my ear.

God! His breath was enough to kill the smell of cabbage cooking. I knew I'd have to breathe soon, so I tried to move away from him, only to stick my stupid nose into Toby's fur coat. He'd been playing 'Roll over' in some fox's dirt like dogs do sometimes an' it was hard to know which was worse, so I tried crawling forward, to maybe leave it behind, but the old man's hand, on the back of my neck, was holding me firm. Don't get me wrong; it's nice to be liked, but it's hell on the lungs, if you get my drift.

It took some effort to drag my mind away from the smell, but gradually the rumble of heavy wheels and the thud of marching feet came through to me.

'Lots of movement, son,' he husked. His breath hung over my head like a cloud, waiting to drop on me the minute I opened my mouth.

'They're moving away,' I muttered between clenched teeth - as if that helped!

Then Zeke answered my prayers. He whispered 'Stay here!' and was gone. I sucked in the clear air like I'd never tasted it before in my whole life. Toby hadn't moved to follow Zeke; although the old man had said nothing to him one way or another, Toby seemed to know what was expected. That was one helluva good dog . . . if only he'd stop rubbing himself in fox's shit.

Zeke had been gone a little while, before Toby slowly changed his position, to watch his master appear out of the brush.

Maybe they could smell each other, I thought. That shouldn't be too much of a chore for either of them.

'More men movin' off the mountain,' grunted Zeke, as he crouched beside me and released another cloud of bad air — this time from the other end. 'Should make it easier fer us, they've left a big gap in their defenses. If we move fast enough, we'll be through before they close it.'

By the time I was on my feet, Zeke had collected his pack, picked up his old Hawken rifle, and was already disappearing into tall timber with Toby at his heels. Now who's the old-timer, I thought wryly, grabbing up my own pack and hurrying along, trying to catch up. The man was like a Goddamned mountain goat.

We kept going for around an hour before Zeke slowed a little, then he came to a huge tree and rested against it.

'Old bellows ain't so good these days,' he murmured, breathing only slightly heavier than normal.

I didn't answer. Truth is I couldn't! My bellows had all they could do to keep me from keeling over right there; they sure-God didn't have anything to spare for idle chitchat. I didn't care how close he came; his breath didn't bother me any. No sir! Nothing was going to stop me from sucking in air, and I do mean nothing!.'

Almost before I'd had time to bring my breathing down to something reasonable, he was off again. This time I was determined to keep up — for all of five minutes, before he began to pull ahead once more.

Suddenly he stopped, and seemed to vanish into the ground. Toby followed suit, dropping onto his stomach and stretching his head along his front paws. From where I was standing, he looked no more dangerous than an old log, so, taking my cue from them, I dropped flat also and struggled to make myself look like part of the landscape. Mind you, the way I was huffing an' puffing, a deaf mute with a bandage around his eyes would be able to find me, with no bother at all.

The old man must have signaled to the dog, because Toby began to work his way forward, still in his crouched position. I followed the dog into the small depression where Zeke waited, staring through the scrub at an encampment set out on a plateau in front of us.

'Weren't here three days ago' he muttered. 'How many men d'you reckon is down there, Josh?'

There was a lot of movement within the encampment, but I couldn't see any field-pieces. Counting the tents and judging by the type of equipment we used, the answer popped into my mind. 'Reckon on two companies,' I replied.

'Wa'al now that's mighty nice of yuh,' grunted Zeke, in a voice that sounded snappy, 'how the Hell many men is two companies supposed to be?'

'Around two hundred, give or take a few.'

'Oh is that all! Looks as if we'll have to wait

fer 'em tuh move off afore we kin cross.'

'We can't wait, Zeke. I have to get this information back to base. Now!'

'You'd best be tappin' 'em over the head with that little pistol of yours then, Sergeant Joshua, because I don't know of any other way tuh git past 'em, lessen we climb down over some almighty steep rocks I know of.'

'Let's do it,' I replied. 'Lead the way, Zeke.'

Muttering something that sounded like, 'Perhaps slavery weren't such a bad thing after all', he led us back up the mountainside, so that we could work our way along the edge of the plateau, without the danger of being seen.

I thought that almost running down the damned mountain in the first place, was bad enough, but believe me, climbing back up was a damn sight worse. By the time we made it to the rocks, standing upright was getting to be a bit of a problem. We'd walked most of the night, and a good part of the day to boot, and to say I was feeling tired was a bit like saying a starving man was kinda peckish. I was just about to tell Zeke that this was as far as I was going right now, when he grabbed my arm. In another second I would have stepped over the edge of a cliff that was so deep I couldn't see the bottom for mist, and believe me, it was damn near straight down!

My head went into a spin and yesterday's breakfast, or supper, depending how you looked at it, almost came up to choke me.

'Did you say we've got to go down there?!' My voice was kind'a strained.

'No! It was your daft idea,' he grumbled, 'ain't no accountin' fer taste.'

'I ain't a damned fly, Zeke!' I protested.

'Maybe you'd better git some practise in then,' he replied, kind'a sharp. 'There's one thing in your favor, at least y'all won't see what you're gettin' into.'

'Why the hell not?'

''Cos we'll be goin' down after dark, is why.' He let out a short barking laugh as he threw his pack to the ground and laid his rifle beside it. 'Just remember this is all your idea, Sergeant Joshua, an', like I said, it's kinda rough country, with a long drop, iffen y'all lose your footin'. Now, stop moanin' an' let's eat.'

There was a lump in my throat and suddenly I weren't hungry. For me that's really something, because hungry is the name I should have been given, according to Mister Jesse. I opened the two packs and soon threw a meal together, and this time Zeke said we could have some Arbuckle, which helped to tow down the ham and beans, which we sopped up with some stale sourdough bread.

Maybe I weren't hungry but I ate it anyway, I'd decided to cancel that cliff from my mind for the time being, but I sure didn't take a second look over the edge of it. No sir!

No sooner had we finished eating and cleared away, than old Zeke lay flat on his back and went to sleep, like he didn't have a worry in the whole Goddamned world. I tried it also, but Toby seemed to take a liking to me. Damned if he didn't come coddling up like we was best buddies or something; and him still smelling of stale fox dirt, which did nothing at all for the gas in my stomach. Though, thinkin' about it, the smell must have helped me to sleep, because next thing I knew, Zeke was shaking me awake and it was full dark.

'Time to go, son,' he grunted, like we were going for a stroll in a meadow. Then he made my day. 'If I don't make it all the way down an' maybe you do,' he said quietly, 'there's a game trail at the foot of these cliffs, just foller it an' you'll be headin' directly for Chattanooga. Remember, fella, iffen you fall, it's all the way to the bottom an' we ain't made to bounce. OK, let's go!'

I already had that kind'a jelly feeling in my legs, but that damned silly old dog was jumping around and wagging his tail like we were on a picnic or something. While Zeke pulled the pack onto his back, picked up the rifle and slipped over the edge like an eel. 'C'mon, son,' he called quietly, 'ain't near as bad as it looked in daylight. There's plenty of hand an' footholds. I've already done this climb a few times.' His voice was getting fainter as he climbed down. I don't know if he was trying to cheer me up, but if he was, it didn't happen.

The dog didn't like it any more than I did. He ran backwards and forwards along the edge whining and whimpering for a while, before making up his mind, then he slithered and skidded over the edge in a slide that rattled small stones down on Zeke, forcing the old man to curse the dog into making less noise.

Now it was my turn. I'd already fixed my pack real tight on my back by using the broken straps as best I could, so I lowered myself over. Toes scrabbling for something to grip. Fingers straining with the tension. My mind was telling me this was crazy, but Zeke had explained that if we'd tried it in daylight we'd stand out like a bug on a bed sheet, and there were plenty of keen-eyed sharp-shooters in the woods below who could pick us off without half trying.

We'd been descending steadily for about half an hour when Zeke cursed somewhere below me, not one of your usual every-day type curses, but more like pain and trouble. There was a rattle and clang of falling metal and I figured Zeke had lost his rifle. Then Toby set up a whimpering and whining; the whole thing sounded bad to me so I tried to move down a little faster. The night was brightening a little because of the three-quarter moon climbing over the lip above me. It helped some, but it still took me a good five minutes to reach Zeke.

In the half-light he seemed to be hanging by one hand from an outcrop of rock, which didn't make much sense, until I saw that his wrist had been trapped in a V-shaped wedge of stone and Zeke was hanging by it. The real bad part had to be that he was slowly turning around until the wrist locked in one direction. Then his body was being forced back the other way, and because he was hanging from the outcrop, Zeke was hanging in space, unable to use his feet to take the weight off his wrist. He was also unable to reach the outcrop with his right hand.

Maybe the wrist was already broken, or perhaps the upper arm had been jerked out of the shoulder socket, either way it was only a matter of time before the wrist joint gave up the struggle and was pulled away from the arm.

Zeke seemed to be looking for something, completely ignoring the fact that he was trapped. Then I realized what he was going to do and the blood ran cold inside me, as the glint of the moon on the blade of his knife struck my eye! He was going to cut himself down by slicing off his own damned wrist!

'Zeke! No!' I shouted, ignoring the fact that I could have alerted anyone on guard below.

'Be with yuh in a minute, Josh,' he replied, as calm as if he was gonna trim a branch from a tree.

I threw off my pack and began to climb. My fingers were already bleeding from coming down the cliff, but I forced them into cracks you wouldn't believe, as I scrabbled upwards.

'You'll never do it, son,' he grunted, an' I could hear the pain in his voice.

'I'll do it, Zeke,' I panted, struggling desperately to get my body higher, 'just you hang in there, fella.'

'Y'all tryin' tuh make me laff, Josh, 'cos I just don't feel like it.' The pain was deep in his voice now and he still held the knife, ready in case he should need it.

I felt his feet touch my shoulders and hope shot through my veins, giving me more power than I ever thought possible.

'I'm gonna do it, Zeke,' I panted, 'let your

feet go over my shoulders and sit on me as I come up under you.'

'Your fingers ain't strong enough to hold us, Josh, we'll both go down.'

'Yeah? We'll see about that, old-timer,' I grunted, as a scream bubbled to my lips with the pain in my hands. My boots were scrabbling on nothing; but slowly, oh so slowly, I could feel his weight settling on my shoulders.

If I thought my fingers were paining before, it was nothing to what was happening now. Two nails broke off completely and more blood began to run down my hands. My brain blanked out against the pain, while my boots continued to try to find some ledge or hollow. Anything, to take the awful weight off my raw fingers.

Then suddenly, the terrible weight of Zeke was gone! The pain in my hands became nothing, as Zeke released his trapped hand, and pulled himself up on to the stone that had gripped him so firmly. I scrambled up on to the ledge beside him and lay back on the small flat space it provided.

My hands were bleeding and the two nails were hanging off my fingers, I pushed them gently back into place and cupped my hands under my arms, trying to stop the stinging, burning pain, rocking backwards

160

and forwards with the ache of it. Man oh man; them nails were aching something awful. I spared a look at Zeke; his hand was swollen to the size of three, with fingers like big fat sausages. My stomach rolled as he twisted the wrist this way and that, checking to see if it was still all in one piece.

'OK, Zeke?' My voice came out all weak and trembly.

'Yeah, Josh. Looks like I get to keep it, thought I'd have to leave it behind, never thought you'd be able to lift me out of that slit' His voice wasn't exactly strong either.

'It was close there for a while, Zeke, you're plumb heavy for your size.'

'Yeah ain't I though. Glad it weren't t'other way around, it'd need a team of hosses tuh lift you, Josh. Say. How'd you feel about a mug of Arbuckle?'

'What about the sharp-shooters down below?'

'Cant see us on this here ledge, Josh, an' what's more, I'm damned iffen I care overmuch.' He tucked his damaged hand into the front of his shirt and slid to the back of the ledge where he began to lay out some dry twigs and sticks. The moon was bright in the valley now, so the fire would hardly be seen, and like Zeke said, I didn't care overmuch either.

It took Zeke a long time to ease the pack from his back and he had a job pouring the water into his billycan too, but he managed it somehow. I couldn't help him because my hands were hurting something awful, what with the nails hanging off and the ends of my fingers raw and bleeding from tearing at the rock face. Fact is I still don't know how I managed to hang on, once Zeke was on my shoulders. Man; he was some weight for a little fella.

Along about then that old dog of his came down on to the ledge, tail wagging and jumping around like he was in a field. Damn near had the pot over twice before he'd be quiet. I tell a man, that Arbuckle tasted real good and, apart from my hands an' Zeke's wrist, it made us feel about as good as we were likely to get. Not near good enough to go down over the overhang though, so we took the long way back to my pack, and we didn't hurry about it, neither.

We were about halfway down the cliff face when Zeke led us into a small cave. The moon had gone and there were angry streaks of color showing in the early morning sky, a sullen red, overlaid with heavy swirling clouds. We didn't need to tell each other that there was some rough weather coming our way — even old Toby was getting restless as flashes of lightning flickered in the distance, followed by soft rumbles of thunder. I haven't seen a dog yet that enjoys a good thunderstorm.

'This'll do us fer now,' grunted Zeke, his voice sounding faint and tired. 'Plenty of logs an' brush around an' I reckon we've enough grub between us to last a few days.' He let out a tired and painful groan as he settled down in one corner and allowed himself to relax. His hand and wrist had gone black, and once he'd even managed to joke that being with me was making him change color.

My hands were very swollen, especially the two fingers with the torn nails, but they didn't pain so much, now that the raw ends had begun to scab over a bit, so I emptied our packs and sorted out the food.

Zeke had a three-day-old jackrabbit wrapped in a piece of shirt. I don't know what color the shirt used to be but it was reddish black right now. Still, three-day-old rabbit ain't so bad, when you don't have much else. It made old Toby's tail work overtime anyway, so that can't be bad.

I managed to gut and skin it; Toby made short work of those bits I can tell you. We didn't have any spare water to wash it, but it didn't smell all that bad. What the hell! A man had to make do with what he'd got. Anyway, it smelled a damned sight better once it started to sizzle, and there wasn't a single piece of it left time we'd finished.

The lightning was picking up pace by this time, with huge crackling flashes cutting down the rocks in front of our tiny shelter, almost blinding us as the heavy claps of thunder followed, setting our ears ringing. Old Toby didn't want anything to do with it; he snuggled over in a tiny slit, as far away from the opening as he could get. Then, burying his head in his paws, he lay there, trembling from head to foot. Zeke crawled over to the dog and wrapped his arms around it. There must be something special in stale fox's dirt, because Zeke was snoring his head off in nothing flat.

I lay back in another corner with my head resting on my pack, knowing that sleep wouldn't come easy. My fingers were throbbing like mad now that I had nothing else to think about . . . Which just shows how wrong a man can be, because the next thing I knew, it was broad daylight . . .

13

We rested for two days in our little cave. We had to! Zeke's wrist, hand and arm had swollen into one solid mass by the time we'd awoken from our sleep. He kept going into a kind'a sleepy faint, muttering and groaning all the while, I tended to him as best I could, but my mind kept wandering off into the past also because my fingers were one big ache where the nails had been pulled clean out of their sockets. They were swollen like you wouldn't believe, and I guess they must have become infected by something, because there was an awful lot of that yellowy stuff weeping out of them.

Food had become a problem, and by the second day, even the tiny drop of water in the canteen had gone. I tried to get Zeke to listen, but he just plain kept flopping about, like a blob of molasses on a plate. I hadn't seen old Toby for a long while, so maybe even he thought the whole thing was hopeless and had walked out on us. Staring around, with tears of pain blurring my eyes, a feeling of hopelessness settled over me, so I just lay down beside Zeke and slept.

It was just before sun-up next day — or was it the day after — when I realized that something was snuffling at my face. My mind scrambled with fear. It could be anything! It took a minute or two before my mind told me just where I was, and less than another minute before old Toby's stale fox dirt crawled up my nose and set me sneezing. I sat up; my head was buzzing like a saw cutting wood, and when I tried to stand everything went haywire.

'Came back then, did you?' I croaked through lips already dry and sore. Toby seemed real happy about something, judging by the way he was whining and jumping about like a two-year-old. Then I saw what he was all fired up about: there was a big haunch of meat lying on the floor, just by the cave opening. And there was me reckoning that old Toby had left us in the lurch! In spite of the pain deep in me, I damn near chuckled. That haunch meant life to Zeke and me; where the hell old Toby'd gotten it from was anyone's guess, but even in the doubtful light of the new dawn it looked good and fresh. 'Hell dog, you're a damned marvel,' I chuckled. My voice came out stronger that time, as hope welled within me.

'You gotta learn to trust ole Toby,' grunted Zeke, 'that dawg's never let me down yet.'

The old man's voice, coming so clear and firm, was like music to my ears. 'We're gonna eat real good today, thanks to Toby,' I said, towing the meat into the cave by wrapping my arms around it. 'That's one helluva dog you've got there, Zeke.'

To my surprise, that tough old mountain man struggled to his feet, and tucking his damaged hand into his shirt, he used the other to help me pull the big haunch over to our tiny fireplace of stones. In no time at all, by blowing on the dying embers, we coaxed the fire to burn and set the last of our logs on it.

Zeke drew his Bowie knife with his good hand and began cutting off man-sized slices. He stuck one piece in his mouth and began sucking with obvious enjoyment. Then he cut another piece and offered it to me, but I shook my head. Don't misunderstand me. I like meat as much as the next man, but not when it could maybe run away, or squeal with pain at the first bite.

Zeke chuckled around the meat as he tossed my piece to Toby, who caught it in mid-air and swallowed it in one go. 'Some people's too blamed fussy, huh, Toby?' He grinned as he continued to carve and toss the slabs of meat on to the hot stones in the fire; and, before many minutes had passed, 'that smell' was in the air, and we really got down to the serious business of eating.

We decided to stay in the cave all that day, resting up. The mist was still down there, in the valley bottom, but we could maybe be spotted from either side. Anyway, we both knew the rest would do us nothing but good and we'd be unlikely to find anything to hide us further down, so we slept, this time with full stomachs.

The sky looked clear and cold as we crouched outside our cave. It was only a half-moon by this time; it was still supplying more light than we needed, but it was time to go. Zeke's hand and arm was beginning to look healthier and my fingers had stopped weeping, so things could be worse. I just hoped we didn't meet up with any Johnny Rebs. We only had my pistol and a couple of knives between us: my fingers wouldn't even go into the trigger guard, never mind shoot the damned thing, and Zeke had already told me that he was worse than useless with a pistol.

We had cut up my shirt so that I could bandage my fingers. Not to keep the dirt out, because the cloth was filthy, but at least it gave them some protection from the raw surface of the rocks. Neither of us was looking forward to the climb down the rock face, and it took old Zeke to make the start.

From then on it was a nightmare. Slipping and sliding, cutting ourselves on sharp rocky outcrops, falling two or three feet at a time, only to land painfully on another rock or boulder, before pushing ourselves to our feet and doing it all over again. I could have sworn that damned dog was more mountain goat than anything else — till I saw his pads. They were leaving a pat of blood on every rock, yet he kept going without a murmur, staying beside Zeke and letting the old man hang on to him when they hit an awkward spot. He was always there; ready to use his body to help Zeke up when he fell.

The fact that I was walking upright came as a surprise to me. Yet we'd been doing it for some time, and looking over my shoulder, I could see the towering cliffs behind me. We were in the valley at last, but I still didn't believe it. There was grass under our feet and we were moving into the lower wooded area, toward the game trail. The morning sun was beginning to climb in the sky, and I knew this was a time when the Confederate scouts would be out. I shambled forward and croaked my fears to Zeke, but he just gave me his lopsided grin and pointed at the dog.

'He'll tell us. You'll see,' he mumbled, 'we've nearly made it, Josh.'

As we walked down the game trail, dewdrops, made heavy by the morning mist, began to fall around us. I opened my mouth to catch some of it, but one taste of the bitter tang of burnt wood and cordite was enough to make me wish I hadn't bothered.

There was a cautious hoarse shout ahead of us and we slipped into the trees beside the trail, crouching low and still; with Toby dropping between us, head between paws, ears pointed and alert, staring at the spot where the noise had come from. We could see three men cutting through the mist and my heart lifted as I saw the dark blue uniform. 'They're Union! Let's call 'em up,' I murmured; pleased to see a friendly face.

'You just hold her right there, Joshua,' muttered Zeke, 'they're far enough away to git the wrong idea, could be we stand up to shout, an' they blow our Goddamned heads off in the excitement.'

He'd made his point, so I sank down again. 'We'll let 'em get real close, then I'll call out, that OK, Zeke?'

'Nope, we'll just send old Toby out. He'll sit in the middle of the trail a'waggin' his tail real friendly, till they come up tuh pet him. Then we'll call out, kind'a quiet like, so's not to upset 'em too much.'

'Sounds about right, Zeke,' I whispered.

The old man put his hand on the dog, ruffling its ears affectionately and muttering away as he petted it. The dog whined quietly a couple of times then, belly down, it eased slowly out onto the trail, whining and wagging its tail in a real friendly fashion.

A young lad was the first to spot it. He came forward, making coaxing noises and offering his hand. When he was close enough, Toby reached forward and gave the hand a friendly lick.

'Hell, I got me a real dawg,' muttered the boy, his voice sounding pleased and excited as he crouched beside Toby and began to fondle him, chatting away all the while, with the dog making small whining noises of pleasure in reply.

'What're y'all doin' there boy?' growled a sergeant as he came out of the trees. 'D'you realize that some sniper could be takin' a bead on you right now, you blamed fool?'

Things were beginning to get out of hand. Something had to be done, before the moment was lost. 'Don't shoot, Sergeant!' I said loudly. 'Sergeant Joshua D here. Member of the scouting party sent out by Lieutenant Savage of the Ninth of foot.'

On my first word the sergeant's rifle was up and lined on the patch where I was hiding. 'Show yourself pronto, mister,' he growled, 'or I'll sieve those bushes right now!'

I pushed tiredly to my feet, hands in the air. 'Take it easy, Sergeant, if I'd meant you any harm you'd have been dead by this time.'

'Anybody there with you, mister?'

'Yep, a friend, name of Zeke, and together we have more information for the lieutenant than you'd ever believe.'

The sergeant was still not convinced and the tension hung in the air, like the feelin' a man gets just before a lightning storm. 'You tellin' it don't make it so,' he grunted. 'Tell your friend to stand up.'

I didn't have to. Zeke slowly rose beside me. 'One thing, Sergeant,' Zeke said quietly, 'don't point that thing at me. Toby won't like it. You could lose an arm doin' that.'

The sergeant stared over his shoulder at the dog, which was no longer wagging its tail. In fact, old Toby didn't look the least bit friendly as he dropped into a crouch, his eyes watching the sergeant intently. 'Yeah, he do look kind'a mean all of a sudden,' replied the man, lowering the gun to his side. 'Did you say you were a sergeant from the Ninth of foot?'

'Yep.'

'Hmm, we'll see about that. There's a man from the Ninth right here, mister. Let's see iffen he knows the right of it. OK?'

I shrugged, pleased that the matter could be put to rights — until I heard him shout. 'Hey, send Sergeant McBain up here, let's see iffen he knows this, Joshua Dee fella.'

'McBain!' The word was out before I had time to think about it.

'Well, well. What do we have here then?' The sneering voice didn't need rememberin'. I stood to attention; he had no right to that honor, he should have been broken down to private long ago.

His next words stopped my scrambled thoughts.

'Ex-Sergeant Dee! The deserter! Fancy y'all comin' back just to face a firin' squad. Tie his arms men. He ain't gonna escape a second time. I already captured him once, when he shot the corporal up there on the mountain.'

Two men jumped forward, dragging my arms behind me they lashed my wrists together and relieved me of my Colt.

'What about this old fella?' asked one of the men. 'Joshua said he was a friend with lots of information about the Johnny Rebs.'

'OK, we'll take him in with us. Strap his arms behind him first though. We don't want him runnin' off, do we?' snapped McBain.

'I don't think we ought to do that,' muttered the first sergeant. 'He seems friendly enough to me. Y'all ain't about tuh run off now, are you, old-timer?'

'Nope, an' old Toby might not like the idea of me bein' tied up anyway. Y'know, Josh ain't no deserter, Sergeant, an' I kin prove it, so don't let nothin' happen to him on the way in. It could be nasty fer you if he turned up dead — even by accident.'

'We'll make sure about that, mister,' replied the sergeant grimly. 'Won't we McBain!'

'OK, you're in charge of the patrol, Price. You do it your way,' growled McBain.'

'Oh I will,' snarled Sergeant Price, anger pushing his voice.

I could see what McBain had in mind, and if there hadn't been so many witnesses about neither Zeke or I would have ever gotten back to camp. We'd been lucky; Sergeant Price didn't seem to like McBain any more than I did, but if I had been listed as a deserter like McBain was claiming then my troubles were a long way from over.

Zeke came up close to me. 'These are friends?' he muttered. 'Josh, fer God's sake, don't make any enemies 'cos I don't wanna meet 'em.' There was a tight grin pasted on my face. 'Soon sort this out, once we git back to camp,' I said, with a confidence I was far from feeling, because if McBain had half a chance, we'd both be dead long before then. My one hope was the dog. Toby would be watching over Zeke like a hawk and God help anyone who tried to get past that hound. My hands were throbbing something awful, being tied so tight, but for now, I'd best keep my mouth shut. The information Zeke and I carried would soon prove that I was not a deserter, in spite of Sergeant McBain's report on me.

14

I'd been in the guard tent for three days. The company surgeon had tended to my hands and they were showing signs of healing. The two fingers without nails still hurt some, but I could put up with that. What really worried me was why I was still under close arrest. Surely by this time old Zeke had managed to convince the officers that our information was vital.

On the heels of my thought, the heavy tarp was pushed aside and Sergeant Price, closely followed by Lieutenant Savage, ducked through the low doorway. I sprang to attention without the need of the sergeant's call of 'Officer Present'.

'At ease,' grunted the lieutenant. A small smile flickered across his face, giving me some hope that the matter of my desertion had been settled.

'Well, well, Sergeant Joshua Dee. Looks as though Sergeant McBain was quite wrong about you, doesn't it? Told us you'd deserted. Even managed to get young Daniel Ervine to support him.'

'Daniel's alive then is he, sir?'

'Oh yes, came in a day behind McBain. Had a fine old tale to tell in the beginning, claimed it was McBain who ran out on you! Changed his mind though, next day he had a different tale, which agreed almost entirely with McBain. I have my own ideas about that, but as there's no clear evidence . . . I can't take the word of a young black over that of a white sergeant now, can I?'

'No sir,' I muttered.

'We'll be watching him though, mark my words. If I get proof he's stepped out of line, I promise you, he won't get away with it.' He smiled again and patted my shoulder. 'Understand you have some big news about the displacement of the enemy; let's go over to the command tent and see what you and your friend have to say, shall we?'

'Zeke hasn't told you?'

'No, 'fraid not. Told me in no uncertain terms that if you were going to be kept a prisoner, I could go and jump into the Tennessee River for all he cared. Even threatened to set that damned dog on me.' He gave a heavy chuckle as we ducked out of the tent. 'A real stubborn man that friend of yours.'

'Wouldn't have been here if I hadn't found old Zeke and his dog, sir.'

A sense of freedom spread over me as I

walked beside the lieutenant, with Sergeant Price just a step behind us. We were three equals going about our duties, and while I fully realized that Lieutenant Savage was way above me in rank, he was treating me no different than he would Sergeant Price or any other N.C.O., and my pride began to swell within me.

There were several officers in the command tent when we entered, and there was old Zeke, sprawled in a chair, not giving a damn for any one of them, with Toby crouched at his feet, same as always, and just as dirty too.

Toby just stared at me, only showing that he knew who I was by a tiny single wag of his tail.

'Well now, young Josh 'Bout time these here brass hats let you out'a that damned tent,' grinned Zeke. 'They sure are hard to convince. Makes a body wonder why the hell y'all bothered to come back here at all.'

Putting my hand on his shoulder, I gave it an affectionate squeeze, before coming to attention in the presence of so many officers.

'So. This is the man Sergeant McBain listed as a deserter?' From his manner, I guessed the man was the senior officer present, and from the cut of his uniform, he was so high up the ladder he probably had to look down through clouds on everybody else. But damn me if he didn't just stroll over and offer me his hand.

'Pleased to meet you, Sergeant Dee,' he said, casual as you please. 'Understand you know a very good friend of mine, Major Jesse Turnball. He told me all about you when I was in conversation with him last month.'

There it was again, I thought. Good old Mister Jesse. 'Uh, hum. Yes sir,' I mumbled, taking his hand kind'a careful-like, because it looked so all fired dainty and smooth, 'is Mister Jesse well, sir?'

The man laughed, a deep rumbling noise from way down. 'Oh yes he's fine, Sergeant. He told me you always call him Mister Jesse. Funny that, he always hated being called mister. Now, what can you tell me about the men on Lookout Mountain? Sergeant McBain led us to believe that there was a full Army strength up there.'

'That's true, sir. We reckoned there was around five thousand men up there at that time. But with respect, I was up there a lot longer than McBain, and I had the good luck to meet up with my friend, Zeke. He knows more about that mountain than anybody.'

'I realize that, Sergeant, but your good friend decided not to tell us anything.

'Isn't that so, Mister Zeke?'

Zeke pushed himself casually out of his chair and helped himself to a cigar as he passed a small table. 'Now Joshua's out've that damned tent I'll tell y'all anythin' you wanna know.' He leaned over the lantern and puffed the cigar until it was drawing to his liking. I could see the old man was really enjoying himself as he strolled over to the map table, set in the center of the big tent.

His damaged wrist was in a sling, so he stuck the cigar between his teeth and talked around it, while his good hand kept stabbing at the map. There was more to Zeke than met the eye. He rattled off all the details like a professional soldier, and for the life of me, I couldn't find a point he'd missed.

'So, Longstreet's men are off the mountain eh? How many do you suppose are still up there, Zeke?' asked the officer.

'We-el me 'n' Joshua reckoned around two thousand or so. That right, Josh?' He cocked a devilish eye at me, a half grin on his face.

'Yes sir, about that,' I muttered.

'That's it then. Thank you gentlemen. You, Sergeant, may return to your duties. Sergeant Price will go with you. He was your replacement, but we'll need all the men we can get for the coming battle. You! Um, Zeke. Feel free to come and go as you please . . . '

'I lost a damned good rifle up there,'

interrupted Zeke, 'you figure I could maybe git a replacement?'

'Certainly, certainly. Least we can do,' replied the officer. 'What type of rifle was it?'

'One of them modern Henry rifles. That's what it was. Right Josh?'

The sly old dog deliberately turned towards me and winked as I slowly nodded. 'Lost all his ammunition also, sir,' I mumbled, trying not to look at Zeke, although I could feel his eyes staring into me. Damn him. Bet he had a grin on his face a mile wide.

'See to it, Sergeant Dee,' replied the officer, dismissing us all with a careless wave of the hand. 'I know when I'm being bamboozled.'

'Bamboozled suh!' Zeke looked like he'd been mortally wounded. 'Why, my wife should die a thousand deaths if I've told a lie to y'all.'

The officer stared at Zeke. 'I know when I'm being bamboozled, Mister,' he replied, 'so just let it lay, OK?'

We left in a hurry, before Zeke made me bust a gut, and Sergeant Price started chuckling as soon as we were out of earshot of the command tent.

'What's so funny?' asked Zeke slyly.

'You are!' laughed Price. 'Bet you've never even seen a Henry rifle in your life, you old reprobate. Fancy usin' that wife of yours to cover a tall story like that. You should be ashamed!'

'I ain't married, so it don't make no never-mind. What's a reprobate, Josh?' asked Zeke, real innocent-like.

'Damned if I know, but it sure sounds bad. Hope it ain't catching,' I replied soberly.

'Now is that some smart way of sayin' I'm a liar, Sergeant Price?' growled Zeke in mock anger.

'No, of course not,' replied Price, 'just maybe y'all ain't too well acquainted to the truth is all.'

'Oh, well, that's all right then,' grumbled Zeke, 'I'm just an ignorant mountain man. Wouldn't know a real lie if it got up an' bit me . . .'

'The officer said young Daniel managed to get back to camp, Sergeant,' I interrupted.

'Yeah, came in a day later than McBain. Was carrying a Henry rifle as it happens. Said it was yours, but McBain took it off him. Swore blind it was his. Young Daniel thought you were dead, don't reckon he'd have left you if he'd known you were only wounded.'

'Yeah? Well McBain's just gonna have to give it back again,' I snarled.

The tone of my voice must have upset old Toby because he growled deep in his throat, which was just about the way I felt also.

'Take it y'all don't like McBain very much, huh?' grunted Zeke. 'My dog didn't like him much neither, an' he's a good judge is Toby. You kin bet your last dollar on that.'

Just as Sergeant Price was handing me my Colt, young Daniel came running up. He skidded to a halt in front of us and came to attention. The big grin on his face didn't seem very soldierly but Price chose to ignore it.

'What d'you want, soldier?' he growled.

'Er, um. Nothin' Sergeant,' grinned Daniel. 'Just wanted to say I'm right glad to see Sergeant Dee is back in one piece. I brung your rifle back Josh — er, Sergeant, but I don't have it right now . . . '

'I know, son,' I cut in. There was still a lot of anger in my voice. 'I'll be dealing with that little matter in my own good time. Thanks for looking after it for me, soldier, now get back to your chores.'

'Don't mess with McBain, Josh,' grunted Price, as Daniel turned and dashed away. 'Heard you did for him once, but he'll be ready for you this time, and I'd say he's a real bad hombre to cross.'

'I'll meet it the only way I know. Head on!' I replied. 'Only this time I'll make damned sure there's no officers around to interfere. You get Zeke fitted up with his new gun and ammunition. I don't reckon he'll be wanting to hang around here, huh Zeke?'

'You're right there, pardner, too damned crowded fer my likin'. If it's all the same to you I'll just collect my things an' move on out. Look to see you around, Josh.' There was no hand shaking or good-byes. Zeke just lifted one casual hand and followed Price without a backward glance. But as I watched them go, with old Toby trailing along as usual, I realized that another friendship had been forged. Maybe we'd meet again, maybe not, but we would both remember that week on the mountain.

It was time to get myself re-established and kitted out. The information we'd brought back would soon be setting the ball rolling, and I wanted to be ready. Part of being ready meant getting my rifle back from McBain; but not yet, my hands were still very painful and I would need every advantage going when I took him on. I stood there a few minutes more before giving myself a mental shake. The time was not yet, but it would come, and you can bet a stack on that.

15

Three weeks dragged by as my hands healed and tiny stubs of nails began to grow. I wore heavy gloves to protect them while we were getting ready for an assault on Missionary Ridge. The attack on Lookout Mountain had proved successful in spite of the heavy fog. It seemed that our information had been right on target, and our armies had swarmed up the cliffs, only to find that most of the Johnny Rebs had been moved over to Missionary Ridge. Our sections had not been involved in what was already being called 'the battle above the clouds', but now preparations were going ahead in earnest and by all accounts it would be real tough going.

I still hadn't challenged McBain about my rifle, and he'd tried to get my dander up, by waving it at me each time we saw each other. Like I said, my hands were still not healed, but the smell of battle was in the air in more ways than one.

Word had it that General Sherman's troops were in trouble due to some ridge or other that they knew nothing about, and General

Hooker's men were bogged down, unable to help.

Maybe my hands weren't ready, but they'd have to do. It was time to get my Henry rifle before I went into battle. I don't rightly know what made me strap on my pistol before I went looking for McBain. It wasn't my habit to wear it around camp; maybe it was my way of telling everybody that I was ready. Young Daniel, who had been hanging around helping me while my hands were too painful to use, spotted the difference in me and scampered off but I didn't think much of it at the time.

McBain and me had something to settle, now! And I knew just where he'd be. By the time I got there, a big crowd had gathered; then I remembered Daniel scuttling away from my tent. He'd passed the word and the men, both black and white, were waiting for what they knew was about to happen. They parted as I came up and I could see McBain in the center. He stared at me, a sneering grin on his face, my rifle held in one huge paw.

'No officer to save you this time, black man,' he taunted, as he waved the gun above his head. 'This time I'm gonna break you in two.'

'Way I remember it, you were the lucky one, McBain. The officer saved you, not me.

Then you shot him in the back for his trouble.'

'You're a Goddamned liar,' he answered, his voice sounding like an animal's snarl. 'Johnny Rebs shot the lieutenant, not me! I'll make you eat those words, you black bastard.'

'Talk's cheap,' I sneered back at him, 'if anybody's the bastard I reckon it's you, McBain. No self-respecting man would own up to birthing a rat like you, 'ceptin' maybe another rat.' That last bit must have got to him, because he charged towards me swinging the rifle like he was about to bust my brains. He'd forgotten my Colt. My hand dipped, fast and neat as my thumb eared back the hammer and the Colt leveled.

McBain stopped like he'd run into a brick wall. All I had to do was lift my thumb an' he'd be dead. Maybe I should have done it, but the moment was past as he jerked his hands into the air. 'You shoot me down now an' you'll hang, black man.' Husky fear was in his voice. 'Look, I'm gonna put the rifle on the ground. All you people remember. I'm unarmed! If he shoots me y'all make sure he hangs.'

McBain slowly placed the gun on the ground and stood up. 'Your turn, mister, or are you scared I'll beat your stupid brains out?' He stepped back a pace or two and started that horrible braying laugh of his. 'Come on, black man, let's see what you're made of. Pure shit I bet.' Then he laughed again.

He really had my dander up by this time, but I guess he knew that well enough. Slowly easing the hammer down, I leaned forward and placed my pistol beside the rifle.

That was when he kicked me in the face. At the last second I saw the heavy boot flashing towards my eyes, and twisted my head so the boot cut across my forehead and cheek instead. The blood rushed into my mouth and down the side of my face as I rolled away from the full force of the blow. Through eyes blurred by tears of pain, I saw him coming for me and rolled some more, as his boot drove into my guts, and then into my chest. I curled up into a ball as the sickness hit me and his boot started to travel towards my head again. Survival was everything! I dived towards the boot and managed to grab it before rolling a second time, taking the foot with me. McBain screamed with pain as I heard a distinct cracking sound and the man crashed face down in the dirt.

Forcing myself to stand, still holding on to the boot, I slammed the heel of my own boot into the joint behind his knee before lifting the leg and slamming it hard into the ground.

I slammed his knee into the ground a second time and it gave me a savage pleasure to hear him shout with the pain of it. Still gripping the foot I threw myself forward, dragging his foot and leg over my own in an arc, that lifted him clean off the ground against my own weight, in a pain-searing lurch that would have broken the spine of a lesser man. The very force of it wrenched his foot from my hand.

I could hardly see him for the blood over my face, but from somewhere close I heard Daniel shout that McBain was trying to get at the guns. I wiped a sleeve across my eyes and saw him. One leg being dragged uselessly behind him, as he scrabbled for my Colt. Sobbing, gasping for breath, and with vomit still in my throat, I dived forward and crashed on to him. He had the pistol now. He'd thumbed back the hammer before twisting it towards me. Doing the only thing possible, I jammed one of my damaged fingers between the striker pin and the cap. The pin slapped deep into my finger, just above the new stump of nail. I yelled my pain but at least it stopped the pin from striking the percussion cap. My face and hand were a mass of pain, and stomach cramps kept biting into me from the kicks.

McBain, realizing the pain of my finger,

began to twist the pistol backwards and forwards as he slowly worked himself from under my body. If he could manage to get on top of me I was finished, and we both knew it. He pushed his face close to mine, a crazy grin plastered on it. 'Bastard! Black bastard! I'm gonna kill you!' he snarled. Then he spat in my face before pushing even closer to me.

It was the second time he'd made that mistake! My head smashed into his with every bit of strength I could manage, and his eyes began to roll backwards. I hit him a second time. My own head was a ball of fire, and the lights flashing in front of my eyes was proof of the power in me.

Slowly McBain's body began to relax and I managed to drag myself to my feet. The pistol was still hanging from my finger and I carefully eased back the hammer. My body was swaying like a tree in the wind, but McBain wasn't moving at all. I shuffled over to him; he was lying on his back. Real peaceful he looked, apart from the fact that his face was covered in his own blood. I drove the toe of my boot into his crotch. He sat up real quick then, so I planted the flat of my boot into his face. It gave me a real satisfied feeling to know his nose would never be the same again. I started to stagger over to collect my beloved rifle, but young Daniel was there before me, picking it up and tucking it under his arm, before allowing me to lean on him. Without his help, I'd have been unable to make it back to my tent. Man! I was sore all over, but come hell or high water, I'd have to be on parade tomorrow, so I rolled into my blanket and slept.

When the bugler roused me my body registered pain everywhere, like I'd been arguing with a stampede. Groaning and gasping, I'd just pushed myself into a standing position, when young Daniel charged into the tent carrying a lantern. He skidded to a stop when he saw the state of me; his eyes grew big with shock and his mouth shaped into a big round 'O'. I could tell he was about to say something about the shape I was in. I pointed a stern finger at him and said, 'Don't!'

His mouth slowly closed, and he had the good sense to choke down what he wanted to say. Which was probably that I looked like something left over from a dog's dinner — but there was other excitement in him also.

'What's new, Daniel?' I grumped.

'Orders to stand ready, is what's new, Sergeant. The lieutenant made me the runner,' he finished importantly.

'So run then, you Goddamned pipsqueak!' I growled. 'Notify all the non-coms. What are you waiting for?'

'Already done it. Seen Sergeant McBain, too. Hot damn, but he's in a worse state than you . . . almost,' he finished lamely. 'Man! You ain't never gonna be ready. Time to hustle, Sergeant.'

'I'll be ready you cheeky imp,' I snapped. 'Leave me be, and get about your business. I'll soon get the kinks out. You'll see.'

A cheeky grin slowly spread over his face. 'Guess what, Joshua?'

'What?'

'I told Sergeant McBain he looked so black an' blue that I couldn't tell him from us. Goddamn! But that made him real mad.' His voice rose in laughter, made tight and high with the excitement and fear of the battle to come.

My hand flipped towards his head, but it stopped short with the pain of movement. 'Get out of here,' I growled, 'and leave me to limber up.'

'Parade's called for on the next bugle, Sergeant, an' we need some breakfast before that,' the lad quipped, as he put the lantern down and dashed off, leaving me to the agony of exercising my aching body into some sort of fitness. Breakfast would have to be missed but at least I'd proved my point to McBain. I glanced down at the rifle lying beside the truckle bed. Maybe it was superstition, I'd heard about that from Mister Jesse, but I wanted that gun with me when I went into battle. Always!

My exercises over, I picked up the rifle and made my painful way into the noise and bustle of the preparations for war. There was an orderly urgency about the preparations, as heavy gun carriages were hooked up and horses led into their traces before trundling off through the mud.

Lieutenant Savage had just left the communications tent. He spotted me and hurried over. He reminded me of young Daniel as his mouth opened in a silent 'O'. 'Good God man! he exclaimed. 'What the hell happened to you?'

'Difference of opinion, sir.'

'Is that all! You look as if the whole Confederate Army has stomped all over you!'

'You should see the other three, sir,' I muttered, trotting out the old soldier's boast.

'McBain?'

'Something like that.'

'Did he get the worst of it?'

'So I'm told.'

'Good! Will you be fit enough? We'll be parading soon and it's going to be pretty rough.'

'I'll be ready, sir.'

Just then, the bugle sounded, and men

were running in all directions, to form up in line ready for battle. Holding myself in against the pain, I hurried to my section.

There was a grim satisfaction in me as I saw McBain limping towards the line in obvious agony. His face was one massive bruise, with his nose flattened over a face that was damn near as black as mine.

Rifles and muskets were loaded and primed, with bayonets glinting in the weak sunshine. We were ordered to march. Away ahead of us were the Confederate rifle pits, already being bombarded with canister and shot. We were taking the middle section, along the front of Missionary Ridge. One moment we were marching, then we broke into a trot. Men called to each other to boost their courage. The noise of voices increased in time with our speeding feet and, as the trot became a charge, our voices lifted to a screaming roar.

The rifle pits suddenly burst into hundreds of puffs of smoke, as every type of small arm, from pistols and flintlocks to repeating rifles and shotguns, poured a lethal rain of metal at us. The second line of pits, set above the first, also began to erupt as they added their noise to the bedlam. We were firing as we ran, screaming our defiance to cover our fear. Men fell on either side of me and more than once I heard the distinctive hum of ball or bullet pass my body; probably to lodge in some other unfortunate man or boy behind me. The air was almost unbreathable, and tight-packed as we were, the riflemen in the pits could hardly miss. Yet still we surged forward, and suddenly we were there! Falling, diving into the pits. Bayonets thrusting forward and back, rifle butts crashing into desperate faces.

We were no longer being fired upon from the second line of pits. Blue and grey were bundled together in the same trench, and the men in the pits above were afraid of killing their own men. A man, crouched in the bottom of the pit, thrust his dripping bayonet at me. I kicked it aside as the butt of my rifle smashed forward and down. He slumped into unconsciousness, or death, I never knew which.

Then we were through. No one thought of stopping the charge. No one gave the order. Lieutenant Savage had fallen before we'd reached the rifle pits, so we charged on, up towards the second line of defense, we were unstoppable, and the Confederates fell back under the force of our mad charge. Men were screaming! It was the shout of victory, as the Johnny Rebs ran towards the summit in confusion. The day was ours and we watched, exhausted, as the rebels scattered and ran.

There was still conflict on either side of us, but darkness was closing in, and we all guessed that the men in gray would withdraw under cover of the coming night. Tired men sank to the ground, to rest just where they were. Tomorrow would come the time for reckoning; men were already calling for mates lost in the rapid charge. Some replied, but too often, there was no reply of 'Yo' to a friend's call; it meant that somewhere on the slopes below us the man would lie, wounded or dead. Yes, tomorrow would come the reckoning, but as I eased my tired, aching body on to the rocky ground, I breathed a sigh of relief.

There was a wound in my thigh where a bayonet had sliced through the fat, but apart from that I was unhurt. Looking for the dead and wounded was for tomorrow. Tonight I was just pleased to be alive. Even the chill of the night air didn't bother me; it would help to clear the air of the stink of battle. I lay back, closed my eyes, made red and sore from the grit of burnt gunpowder, and allowed my battered body to relax.

A part of me wondered how this could ever have happened, or how I could lie here so calm, with the dead and dying around me. Men who would never see loved ones again.

Did we know what we were fighting for? I thought I did, but how could I be sure? Only time would tell that story. The thoughts slowly drifted away on the mist of sleep . . .

It seemed to me that I'd hardly closed my eyes, before the haunting sound of the bugle made me open them again, to stare at the sullen, smoky red of the dawning sky. Clawing myself upright with the help of a convenient rock, I stared around at the ruins of shattered and smoldering trees, as the memory came flooding back.

The blood had congealed on my thigh. It was just another ache to go with the gash on my face. I reckoned McBain had loosened a few teeth with his kick, and there was a raw place inside my mouth where the teeth had cut into it. I spat, to try to get rid of the filthy taste. It must be still bleeding; the thought penetrated the foggy haze of exhaustion as I wiped my hand across my mouth and saw the dirty red of blood on it.

We had all been carried forward on a wave of sheer terror and excitement yesterday. Now men were wandering about, stoop-shouldered and dejected. I pulled myself upright and shouted. My voice came out like the croak of a frog.

I hawked and spat a second time. 'Right! You men. Start back down. Now! Check every man you come across, and remember, we don't get any grub till we're back in camp.' My voice had gradually grown stronger with use. 'Come on now, men. We showed 'em yesterday an' we won. Let's git back down now.'

The men accepted my lead and, one by one, they began to shamble back down. It was a sorrowful chore as we turned over the dead and dying, seeing friends and comrades who hadn't made it to the top, but there were whoops of joy also, as men found friends with only minor wounds and began to help them down the hill.

Near the bottom, three dead men were sprawled across the body of a boy. I was about to move around them when a hand moved. Pulling aside two of the bodies, I was shocked to see young Daniel. A large caliber ball had taken him in the back. Either he'd been running away or he'd been shot in the back by one of his own. Kneeling beside him, I gently turned the boy over. His eyes flickered open. There was a trickle of blood from his mouth.

'Hey now Danny,' I murmured, as agony pulled at my gut at the sight of the big wound in his chest where the ball had come out. 'Y'all sure copped a packet this time, old son.'

He coughed, and more blood trickled

down his chin. 'That you, Josh?' he whispered, as his hand gripped my wrist. 'Guess I'm goin' huh?'

I eased his hand off my wrist and slipped my arm under his shoulder, holding him close to ease the pain and to make him feel that someone was there. My other hand dropped over the wound, trying to stop the flow of blood.

'Stay with me, Josh,' the boy muttered. 'I don't mind dyin' so much, it's just that I didn't figure to git it in the back! War's hell ain't it?'

'Sure is, son. You got anyone I could maybe tell?'

He smiled, kind'a wistful an' sad. 'No Josh, leastways, I do have kin somewhere, but I was sold on when I was jest a babe. Owner didn't need no pickaninnies around. You'm my kin now, Josh.'

His words hit me solid, and told me again why this war had to be fought, and won. Nobody should be allowed to take a baby from its kin and sell it, just because they didn't want young-uns around.

Young Daniel's voice was getting quieter now. He was drifting, somewhere way back, and his eyes seemed to be dulling out some.

'We'll get you some help, Danny.' My voice was hoarse and didn't hold conviction.

Danny saw through it and smiled. 'Ain't no use tryin' tuh kid me, Josh.' Suddenly his eyes brightened. 'Leave you to see to McBain . . . watch your back now, Josh, remembe — ' The blood flowing from his mouth stopped him finishing it. His eyes clouded over and he slumped in my arms.

My tears dripped unashamed onto his face as I lay him down. I well knew who had done for young Daniel, but there was no proof; that was the rub. No proof, but one day there'd be a reckoning.

My mind carried me back to yesterday. Me with a pistol in my hand and how maybe young Daniel would be alive today if I'd used it. I shook the useless thoughts aside. Other men called for my help as more wounded were found, drawing my mind back to getting the wounded off the hill before the cold got to them.

Other soldiers were helping men in blue, and gray also, back to Chattanooga. I called to the men around me. 'Look below there,' I shouted. 'Are we gonna be last to taste some chow, boys? C'mon now. Let's move it!'

My call set new heart into almost everybody around me, while my own eyes were blurred with tears for young Danny. Slowly we came down from the ridge, and it wasn't long before we were straggling towards the encampment. As we came closer, the smell of chow cooking really made us all pick up the pace; hunger can do that to a man, even on a battlefield. We'd have to go back again, to make a real search and count our losses; but for now every man, wounded or whole, had but one thought in mind. That appetizing smell . . .

We managed to make our burial detail at Missionary Ridge before the really bad weather set in, so most of the dead received some sort of Christian burial. I made it my own personal chore to bury young Daniel. Even put up a marker for him. Not even McBain had anything to say about that. Both he and I knew that things weren't finished between us. Like I said, one day there'd be a reckoning.

Our Generals decided that we'd make our winter quarters at Chattanooga. December was upon us and, as we were no longer under siege, our provisions would soon be brought in. The word was that the Confederate Army had chosen Dalton, Ga; for their winter quarters, so this was the time to put our artillery into good order, stock up on ammunition and generally prepare for the battles to come.

There was a general hubbub of hammering and banging as horses were being shod.

Wheels of gun carriages, smashed by cannon fire, or broken in the deep mud of the battlegrounds, were being re-made and fitted, while caissons were loaded with their deadly cargoes. Everyone seemed to think that the New Year of 1864 would bring an end to the war, and as one month followed the next with no major battles being fought, men became more and more optimistic.

It was May, 1864, before we began to move from our winter quarters and we realized that our hopes or fears were going to be proved, one way or another, as gun carriages were being hitched up and driven away, closely followed by the caissons. Men were everywhere, marching and parading, cleaning small arms and being kitted out with everything possible.

May 1864 was when we first heard the news that we were going to march into Georgia, aiming for the city of Atlanta. And just like Mister Jesse said back there, in what was now being called. West Virginia, brother was killing brother and father killing son, and now we were going to burn a fifty-mile wide path clear through Georgia to the coast.

I faced the front and marched as a tiny part of the combined Armies of the Cumberland, the Tennessee and the Ohio. In all, about 100,000 men were about to sweep through

Georgia to the sea. I was slowly coming back to where I'd started. The maps I'd studied with Mister Jesse for all those months was fixed in my brain. Atlanta; Savanna; Columbia, in South Carolina; and then into North Carolina. Full circle, to the place I'd always known as home! Out there in front were the Confederate soldiers; their big guns could be heard as we marched towards Atlanta, our troops forcing their way through, following the rail lines towards Dalton.

On the 9th of May we attacked a place known as 'Buzzard's Roost', with Thomas's Army of the Cumberland, but we were thrown back by the fierce fighting of the Confederate soldiers.

No one who has experienced such a battle will ever manage to describe the sheer bedlam of noise and terror, as ball and canister screamed through the air. To be followed by the explosions, when the thousands of small pieces of metal, released from the canisters, set up their howling and moaning as they spin through the air, cutting men to pieces, leaving them torn and bleeding, limbless or dead.

Thousands of rifles also played their part. Their crackling explosions almost lost in the deep booming sound of the big guns. Their lack of noise doing nothing to stop the deadly drone of the rifle balls and bullets, as they cut down man and boy alike; and many a man hugged the torn earth that day and prayed to their God.

Our betters were already calling the battle, 'The Door of Death', yet slowly we pushed on. We had losses, sure, but we seemed unstoppable.

Then the rains came, turning Georgia's soil into thick, sticky mud. Each time we paused, I'd find McBain in the background, waiting, hoping I'd do something stupid. He was afraid young Danny had found time to tell me how he'd come to be shot from behind, but always there was the need of proof. He was still senior sergeant and my word would not carry against him. Things went from bad to worse when a new officer took over from Lieutenant Savage. Either he didn't know about McBain's little quirks, or didn't care one way or the other. Only once did I try to hint that McBain was not to be trusted, and that was enough!

Lieutenant Marcus Wilding marched up and down in front of me for over an hour, pulling at his beard, and twisting his rather long moustaches all the while.

'You are an ingrate,' he shouted. 'The man is fighting for your freedom, not his! Yours! And every other black slave. Yet, you castigate him with your scandalous lies. You should be flogged, and if I hear any more of this, you damn well will be. Now get about your business, before I have you reduced in the ranks!' Then he turned his back on me and stomped off.

Don't rightly know what half of those big words meant, but I had no trouble getting the picture. It was back to the 'Yassah, Nosah,' bit to satisfy him, with no sympathy if I stepped out of line, and McBain would just love to see me in big trouble with an officer like Marcus Wilding. So for now I'd have to walk small an' keep my big mouth shut.

One thing worried me though. My back was a damned sight bigger target than young Danny's, so I'd have to make quite sure Sergeant McBain was not behind me when we went into battle. So far, I'd been lucky. In each battle since Chattanooga, McBain had been in charge of a different troop. I had Sergeant Price to thank for that. He was our new section sergeant, and a real nice fella, but even he found it hard to believe that McBain had been responsible for Danny's death.

The rain was holding up our advance, and as day followed day without a break in the weather, men, worn down by war, soaked to the skin from morning till night, were falling out with each other. It was my job to make sure that the arguments didn't start the men fighting, and for a while, I managed well enough until two men from McBain's section wandered through the thick mud into our camp. Then for no reason at all they started arguing with each other.

I arrived just as they started name-calling. Then one threw a punch that was hard enough to knock the other into the mud. Cursing and swearing the second man climbed to his feet and charged, knife in hand, at the man who had punched him. It was time for me to step in. They were both on the skinny side so apart from the knife — a Bowie like my own — I didn't figure there was gonna be much of a problem. I yelled for them to quit it, but they took no notice so I grabbed the unarmed one and threw him into the mud. Then I closed on the one with the knife. By this time, there was a crowd around us, yelling and calling advice. Slapping the guy across the face with one hand, I grabbed the knife-wrist in the other. Twisting the knife out of his hand, I allowed it to slide into my own.

This is almost too easy, I thought; grabbing the front of his shirt while I still held the knife, point forward, in my other hand.

Suddenly the man grabbed the front of my own shirt with both hands and threw himself backward into the mud. Taken completely by surprise I fell forward on top of him. Still gripping my shirt, he started to shout into my face. 'Please Sergeant. Don't kill me! Get him off me someone. He's gonna stick me with that knife of his. Help!'

On the heels of his shout, McBain's voice cut across my scrambled thoughts, like lightning through the night.

'On your feet at once, Sergeant!'

I released the man and scrambled to my feet, still holding the Bowie.

'This ain't what you think, Sergeant,' I snapped, coming to attention.

'Pr'aps we'll let the officer of the day be judge of that, mister.' I could hear the vicious laughter in his voice. 'Attacking a soldier with a knife? Making unfair use of your rank?'

I turned towards him, to make my excuses.

'Stand still!' Lieutenant Wilding's voice stopped me before I'd even started. 'Place that man under arrest, Sergeant, confiscate that knife, and disarm him. Select two men and march him to the guard tent. Move it!'

McBain snatched the knife and removed my Colt from its holster. My knife sheath was empty, so I figured that my own blade had fallen into the mud when the soldier had pulled me to the ground. I didn't give much thought to it as McBain handed the weapons to the officer; my mind was so scrambled.

McBain selected two troopers, and with Lieutenant Wilding leading the way, I was marched to the guard tent and tied hand and foot.

The lieutenant left to make his report and the two escorts were dismissed, leaving me alone with McBain. He pushed me to the ground; with my hands and feet tied, it was an easy thing to do.

'Oh man! You're in it this time, right up to that dirty black neck of yours,' he gloated, 'attacking a man with your own knife, Dee. Now that was very silly of you.'

The daylight had registered a little while back. McBain had done some very careful planning, but he'd slipped up. My knife had my initials burnt into the handle. 'You can't prove it was my knife, McBain,' I growled, 'and the men will give the true story when they're called.'

McBain was already shaking his head, that nasty sneering grin pasted to his face. He slipped a knife from beneath his tunic. A Bowie grimed with mud. 'That nice officer has your knife, Sergeant. This is the one you were fightin' over. As for the men, I'm told that we'll be pushin' on in maybe one or two days, so they just won't be around. Who's gonna be bothered about a court martial when there's a war to be won?' He chuckled.

He raised his hand, pointing it at me like it was a gun. 'Bang! An' you're dead, you black bastard. I've bin longin' fer this day to come. Knew it would if I waited long enough. Just like little Danny. Bang!'

I was trembling from head to foot with useless anger. 'I knew you killed Danny you slimy bastard,' I snarled at him. 'I'll live to have you, McBain. I'll cut your filthy heart out.'

He stopped smiling for a second, as if a ghost had walked over his grave. Then he drove his boot into my groin. 'You won't ever git the chance, damn you,' he snarled. Then he kicked me a second time, but I managed to take most of it on my thigh.

Something made me keep staring into his face, and although I was on the ground, he couldn't seem to pull his eyes away. I forced the pain from my mind and held him with my eyes, like a snake holds its prey, and all the time I kept muttering 'I'll 'ave you, McBain.'

He was about to kick me a third time, when the lieutenant came into the tent.

This time it was my turn to pull a trick. I started groaning with the pain of my groin, and it didn't take much doing neither. 'Please don't kick me again, Sergeant,' I moaned. Then I put on my 'Down Home' talk. 'Y'all know real fine I ain't gotten any money yet,

Mister McBain, suh, but I'll sure-God pay y'all just like always, once I git my Army pay.'

'What the hell is this, Sergeant?' snapped the officer.

'I . . . I, don't know,' muttered McBain.

'Oh my God, ah sure is sorry, Lieutenant suh,' I interrupted before McBain could think of anything to say. 'Ah knows that the Sergeant has to pay y'all your share of all the money he collects, 'cos he just finished a'tellin' me so. It ain't his fault we'uns ain't paid yet, so don't y'all get to blamin' him none, no sir. He'll pay y'all just as soon as he gits it, huh? Sergeant suh.'

'Stop gabbling on, man,' snapped the puzzled officer. 'What's all this about money, McBain?' There was suspicion in his voice. It was well known that certain sergeants demanded payment from some of the soldiers, to get them out of trouble, or off tiresome duties.

'I don't know what the hell he's talkin' about, sir,' replied McBain, his face a mass of confusion.

I must have accidentally hit on a sore spot because the sergeant was beginning to sweat. 'No sah,' I interrupted again, 'ah'm sure the sergeant don't know nothin' about it — if he says so — but y'all know full well suh. We just ain't bin paid yet.'

'Stop this nonsense at once!' roared the officer. He withdrew the Bowie from under his tunic. 'Sergeant McBain. This is not the knife Sergeant Dee had in his hand when we arrested him!'

McBain's eyes flickered from the knife to the officer, the worry on his face beginning to show. 'I don't understand, sir,' he mumbled.

'Neither do I, mister, and what's more, neither does Major Griffin! This knife is spotless. Not the slightest sign of any mud or dirt anywhere man. So where did you get it?'

'But, we saw Dee with it in his hand, sir.'

'No we did not! You made me look a fool in front of Major Griffin, Sergeant; I'm beginning to wonder if this man is telling the truth. That you are collecting money from him. That you have maneuvered him into this position because he hasn't paid recently.'

'But sir . . . '

'Shut up, Sergeant. This matter will be resolved at a later date. Release this man and send him about his duties, and, McBain, if I ever find out that this whole thing was set up on purpose . . . ' It seemed that words failed the Lieutenant at that point, because he turned and stalked out of the tent.

'You crafty swine,' snarled McBain. 'I'll get you yet. There's a lot of war ahead of us, and at the end of it, you'll be dead!'

'We'll see,' I told him without raising my voice, 'now cut these damned ropes, and do it carefully, McBain. Lieutenant Wilding ain't so pleased with your antics just now, he'd love to take his spite out on you and so would I.'

I could see by McBain's eyes that he was weighing up his chances, as he leaned over me with the Bowie in his hand and I was ready to do what I could, but just then Sergeant Price stuck his head through the flap in the tent.

'Don't take all day, McBain,' growled Price, 'I need that man on parade. We're moving forward to the Chattahoochee River any time now, so get those ropes off him. Pronto.' And, as McBain still hesitated, Price raised his voice. 'I said pronto! McBain.'

I gave McBain my best lopsided smile, as he growled deep in his throat and cut the ropes. 'Your best chance just up and went,' I muttered into his face, as I took the knife and cut the ropes around my legs. Still holding the knife, with the blade pointing towards his throat, I deliberately winked at him as I flicked the blade, cross-wise, real close, making him flinch with the suddenness of it. 'We'll see who gets to die, McBain,' I hissed through my teeth.

That seemed to be enough for him. He straightened up, turned on his heel and stomped out of the tent.

'You need to watch that one,' muttered Price, as he offered me his hand and pulled me to my feet. 'He's a bad one to cross, Joshua.'

'I'm watching, y'all can bet a stack on that, Sergeant,' I replied as we left the tent.

16

The following dawn, our main army crossed the Chattahoochee River, on the Northwestern side of Atlanta, while the Army of the Cumberland, under Major Thomas, crossed Peachtree Creek. We quickly established our position, but the Confederates attacked us like crazy men on all fronts. By nightfall, some 8,000 men had died, and the word went out that we were in for a long bloody struggle.

On the 8th of August, the big guns were being pulled and tugged into position around Atlanta, and on the 9th, they began their deafening roar, from the North and West. The dreadful noise continued by day and night. Atlanta was to be smashed into the ground.

On, or about, the 30th of August, Hardee's Johnny Rebs tore into us. They fought like madmen, but so did we. From the head count we did later it was said, that of the 24,000 Johnny Rebs who had fought us that day, only about 5,000 managed to escape with their lives. On the 2nd of September, a fiercely burning Atlanta surrendered.

Battle weary men trudged through the

streets looking for lone snipers, or officers with their dispatch bags. Dirty men with crude bandages on arms or legs foraged for food in the burning ruins, while some were looking for booty, stealing rings or trinkets from the dead and dying. Other men were seeking women to satisfy a more basic need.

My mind tried to ignore these things as I trudged through the manmade hell. What madness was this? I asked myself, as I passed children, lying like broken dolls in the muck of the streets, ignored by filthy men squabbling over the pitiful items found in dead men's pockets. I saw an officer of the Confederacy sitting against a wall. He only had one half of his face; the rest of it had gone, torn away by flying steel. In his hand was a scrap of paper; I thought it might be orders, information of troop movements or something like that.

Pulling the paper from his stiffening fingers, I carefully spread it out. It was blood-smeared, like you'd expect, but the words were plain to see. It wasn't orders, it was personal, but I read it anyway. It was one of those poems people are always talking about, and Mister Jesse was so fond of, that he'd spend many an evening reading them to me. I felt kind'a sad as I read the words on that piece of paper . . .

Oh my God what tragedies, this war
has brought about,
With brother killing brother, and in
their death-throes shout,
A curse of pain, of blasphemy. A plea
against our destiny from friend and foe
alike,
Oh my Lord when will it end? When
will my hammer strike?
I saw death's awful chamber, at Chatta-
nooga's battle,
At Lookout Mountain in the clouds,
where men were slain like cattle.
I staggered onward, from 'The Ridge',
and Chickamauga Creek,
The choking smoke, the grit, the smell,
left me torn and weak.
But now my brain is numb with shock,
as I slowly turn,
The tears run, scalding down my face,
as I watch Atlanta burn.

It seemed to me that there was going to be
more of this kind of stuff, because there was a
long squiggly line down the page. I figured
that whatever took away his face, did it right
about then, where that squiggly line was. It
was easy to see that this fella had been
through hell, and regretted it. That little
poem told me that the dead man never

should have become a soldier. More your home town family man, and if Atlanta had been his home town, then I could understand his sorrow, because what had been a beautiful place was fast becoming a burnt out shell that might never be rebuilt.

My weary eyes were sore and weepy from the grit and smoke all around me. There's no explaining the awful taste of burnt gunpowder at the back of a man's throat. You have to taste it to know it. Death and destruction lay everywhere; somewhere close a building crashed to the ground, giving up to the raging fires, and sending even more smoke and hot dust into the air, while other buildings seemed to shimmer in the heat haze before bursting into flame.

My attention was caught by a sharp female scream. I don't know why it should have cut into my morose thoughts, but it did. My eyes squinted down even more, as I searched for the place where the scream had come from.

Across the street, three men in blue were dragging a woman towards a stone building, and she didn't want to go! Man! She was fighting like a wildcat. Biting, snapping and kicking like a mad thing. I figured that those three men were gonna have one tough time, getting what they wanted from that vixen.

Then I noticed that the men were all white,

while the woman was black. Well that kind'a got my dander up; I was supposed to be fighting a war to stop this sort of thing happening. Maybe I'd not be so het up if the woman had been white, but that was neither here nor there. I only knew that my big flat feet were already carrying me across the street as I stuffed the scrap of paper into my pocket.

My good Henry rifle was gripped tightly in one hand, while the other rested on the handle of my Colt, but I deliberately kept my voice friendly as I approached. 'Hold up there fellas,' I called, 'just where d'you happen to be taking that young lady?'

The men stopped and turned towards me, and I could see the woman for the first time. She stared at me, all haughty and unafraid. I could feel her contempt pour over me, like green slime in a pond, but I also felt something else — like I'd just been offered the most wonderful gift in God's creation — or kicked in the stomach! Although there was dirt on her dress and face, from the burning buildings and such, she still looked clean an' regal somehow, untouched and pure, like the dark side of a beautiful peach, with just a smudge of dirt on the perfect bronzed skin.

I took in the beautiful, dark, sloe-black

eyes, full pouting lips and the firm, well-shaped body in nothing flat, and my guts did a flip-flop. This woman was too beautiful to be true! My mind was still racing along as I snapped, 'I asked you a question soldiers. Where are you taking this young lady?'

One of the men gave me a knowing smile. 'Ain't no lady, Sarge. Lady's maid more like, we'm just gonna have us a leetle fun is all.'

I stepped up real close. 'Let her go at once, and get about your business.' My voice was parade ground sharp.

'This is our business just now, fella, so I'll ask you to stand aside.' The man was big enough to stare me in the eye, and that's big! He was also heavily built, and while I'd be pleased to take him on alone, I reckoned the other two gave them too much of an edge.

The big man thought so too; he had a wide sneering grin on his face. 'Don't worry black boy, we'll let you have her when we've finished, won't we boys?' He turned to his mates with a sly chuckle. 'We like to share with our black friends. Don't we?'

That's when the butt of my good Henry rifle slapped him in the teeth, real hard, and he keeled over without a sound. I remember thinking that he'd need to see the surgeon real soon, once he woke up. The barrel of my rifle followed through, and came slashing down across the first man's nose. It would never be the same again; the man would spend the rest of his life breathing only through his mouth. The third one was about to run, when I levered a cartridge into the magazine. I didn't have to tell him to stand still. He froze, with the barrel of my rifle about three inches from his throat.

'I figure you ought to help your mates back to camp, friend, don't you?' I asked quietly, 'and tomorrow morning, put yourselves on report for insubordination. Understand soldier!'

'Y-yes Sergeant,' the man muttered, as he tried to choke down a mixture of anger and fear.

'Well get to it then!' I snapped.

I smiled at the woman, expecting a grateful 'thank you' at least, but she glared at me like I'd just crawled from under a stone.

'Just want me all to yourself, is that it, Sergeant? Well you just try, and I'll take that gun an' stuff it down your Goddamned throat!' Then she turned and walked off, cool as you please.

I had a big daft grin on my face as she sashayed away. At least she didn't say she'd shove the gun up somewhere, which to my mind showed her good breeding. My grin widened at the thought. Then she suddenly turned around and caught me at it.

'Did I say somethin' funny, Sojer-boy?' she asked, standing with hand on hip, and her head tilted, just so. She'd caught me out a real beauty, turning around sudden like that, and if I weren't so Goddamned black, my face would have been as red as a turkey cock's comb.

'Y'all lost your tongue, Sojer-boy?' She flickered her eyes like women do.

'No Ma'am,' I replied, still grinning.

'Well, wipe that silly grin offen yore face then, mister — if you're gonna escort a lady safely to her home. You are gonna do that small thing now, ain't yuh?' One eyebrow came up in a big curve.

'Yes Ma'am!' I replied, quick smart, as I stepped up beside her, still grinning from ear to ear; and damn me, but I couldn't get rid of that silly grin no matter how I tried.

We didn't have far to go, which was a pity, because I kind'a enjoyed sauntering along beside her, my every movement telling anybody who might get ideas to forget it. I was still strolling along like that, when I realized she'd stopped at a big oak-paneled doorway, and I felt all kinds of a fool as I hurried back to where she was waiting.

'Thought y'all wasn't gonna bother tuh stop, mister,' she said, kind'a cool an' sarcastic. 'This is where I live, big man.'

This time it was my turn to come the fancy-Dan. 'No Ma'am,' I said, 'this is where you maybe used to live, but not any more.' I stepped back and stared up at the building. All that was left was one wall with the oak-paneled door in it. 'Y'all open that door and the whole wall will fall on you, lady.' My grin was back again; I could feel it stretching the dirt on my face.

'Man! Y'all sure do find some strange things to smile at Sojer. I'm homeless and you're laughin'?'

'No Ma'am! I ain't really laughing, I just feel that today might just be a lucky one for me, and I'm kind'a pleased about it.'

'Oh is that all? Pr'aps you feel lucky enough to find me a place to stay in this God-forsaken junk heap, fella.'

'Joshua.'

'Huh?'

'That's my name, Ma'am. Joshua D. Sergeant. What's yours?'

'None of your damned business. Joshua D! What the hell does the D stand for?'

'Just that Ma'am, I was number four. A, B, C, D, like the alphabet. Y'know?' I was grinning again.

'Of course I know the alphabet, Joshua D.

222

D'you think I'm some ignorant slave, or somethin'?'

'No Ma'am!'

'I should hope not! Y'all gonna find me a place to stay? Or are we gonna stand in front of this here door till the whole thing falls on us?'

Finding a place for her in Atlanta just now was going to be a problem. The way the buildings were burning, it just stood to reason that there was bound to be some overcrowding. I'd invite her back to my tent for the night but she might get the wrong idea. Me, too, now I came to think about it.

She was getting impatient, I could tell by the way she was tapping her foot; so, stretching the grin even further, I took her arm and started leading her along the road. Seemed to her like I knew just where I was going. So how deceitful can a man get?

By sheer good luck, we came across a stone church. It had remained undamaged through the bombardment and a few people were straggling towards it. I helped her up the steps and pushed the door open for her. Three men stood in the passage, and they weren't pleased to see us — until I showed them the muzzle of my rifle. I stared at them and waited, as they slowly moved and allowed us to pass.

'Look to see you here in the morning, Ma'am,' I said evenly. Then I turned to the men. 'Hope no harm comes to the lady, friends. Otherwise, I just might look to you gents for some answers. You catch my drift?'

The men looked at each other before nodding. Then the one with the dog collar made a steeple of his fingers and kind'a bowed over them. 'Have no fear, all God's children are welcome here.' His voice came out all deep and hollow, so I knew he was lying through his teeth. I tapped him on the chest with the barrel of my rifle.

'Your God might feel like that, mister. You just make sure that everybody else agrees with him. Otherwise, y'all might get to meet him far quicker than you realize. Sabe?'

The preacher kind'a swallowed, and twisted his neck, like he had a lump in his throat 'I-I quite understand young man,' he mumbled, 'you really don't need to be so aggressive you know.'

'You think this is aggressive?' I showed him my teeth to prove I was happy. 'I'm just a pussy-cat, fella, but don't make me angry, you won't like it one little bit.' I turned to say goodbye to the lady but she'd gone into the hall, so the tough act I'd put on, just for her, went unnoticed, an' that made me kind'a mad, so I put the muzzle of my rifle under the vicar's nose. 'Hope you have a real good memory, friend,' I growled, as I backed out the doorway and headed towards the encampment.

I'd see that lady around somewhere tomorrow, and I'd find out who she was, or my name wasn't Joshua D. I stuck a cigar in the corner of my mouth and struck a stinker on the seat of my pants. Maybe Atlanta was burning, I thought, as I sucked the smoke into my lungs, but there was life here, too; maybe the beginning of a new life for me. The woman's face was tacked into my brain like a nail in a coffin, and that suited me just fine. I grinned around my cigar. Maybe life weren't so bad after all.

17

We camped outside the town for near on a month and I got to know the lady a lot better. Even found out her first name, and that was no bad chore either; couldn't get her to tell me her second one though and you can bet that I tried real hard. I was beginning to believe she was a princess or something, she was so Goddamned secretive.

'Pears her name was Lily, which she seemed a bit ashamed of. I have to admit it didn't suit her one little bit. Tigress would have been nearer the mark, judging by her temper — but I didn't tell her that — I ain't exactly stupid. She had worked as a Lady's Maid and it seems like she enjoyed it too, because when I told her why we were fighting this here war, it was like setting light to a barrel of gunpowder.

'Oh now. That's just fine, Sojer-boy,' she yelled. 'Y'all fight a war tuh set us folks free huh? So then, what happens? I had a damned good job, with real nice folks. I get to eat regular an' sleep in a fine clean bed. Then along comes Mister Hero an' sets me free. Free! Only now I got no job, no place to sleep an' nothin' to eat neither, an' y'all call that progress?'

It was a waste of time trying to explain to her the 'wider issues,' as Mister Jesse called them. Man! I couldn't get a word in edgewise for the first two days, but things brightened up after that.

I tell the world, this was one loving woman, and by the time the troops were ready to move on, we'd formed quite an understanding. Mind you, she weren't quite so understandin' when we were told to blow up the few remaining factories and set fire to what was left.

Fact is, I weren't sure who scared me the most, Lily or the general; but in spite of her screeching, we still kissed each other goodbye, and promised to meet again when the war was over. Seeing tears in her eyes for the first time was quite something. Kind'a choked me up some too. Goddamn! I'd like to know where that lump in my throat keeps coming from, just when I don't need it. There it was again, big as ever, as I looked over my shoulder and saw her waving a piece of cloth at me when we started our march towards Savannah. Trying to swallow just don't shift it no-how; you just have to wait for it to go away.

The orders were to burn everything we

didn't need for twenty-five miles in either direction as we moved forward. It tore a man's soul apart, to see good crops and farms going up in smoke and flames, although there were some of the troops who seemed to take great pleasure in the destruction. Families, who couldn't believe this was happening, watched in dumb shock as their life's work was wiped away by the fires. Women and girls, some still in their early teens and some even younger, were sorely treated by many of the troops; while others just ran before us, or were cut down by marauding bands of Confederate cavalry as they tried everything they could to stop our advance towards Savannah.

There was nothing noble or heroic about it. Our commanders had boasted that we would be in Savannah by Christmas, and by God it looked like they were gonna be on target. Rail lines and sleepers were torn up; stations, watering points and telegraph lines were smashed and burned. It tore at a man's heart to look behind us and see blackened earth, for as far as the eye could see. Then we'd face the front again and look at the crops before us. More of the same, ready for the torches.

Our armies massed outside Savannah in early December as over 60,000 men prepared to attack the city; and on the 13th, a section of our forces stormed Fort McAllister, and by the 21st December, the Confederates abandoned the city.

The hand-drawn maps Mister Jesse had given me, way back in Kentucky, told me that we were close to the Southern tip of South Carolina. More and more I felt that 'comin' home' feeling and I wondered how my Pa was getting along with the white folks at the farm I'd run from, nigh on three years ago. I crouched over the map and traced my way up through South Carolina toward Washington, thinking that maybe we'd head towards Charleston and Sumter, or perhaps Columbia. Either way, we were getting closer and closer to North Carolina. Yep, the map told me that I'd bin traveling full circle, and if we kept going like I figgered we would, I'd end right back where I started.

So far, I'd been very lucky. Apart from that one bayonet wound, and the scratch on my skull, I'd come through without a ball or bullet to knock me down. How much longer would my luck carry me? Would I ever get back to Atlanta where Lily was waiting? Or would McBain get his wish, and still nail me somewhere along the way? I knew he was biding his time, but because of the casualties, our regiment had been broken up and spread among other sections of the army. I knew he was out there somewhere, just waiting for me to make a mistake.

The fact that we no longer exchanged prisoners meant that our captives had to be kept somewhere safe, and the white section of the army guarded these men, because it was generally agreed that to put black troops in charge of white prisoners would cause too many problems. The wounded were different. No wounded man or woman would be too particular who dressed their wounds, and the surgeons were too busy with our own men to bother much with enemy wounded.

First time I walked into what was laughingly called the infirmary, the smell hit me straight in the guts. I'd just finished a meal of cold pork. Believe me! Eating that was just a waste of time. I hung about outside for a long time before I stuck a cigar in my face, lit up and used the smoke to help kill the awful smell; but a man gets used to almost anything after a while and this was no different. Before long, I was bandaging and wrapping arms and legs with the best of them.

Looking around in that crowded place of pain and misery, I wondered again if this was worthwhile, because I was remembering Lily's words. 'Free? Yeah, but with no job, no money and no place to go. So what's good about it?'

My attention was caught by a low moan, a short distance along the crowded, badly lit room, and I made my careful way towards the man on the floor. He wore the tattered and bloody uniform of a Confederate Cavalry Officer. At least the top half was still there. The trousers ended just above the knee, and so did his legs. The stumps had been tied into a kind of leather pocket. The smell was of gangrene; I'd smelled it a time or two before, and from the look of him, the man didn't have long to go, so I knelt beside him and turned his head, figuring to give him a few drags of my cigar. Even that small thing can help when there's nothing else. The face came around easy; the eyes were blank with pain.

'Mister John!' The words were forced out of me, as I recognized the owner of the estate where I'd been born.

His eyes flickered at the sound of my voice. 'Joshua? Is that you?' His voice was so weak I could hardly hear it but the hand that gripped my arm was still strong. 'Joshua D!' It came out as a sigh. 'My Lord but it's a small world, boy.' The eyes were open wide now, pleading for help.

'Take these damned boots off me, boy. Bandage my legs up good and tight to stop the bleeding, then I'll be walking in no time. Fetch your Pa, there's a good lad.'

His voice tailed off, muttering and mumbling, and I knew he was rambling, back to the time when I was just a button and his leg had been cut by the blade of a plow.

Then his eyes cleared again and he was back with us. 'Listen Joshua,' he muttered. 'Matthew has been taken prisoner. He's in the compound. Try to get permission to let him come to me, if you can.'

Then he set off mumbling again, and I leaned real close, so that I could make out what he was whispering. 'This war, lad,' he muttered. 'Never should have been like this. Always did the best I could for my people. Did I ever cause you harm, Joshua? If I did, it was without knowing and I'm truly sorry. There's no need for all this useless bloodshed.' He coughed and there was blood on his lips as I laid him back down and patted his shoulder. 'I'll do my best to get Master Matthew,' I promised. But he didn't answer. Just kept rambling on about the farm, like he was still there and Master Matthew was just a young shaver.

The duty officer, a Captain Marchant, was a nice enough fella, and he knew of my friendship with Major Jesse, which maybe helped to get me into the compound. It also seemed like he was man enough to understand my feelings for Mister John, and when I explained that his life was slipping away fast, he brushed aside the rules and took me straight into the prison buildings.

Man! I have never, in my worst dreams, seen such terrible conditions. The place stank so bad that even the Infirmary was an improvement. Dull-eyed men were crammed so tightly together that they'd have a hard time even sitting on the stinking floor to sleep. There was no room at all to lie down, and who'd want to anyway? Their clothes were covered with mud and human filth, but the worst thing was the silence. No one was talking or cursing, just plain hopeless silence, as empty eyes stared at nothing. At each barred cage, I called Master Matthew's name, but there was no reply.

There was the crack of a bullwhip up ahead, followed by a high squeal of pain. The heavy sneering laugh registered with me. McBain had found another way to take his pleasure. The man came lumbering through the narrow corridor, a coiled bullwhip in his hand. He was using the stock to push a boy, dressed in a tattered soldier's uniform, ahead of him. It was obvious that the lad had been crying, and was terrified of the hulking man behind him.

McBain stopped when he saw the officer, and a wariness stiffened his body when he saw me. His hand came up in a sloppy salute.

'Where are you taking that lad, Sergeant?' Captain Marchant's voice was harsh, showing his dislike for McBain.

'Interrogation, sir,' replied McBain, as his eyes kept flickering between us and it was easy to see that he was wondering why I was here.

'Why should you want to question a mere boy? What information could he possibly have, that would help us with our battle plans?'

McBain had a sly half-grin on his face. 'Don't rightly know until I've questioned him, sir. Do I?'

'Don't be insubordinate, Sergeant McBain,' snapped the captain. 'Put this soldier back into the cells, and in future there will be no interrogation unless I say so. Is that understood?'

'Yes sir!' McBain must have realized that he had overstepped the mark. He snapped to attention, and hustled the boy back along the corridor.

'There's something about that fellow I don't cotton to, but I can't put my finger on it,' muttered the captain, as we continued to look for Master Matthew.

'Sir, when you think of Sergeant McBain, think how often he has a young boy with him. I used to do some wondering about that myself, till I found out why.'

It didn't get a reaction from the captain, and we continued to go from cell to cell, calling out Master Matthew's name. Then, quite suddenly, he stopped.

'Good God man! You don't mean-?' He let the words hang in the air, like it was too bad to believe.

'Damn-me, you can't mean it, Sergeant! You mean — with boys?'

I didn't say a word. The last time I'd tried to tell an officer what McBain was up to, I'd damn near had my baby-makers chewed off.

'I'll keep my eye on Sergeant McBain in the future, Sergeant. If I see so much as a suggestion of that sort of thing I'll have him before a court martial.'

'Two other officers threatened to have him under court-martial, sir. They were both shot — in the back!' I replied quietly.

'A-are you saying,' His face grew red with emotion, 'tha-that — '

'I'm saying nothing, sir. Only don't let him know what you intend to do, an' if you do — watch your back.'

I called again for Matthew and a weak 'Yo' answered my call. There was some pushing and shoving from the back of the cell, before a dirty bedraggled cavalry captain managed to push through the tightly packed bunch. He squinted at me in the dim light. 'I know you from somewhere, mister. What d'you want? Come to gloat have you?'

'No sir!' I replied. 'I'm Joshua D from the plantation, remember?'

He stared some more. 'Well hell, yes. How are you, boy? What do you want with me?'

'I ain't a boy any more Master Matthew.' My voice told him I wasn't best pleased with the term. 'I'm a sergeant in the Union Army and proud of it, so don't be calling me boy!'

'Hell, I didn't mean anything special by it, Joshua, you know that well enough. Why did y'all come looking for me anyway?'

'Mister John. I mean your daddy. He's at the Infirmary, in a bad way, and was asking to see you. I promised I'd try.'

His hand gripped mine through the bars, his eyes pleading. 'Can I see him, Josh?'

'Captain Marchant here, says so. If you promise to come back here without causing any bother. He's breaking all the rules to help your daddy, so I'd expect a man of your breeding to stand by your word, if y'all gave it.'

He was tired and weak. His clothes were ripped and filthy, but he snapped to attention and saluted Captain Marchant, like he was in his best uniform and on parade.

'I'd be mighty obliged for your kindness, Captain, and you have my word, sir.'

Captain Marchant returned the salute. 'Your thanks should be for Sergeant Joshua. Captain. He's the one who took the trouble to seek me out and get the permission.' He fitted a key into the lock and opened the door, just enough for Matthew to slip through, before relocking it. 'You have an hour, Captain. Don't let me down,' he called as we hurried away.

I stopped and turned, raising my hand to the Captain. 'No one will let you down, sir, and thank you most kindly,' I shouted, before we hurried out of the building and across the compound towards the Infirmary.

'Is he very bad, Joshua?'

'About as bad as it gets, Master Matthew. I don't figure he's gotten too much time left. Be prepared, sir, both his legs are gone from below the knees, and gangrene is having its way with him.'

'Oh God, Joshua D. Why the hell are we fighting this stupid war?'

'Slavery, that's why.'

'No, Josh, that isn't the real reason,' he panted as we hurried along. 'That's the excuse.'

'Slavery ain't a good thing, Master Matthew.'

'Maybe so, but it's still only an excuse.'

I didn't get time to figure out what he meant by that, because we had entered the Infirmary and we needed all our care to make sure we didn't step on any of the bodies lying on the floor.

Mister John was still mumbling away, but he was much weaker.

Master Matthew knelt beside him.

I stayed well back out of the way when they clasped hands. I could see that Matthew had tears running down his face. This was too personal. It was between father and son.

Besides, I had a few tears running down my own face, because, like Mister John had said, he'd never treated us badly. He was a good man, who was just doing what he thought was right at the time. I heard some mention of Master Luke. Then Mister John gave out a groan, an' Matthew lifted him, hugging him close.

Time he laid Mister John back down on the floor, he was dead, and great sobs was shaking Master Matthew's shoulders as he leaned over his daddy. Like I said, I was some cut up my own self, but I'd done the best I could, so I tapped Master Matthew on the shoulder. 'We'd best be leaving now, sir,' I muttered.

Matthew nodded, as he tried to tidy up his daddy's muddy tunic and cross his arms over his chest. 'Do your best to see he gets a good funeral, Joshua, please,' he said, as more sobs shook him. 'We never meant harm to you, or your people, you know that don't you?'

'Sure do, Master Matthew,' I mumbled; that Goddamned lump was there again so's I could hardly speak. 'I'll do the best I can; sir, we have to go now.' He leaned against me, still being shaken by sobs, as we walked back to his cell together.

'I won't forget this, Josh. We're on different sides, but we're family. Leastwise that's how Pa always put it. He always said we were all God's children, and we all believed him.' He held out his hand to me at the cell door, and I gripped it hard. 'Good luck, Master Matthew,' I muttered. That damned lump was still choking me as the door clanged shut, and he pushed his way back through the dull-eyed prisoners, towards the small rear window.

I looked in on Captain Marchant as I passed his office; to let him know I'd put Master Matthew back in the cell like I promised. He called me in, and offered me a cigar, which we lit in companionable silence, both remembering Master Matthew; he pulled a bottle of malt whiskey out of a drawer and poured a goodly measure into two glasses.

The glasses lay between us, but I made no move to pick one up. I'd never been offered a glass of whiskey or any other kind of brew — except root beer — by a white man in my life. It was something that just never happened, and I wasn't about to make the mistake of drinking that good whiskey without his say-so.

The captain picked up one glass, and also waited.

'Won't you take a drink with me, Sergeant Joshua?' He asked quietly.

'D'you think I should, sir?'

'I do. We're equals, you and I; my rank may be higher than yours, but under these clothes we're equals.' He raised his glass. 'That's what this awful war is all about, and let's hope it's over soon.' He lifted the glass higher. 'To the end of wars, Joshua D!' he said by way of a toast.

I picked up my glass. 'I'll drink to that, sir,' I muttered as I lifted the glass, and felt the comforting jolt clear down to my boots.

Walking back to my tent, I allowed my mind to wander back over the last three years, thinking of those two white women and the way overseers used to beat slaves on the other farms and plantations. I didn't ever think that one day I'd be taking a drink with a white man. An officer of the army to boot. It sure does beat everything, the way things turn out sometimes.

The cigar tasted sweet as I sucked the smoke into my lungs. Maybe, just maybe, this here war would make a difference, but one thing was for sure, the old ways had gone for good.

18

The rains held us up clear through to the beginning of January, before the men at the top grew restless at the delay. The troops were beginning to get edgy also. What was left of Savannah wasn't worth looking at, and there weren't any women to satisfy their hunger.

I'd managed to get Mister John decently buried and Master Matthew was real grateful for that, but there was no time to see him again, because we were preparing for our march towards Columbia, in South Carolina.

The rain was falling down in great sheets when we started our march. We'd spent weeks waiting for the weather to break, but damn me if that morning weren't the worst one yet, and to make matters worse, it wasn't long before we hit the coastal swamps. There was no let up though. Day after day, we'd plow our way over a soggy pathway of the rushes and straw we had laid to help the big guns through the mud and water; sometimes up to our waists in the soggy mess.

The cannons had to be hauled out and pushed forward, horses and men tearing their hearts out to keep up the ten miles each day demanded by our officers. Thing was, while we were up to our asses in muck, they were perched up there on their hosses, telling us to get moving and not to take all day about it.

Cooking was another problem. With all that rain, we couldn't get a hot meal very often; but the officers! That was a different kettle of fish altogether. Their servants would ride ahead, set up their nice big tents on a dry hummock of land, and have a real hot meal ready for the gentlemen.

By the time we arrived, footsore and weary, we'd fall on our faces in the mud, and sleep, while they washed up and enjoyed their meal. The officer's clothes would be dried by the servants, ready for the next day's march, while ours would go on soaking up the water, so that legs and arms would be rubbed raw by the wet cloth, making real good feeding places for leeches and such.

On the 15th of February, our armies started the attack on Columbia. Again, the mind-numbing fear gripped us as we charged towards the enemy with bayonets ready, the screams tearing at our throats to cover the thoughts of death; and once more there was the tiny flicker of flame from rifles, as men fired into our charging bodies. Bayonets reflecting redly in the weak sunshine, as the men in gray threw themselves at us. Others fell, caught by our bullets, before they could engage us in the awful hand to hand fighting; when frightened faces and screaming mouths were closed forever, in the horror of death, and other men trampled over their soft bodies, eager to get this thing over with. Maybe to pray to their Gods once more, because they weren't the ones labeled for death this time.

By the 17th, Columbia was burning. We crept through the streets looking for snipers, moving through burned buildings, with the sulfur from scorched timbers stinging a man's eyes and clogging the throat; it sure takes some explaining.

The sharp crack of a rifle and the spiteful whine of a bullet spanging off a wall, close enough to feel the wind of its passing, kind'a jolts the stomach enough to make a man hunt for a latrine quick-smart, and a body ain't even safe there neither. We've found more than one man with his kegs at half-mast and a hole in his head.

I was passing a stone-built mail depot, when a bullet ricocheted offen the wall, spitting stone dust into my face. I went to ground behind a big smoldering log, as two more bullets slammed into it from different directions. Another bullet pulled at the heel of my boot; it was getting time to find that latrine I'd been thinking about.

I'd just about brought my eyes up level with the top of the log, trying to spot one of the snipers, when another bullet slapped into it, spitting wood chips into my face. I was caught in the open between the wall of the depot and the big log. Burrowing as close to the stinking log as possible without setting myself on fire, I looked for a line of retreat. The wall was solid, without window or door, around fifty feet long with no way over or around it. I was slap dab in the middle, and there was an awful feeling in my gut, that as soon as I tried to run for cover, I'd be carrying more lead in my body than I could ever get into the magazine of my rifle.

A flurry of shots from farther down the street made me hope that the sharpshooters would take their minds offen me for a while. It didn't work! I'd only just started to raise my body, for a quick run to the corner of the wall, when a bullet cut across my back, close enough to burn the skin. There were three men over yonder who wanted my hide! Well they'd have to think again.

Sliding along beside the log, I noticed that it curved upwards in the center, so that it was hardly touching the ground. My Bowie knife slid into the sandy soil real easy, and in no time at all I'd cleared a good sized hollow under the log; big enough to get my hand through to the other side anyway.

I kept scraping away with that old Bowie until I could ease my body under the log. With the heat of the smoldering timber drying out the sandy soil, it didn't take too much doing. They were still watching, because every once in a while, a bullet would thump into the timber to let me know of their interest.

Easing my way into the tight little slot made me realize why the earth had been so easy to shift. It was like an oven in there as I waited for one of them to make a mistake. There was no room to move in the tiny space, and if one of the snipers aimed too low, the bullet would cut into my hiding place, nailing me for sure. Five minutes dragged by and sweat was pouring off me. Iffen I had to stay here much longer I'd end up as one big blob of fat, melting into the earth.

Through the tiny slit I saw sunlight glint on metal. A few seconds later, a puff of smoke, followed by the smack of a bullet hitting the log, told me that one of the snipers was stretched out on a crumbling stone wall, and he was careless enough to be wearing a wide brimmed hat with the front turned up. I'd take him last. That hat-brim would make a first rate target. I grinned at my own confidence. Three good shots out there. All under cover, and I was deciding which one I'd take last!

Then another problem showed itself. The wind had picked up some and it was fanning the log into flame. So maybe I shouldn't be so Goddamned choosy and just shoot the fella with the big hat.

About then some slight movement caught the corner of my eye. Someone had shifted his position; maybe he had leg cramp or something. Anyway, I honed in on a window in the building opposite. My eye had picked up the man's reflection in a broken windowpane swinging in the breeze. The third man didn't show himself at all, so, inch by inch, my rifle moved around, to center on the one in the building, by the windowpane.

The way my rifle was almost buried in the soil would have made it hard to see, even close-up, but I wasn't about to make any sudden moves. As soon as my gun fired, they'd know just where to shoot, so it had to be fast, and good. At the same time I was hoping to God I'd get a bead on the third one before he nailed me!

Smoke from the log began to feed into the hollow, and now the odd ember was beginning to pop and crackle, throwing hot sparks into my face. Life sure was a bitch and time was running out. I fired, but didn't wait to see if I'd scored a hit. Jacking a cartridge into the breach I flipped the rifle towards the man on the wall, and damn me if he didn't jerk his head up, to see where my shot had come from.

The pinned up hat-brim fitted into my sight real neat. My rifle dropped half an inch lower, and his face kind'a crumpled up, before he rolled off the wall.

A bullet spanged into the log real close and a second slapped into my leg. I was lucky. The guy was using a Sharps single shot. He was fast, but not fast enough. I'd put a pattern of three into him before he could finish closing the loading gate for his third shot. He staggered out of cover still trying to get off his shot when I planted one right on the nose. The man hit the floor and he wouldn't be getting up again.

When I scrambled out from under the log, my clothes were smoldering and my leg hurt like hell as I limped behind the wall for cover. The bullet had passed through the muscle, and judging from the hole it left in my leg, I reckoned it had to be a 50 caliber, man! Those damned Sharps were some heavy guns and no mistake. Could even tear a man's leg off if it hit the bone.

I was still sitting on my rear end trying to stop the bleeding when a shadow fell across me. My six-gun came up real fast, my thumb slipped the hammer on to full cock and Sergeant McBain's sneering laugh was cut off short by my speed.

'Gettin' scared, Sergeant?' he snarled.

'I ain't ever gonna get as white-scared as y'all, McBain,' I fleered back at him. 'I don't trust you, mister, and iffen you come up on my blind side again I'll blow your stupid head off.'

My gun slipped back into its holster almost as fast as I'd hauled it out.

'That kind of speed won't help you none when the time comes, boy,' he sneered, 'y'all won't even know it's gonna happen.' He laughed again as he swaggered off; I had me a feeling that he had some plans already laid down. I'd really have to watch that bastard and no mistake.

Crow-hopping to the tent where the surgeon was attending the wounded, I squatted on the ground to wait my turn. An orderly was doing the rounds, checking on the walking wounded. He cut the wrapping from around my leg and stared at the bullet hole. 'Is that all?' he grunted.

'Sure hope so.'

'Y'all figure it's worth the bother, Sergeant?'

'It's bothering me.'

He stuck his thumb on the hole and spread it out; I gave a bit of a jerk as the pain bit home.

'Painful, huh?' he muttered, like he couldn't give a good Goddamn whether it hurt or not.

'You ain't helping any,' I grunted as he prized it apart some more.

'Don't seem too bad, sergeant. Flea bit you did it?' He tilted a bottle over the opening, and some milky looking liquid ran into the hole.

Goddamn! That must have been liquid fire. The pain lifted my ass a clear foot above the ground, before I walloped back down with a yell of agony.

'That hurt did it?' he asked without interest as he kneaded the stuff through the hole. 'Just a drop of disinfectant, nothing to make a fuss about.'

I gritted my teeth as he gave the hole a second dose. From where he was standing, maybe, it didn't feel like hell, but I'd sure love to do some pouring on him for a change.

My leg healed up real quick, so maybe I was just putting him down because I didn't like the treatment he'd dished out. Then again, if my leg hadn't healed so fast I wouldn't have been marching towards Fayetteville; but, like Mister Jesse used to say, 'trying to dodge fate was just one big waste of time.

The Johnny Rebs were on the run now. Sure, they'd stop every once in a while and fight like demons, but they were poorly armed and mostly half starved. The Union had captured most of the armaments factories, so our ordnance was getting better and better; the food had also improved. Each town we captured was looted of everything eatable, and drinkable, so there was very little left behind for the townspeople, or the defeated prisoners of war.

Fayetteville was gonna be the first battle in North Carolina. This was real close to my home stamping grounds, and there was a great hope in me that once we'd taken Fayetteville, our troops would be ordered to move sharp left, towards Greensboro. I'd be just a spit an' a holler away from the old farm then.

Inside me was a deep longing to see my daddy once more, to let him see the man I'd become and to feel his arms wrapped around me, like when I was just a button. I was a man full-grown, sure, but there were things in my heart that I needed to cry over, and a man can only do that with his daddy, or maybe his mom. Perhaps I'd get lucky!

We attacked Fayetteville that night, laying down a heavy field of gunfire, before the troops charged forward through the early morning mist, bullets once again seeking our bodies as we dived into holes and hollows, slowly forcing the Johnny Rebs to give ground. There was a lull in the fighting as the mist deepened, blanking out any noise. It closed in around me more and more, so that I was alone, locked in my own tiny silent world, so close to enemy and friend, yet isolated. My eyes aching from staring into the mist, just waiting for something to happen.

An officer was suddenly standing in front of me, a leveled pistol in his hand. I snapped a shot at him, but missed. My mind blanked out. The pistol was pointed at my head and there was no time for me to jack another cartridge into the chamber! This was as far as I was going and my body tensed, waiting for the bullet to smash the life from me. Yet still, the man didn't fire. We must have been facing each other for just a few seconds, yet it seemed like hours. Him with his gun pointing at my face, me unable to jack a cartridge into my rifle, but with the bayonet pointing at his stomach. Then he just charged at me!

I swear to God, he just ran straight on to

my bayonet, with a force that almost knocked me over. His mouth was open in a silent scream, as the weight of his body wrenched the rifle out of my hands. I just stared at him in wonderment. I slowly dropped to my knees. He could have killed me, yet he chose to die himself. It was beyond my understanding.

He grabbed my arm and pulled me close. His lips were moving, so I leaned down close to him. There was a wad of paper in one hand, which he pushed into mine.

'Take them to my Abigail. Please!' Even in the mist, I could see the pleading in his eyes. Then he said the damnedest thing I ever heard in my whole life. 'Thank you for killing me, my friend,' he mumbled, so quiet that I could hardly hear, 'there were no bullets in my gun, b-but I had to — die.' He went quiet and I thought he'd gone, but then he opened his eyes real wide. 'P-Please! Take my letter to m-my dear wife — Promise me you will!'

I stared hard at the guy, thinking he must be war crazy. I looked at the bundle of paper in my hand and then at him, trying to understand. He nodded and squeezed my hand. 'Read it! You'll understand then. Please do this for me.'

God, the fella's eyes were just begging me to understand, so I nodded; don't know why,

I just did. Then he smiled. 'Thank you my friend,' he muttered, and died! I stayed like that for quite a while, just kneeling beside him, holding the letters in my hand, hardly believing that I was still alive, when there was no good reason why I should be.

After a while I stood up and pulled my bayonet from his body; that was some chore, because he'd dived on it so hard that the muzzle of the rifle had followed the bayonet. Then I stumbled off, still carrying the bundle of papers in my hand.

It was much later that same night, when Fayetteville had been taken, that I lay in my small tent and decided to read the letters; to find out what was so important about them, that a man had rammed himself on my bayonet, when he could just as easily have killed me.

It started simply enough, with the address.

To Mistress Abigail York
York Farm
Conecuh River
Alabama May 20th 1864

My Dearest Abbey
How can I explain to you the horrors of this dreadful conflict, which I now see as beyond all reason?
My heart is heavy with grief as I see

young men — some even younger than our dear son, Nathaniel — dying, with their poor bodies torn asunder by the blasts of the big guns.

I swear to you my love, that if I had but realized the total uselessness of this war I would never have left the peaceful tranquility of our small farm.

Each time I close my eyes to sleep, I see again our fields, their crops ripening in the summer sunshine. I see our son, a fine sapling, strong and true spreading into maturity as he worked beside us, gathering the crops from God's good earth —

I must go now dearest one. The bugler calls us to arms, I will continue when I am able.

August 10 1864

The battle is over once more dear heart and I am unscathed, for which I give thanks to the good Lord's mercy.

Our son is rarely out of my thoughts these days, and it pains me greatly that we should be on opposite sides in this war. But although we are both hot blooded, my dear, I am sure the harsh words we exchanged before he left to join the Union Army will not stay between us, once we are re-united, and this filthy war is behind us.

In all conscience my dearest one, I have to say that I was caught up in the furor of North and South. My thoughts now, are that Nathan was right. Slavery should be abolished, and why I am still fighting in this conflict is beyond my understanding.

We, who have never impressed another human being to do our bidding in the whole of our life together, yet our family is split asunder because of it.

I still see the tears in your eyes, as they were the day our only child stormed out to go to war — Again I have to stop, my love, but please God I shall live to continue my letter.

December 20 1864

The war is not going well for the Confederacy my dearest, and no one has time to take mail to loved ones, but I shall continue with my letter until such time as it is possible to send it to you with some scant hope of it ever arriving.

I have sustained minor wounds since I last wrote, but they were no cause for alarm and I am now fit to continue the conflict, and so once more I have to enter the battle or be branded a deserter.

March / April? 1865 Fayetteville

I no longer know for sure whether it is March or April as the fight goes even more against us.

I am spent, my love, I am lost beyond redemption and can hardly bring myself to write about the most awful of happenings — But I must — for only in the telling can I cleanse my guilty soul.

It has been two weeks now since the last battle but it could have been yesterday for all my mind cares. Oh Abbey, Abbey, dearest one, please try to understand.

The battle had been continuous for over three days and our losses were many. The men were drawn and battle weary, with eyes smarting from the smoke and soot, legs barely able to hold us as we stood our ground.

Our comrades lay around us, so many that we were unable to stand without placing our feet upon their bodies.

A young officer, well mounted, charged towards me. The smoke and filth swirling about him as if he were the devil of darkness. I was unable to bring my pistol to aim and his saber was about to sever my head from my body. Yet, he paused in the slash that would have taken my life. Paused for that vital second, and though I could not understand the reason, I used his hesitation to bring my pistol into line and fire.

My bullet struck him in the chest, sweeping him from his mount as the awful realization came to me, and I charged forward to cup our son's body to my breast. Oh dear heart what can I say to you that might ease the pain of the awful truth?

He smiled at me, that lop-sided grin he always had. Remember? Then he said, 'Hell Pa, it was you or me, an' Ma needs you more than I.' Then he died. Died my love. In my arms, and by my bullet. I cannot live with it much longer, it haunts my every waking hour and though I am deliberately careless on the battlefield, no one can seem to take my pain away with a well-placed bullet.

I cannot support my grief any longer, so, on this day, my darling Abigail, this day I shall die. Fayetteville is presently under attack and it is time to meet my maker.

Please do not think too badly of me my darling one. My pain and remorse is too great to bear so I cannot go on.

I can only hope that the person who ends my life will honor my last request and will, some day, deliver this letter to you.

Do not think badly of him either, whoever he may be, because he will be ending my unbearable suffering and I shall *not defend myself against him.*

I could never stand before you and ask for your forgiveness, and even if you could find it in your kind heart to do so, I could never forgive myself, or forget the great wrong I have done to our son and to you. The two people I love more than life itself.

Goodbye. God bless you and keep you from all harm my lovely Abigail.

Yours Always

Your loving husband. Amos.

(Lieutenant Amos B York)

I stared long and hard at that letter. Even wished I'd never learned to read. Maybe this education thing weren't so all fired good as people made out, words could tear a man apart, but if you couldn't read 'em, you'd never know the gut-wrenching pain. A deep sigh shook me as I folded the stained pages and tucked them inside my tunic. One thing I was sure of. The letter would get delivered; I owed it to the fella. If he hadn't decided to dive onto the end of my bayonet, he could have blown my stupid head off.

Yeah, I'd deliver the letter for all the good it would do, but for now there was a war to fight I blew out the lantern, rolled onto my back and fell asleep listening to the sound of the wind.

19

As it turned out, we didn't head for Greensboro like I'd hoped, but cut towards Richmond. We were beginning to think the war was over as we drove units of the Confederacy ahead of us — until some of our troops reached Bentonville.

The Johnny Rebs hit our left flank like madmen on the 19th of March. Hell! We didn't even know there were that many Confederate troops left this far South, and by the time we got to the left flank the following day, our troops were on the run, but we had numbers on our side and better artillery to boot.

We had marched nigh on 450 miles since leaving Savannah, but there was no stopping us as we fought our way into Bentonville, and to make matters worse for the Johnny Rebs, we were joined by another body of men from the Wilmington expedition. By nightfall we'd taken the town and set our pickets.

The weather was still bad, so we were rested for three weeks while we cleaned our big guns and made running repairs to our kit, which was beginning to fall to pieces. We even managed to get some hot food inside us once in a while, as we waited for the mud to dry up enough to be able to support the big guns. Then we started for Petersburg and Richmond, to join up with General Grant's men.

We were near to four days out from Petersburg when we saw flashes of the heavy artillery and the great pall of smoke hanging over the town. If we'd had the idea the war was about over I figured it was time to change our minds, because there was some real heavy activity ahead.

Seemed like there was a bit of trouble afoot and our officers wanted us to move it along. We made the four-day march in three, and closed on the Johnny Rebs' trenches on April 1st. I hadn't done much thinking about my own worries until I heard Sergeant McBain's laugh close beside me.

'I'm back, black boy, right here beside y'all for the big push.' He laughed again. 'Bet you thought I was long gone an' you didn't have to worry about me, huh?'

I glanced around, shocked out of my thoughts.

'Lookin' fer your good friend Sergeant Price, black boy?' He chuckled again. 'He died! Funny thing though, he must have bin runnin' away. He got his in the back, just like young Daniel did. Remember?'

He seemed to think that was real funny because he let loose with a big belly laugh. 'Watch your back black boy. This next fight's gonna be a real big 'un, anythin' can happen.' He sniggered. 'Hear tell that you've managed to get yourself hooked up to a real purty dusky maiden, fella, should keep an eye on her was I you. It ain't only little boys I like y'know. Black velvet comes real high on my list.'

He could see that he'd gotten to me, by the way my hand dropped to my pistol.

'Go on, draw it!' he snarled. 'I'd just love to have that officer over there see you do it.'

Caught off guard, I glanced sideways and the butt of his rifle smashed into my guts. Half an inch lower an' I'd have been rolling on the ground, screaming in agony. Even as I was falling my hand reached for my .44 but his rifle smashed down, and a shout of pain was forced from me as my wrist cracked. The stunning pain held me in my crouched position holding my damaged wrist, and I could put up no defense as he tucked the butt of his rifle under my chin and forced my head up.

'Listen black boy,' he hissed. 'Petersburg would be a nice place to leave you, with your black face in the mud. With a broken wrist you ain't likely to cause me any problems, so

I'll say goodbye for now, I might not get the chance once the battle starts.' He slapped the butt of his rifle into my chest and I fell on my back in the mud, still gripped by the pain in my guts and wrist. 'That's it, black boy. Stay in the mud where y'all belong,' he sneered, as he sauntered away. 'See you dead . . . real soon I hope.'

His loud harsh laugh echoed in my brain long after he'd left me lying in the black oily mud, with the things he'd said searing my mind. I was frightened — not for myself, but for that lovely girl back there in Savannah. We hadn't been together long, but her hooks were into me real firm. Man! I was just living for the day I could get back there, and I was sore afraid that something real bad could happen to her while I was away. Nothing could be worse than McBain getting to her, but he'd have to kill me first.

It took me a long time to get on my hind legs and find the surgeon, who strapped up my wrist so's I could go into battle. I told him I'd slipped in the mud and fallen on it.

'Not just trying to dodge the next battle are you, Sergeant?' he asked slyly.

'No sir, one battle is pretty much like the next,' I told him, 'it only takes one bullet in the right place.'

'Yeah, that's true, Sergeant.' The voice still

held a sarcastic note. 'But the next battle could be the one for you, if you see what I mean.'

'Or you — sir!' I replied, keeping my voice as civil as I could.

He chuckled. 'That's right, Sergeant. Kind'a makes a man think when it's put like that, huh?'

'It only takes one for any of us, sir, an' I'll be facing the Johnny Rebs if I get mine. How about you, sir?'

The surgeon's smile thinned out, as a frown puckered his forehead. 'You being insubordinate, Sergeant?'

I let my face show surprise. 'Well gosh, no sir! Just havin' a friendly conversation while you strap me up is all, Captain. Thank you most kindly,' I ended as he finished the work on my wrist and stepped away from me.

'Humph,' he muttered, as I saluted him. 'If your shooting arm is as sharp as your tongue, Sergeant, you'll come out the other side well enough. Carry on.'

There was a touch of a smile around my mouth as I left the Infirmary. I reckoned the captain took my meaning well enough. That was Jesse Turnball's way of making a point. Sure left a guy feeling kind'a superior somehow; maybe this education thing weren't so bad after all.

We heard on the grapevine that Sheridan had been in one hell of a battle along the White Oak Road and that Pickett's division, which had taken the full brunt of the attack, had been completely wiped out. April the second dawned, wet and dismal, as the Army of the Potomac began to push their way towards the Confederate trenches, and finally captured Petersburg. On April the third our own black troops headed the march into Richmond.

Union soldiers were all over the place, but we still couldn't stop the Johnny Rebs from setting fire to the factories and military stores, before retreating across the bridge towards Appomattox Station. Suddenly the fires began to spread in the freshening wind. Men were screaming and dying as bullets flew, and flames wiped out what was left of Richmond. By the following morning, there was hardly a whole building standing: just chimney walls, smoke-grimed and crumbling, their blackened stacks pointing, like accusing fingers, towards the sky. It sure was a sickening sight to see. I'd been on a few trips to Richmond with the Franklyns, when I'd been their driver. It had been a proud place then and no mistake.

Was that only four years ago? Man, how

things can change. I find it hard to realize that it was only just over two and a half years ago, when I was a runaway slave and could hardly speak decent American, much less read it. Now I was a sergeant in the Union Army, and my way of speaking was as good as that of any working class white man. The war seemed to be about over now, but would it make any difference? Would black people be equal to the whites? My mind remembered Lily's words, back there in Atlanta. I hoped she was wrong, but somewhere in the background of my mind was this nagging doubt, as I stared around at the ruins. Yesterday had been Palm Sunday, but no one had even remembered it. My daddy had been strong on the good book, so I remembered; but who else? I wondered.

Thinking of Lily gave my sagging spirits a bit of a lift. The war was almost over. It had to be! There was nothing left to fight for. I'd soon be galloping back over the trail to Atlanta. My injured wrist was throbbing and it drew my mind to McBain's threat. I'd have to do something about him, before it was too late.

Every time I thought about that man, it seemed he'd be there, and it was no different this time. A hand slapped me on the back and his harsh sneering voice grated in my ear.

266

'Heard the news black boy? Lee's surrendered. Be able to chase off after your little bit of black velvet soon — if I don't beat you to it.'

His big belly laugh choked off as my hand dipped down real fast and my .44 snugged up under his chin. Bad wrist or no, I was still wicked fast on the draw.

'You want I should blow your face off, McBain?' I growled, real anger, and maybe a little fear too, tugging at my voice.

His eyes got big and round, kind'a scared also, which pleased me some.

'Don't git too big for your britches, Sergeant,' he growled back, as the fear began to leave him. 'Like I said, this war is almost over and things'll soon get back to the way they was, an' you'll be just a no-account black boy again.' He slowly pushed my gun aside. 'Y'all don't really think this here war is gonna make any difference to that, do you? Goddamn! How stupid can you get?'

'It's what this war was about,' I replied, almost defensively.

'Is that what y'all believe? Hell no! This war was about takin' all this good land and grand houses from these no-good rich Southerners. I'll still be able to kick your ass when all this is over, you'll see. Black is black an', white is white, no Goddamned war is gonna change

267

that. Once the Northerners have taken over all this good land, everything will go back to the way it was. Now. Git out of my way, black boy, before I lose my temper.'

And, by God, I let him go! With his harsh laugh ringing in my ears and ever growing doubts in my mind. I knew for sure, that whatever happened in the future, I had to get to Llly before McBain did.

Although Lee surrendered at Appomattox Courthouse on the 9th of April, it took until the 26th of May before General Kirby Smith made the final surrender of all Confederate forces West of the Mississippi.

The war was over, but already a new breed of coyote was beginning to invade the South; they were called carpet-baggers. Men in fancy-dan clothes were taking over huge properties, dispossessing the old Southern families. Killing and looting was ripping the Southern states apart, and I could see McBain's words coming true.

I was finally mustered out of the army in June. Still in my uniform, but with no chevrons on my arm. I felt a sense of loss somehow, a sense of isolation. The army no longer wanted or needed me and my color was probably an embarrassment.

I was a civilian again. I had money in my pocket, sure, but it was only my back pay, so right now I felt flush, but still kind'a unwanted, if you see what I mean, and Lily's words began to eat into me. 'I'm free! Thank you Lord,' she'd said. 'So what the hell's the good of that, if I don't have a job to put food on the table? Big deal!' she'd said, and she was right. I headed for the livery stable, carrying my good Henry rifle in one hand and a small pack, holding everything I possessed, in the other, my Army Colt .44 was strapped around my waist like it was part of me, sitting comfortable, and easy to reach.

The town was teeming with ex-soldiers, all in blue, but with the chevrons missing, along with legs or arms. Men and boys damaged forever and for what? If McBain's words were true, it had all been for nothing, making all these wounded men outcasts like me. I found that hard to accept. Surely, I thought, things had to change now. The old ways just had to go.

Three men were approaching me. They had badges on their vests and Stetsons on their heads instead of the kepis I'd been used to seeing, and they looked like trouble. They stopped in front of me, and I could see the darker marks on their tunics where chevrons had been removed. I nodded a 'Howdy' to them and gave 'em a slight smile, although I didn't feel one little bit friendly.

They were blocking my path, so I asked. 'Something I can do for you, gents?'

The smallest of the three sniggered. 'Yeah fella, y'all seems to be carryin' a lot of hardware. Town rule says no guns, so what say y'all just pass 'em over, like a good lil-old black boy, huh?'

I took a quick look around me; there were men all over the place carrying weapons. I nodded towards some of them. 'Seems like nobody's taking much notice, friend, or am I special?' My voice was slow and even, almost calm, but it weren't the way I felt inside, no-sir! The smaller guy seemed to be in charge, because the other two wasn't saying a blamed thing.

'You do see 'em?' I prompted.

The little fella shrugged. 'Oh sure, I see 'em pilgrim, but they're white — if you get my drift.'

I was getting his drift all right, and I could also feel my dander beginning to come to the boil.

'What do they call you, boy?'

'Who wants to know?'

While we'd been talking I'd slowly dropped my pack to the ground and eased my rifle around, so that I was holding it with both hands. The man glanced at his two companions, as if gaining courage from them.

I'd seen that happen many times before, from men going into a battle; it told of a nagging uncertainty.

He sniggered again; it seemed to be a habit with him. 'He wants to know who we are boys, ain't that a laugh?'

'I ain't laughin', I told him, allowing my language to match his. 'Put up or shut up, an' git out'a my damned way, mister.' My voice was still even — like I'd learned to keep it, when I was giving the men under me a lecture on discipline.

The small guy had heard that tone before and his head swiveled slowly towards me. His voice fell to a hissing whisper. 'Don't y'all ever take that tone tuh me, black boy, or I'll — '

That was when the butt of my rifle hit him hard in the mouth and he dropped into the mud without a sound. I stared hard at the other two, my eyes daring them to start something. 'I ain't got any beef with you two gents,' I told them, 'so what say we call it a day?'

The two glanced at each other, and one shrugged. 'Wes always did have too much mouth, high time he had it closed for him.'

The other man nodded his agreement. 'I should get out of town though, if I was you, Sergeant Joshua. He's bin made the town constable and he likes to throw his weight about; fact is, he's a right pain in the butt. We don't like working with him, but a job's a job an' we're out of the army just like you.'

I touched my kepi and picked up my pack. 'Appreciate the advice, mister. Come morning I'll be long gone. You seem to know me, friend. How come?'

'Yep, same outfit, white section. You were a good sergeant, Joshua Dee. Hope y'all don't meet too many like him,' he nodded towards the man on the ground, 'nothin's gonna change his attitude.'

'My sentiments exactly,' I grunted, 'see you around.'

'You won't be stayin' around though, will you Josh?'

I grinned, the first time I'd really felt like grinning since I'd been mustered out. 'No, guess not, fella, I'll sleep in the livery. Horses don't have a color problem. So-long.'

I was lucky; the be-whiskered old-timer in the livery stables had watched life go by for a long time, so we were able to come to an agreement about a big roman-nosed skewbald that looked as if it could run forever. There was a lot to choose from, so I managed to beat the old guy down to something I could afford. I even managed to talk him out of an old saddle, a blanket and the rest of the tack.

'Six months ago I could have got twice the money fer that nag,' the old man grumbled, as he took my coin.

'Yeah, that's maybe true, old-timer,' I grinned, but that was six months ago, and my guess says the money would have been in Confederate scrip; an' you know full well it ain't worth the paper it's printed on now, whereas my coin is good silver cartwheels.'

'Yeah, yeah,' he interrupted, 'y'all is too damned edificated fer the likes of me, fella, so let's say we've got ourselves a decent deal an let it go at that, huh?'

He spat on his hand and stuck it under my nose, so we clinched the deal with a handshake.

'Any chance of me bedding down here for the night, to keep the hoss company, fella?'

'Hosses don't usually git lonesome, mister,' he replied, as a crafty gleam crept into the washed-out blue eyes. 'Was you figgerin' 'on payin' fer the use of my straw? You could get a good mug of coffee thrown in fer supper. Might even throw in some ham an' aigs fer breakfast, fer another ten cents.'

Knowing how this man liked to dicker, I grinned back at him. 'Make it two cups of

Arbuckle tonight an' another two in the mornin.'

'Make it fifteen cents,' he came back, quick smart.

'Twelve an' you throw in a few pancakes an' some molasses,' I countered.

'Done!' he replied, as he spit on his hand again and we shook on it.

'Hot damn, but you're the kind of a man I like to do business with, stranger, even if you are a damned Yankee. By grab, you sure know the way to dicker, an' no mistake.'

'Nobody's damned Yankee or Johnny Reb any more, old-timer,' I said seriously. 'I reckon we're all straightforward, honest-to-God Americans now, don't you?'

'Like to think so, pilgrim. Was a time when color made the big difference, but now? Well, there's gonna be a lot of bitterness comin' along, an' the carpet-baggers, thieves and rogues from both sides ain't gonna make things any better are they? Many a mother has lost her kinfolk in this struggle. Me! I'm just gonna spend the rest of my time dickerin' fer hosses and saddles, it's a lot simpler.' The Hostler patted my shoulder as he turned away, shaking his head in sorrow at his thoughts.

The old man made a lot of sense. The bitterness and loss would take a long time to go away, and in my heart, I knew that what McBain had said was true. Nothing had really changed.

As I lay in the straw that night, with the sharp tangy smell of the livery around me, I made up my mind to shake the dust of this town from my feet. As soon as I had found my father and Lily, we'd all head West, and lose ourselves in Indian country, far away from the frictions of North and South, aye and black and white, too. It was the only way we could be sure to live our lives in peace. With that thought in my mind sleep soon snuck up on me.

20

The old-timer roused me with the smell of hot fresh coffee, mixing together with the crackle and spit of ham in a hot skillet. Man, did that smell good! And he weren't no skinflint; I'll give him that. Plenty of ham and four eggs, with a plate of sourdough to mop up the grease, followed by a pile of pancakes and a plentiful supply of molasses and four mugs of good strong coffee to swill it down. At twelve cents it was a steal, but I dassent give him a cent more. We'd made a deal and we'd both be respecting that.

The sky was just beginning to lighten up a little as I said goodbye to the old man and led the roman-nosed skewbald out into the cold of the morning. I swung into the saddle and the hoss showed his dislike of a cold blanket by crow-hopping around. I could tell he was a bit put out because he even tried to dump me a couple of times, but I wasn't having any of that and the hoss soon realized who was the segundo on this trip. I raised a hand in silent farewell to the old man and nipped the skewbald with a pair of spurs; which was something else I'd also managed to coax into the deal. All things considered, I figgered that I'd come out of the bargain pretty good — for a non-com that is. We were soon leaving the dust and smoke of Petersburg behind us and heading towards Danville. Then Greensboro; almost back to where I was born. And although Lily was on my mind and I was using the shortest route possible to get to Atlanta, I couldn't pass my old home without checking in at the Franklyn Estate, to see if my daddy was still there. He'd always figured strong in my plans; maybe he'd come with me and maybe not, but I had to know one way or the other . . .

My route was taking me through some of the country's strongest Confederacy areas, and I had to remember that there was a notice of rape out on me. Whether it would still hold, or even be remembered, was doubtful; but I played it safe, and skirted around any town in my path, until the food ran out.

Greensboro was an up and coming town when I last saw it as a driver for the Franklins, and I had my doubts about going in; but food was needed, so I eased into town just before sun-up, figuring that the place would be quiet so early in the morning. So how wrong can a body get? The town was teeming, like an anthill that had just been kicked by a hoss. Men were hoppity-go-pegging all over the place. I've never seen so many one-legged men in my life, aye and one-armed men also. Seemed like every other fella was wearing a bandage of some sort. Then there were others even worse off. Sprawled in bath chairs, with no legs at all.

The ones that were whole glared at me as I rode slowly down Main Street, and the only black men I saw were swamping out, ready for the day's business. They were still dressed in the raggedy clothes I remembered. The town was bigger, but apart from that, the order of the day was still the same; the black men did the dirty chores, while the whites stood around and bossed them.

I tied up at the mercantile hitch-rail and stepped up onto the sidewalk. A white man in an old confederate officer's uniform with two Colt .44s strapped around his waist watched me as I approached. I stepped to one side, to go around him, but he stepped sideways also and we stopped, facing each other.

Mister Jesse's voice seemed to come out of nowhere. 'Don't ever look down, Josh,' it said, and I didn't, my eyes fixed on his, and nothing happened for a few heartbeats. The man turned his head to one side as he studied me, then came the sound of a voice I knew so well.

'By all that's holy,' he said, kind'a like he couldn't believe his own eyes. 'It's Joshua isn't it?'

'Mister Luke?' I couldn't believe it either!

'Well, damn me, fella, I never thought to see y'all agin,' he almost shouted, as he stepped forward and flung his arms around me, like he'd found a long lost brother.

Although I was locked in his embrace, it still didn't seem right somehow. After all, I'd run from the estate with the cry of rape in my ears, surely his mother would have told him about that? Then the answer came from Luke himself.

'Man! I just rode in from Fayetteville this very morning. They let me out of prison just yesterday.' He held me away from himself. 'Have you heard anything of Pa, or Matthew, Josh?'

'Yeah, sure I have, Luke. Let me get my grub bought and paid for. We can talk as we go. OK?'

A frown of annoyance flickered across his face. He didn't like me dropping the mister, but that was too bad. He didn't like me not answering his question right smart, either. Luke had changed some, and not for the better.

He still stood in my way. 'I want to know now, Josh. Now! Not when you've finished what you want to do! Are you understandin' me, fella?'

A glance around told me I'd best be careful here. Quite a few of the men had paused on the boardwalk, listening to our conversation, and from what I'd seen of the town, the quicker I was out of it, the better.

'Sure, sure, Luke,' I muttered, 'but y'all don't want the whole world to be listening in, do you? Let's just stroll into the store. What I have to say ain't for stranger's ears. Your daddy always used to say 'Private business is private, keep it in the family',' and as he began to hesitate, I stepped around him and started for the store, knowing he would follow.

I bought my goods quickly; I could feel the resentment in the storekeeper's attitude and knew that if Luke had not been there, the crusty-faced old man would have refused to serve me. I could also see that Luke was getting impatient.

Telling him about how his daddy had died was tough for me, but it hit Luke like a bullet in the guts, I had to help him to his horse and boost him into the saddle.

'Remember, Luke. Your brother was alive last time I saw him, so he should be coming home right behind you.'

'You comin' back home, Josh?' He sounded

like a small boy, drifting alone in the wilderness of life, and there was a sorrow in me for the times we'd had together, and lost.

'Just to see my daddy is all, Luke, then I'll be long gone, fella. Times they is a-changin'.'

He nodded, glumly, and rode slowly off without saying another word.

Watching him ride away, it seemed somehow odd that I had to lower my standard of speech to get to his level. I'd lost all the 'Yassah and isacomin' bass', but I noticed that the black men in Greensboro hadn't. This would be a good place to leave behind; the Southern attitudes were as strong as ever here, so I strapped my provisions to my saddle and swung aboard. Even so, I saw a couple of men dressed in dirty gray uniforms, glaring at me and fingering their pistols. Maybe I just looked too big to tackle. Probably too tough also, with a three day beard on my face and my pistol slung real low on my hip, the way Mister Jesse had worn his.

Aggie didn't seem to care too much for the town either, because we left Greensboro behind at a fine old pace.

Aggie is the name I gave the skewbald. Now I know he's a big roman-nosed stallion, but my aunt Aggie was big, with a roman nose to boot. OK, she wasn't a man . . . maybe! But nobody would have guessed it, and both the hoss and Aggie was real humpy in the mornings, even threw me once — the hoss I mean — so I named him Aggie out of spite. It sure took him down a peg or two because he ain't tried to buck me off since.

I took a wide sweep around Winston and Salem, heading towards the hills, as dusk settled in. Food was on my mind, so I close-hobbled Aggie and started a small fire and soon the appetizing smells of the meat I'd purchased in Greensboro, began to waft around me and the feeling of 'coming home' made me relax.

Just a short way ahead was the North Field; the place where I'd driven the buckboard into the man who'd been chasing me, before I'd started running, all that long time ago. From there, it was only a matter of cutting back over the long flat road to my daddy's shack. I could have made it tonight but figured it was safer to wait until morning. There was no knowing how many changes had taken place while I'd been away, and maybe; just maybe; people were still looking for me.

I finished the last of my meal and lay back under the big bright stars I remembered so well. The coffee tasted good and strong, the cigar helped to cool my nerves, as the night closed tighter around me. I was coming home, but to what? My hoss sounded at peace as he made a meal of the long grass and the soft sound of his chomping and blowing set me to dozing. So I finished my coffee and threw the stub of my cigar into the dying embers of the fire, before tucking my Henry rifle under my arm and leg . . . just in case I was bothered in the night. The saddle was my pillow and the stars my candle, as I settled to sleep.

Being a very light sleeper I figured nothing much could surprise me . . . So I was wrong again!

Next thing I knew was the cold muzzle of a pistol being pressed against my cheek. I started to move, but the gun pressed harder.

'Y'all wanna die quick, mister? Or do we talk some, first.'

I lay still; that deep, 'down home' Southern voice didn't sound friendly. 'You move around real quiet, mister,' I countered.

He cackled, so I set him as an older man, hillbilly type.

'Almost didn't make it though, I've snuck up on some men in my time, fella, but y'all almost caught me out . . . I said almost.' His voice had hardened as I started to move, so I settled back again.

'No need to be so unfriendly, fella, you

want some grub? It's okay by me.'

'You just roll over on your stomach, stranger, an' git your hands behind your back. Don't worry about the rifle, I'll take good care of it fer now.' As I hesitated the gun pressed harder. 'Do it!'

My mind registered that there was only one man, but if he was allowed to tie my hands behind me I'd be at his mercy, so I started to roll, slowly over on to my belly. The barrel of the gun had to leave my neck for a moment while I turned. That was when I lifted my legs straight up into the air and threw my body over his. My weight pinned him to the ground for a moment so I flung one arm around his scrawny neck and began to squeeze, while my other hand searched desperately for his gun hand.

He let out a squeal of fright and pain. Like I said, he was old, thin and scrawny, but by God he twisted and squirmed like an eel. He hadn't fired his pistol and I could feel his hand slipping and ducking away from mine as I grabbed, and grabbed again.

Then he made a mistake. He hit me over the head with his gun. I hardly felt it! A real gun would have split my head open, now I knew why he hadn't fired. It wasn't a gun at all! It was just a Goddamned lightweight piece of metal.

My dander began to boil; the son-of-a-bitch had almost fooled me, with a useless piece of hollow bar. The shadow of his face was in front of me as he squealed again in his fear. My forehead hit his nose with a meaty thump and he sagged in my arms without a sound.

He seemed to be unconscious, but I let him loose very carefully. This was one sneaky sidewinder. He was just as likely to be faking it. Still being careful, I eased my rifle away from him and started to stand up, when another voice behind me quavered. 'Don't y'all be doin' anythin' stupid, son. I'm about ready to plant a musket ball in your wishbone.'

I'd had more than enough of old-timers trying to pull a rusty on me for one night, so, from my semi-crouched position, I swung around, holding my arm and my rifle out straight in front of me. The butt of the rifle slapped into the man, fetching him an awful crack in the ribs, and he flopped to the ground with a groan of agony and passed out.

I was mad clear through. Kicking some spare wood into the still flickering fire, I soon had a good blaze going, and grabbing the two men by the scruff of their scrawny necks, I dragged them up to the blaze. Neither one would have weighed 100lbs soaking wet, but they'd sure upset my good night's sleep, and could have walked off with all my gear to boot. I had a bit of a shock when I discovered that the second one really did have a loaded musket, all primed and ready to fire. He must have thought he had me dead to rights, which just goes to show, once again, how wrong a body can be. I didn't expect him to have a gun and he didn't expect me to be crazy enough to argue with a loaded musket pointed at my back.

I must have hit 'em real hard, because dawn was lightening the sky before they started to moan and groan. The skillet was on, and the coffee was sending its aroma into the morning mist by the time they were able to sit up and take notice.

'You got any of that Arbuckle to spare, mister?' wheezed the one I'd hit with my head.

'Are you joshing me, fella? You threaten to blow my brains out, then you expect to drink my coffee!'

'Couldn't blow your brains out with a bit of hollow pipe now, could I? I was just funnin' is all.'

'Yeah? Well I ain't laughing.'

'Hell of a way to treat an old fella. Bust his nose an' not even offer him a cup of Java.' He pushed at his nose, 'Old sniffer ain't never gonna be the same again I reckon. Hurts, too.'

'You think that's bad, Mort?' growled his friend. 'Reckon I've picked up a couple of busted ribs. Told yuh we ought to have hailed the camp, an' come in peaceful like . . . That ham sure smells good!'

I was beginning to think these two galoots were going to blame me for their misfortunes. 'Like your friend said, you could have hailed the camp, you old goat,' I growled.

'Told yuh, Mort,' grunted the one with the busted ribs.

'Hell, he wouldn't have given us old coots any of his coffee, Sam,' protested Mort. 'He'd have shot our asses off with that rifle of his.'

'I've never refused a man a mug of coffee in my life, you damned old reprobate,' I growled

'Told yuh,' grunted Sam.

'You're always tellin' me somethin'. He's a bloody know-all, mister,' replied Mort indignantly.

'I told you the North would win this here war, didn't I?' replied Sam.

'Yeah, like last week you did. We all knew it by then. Any chance of that coffee, mister? Some ham an' beans wouldn't come amiss neither,' coaxed Mort.

I could hardly believe the gall of these two

old coots, but I slapped some extra ham and beans in the skillet anyway. They weren't getting any eggs; I'd paid real heavy coin for the few I had.

Suddenly I thought of Jesse Turnball and how well he'd treated me when I was starving. A vagrant thought flitted through my mind about how he'd pulled those eggs from my ear. Mort was sitting nearest to me, and my hands were close to my pack. I had a half-grin on my face as I reached towards Mort's ear.

'Fancy an egg, old-timer?' I asked as the egg appeared in my hand.

'Damn me, Sam. Did y'all see that?' Mort asked. 'You're the second fella who's pulled that stroke on me, mister.'

'Yeah?' The comment aroused my interest.

'Yeah. Fella with a goatee beard, name of — '

'Turnball?' I interrupted.

'Yeah, that's the fella right enough, real slick he was. Had some of his cure-all also. Real fine sippin' whiskey that was.'

'Where did you meet up with him, Mort?' I was excited by the news; it was a long time since I'd thought of how Jesse was making out.

'Why down Atlanta way, just before he was captured. Heard tell he was a Union spy. Don't reckon he was though, seemed a real nice fella to me. Anyway, they carted him off to the prisoners' compound. That's when me an' Sam got to drink most of this elixir stuff he kept in the wagon. Man! Was that a mistake, damn near blew the tops of our heads off. Ain't that so, Sam?'

'Told yuh it would at the time,' grunted Sam complacently.

My mind struggled with the thought of Jesse being captured by the Confederates, as I passed the skillet over to Mort and allowed them to help themselves to my grub. I hoped that by this time he'd be released, but I'd heard of some nasty things happening to prisoners on both sides, especially spies.

My mind was made up as I watched the two old-timers shoveling food into their mouths. I'd see my daddy if I could, then hightail it to Atlanta. The things I had to do was piling up on me, and always in the background of my mind; was McBain, but if Jesse was in trouble, well, I owed him a deal more than I could ever repay.

There was no more time to spare, so I collected my gear and saddled up. Mort and Sam waved a careless hand each as I swung into the saddle; they looked too full to move, and my stores had taken a real beating, but the news about Jesse had been worth it.

21

Aggie seemed to sense the excitement in me as I set out towards the North Field; he quickly settled into a mile-eating lope that he could keep up all day if he felt like it. The North Field looked neglected, not the way it used to be, and a foreboding began to settle in my gut. My daddy would never have allowed the workers to let the fields get in this condition. Then I remembered. The workers had been slaves. There were no slaves any more; they were all free men. So, who was going to work the huge plantations in the future? I had quite a time getting all the changes planted in my mind. I was all mixed up with what used to be, and the way it was going to be from now on.

My concentration was being dimmed by my thoughts. Aggie was loping along the road towards my daddy's place and I hadn't even realized it. The shack gradually grew out of the ground mist. Not neat and tidy like it used to be, the place was practically falling down; the chimney was leaning at a crazy angle, and the door was hanging off its hinges. There'd been a fire here at some time, because the walls were dirty and smoke-blackened. A fear was mixed with the excitement in my gut as I slid from the saddle and eased open the sagging door. 'Pa?' I called anxiously. 'Pa, are you to home?'

There was a scuffing sound, and a kind of grunt, that set me reaching for my .44. 'Who's there?!' My voice was set sharp and demanding. But my heart jumped into my throat near choking me, as I heard that well remembered voice. Older and kind'a wavering, but it was still the voice of my daddy.

'Glory be! Is that y'all, Joshua, son?'

I was through that door like shot out of a cannon. The joy in me was ready to burst my heart, but the sight that met my eyes stopped me cold. That fine, big tower of strength I remembered so well had been reduced to a quivering wreck that had to use two sticks, just to get around. The wheals on his face where the whip had lashed him were still deep and easy to see. My poor daddy had been whipped, and whipped again. This huge man felt like a mere boy to me, as I hugged his thin, beaten body in my arms and we cried together.

After a long while, I picked him up and carried him to the rickety old chair he'd been using. Tears were still coursing down my cheeks as I knelt beside him, holding him close. 'They sure beat you bad, daddy,' I muttered, dropping almost automatically into the old 'down home' way of talking through a throat made sore by my grief. 'Oh man! I should never have left you to face them two wildcats.'

'Nothin' you could have done, son. They enjoyed the beatin's even more than they enjoyed messin' around with you. Tell me, son, have y'all brought any vittles' with you? It's bin a long time since I tasted any food.'

This was something I could do; it wasn't much, but it was something. 'Y'all just sit there, daddy, I'll rustle you up the best Goddamned meal you've eaten in a coon's age,' I mumbled.

'That'll be real nice, Joshua,' he replied as he seemed to drift into a doze. 'All this excitement has plumb worn me out. It's real good tuh see y'all again son, it sure is.'

I hurried out to my horse and collected my pack. The fire was no problem, and in no time at all, the smell of cooking had my Pa drooling. He sure perked up when a full plate of vittles was placed in front of him. And by God, he could still pack the grub away; trying to question him was a waste of time while he was eating, and it was some time later, while he was sipping at yet another cup of Java, that I saw concern flit across his face.

'Son y'all have tuh git out of here,' he muttered, trying to struggle to his feet. 'Them she-males find you, they'll hang you for sure.'

'Do they still come here, Pa?'

'Oh yeah, the war ain't stopped their shenanigans, it's open house at the farmstead an' they don't care iffen it's Yankees or Johnny Rebs so long as they're happy.'

'But, why would they come here?'

'Nothin's changed, their whuppin' hands are still as strong as ever.'

My mind hardened over at the thought. 'Are they likely to come here today?'

'As like as not, and they still want to see you hangin' from a tree, don't ever forget that, and there's men who'd be more than willin' to help hang a black fella.'

'I need a carriage, or buckboard, to get you away from this place, Pa.'

My daddy was shaking his head. 'I ain't in no fit state to go any place, son.'

'You sure ain't staying here. I ain't leaving you at their mercy a second time.'

Just then, I heard the clatter of hooves and the swirl of carriage wheels on the gravel outside, and my daddy started shaking, in his concern for me. 'It's them two back agin, son. You'd best be gettin' out of here, quick smart.'

I could hear their high-pitched voices now.

293

They were firing questions at each other about my horse. Then there were men's voices, and I moved toward the door, loosening my Colt in its holster as I stepped into the sunlight and saw two men climbing down from the carriage. Both were dressed in union blue, with flapped holsters strapped to their sides.

In the back were the two females I hated more than anyone else in the world. Still all dressed up in their finery, with bows and tassels everywhere, looking as if they would break at the slightest touch; but I knew them for what they were, hard vicious vixens, ready to tear a man apart, and enjoy doing it.

The men turned at the women's squeal of surprise and their hands dropped to their weapons, but eased off a little when they saw my blue uniform and the color of my skin.

'What are you doin' around here, boy?' asked the bigger of the two, the sneer heavy in his voice. 'Come to try to get work? Or are you just looking around for something to steal?'

'Stealin's my guess,' sneered the other one. 'Most of 'em's thieves, a good whuppin' is what they need.'

I could tell by the cut of their uniforms that they were ex-officers of the Union Army, and again it made me wonder why men like these had fought for the freedom of slaves. Maybe McBain was right and it was just an excuse to take over the huge land tracts of the South. These thoughts didn't stop me from watching their every move. I was like a stalking cougar, poised, ready to pounce at the slightest sign of trouble, but not wanting to unless they pushed me into a corner.

My silence served to anger the heavier of the two. 'The war's over now, boy,' he snapped. 'Time y'all learned your place again.' He reached up and pulled the horsewhip from its slot, swung it high and made it crack, in one swift movement.

'Here comes your lesson, boy!' he growled as he raised the whip a second time.

My hand dipped down and up real slick. The bullet busted his elbow and he fell to the floor with a scream of agony, writhing about nursing his shattered arm. My pistol settled on the other fella, as he made a stab at reaching for his piece.

'You try it an' I'll take your damned head off,' I growled.

He weighed up his chances and decided not to try, but he kept his hand poised above his pistol. Meanwhile the two women set up a hysterical screeching, like they'd never seen blood before.

My pistol twitched towards them. 'Shut the

row,' I snapped, 'and get out of there. Now!'

They snapped their mouths shut real quick when they looked down the barrel of my pistol.

The man with his hand still poised above his Colt thought he saw his chance while I was occupied with the two women. His hand dipped down.

He was wrong! He stood no chance at all. My thumb flipped the hammer and he died with a bullet through the throat.

Blood splattered Emily Franklyn's nice white dress and she started screaming again . . . until she heard the double snick of my Colt hammer coming on to full cock.

'Y'all won't get away with this,' Norah Franklyn panted, 'you'll be hunted down and hanged, you black bastard, I . . . '

'Just call me Joshua D,' I growled.

The two women stared at each other, and I have to confess to a savage enjoyment as I watched the different expressions chasing each other across their faces as they realized what I'd said. Surprise, shock and horror followed one after the other. Both thought they were about to die and they fell to their knees, closing their hands in front of their breasts, silently begging me to spare their miserable lives.

'I've seen what you did to my daddy, you

pair of white bitches.' My voice was harsh with suppressed emotion as I picked up the whip, which lay where the wounded man had dropped it. 'You like whipping defenseless people, don't you? I just wonder how you'd like to feel the cut of a lash across your Lily-white shoulders.' The whip cracked under the flick of my wrist; I'd learned to be an expert with it in the years I'd driven these two women around, I could pick a fly off a bronc's nose without causing the hoss a moment's pain.

There was a deep anger in me, and a perverse pleasure also, in making these two bitches squirm. The lash flicked out and Mistress Emily's hat was whisked from her head, making her squeal in fright.

The anger was building into recklessness. Again, the whip cracked. Norah shrieked in agony as the tip stole a piece of flesh from her shoulder. Recklessness was turning into madness as I stared at Emily's right eye. My arm came back. I could pluck it out, without damaging the skin around it. The whip twirled and I could see the stark fear in the eye I was about to cut out.

The hoarse shout of 'No!' halted my hand even as my wrist flexed to make the strike; and my father had staggered out of the shack, he was leaning against the door-post, almost falling down from the effort.

'They deserve all they get, Pa.' My voice was perverse. I was determined to exact punishment for what they had done to my daddy.

'Do we have to act like dogs because they do, son?' His voice was trembly, but there was determination there also. 'Stand above it, son, remember the good Lord's words.'

'He said an eye for an eye, as I remember,' I replied, but I threw the whip from me, my madness gone. The women knew it too because they began to cry with relief, telling my father that they'd never even think of whipping him, not ever again.

I ignored their promises; things would soon change if they managed to get the upper hand again, but I didn't intend giving them the chance. Picking my father up in my arms, I placed him in the carriage. Then I tied my horse on a loose rein at the back, before going into the shack and collecting my pack. I should have taken more care; the wounded man had struggled to his feet, and was holding his pistol against my father's side by the time I'd returned. His face was pinched with pain, but it held a sneer of triumph too.

'You shuck that damned Colt, boy, or I'll blow a hole in this old fella big enough to drive a pony an' trap through,' he threatened.

It stopped me for a moment; my pack was in my left hand, leaving my right free to get at my pistol, but I'd never make it fast enough to stop him killing my Pa. The man was weak with shock from his bullet wound, and he was hanging on to consciousness by sheer will power.

'Make up your mind, fella.' The sound came out as a gasping croak, but the women didn't realize how close the man was to collapsing, they thought they had the upper hand.

'Kill the old bastard, Rafe,' screamed Norah in an excited frenzy. 'Let us deal with Joshua D in our own time.'

'Yes, yes, go on, put a bullet in the old man,' panted her mother.

I strolled towards them like I had all the time in the world. 'You just do that, Rafe, and one second later you'll be dead also. Do it or drop your weapon. Now, mister! You only get this one chance.'

All this time, I had been slowly walking towards the carriage. The nearer I got the more undecided the man became. My daddy knew what I was about to try and his arm flicked backwards, pushing the gun out of his side for a moment.

The man had been watching my gun hand. It was a mistake! The pack in my left hand smacked into the side of his head, with all the force I could put behind it, sending him reeling away, almost out on his feet. This was like the war. There would be no more messing about.

He had fallen into Mistress Emily. She was trying to prop him up while he attempted to bring his piece into line when my bullet smashed into his head, splattering blood and brains all over the woman, who began to shriek and scream uncontrollably as the body fell against her, dragging her down and pinning her to the ground.

Her daughter began to vomit, as the mother, still screaming, frantically tried to fight her way out from under the dead man, causing more and more blood to pour over her white dress.

'Oh God, help me, Norah,' she screamed. 'I'm bleeding! Oh save me you bitch, I'm dying.'

There was no feeling in me for the two women; and, as I climbed into the carriage beside my father, Norah tried to grab my ankle, She looked a mess with tears and vomit running down a face made fat through over-eating. I snatched my foot away from her and slapped it into her face. She staggered backwards, tripping over the other dead man, and crashing down upon her mother, where she too started to scream, as her hand pressed into the mess that had been a man's face such a short time ago.

The horse was getting restive, so I released the brake and slapped the reins, setting it going at a fast trot, while my father clung, with all his feeble strength, to the seat-rail. Once again I was running. But this time I was a seasoned soldier and no one had better get in my way.

22

We had been travelling for quite a while; I was heading for the city of Charlotte, avoiding any towns or large settlements on the way. The food still in my pack would be enough to keep us going for a few days, but then I'd have to take a chance and hope to find a small settlement, or travelling merchant, where I could buy more.

Charlotte, being a city, would be used to all sorts of people coming and going, including many travelers and displaced soldiers. We would not be so noticeable there; and unless they were very lucky, the two women I'd left in the dirt back at my daddy's shack would take hours to get back to the farmstead to call for help.

Pa was the big worry. After my dash away from the old shack, I stopped, and laid him on the back seat, wrapping him in the travelling blankets that were always kept in the carriage to cover the feet and legs of passengers in the cold weather. It wasn't very comfortable, but it was better than sitting on the buck-seat beside me.

We nooned beside a small stream, drinking

scalding coffee and munching on the remains of the meat I had cooked the day before. My daddy ate well enough, but I could see that the ride had already taken its toll of him. Atlanta was a long way ahead and we'd hardly covered a quarter of the distance, but my daddy already seemed spent, so once the meal was finished I packed him into the rear seat, and surrounded him with the heavy blankets. There was an old tarp tied to the back of the carriage, so I wrapped it around him also before starting off again.

An ominous darkness began to build in the sky as heavy clouds rolled in, blotting out the mid-day sun. Some of the spring and summer storms could really cause havoc to the crops, and the sky looked about ready to drop one of those storms on us. I wasn't worried for myself, but a soaking was the last thing my Pa needed right now, so I left the dirt road and moved off to my right, towards some hills and forested slopes I could see in the distance.

The rain hit long before I was anywhere near the protection of the trees, and soon I was driving through deep, boggy mud, as the rain, driven by a high wind, did everything it could to drag me from my perch. I glanced back to where my daddy was curled up, in the corner of the back seat; I could hardly see him through the driving rain, although the high wind had torn the overhead canopy away. The horse was also having difficulty in dragging the heavy carriage through the clinging mud.

There was a small stand of trees ahead, so I steered the carriage into them. It was no real protection from the elements, but at least it broke the solid blast of the wind. I set the hand brake and climbed down, feeling my cold feet sinking deep into the mud. Easing my daddy out of the seat, I carried him into the scant shelter the trees provided. The blankets were of little use, soaked as they were, so I used the large tarp to wrap my Pa in. It was wet, sure, but it would soon dry off inside; and even the soaking wet blankets, thrown over the tarp, would help to keep what little warmth there was trapped inside it. It was the best I could do, and anything was better than leaving him back there to be flogged to death.

Slipping and sliding, through mud that seemed determined to tear the boots from my feet, I managed to untie my own mount and remove the other horse from the shafts, before leading them into the doubtful shelter of the trees, where they turned their backs on the driving rain and hung their heads. A picture of complete dejection as they waited, with the patience of all animals, for the wind and rain to subside.

Making coffee was out of the question, but there was still a little of the meat left, so we munched away at it. Somewhere out there were two women; if they were getting this they'd probably die from the cold. I must confess that the prospect cheered me up a little. I also knew that if they ever managed to get back to the farm, I'd be a hunted man, with half the county looking for me. I pulled my mind from that problem and managed to get a little sleep in spite of the rain but I was aware that the storm was moving on. Distant lightning flashes and rumbles of thunder told me that the storm was following the Southern run, towards Savannah, before I really slept.

*   *   *

The dawn light showed a clear sky. The storm had gone and soon my skillet was nestling into a cheery fire. I'd already moved my Pa towards the fire, by simply catching hold of the rolled tarp, and dragging it down the slight slope. Easing the tarp aside I could see his face; it looked cold and pinched. Maybe the smell of food cooking, and the sharp tang of coffee in the air would help to raise his spirits.

A slice of ham hit the skillet and started to

sizzle, but my daddy hadn't moved, so I eased the tarp away from his face. That's when I noticed that he wasn't breathing! A quick check told me that Pa was gone. His pain was over, but I was mad clear through.

I cried then hot scalding tears fell onto my pa's face. A man I'd always looked up to was dead because of two wanton females; and I knew that, if I ever saw them again, I would tear them apart with my bare hands. The ham burnt to a cinder without my noticing as the world closed down around me and my daddy. I guess I stayed that way, holding him — as if I could drive my own warmth into his cold body and fetch him back to life — for over an hour. Till the hot sun on my back eventually stirred me, forcing me to move my aching limbs.

There was always a shovel strapped to the back of the carriage. It was kept there in case of flash storms, so that a man could dig his way out of deep mud or snow. I kicked the glowing skillet off the fire as I passed it to get the shovel. I knew that this mud could be like stone in an hour or two, so if I was going to dig a grave for my Pa, now was the time. I threw off my damp coat and shirt, allowing the warm sun to dry my body as I dug a good deep hole, and soon I was leaning on the shovel with sweat pouring from me as I stared into my Pa's last resting-place.

It was well past noon by the time I'd covered him, and said the kind of prayers I knew he would have wanted. Already, my mind was moving on. The death of my Pa was bad, sure, but I'd seen so many dead folks in the past few years; and in my heart I knew that the giant of a man that had been my father would not have wanted to linger, unable to care for himself.

So now, it was time for me to look ahead. If those two women had been lucky, there would be a posse of men hunting me by this time, and they'd be looking for the carriage, so it had to be destroyed. Using the shovel, I smashed it to pieces and scattered the debris among the trees. Saving some of the pieces, I stoked up my almost dead fire and cooked the last of my food.

I'd take the second horse with me for a while, to confuse any followers, but would turn it loose before I arrived at Charlotte. I did not want the charge of horse stealing against me, there was already enough to hang me twice over as it was.

Evening shadows were closing in by the time I had saddled up and was ready to ride. Taking a last look at the pile of earth that hid my father's body, I collected the lead-rein of the second horse and headed for the trail to Charlotte. With a bit of luck I would lose any pursuers there, and ride on my way without looking over my shoulder all the time.

I rode all night, between a steady lope and a trot, changing horses from time to time to give them a rest from my weight, and in the dawn's early light, I made a breakfast of coffee before hitting the saddle once again. By keeping the horses to a fast walk in the heat of the day and picking up speed in the evening we were covering a lot of ground. And as the outskirts of Charlotte came into sight, I turned the carriage horse loose, driving it off into the hills close by, where it promptly settled to grazing.

I was right about Charlotte. Nobody took a second look at me as I rode in. From all the signs it had been a major Naval Ordinance depot for the Confederacy, but there were more blue uniforms than gray about, with a generous mixing of black, white, and Chinese with all colors in between. The storekeepers and the Hostler, where Aggie spent a restful night, took my coin without raising an eyebrow over my uniform or color. Maybe this was the beginning of the changes we had been promised in exchange for all the blood spilt in the war.

It would take time to spread to all the small settlements of mainly white people, but this town at least showed some hope for the future, and I found myself moving around easily for the first time since I had been mustered out of the army.

One thing was for sure, the cost of food, cartridges and hoss-feed was eating into my small reserve of coin, so with a full pack, a full stomach, but an empty pocket, I headed out of the city. I lifted Aggie into a trot and left the bustle of Charlotte behind me, riding towards the setting sun and the town of Anderson, midway between Charlotte and Atlanta and nestling in the foothills of the Blue Ridge Mountains.

My tension was beginning to ease. Maybe I was worrying over nothing at all, but nagging in the back of my mind was McBain. Would he try to make good his threat by going back to Atlanta? It seemed unlikely, but this was a man who had shot at least three members of his own regiment, in the back, out of pure spite. It surely made a man wonder just how far he'd go to get his own bitter brand of satisfaction.

I'd purchased a Stetson in Charlotte and given my kepi to a black urchin I'd seen searching through bins on the street corners. As the Westering sun settled lower and lower in the sky I found that the wide brim had some big advantages as I tilted the headgear to shield my eyes.

Although the signs of war were everywhere, I still figured it was a good place to live. Trouble was, I needed coin but there was no way I could get it. My mind turned away from serving white folks, whether it was cotton picking or driving 'em around in their smart buggies or carriages. No, those days were gone forever.

My mind picked over the possibilities as I rode into the sunset, seeking for something I could do well. Farming was out; a man needed coin to own a farm; and anyway, I didn't know the first damned thing about running one.

I rode into a small coulee and dismounted as the dusk turned to darkness, close-hobbled the bronc, and set about making some supper before turning in. It was kind'a quiet and private in the coulee, apart from the sizzle of my favorite kind of pig in the skillet. Throwing a decent handful of coffee into the coffeepot I sat back and lit up a cigar while it brewed. Soon the aroma of the coffee mixing with the cigar and that special smell of pig was making my taste buds tingle. Some good beans and two eggs added to the skillet really set the old mouth watering, so I nipped the glowing end off my cigar and set too with a will.

In no time at all I was snugged back on my bedroll, feeling as fat as a bed bug in a rooming house, as I re-lit the dag-end of my cigar. Man! It felt good just to be alive, but I still hadn't solved the problem of how to earn a living.

A branch or twig snapped somewhere close. Rolling from the bedroll, my Colt flicked into my hand in instant reflex as I slid into a crouch and headed silently towards the sound the cigar was still smoldering behind me, where I'd spit it out at the first sound.

As it turned out, there was nothing to worry about; my bronc had stepped on the branch while it was shuffling about, searching for some good grazing, but it served to tell me two things I was good at. My gun hand was fast and I could move around without making a sound; like a hunter. A man hunter perhaps?

Satisfied there was no one to bother me I returned to my bedroll, picked up the cigar stub and puffed it into life, before settling back with my head on the saddle.

The idea kept picking at me. A man hunter! It wouldn't have to be for long. Just so's I could get enough coin together to buy a small parcel of land. Maybe I didn't know from diddley about farming but I could learn. The Homestead Act of '62 said that a citizen who was over twenty one could buy a hundred and sixty acres, for just the administration fee of a dollar twenty-five an acre. We'd been told about the act in the army. I suppose the officers thought it would give us an extra reason to fight, but who needed one?

The sums clicked together in my head. Maybe four sets of bounty would be enough to buy me a one-sixty acre spread; I could become a farmer and offer Lily a home of our own. It was a nice thought. My hand slipped the pistol from its holster and I stared at it in the flickering light of the dying fire. It looked wicked, black and deadly, but others were doing it and I was entitled to a life too, wasn't I? The gun flicked away. I pulled the Stetson over my eyes and slept on the idea.

I awoke as usual, just as the false dawn was coloring the sky, before that big old moon dropped below the horizon and the sun climbed up the other side. The idea of becoming a bounty hunter hadn't left me; there were hundreds of deserters with money on their heads. Bad men, that had used the war as an excuse to pillage small communities. There was even a bounty on Indians, but my mind turned from that.

The idea of becoming a man hunter was new to me, but one thing was sure, a great deal would depend on my gun-speed. So before dragging out the old skillet and coffee pot, I put in a spot of practice, to see just how fast I'd be able to un-limber my pistol. After an hour or so, my arm was aching like you wouldn't believe, so I gave it up in favor of some grub; then I saddled up and headed for Anderson at a good fast clip.

23

Anderson was a border town between South Carolina and Georgia. It was close enough to Atlanta to feel the impact of all the burning and killing in our army's march Southward, and I reckoned that my uniform might get me some trouble.

The town owed its existence to the big Southern farmers, so a blue uniform would hardly be welcome. So I decided to give the place a wide berth.

It was around noon on the second day after passing Anderson, when I saw a small group of riders heading in my direction. I had a feeling they knew just where they were going. It was flat open country hereabouts, and the stubble of scorched cotton plants was sticking out of the ground, while burnt tendrils of cotton were being whisked around them by the short gusts of wind.

If the men were looking for me, the miles of flat open ground was no place to be, yet if I pushed my horse into a run they'd be sure to give chase. Using my knees, I directed the bronc onto a different angle, so that I'd pass behind them. My fears were justified, because they changed course also and I could now see that there were four of them, still heading directly towards me; and as we closed, I could see they were wearing Confederate gray. They gradually spread out in line abreast and halted; my hand eased the Colt in its holster as I drew to a halt about twenty feet in front of them.

Now I could recognize Matthew Franklyn, and his brother Luke. The other two I didn't know, but they were all here for the same reason.

I nodded. 'Matthew, Luke,' I said evenly enough. 'I don't know your friends, but I wish y'all good morning, gents.'

None of them answered the greeting. I didn't expect them to.

'Reckon y'all know why we're here, Joshua D,' Matthew said.

'Maybe so, maybe not, Matthew. Suppose you tell me why.'

'It's about my family, Joshua. Sister Norah tells us y'all raped our mother before you left to join the Northern Army, also tried to rape Norah. That true, Joshua?'

'Ain't so, Matthew.'

'Why'd they say is was so, iffen it ain't true?'

'Beats the hell out of me. Women say the darndest things sometimes.'

'You also stole a slave, you deny that too?'

'Yep, sure do. Ain't no such thing as a slave now, you should know that.'

'To hell with all this palaver,' snarled Luke. 'Let's find a tree, and hang the black bastard; ain't no way our folks would lie about this, Matthew.'

One of the other two, grumbled agreement. 'Time we started to teach 'em what's what again,' he growled.

I took a good long look at that one, he was short and stumpy, an ex-officer, but not a good one, judging by his sloppy appearance. His round mottled face showed signs of too many short drinks in long glasses. His pistol was in a buttoned-down holster, so unless he made some move to make the pistol ready for use I wouldn't have to worry about him too much.

The other one was just about the opposite in every way. A tall, lean beanpole of a man, with a long doleful face and a hooked nose, his face was made to look even longer by the tall, undented Stetson, with the sides of the brim pinned up against the crown. He had a big prominent Adam's apple that seemed to gallop up and down his throat every time he swallowed. He seemed relaxed, lazy, almost half-asleep, but that didn't ring true, because the gun on his hip was set just so. The flap

316

had been cut away from the holster, and the side of it had been cut into a deep curve which allowed the trigger guard to ride free, and the bottom of the holster was held tight to his leg by a leather thong, looped through a hole. Everything about the rig spoke of care and attention to detail. This fella I'd have to watch real careful.

My study of the men didn't take much time, but I could see they were getting restless.

'I'm giving you this one chance to explain yourself, Joshua, because you tried hard for Pa back there in the prison, and I appreciated it,' growled Matthew. 'So speak up man, let's hear from you.'

That was his parade-ground voice, but I wasn't about to let it worry me. My good friend, Luke, had turned into a mealy-mouthed officer who'd always hide behind his rank, and he'd be almost as slow in unlimbering his pistol as the stumpy one. No, the beanpole and Matthew would be the two to watch. I'd never seen a gun holster tied down that way before; maybe I'd copy it if I started bounty hunting — if I ever rode away from this, of course, which didn't seem likely.

Matthew interrupted my thoughts a second time. 'Come on, man, speak your piece if you have anything to say, before it's too late,' he snapped.

'Of course he don't have anything to say,' Luke scoffed. 'We're just wasting time. Let's hang the bastard and be done with it.'

The thin man pushed his mount in front of Luke's horse; his voice was thin and nasal. 'Y'all just hold on there a minute, fella, ain't nobody goin' off half-cocked here. I'm the elected constable hereabouts, an' I decide what's gonna happen to this hairpin.'

'Told you we should have left him behind,' growled Luke, acting like the spoilt kid he was, but he had respect for the thin man, because he soon shut his mouth when the guy faced him down.

Satisfied that he would get no more lip from Luke, he leaned forward, resting a hand on the pommel of his saddle, and switched his gaze back to me; the slate blue eyes had about as much expression as a piece of flint on a rainy day. I was right; this was a fella to watch, real careful.

'Now, mister, if y'all have a tale to tell this is the time to do it. No lies now, gimme it straight from the shoulder an' I'll listen. Try slippin' me a windy and I'll know it. Understand?'

I understood all right. Those eyes felt like they were dipping into my soul, so I sat easy in the saddle and told him my story from beginning to end. Twice Luke swore and tried to interrupt. Once he even dropped his hand to the pistol at his side, but one look from the beanpole stopped him in his tracks.

'That it?' grunted the man, as I ran out of steam.

'That about covers it,' I replied evenly, 'except that the slave I was supposed to have stolen was my own father, beat so bad that he died in my arms.' I stared hard at Matthew. 'And you know good and well that my daddy was always well respected by yours, there had never been a call for beating anybody in your daddy's day, Matthew.'

'Why did the women beat him then?' snapped Luke.

'They liked to do it, simple as that, fella. Now I'm through talking, and I'm heading for Atlanta; if I have to go through you to do it, then that's what I'll do.'

'Reckon you'd try too,' replied the thin man quietly, 'but you don't have to. I know when a man's tellin' the truth, so y'all kin ride on your way, Joshua.'

'The hell he can!' Luke squalled, his hand diving for his pistol as he spoke.

But he was way too slow. The thin man was so fast; the pistol seemed to grow in his hand.

I didn't even see it happen until it was way too late.

I was lucky. The pistol was pointing at Luke, so I stayed my hand; this was no time to die a hero.

'Like I said,' continued the thin man, as if nothing exciting had happened, 'no one is gonna stop you from leaving. Ain't that so, Matthew?'

'That's right. I believe you, Josh. I had my doubts when the women folk tried to explain it, but you understand, I had to make sure. You'd have done the same, fella.' Matthew shrugged his shoulders as the regret showed in his voice. 'Even if Pa had lived, he couldn't have faced this, so maybe he's better off dead. So long, Joshua, ride easy, man,' he mumbled, as he pulled his mount out of line, turned, and loped away, shoulders slumped in dejection.

I felt the tension easing from my shoulders as Matthew rode away. I jerked my mind back to the men in front of me as Luke cursed and turned his mount in a swirl of dust to gallop after his brother, raising a squeal of pain from the horse as he applied the quirt to its flanks in his temper.

The short man also pulled his horse around, but anger and frustration showed in the mottled red of his face as he glared at me.

'We'll be seein' y'all, black boy!' he snarled, as he fed steel to his mount and followed the other two.

I logged his remarks away in the back of my mind; the guy was another McBain, and Luke wasn't about to give up either.

The gun in the thin man's hand disappeared as fast as he had drawn it. I had been right about him, but I'd have been dead long before my pistol had cleared leather. He seemed to be reading my thoughts.

'You would still have tried, mister.'

I nodded. 'A man's got to try.'

'Yeah, I know, but ride easy, friend.'

'I'll do that, and thank you kindly for taking the trouble to listen, I appreciate it.'

He touched the brim of his Stetson in a careless salute, before backing his horse away and riding off after the others. This had to be my lucky day. Like the man said, I'd have tried, but . . .

24

I made camp early that night in a small stand of trees and spent some time carving away at my holster, paring down a deep curve, to leave the trigger guard free. There was a three-band leather strip around my Stetson that could be tightened to make the hat fit properly, but being a big built man I didn't hardly need it. So, pulling it out of the metal eyelets, I threaded the strip through a hole I'd made in the bottom of the holster and looped it off before tying it around my leg.

I could hardly believe the difference it made to my gun-speed, and I didn't have to hold my holster with my left hand either, which left it free to fan the hammer as the pistol came up. Man! That gun came out slicker than spit on a hot griddle, and after about an hour's practice I reckoned I'd be a fair match for anybody, including the thin man . . . maybe.

I was like a kid with a toy. Even after I'd eaten supper and stretched out on my blanket with the saddle for a pillow, my hand kept flicking down like a snake's tongue, lifting the pistol out and cocking the hammer in one easy movement, something that was almost impossible before.

The thoughts of becoming a bounty hunter had firmed up in my mind. Maybe Lily wouldn't agree with my ideas, but it was for me to decide how I was going to earn a living, although I had to admit to myself that if Lily decided to go against the idea, she'd let me know. She had one God-awful temper that one and no mistake.

Thinking of her set me worrying about McBain again and sleep was slow in coming because of it. Which was maybe just as well, because as I leaned toward the dying embers of my fire, looking for a glowing twig to light the dead stub of cigar I'd been sucking on for the last half-hour, there was the spiteful crack of a carbine. The bullet snicked off the top of the saddle pommel and spanged off into the darkness. I rolled away from the flickering light of the fire, aware that if I had not moved to light the cigar at that moment, my brains — if I ever had any — would have been decorating my saddle about now.

As I rolled, my hand collected the Henry rifle, which always lay beside me while I was bedded down. The other hand dropped to an empty holster. My Colt must have fallen out as I rolled, but this was no time to hang around looking for it. I discovered that this was one of the faults of a cut-away holster. There's always one, I thought, rolling towards a hollow near a fallen tree trunk that I'd marked off during the daylight hours.

A man who has spent almost three years defending his life in wartime will, almost without thinking about it, log in his mind all the good points of cover close to his bed, in case of a night attack, and my training had worked for me this time also.

I'd heard some muttered curses right after the sharp crack of the rifle. So unless the attacker had moved, I had his position spotted; and, as the hollow behind the fallen tree was in deep shadow, I rested there, listening to the sounds of the night, allowing my night vision to build by staring into the deep shadow of the hollow. Nothing moved out there, my whole body was strained, tuned to hear the slightest sound; but the night animals knew there was danger, because the normal slight sounds made by them had not re-started.

An hour passed on leaden feet. Apart from their unfortunate choice of shooting just as I had decided to move, my hunters were very good. Soon that big old moon would be climbing higher, bathing this small patch of trees in moonlight.

I was prepared to bet that there was more

than one man out there waiting for me, and once the moon brightened the place up I'd lose my advantage; some sort of diversion was needed, something to cause whoever was out there to make a mistake. I moved my hand along the ground an inch at a time, searching for a rock or heavy piece of wood; something to throw, to make a noise that might set them moving towards it. There was nothing suitable, so I slid slowly along the length of the tree, searching the ground as I went, and all the time that big old moon was climbing higher and higher. My searching hand found nothing except loose soil, but there was an idea digging in the back of my brain that might work. A few cartridges tossed into the faintly glowing embers of my fire, which was just a few short yards away, might tempt 'em to open fire, but first I had to get over the tree to the other side. Be a real big laugh for someone if one of the exploding cartridges tagged me. Easing back along the trunk again I found a smooth clear place where there were no branches to get in my way. The trunk was big here, almost two feet thick if I was any judge. My Stetson was back by the fire, lost in my mad dive for safety. Lifting my head close to the top of my cover, I allowed the hand holding my rifle to slide over the trunk until I could rest the gun on the ground the other side. Now it was my turn. I had two choices, to go over fast and take some chances, or slide over as slowly and as quietly as possible. Either way I could end up very dead, and that big old moon was still climbing higher and higher in the night sky. Soon it would be shining right down on my hiding place; they'd have me for sure then.

It was spit or close the window time, so, keeping as flat along the tree as possible, I fast-rolled over to the other side. Nothing! No crack of pistol or rifle split the quiet of the night! I began to breathe easy again. Either they were concentrating on creeping up on me, which was possible. Or they hadn't spotted my move, that was very likely. Or they'd given up and left. That was just wishful thinking, but whatever the reason, it was time for me to make my play. Slipping three cartridges out of my belt loops, I peered over the top of the trunk; staring at the smoldering fire did nothing at all for my night sight, but it had to be done.

Staking everything on one long over-arm throw, I tossed the cartridges towards the fire. There was a slight disturbance, and it looked as if at least one had fallen on target. It would take a few moments for the heat to explode the cartridges, so I picked up my rifle and waited, staring away from the fire, to regain what night sight I could.

The time seemed to drag waiting for the cartridges to explode, and I began to wonder if my eyes had been playing tricks with me. Maybe I'd missed the fire altogether! I was about to make a second try when the explosions almost frightened the wits out of me, and there was a startled yell from the bushes opposite my hiding-place, followed by the wicked wink of fire as a pistol opened up in reply to the decoy. My rifle centered on the pistol flame and I placed a pattern of three bullets into it.

The pistol stopped firing and a loud curse echoed in the silence, followed by a crash of something heavy falling into the dryness of the bush. Only one! The thought flashed through my mind as I moved further along the trunk. It didn't make any kind of sense. One man would hardly try to attack another in the darkness. There would have to be two, or even three. My eyes flashed around the tiny clearing, searching for some movement, some sign of warning, but there was nothing!

Time dragged on. The moon was shining into the clearing now, but still nothing moved; if there was anyone else out there they were good, very good. My limbs were beginning to ache, half crouched as I was behind the tree trunk. The insects were beginning to make their night noises again so maybe I was mistaken! Perhaps there had only been one attacker! Yet still, I waited.

The urge to move was getting to me when I suddenly thought of my horse. Was that it? Maybe they'd decided to leave me afoot! I'd be easy to kill then. A rifleman could wait until I decided to come out of the timber, into miles of flat open country where they could pick me off in their own sweet time with a rifle.

Slipping along to the end of the fallen tree, I moved into the timber, striking a path towards Aggie. I heard him blow softly through his nose even before I spotted him between the trees. Aggie's head was turned away from me but its ears were pricked forward. The horse was staring at something, or someone! Easing back into cover, I watched and waited, hoping that whatever was holding Aggie's interest would show itself soon.

There was a whisper of sound behind me. I started to turn and my world exploded into a blaze of colored lights, before the blackness dragged me down into unconsciousness . . .

★ ★ ★

It felt as if a mad Indian was using my head as a war-drum and a thousand woodpeckers were joining in, just for the fun of it. Managing to stop myself from giving out with a groan of agony took some doing, but again my war experiences came to my aid. A groan could mean a bullet on the battlefield, and without putting too fine a point on it, that's just what this was.

Prizing my eyes open a crack took some doing. Although the moon was on the wane, it hurt like hell. Things kind'a swirled around there for a while, but they gradually leveled off. I could see two humps, close to what was left of the fire, which meant that there had to be three of them originally, because the one I had shot at stood no chance at all of being able to move around. Not exactly clever figuring I know, but you have to understand that I was not at my best right then.

Trying to get up was a waste of time. Apart from almost losing last night's supper, I was tied hand and foot, so it seemed that Luke, and whoever was with him, had the winning hand. The mad Indian had begun to run out of steam, but the woodpeckers were still in there banging away like they'd never get tired. I lifted my head and stared at the two big lumps by the fire. They were still sleeping so I began to roll away from my spot on the ground, heading for the fallen tree again.

My movements must have roused the mad Indian because he had another go at his war-drum, and about then something hard dug into my spine; it hurt like hell, so I wriggled around to try to remove it and my bound hands came into contact with my lost pistol, which was kind'a lucky — except that my hands were bound.

After another quick look towards the sleeping men, I continued to roll, taking the Colt with me into the hollow. I had no idea how I was going to make use of the gun, but managed to hide it under a heavy branch before rolling as far away from the spot as possible.

In my hurry, I must have made a noise, because one of the men grunted and sat up. It was the short one with the mottled face I'd seen earlier. He hawked and spat, before realizing that I was no longer where they had left me. The man cursed, and drew his pistol as he stumbled to his feet, waking the second man in his efforts.

'What the hell's gotten into you, Clay?' the man grunted, staring at his partner.

'Thought our prisoner had escaped,' replied Clay, relief sounding in his voice. 'Looks like he was tryin' to but didn't make it,' he added with a laugh, as he holstered his pistol and came towards me.

The other fella also sat up and stared in my direction. 'When I tie 'em they stay that way,' he grunted, as he also climbed to his feet.

I had expected it to be Luke, so it surprised me to see someone else.

'Bounty hunters huh? Luke paying a bounty on my hide now?' I asked.

'Yep,' replied Clay, as he stared down at me. 'Me an' Tom here have agreed to split the bounty on you, black boy.'

'So where's Luke?'

'None of your damned business.'

'Who was the guy I shot?'

'That was Luke,' replied Tom, as he also strolled over to stare at me, like he hadn't ever seen a black man before.

'Is he dead?'

'As he'll ever be,' replied Tom.

'So who's gonna pay the bounty?'

'Reckon Matthew will, when we tell him you put three bullets into his baby brother,' answered Clay.

'So where's Matthew?'

'Chock full of questions, ain't yuh, boy,' growled Clay. 'He'll be along soon. He still figures he has to look after his little brother but he don't know the mean, nasty little bastard like I do. Now I'm through talkin' so shut it.'

'Like to know where I stand, mister. That's when he kicked me real hard between my legs. The pain shot up into my stomach like liquid fire and it set me squealing like a stuck pig.

'I said shut up, black boy, or do you want some more?' snarled Clay. 'That's enough talkin' on an empty stomach, but after a bite of food we're gonna hang you black boy, so think on that.' He swung the boot a second time, but in spite of the pain running through me I managed to take it on the inside of my thigh. I still howled like a banshee, but it didn't hurt near so bad. Being prepared for it made a lot of difference.

The two men soon had a fire going, and shortly after, the rich smell of ham and eggs, mingling with the tangy smell of freshly brewed Arbuckle, was drifting around the tiny clearing. The pain in my groin and stomach began to ease a little. The smell of food cooking didn't do much for my appetite. I was in big trouble, so filling my stomach was the last thing on my mind.

Matthew had been on my side back there on the plains, but now I'd killed Luke it would be a different story. Like Clay had said. Matthew only knew his brother from before the war, so he had no idea how completely Luke had changed.

I'd tried to get my hands out of the ropes when I'd first discovered that I was a prisoner, but it was a waste of time. Tom was right when he said he knew how to tie a man, and while my hands were tied behind my back, the gun under the branch of the fallen tree was no good to me.

Their breakfast was soon over; Clay had been pitching remarks at me all the while. Things like, 'Ain't much use feeding y'all, you'd never get to keep it', or, 'We won't keep y'all hanging about much longer, boy!' They must have thought these remarks were funny because they both brayed with laughter every time. 'What's the matter, boy,' hooted Tom, 'lost your sense of humor?'

When they found that I didn't rise to their baiting, they soon got tired of it, and eventually Clay threw the dregs of his cup into the fire and picked up a coiled lariat that was laying beside him. 'Let's get it done, Tom,' he grunted. 'Go fetch his nag; the quicker we get him back to the Franklyn farm, the sooner we get paid.'

'Be a big laugh if Matthew don't pay you anyway,' I grunted.

Tom stopped and glared at me. 'One thing's for sure, you won't be the one that's laughing, black boy,' he growled.

'No, but it would be real funny if the law

grabbed y'all for murder!'

Tom glared at me, then turned his attention to Clay. 'We are gonna git paid fer this ain't we?' he growled, the uncertainty showing in his voice.

'Why sure we are,' replied Clay. 'You heard Luke promise us a thousand dollars bounty, just like I did.'

'Oh yeah! I heard him and you heard him, but will Matthew Franklyn pony up the money?'

'Good question, Clay,' I offered.

'He ain't likely to duck out on the deal is he? Especially when we tell him this jasper killed his little brother,' replied Clay, glaring at me, but there was an uncertain bluster in his voice.

I found the room for a chuckle from somewhere — believe me, I didn't feel like chuckling, No sir!

'What's so funny?' snarled Clay. 'From where I'm standin' you ain't got nothing to laugh at.'

Shrugging my shoulders, I pasted a grin on my face, and that took some doing. 'I got nothing to lose, Clay old buddy. Either way I'm just as dead. Now you and Tom here. Why, y'all gotta watch which way you jump.'

'How d'you figure that?' Tom hadn't gone to fetch the horse yet; he was getting curious, which suited me just fine, because I had to prove to them that hanging me was not a good idea.

'Look at it this way, fellas. If you hang me and tote my cadaver back to the Franklyn spread, Matthew could just say 'Thank y'all very much' and send you on your way, because you ain't got nothin' to bargain with, except a body that's already dead. Or he could call in the law and complain that you two are murderers. Either way you draw the short straw.' I shut up about then, because I could see they were giving my spiel a lot of thought and it didn't pay to over-cook things.

Clay snapped his fingers. I could see his wonderful idea taking shape — he'd make a lousy poker player,t's for sure.

'We'll just take him back to the Franklyn spread alive,' he chuckled. 'That way we can't lose. Either Matthew Franklyn, or his momma, pays us a thousand dollars like his brother promised, or we ride away with the prisoner!'

'That's more like it,' growled Tom. 'I'll bet Luke's old lady will pay real good for her son's killer. Maybe even more than a thousand, huh?'

'Go get the hoss, Tom, and we'll be on our way,' grunted Clay. 'The quicker we get this hairpin back to the Franklyn spread the better.'

Well, I'd managed to put off getting hung for the time being, but I still had to make my escape. Maybe I'd slipped out of the skillet and into the Goddamned fire. My one thought was that the two men had said Matthew would be sure to come after his brother. Whether he'd feel so kindly towards me when he heard that I was responsible for Luke's death was doubtful, but any chance was better than no chance at all.

By the time they'd untied my legs and boosted me into the saddle, I'd reconciled myself to the situation. All I had to do now was figure out a way to escape. Aggie was quiet enough because we'd come to an agreement about him trying to buck me off in the mornings. If I didn't bounce my heels into his sides, Aggie didn't get uppity. The idea had worked out pretty well up to now, so I kept my heels well away from his flanks. The last thing I wanted to do was to upset Aggie while my hands were tied behind my back.

Tom had fixed a lead rope to Aggie and was about to mount when I hit him with my next bit of spiel — I'd sure learned a lot of helpful hints from Mister Jesse and no mistake.

'Y'all gonna leave me with my hands tied behind my back, fellas?' I made it sound like it was a real stupid thing to do.

Tom paused with his foot in the stirrup. 'You think we're gonna cut you loose?'

'Nope,' I replied; as if I didn't give a good Goddamn about it one way or the other. 'Just wondered is all. Wouldn't want to fall off and break my neck, this hoss can be right uppity at times, he could pitch me off real easy tied thisaway.'

'Be a real pity,' grunted Clay; he could be real sarcastic when he put his mind to it.

'Yeah, wouldn't it though,' I responded, 'be goodbye to a thousand cartwheels for you boys.' My grin made Tom start thinking again.

'You got somethin' else to say pilgrim?' he growled. 'D'you think we care a damn whether you break your stupid neck or not?'

'I don't see even Momma Franklyn paying good coin for a fella with a broken neck. Do you?'

I took a real chance with Aggie then, and rubbed a heel ever so gently into its flank. Aggie responded beautifully by crow-hopping a couple of times, as if to say, 'I'm warning you, mister.' Which was fine by me.

Tom walked over and grinned up at me. 'You know, it's nice to have a fella like you around, thinkin' real hard to help us out all the time. Maybe we should tie your hands to the pommel, hoss can't buck y'all off then, huh?'

'Might be an idea at that,' I shrugged. 'You're the boss.'

'Yeah,' grinned Tom, 'that bein' so I figure we'd better tie your legs together under the hoss as well, be a pity to have y'all run off on that nag of yours, now, wouldn't it?' He gave a deep chuckle as he collected his lariat and lashed my feet together under Aggie before he untied the ropes on my wrists and tied them to the pommel.

My spirits took a nosedive; I'd over-cooked it!

Tom patted my hands, still grinning. 'We didn't all come up with the last rain, sonny, but thank you kindly for bein' so helpful.' He swung into his saddle and jerked the lead rein. He was still smiling as he looked back at me. 'Be sure of one thing, fella, I want a thousand cartwheels for your hide an' I'm gonna get it, an' all your clever speechifyin' ain't gonna help y'all one little bit.' He jerked the lead rope and we started on the return trip to the Franklyn spread, back to a place I'd rather not go.

25

We traveled for the whole of that day at a snail's pace, stopping only for a bite to eat at noon. It was obvious that the two men were hoping Matthew Franklyn would turn up and save them the long trek to the farmstead. They wanted to collect their money and be on their way.

I racked my brain, trying to figure out a way to escape. But they gave me no chance at all, and come sundown — a time when I thought there might be a chance — they played it real cagey, untying my hands to release me from the pommel and re-tying them again before releasing my feet. Finally they sat me on the ground with my back to a tree, tied my arms around it and lashed my feet together.

The food smelled good, but they weren't in a sharing mood, so nothin' came my way. The two men talked far into the night, sharing a bottle of something, discussing what they would do with their reward. Gradually their speech became more and more slurred, until finally, the talking stopped and snores took over.

I struggled for a long time with my bonds, but it was no use; the ropes were as tight as when I'd started. My head slumped forward onto my chest as I tried to doze. Real sleep was impossible, but I had to try to keep my wits about me, in case a chance did come my way. It was around two in the morning when I slowly became aware of the complete silence! The insect world had suddenly stopped making their noises and I became sharply awake, my mind tuned to pick up the slightest sound.

Then I heard it! A whisper of sound from behind the tree I was tied to. My mind jumped to thoughts of a wild animal; until I felt the rope securing my arms to the tree fall slack. A moment later a knife slipped between my wrists, so apart from my ankles, I was free! Then a strong pair of hands hooked under my arms and drew me backward into the bushes.

'Easy now Josh, I'll have y'all free in no time,' whispered Matthew, as the knife sawed through the rope around my ankles. He tapped my shoulder. 'Let's go, man,' he murmured, and although the pins and needles were chasing each other through my arms and legs, I managed to follow his shadowy form through the bushes, to where the horses were tied, without a stumble or noise to betray us.

They'd not even bothered to remove the saddle or bridle from my mount, and it was close-hobbled to boot. Maybe it was just as well, because I was able to lead Aggie away without any fuss at all, once I'd cut the hobbles with Matthew's knife, and we eased quietly away from the camp without speaking. My mind was playing hop, skip and jump. Matthew could not know I'd killed his brother, and maybe he wouldn't have helped me if he had known about it. So I wasn't about to tell him, if you get my drift; I ain't exactly stupid and my only weapon was back there under the branch of that fallen tree, Tom had my Henry rifle, and Clay had claimed my Bowie knife.

We rode stirrup to stirrup for a while without speaking, which suited me just fine, but it had to come.

'You know I only helped you to get away from Luke because you helped Pa and me, don't you Josh? I believed what you said about Momma and Norah, but Luke was sure you were lying.'

'He wanted me to be lying.'

'Maybe. He ain't the same as he used to be, Josh. He's gotten kind'a vicious. Why's he so set against you?'

'Dunno. I thought we were friends; even

saved his life when you threw him in the pond, remember? 'Pears he only thought of me as his own personal slave. Why didn't you ride into the camp and tell Luke you wanted me freed, Matthew?'

'I knew Luke wouldn't agree, and I didn't want him to know I was going to let you go. Those others are bounty hunters, they would have wanted their money anyway, so they could have caused me some trouble. Fact is, I don't have any money right now and neither does Luke.'

We slowed to a fast walk.

'I reckon we're even now, Josh, and you've got to understand that I can't stand for you against Luke any longer. You're on your own now, fella. I'm riding back to Anderson so maybe we'll never meet again, but you have to know I'm standing by Luke from now on. If we ever meet again, we'll probably be enemies. So long, fella.'

'Not riding back to Luke's camp?'

'No. Like I said, I don't want him to know I've even been near the camp. I'll make it seem like a big surprise when he rides into Anderson.'

You don't know just how big a surprise it's gonna be, I thought, breathing a quiet sigh of relief. 'Ride safe,' I called, as he turned his mount away from me and galloped off into the dawn's first light.

It looked as if keeping my mouth shut had done me a real big favor, especially as he was riding back to Anderson. My way was back to the Colt I'd pushed under the branch back at my last camp. Then I was going to do some hunting myself. Time I'd finished, either Clay and Tom would be dead, or I would. If I won, Matthew would not know about Luke's death for some time, and if Clay and Tom outsmarted me, it wouldn't matter anyway.

There was a good Henry rifle I'd carried a long way during the war; I wanted it back. There was also my pack of grub to consider and all my spare ammunition, except the few rounds in my gun-belt. There was a deep ache in my groin where Clay's boot had landed, to be dished out with interest if I had my way. Aggie was setting a good pace, so I let him get on with it while I scoured the countryside, looking for possible trouble ahead. Trouble had stuck with me, like an itch I couldn't scratch, for some time now, and an empty holster was not exactly comforting, but I was free again and that was the important thing.

The sun was climbing high in the sky when I eventually pulled to a halt in the small stand of trees, and slipped quickly from the saddle to retrieve my pistol. It was still where I'd put it, so I squatted right there on the branch and used my neckerchief to clean off the sandy soil and wipe the cartridges and caps, making sure that not even the tiniest bit of grit was left in, or on, the gun.

Re-setting the holster and tying it off at just at the right angle only took a few moments. I dusted that out too, so's the pistol slid into my hand and back into the holster without catching or clinging. Then I practiced my draw for over an hour. Satisfied, I tightened my belt against the hunger pangs and went to look for Luke's body.

I found the bush he had fallen into, but could find no sign of the cadaver. So maybe the two hombres I was after had taken the trouble to roll Luke's body into a hollow somewhere. After another short search I decided that the new Luke didn't deserve too much of my time anyway, so I mounted, and, touching my spurs to Aggie's flanks, we set off at a fast canter.

The horse must have sensed my mood because he didn't even try to hump or buck, which was just as well for him; and once he'd gotten into his stride, Aggie settled into a long lope. The horse was big and he was good, the miles fairly flew by under the smooth rhythm off its hooves. Even so, it was well past midnight before I rode into the wooded section where I had been held prisoner. The camp was deserted and it was useless to go farther in the darkness, so I rested against the same tree I had been tied to earlier, and dozed the hours of darkness away, my stomach grumbling now and then at the lack of attention it was getting. It didn't help to hear Aggie contentedly munching away at the long grass growing around the tree-roots, but I'd been hungry before. A cigar would have helped, but they'd gone the same way as my rifle and Bowie knife. Just another thing to make me eager to meet up with those two bounty hunters again.

I must have dozed for a short while because the next time I looked around, the false dawn was tingeing the sky with a mixture of cobalt and gold; and the light was good enough for me to hunt for sign, and it didn't take much finding. From the spoor I reckoned they were about four hours ahead of me, but riding slow and easy. They'd seen no reason to cover their tracks because they were following the long sweeping curve Matthew and I had taken when he'd rescued me, and the overlapping hoof marks were not difficult to see. Tom and Clay were riding as hunters, they didn't expect to be the prey.

We must have passed within two miles of each other in the hours before midnight.

Soon they would come to the point where Matthew and I parted company, and then they'd have to choose which trail to follow. Back to Anderson, or on towards the stand of timber where they had first captured me.

If they rode carefully enough, sooner or later they would spot my other set of tracks, which would bring them back towards me. So what I needed was a decent place to wait for them, something that would hide both myself and my bronc, until they were close enough for me to use my pistol.

Hitting something over twenty feet away with a pistol, even an Army Colt, is a matter of luck, whereas a rifle could cut a man to pieces at three times the distance with no trouble at all. So, I needed something a bit special, where I could hide until they rode up real close, without suspecting a thing. There was a small stand of trees to my left, but with all this open country around they'd hardly ride into woodland, especially as my returning tracks bypassed the stand of timber by at least a quarter of a mile.

After giving the matter a lot of thought, I took Aggie into the timber and tied him in a brush-choked coulee. Taking the saddle and blanket off him I dumped the saddle and my Stetson in the brush, but took the blanket with me, using it together with a small leafy branch to dust out my tracks as I backed away. The wind soon wiped out the small traces I'd left behind, leaving me satisfied that no one would find my spoor.

I worked my way back to my cross-tracks, then backtracked on foot, until I came to a deep sandy hollow I'd noticed earlier, beside the trail. Standing in the hollow, I spent a good fifteen minutes looking for anything that might give my plan away. By kneeling, I could just see over the hollow; sooner or later, the two men I wanted would be riding right alongside my hiding-place, and they wouldn't know I was anywhere around.

Folding the blanket in three so that it gave me a long tube, I laid it in the bottom of the hollow, and spent another half-hour scooping the sandy soil from the edges of the depression over it. I was sweating like a bull on heat by the time I'd finished that chore, but it was going to be a damned sight hotter inside the tube.

I took a last long look around. Nothing moved as far as the eye could see, but it was time to slide into the tube, to see if my plan would work. Once in the tube I'd have to lay still; the smallest movement would disturb the soil, which had already dried out, and the loss of soil would leave the blanket uncovered. Slowly and carefully, I eased my

347

body into the blanket. It was like sliding into an oven; it sure made me feel sorry for turkeys. The Colt was in my hand and resting against my face, ready for instant use as the two men rode by, if they ever did. I was taking a chance that they'd still follow my trail, which wasn't unreasonable under the circumstances, since they wanted the money Luke had placed on my hide.

An hour passed, and another followed. The sun was blazing down and I was cooking, sweat was streaming down my face and breathing was becoming a real chore. I'd about convinced myself that I'd made a big mistake, when the jingle of bit chains sounded in the still air. From here on I'd have to depend on my ears, so I eased the end of the blanket over my face and waited.

Hot! Man! You wouldn't believe how hot it was under that damned blanket with the front closed up. The heat seared my lungs with each breath, so I stopped breathing ... almost, just taking in enough of that scalding air to stay alive, as the two horses ambled past on the trail above my hiding place.

The mumble of the men talking helped me to judge their position, and it was easy to tell that they were not on their guard — and why should they be? They could see for miles out there.

I eased the blanket back from my face; the horses' hindquarters were just beyond the hollow as I slid all the way out and stood up. They thought they had the whole country to themselves . . . until they heard my Colt snick on to full cock.

'Just don't move, or I'll blow you out of the saddles without even thinking about it.' My voice had a real snarl to it; I owed these guys plenty and I wasn't about to pussyfoot around.

It did me a power of good to see their backs stiffen with shock as their hands began to climb slowly towards their shoulders. 'Higher!' I snapped. They obliged and their hands kept climbing until they were level with their ears.

'Don't even think about turning around, fellas, you'd never make it,' I growled.

'You'd give it to us in the back?' Clay sounded as if it was the last thing he'd ever think of doing.

'Try me!'

'I believe you,' grunted Tom. 'Do the same if I was in your boots. We gonna get some sort of a chance here?'

'We'll just have to see about that. You, Tom. Shuck your pistol. Careful now, I'm nervous.

Do it left-handed an' remember, I only have to lift my thumb off the hammer and you're dead.'

'I know mister, I can feel the itch in my back already.'

As Tom lifted his pistol out of the holster with two fingers of his left hand, and held it well away from his body, ready to let it drop to the ground, I saw Clay's right shoulder drop slightly. He was about to try his hand while I was watching Tom.

'You'd never make it, but you can try, if you're feeling lucky,' I growled, half hoping he'd make his play. But Clay wasn't feeling that lucky and he pushed his hands higher just to prove it.

'Your turn, fella,' I grunted, as Tom's pistol hit the dirt. 'Don't be a hero, you might get your chance later.' Clay would never have made a decent draw. From the time he took to undo the flap on his holster and un-limber his side arm, I could have lit a cigar and still beat him to it — if I'd had one to light.

I stared at the backs of the two men. It was true that they had no sidearms, but there were two rifles in the saddle boots and I had no way of knowing what other pistols they might have hidden in their gear, so I couldn't allow them to dismount in the usual way.

'Okay, one at a time. You first, Clay. Slide

over the bronc's rump, real easy now, don't make me nervous.'

'Y'all can't expect me to do that, fella, the bronc's likely to fetch me a kick in the guts.'

'Be a real pity, Clay. Just do it. OK?'

The hoss crow-hopped a little when Clay slid over its rump. But the man managed to dodge the hooves as the bronc shied away and trotted forward a few yards, before starting to crop the sparse new grass that was beginning to show in the dried out sandy soil between the burnt cotton stumps.

'Your turn, mister,' I grunted at Tom.

He slid over with no argument and easily avoided the flaying hooves.

'OK. Now what? Y'all gonna shoot us in the back, mister?' asked Tom.

'Nope; you boys just walk on over and holster your pistols, and when you turn around, start shooting!'

'Hell that don't give us no chance at all,' snarled Clay, but there was a whine in his voice that said he was real scared.

'It's the only chance you get, and it's more than you gave me, so get to it or take it in the back.' My voice sounded like I meant it, because I wanted 'em to try me. Whether I'd have done it or not is another thing all together, but neither Clay, nor his partner, was willing to put it to the test.

They both walked slowly over to their pistols and picked them up. Clay threw himself forward and rolled on to his back, gun coming up at full cock. My bullet took him between the eyes and he died without getting off a shot.

Tom was a few seconds behind Clay as he turned in a crouched position, his pistol in his left hand, the right lifted flat above the hammer, ready to slap it back in a quick fanning motion. He was fast, but he was unbalanced. A bullet plucked at my pants-leg and a second tugged my holster. His eyes widened and he grunted in shock as my first slug slapped into his shoulder, half-turning him into my second, which made a real mess of his throat.

My legs were trembling and I felt a sickness in me. I'd killed men before, lots of 'em in the heat of battle, but this was different; somehow more personal. I stood there for quite a while, just staring at their bodies, waiting for the shakes to leave me. Then at last I stared around the empty landscape, almost without seeing it, but with the instincts of an animal, making sure that there was no one out there likely to do me harm.

Walking over to the cadavers was quite a chore, but I needed a smoke real bad and Tom had my cigars in his pocket. Kneeling beside him I fished out a smoke and used one of his stinkers to light up. Man! That smoke tasted real good as I sucked it into my lungs. Made my head spin too, for a while, but what the hell! I was alive and they were dead! So I sat between 'em and enjoyed my cigar.

The two horses were in fine fettle and there was no sign of a brand on 'em. The saddles and gear were all in good condition also, and I was real pleased to get my Henry rifle back. The Starr carbine belonging to Tom was OK, but it fired a .54 caliber linen cartridge, so I'd probably sell it in Atlanta.

Thinking along these lines made me remember my bounty hunter ideas; maybe there was a 'flier' out on these two. It was worth a try, so I decided to strap 'em to their own nags and take 'em to Atlanta; maybe I'd get lucky for a change. I rolled Clay over and searched him first, for guns, knives and such. Man! My luck was really in. There was a real sharp gutting knife in his boot, and over 300 dollars in coin in his pockets, a bottle of stinkers and three of my cigars.

Tom's body had even more booty: an Allen and Thurber pepperbox .34. My own Bowie; I slid that back into the sheath attached to my gun rig. 700 silver cartwheels and the rest of my cigars. Man! This bounty hunting was one good paying business. Even if I didn't collect any money on the two dead men I had at least three years' pay, once I'd sold the horses and guns.

Loading the cadavers on the horses was a bit of a chore, but I eventually managed to throw them across their saddles, and tie 'em hand to foot under the bellies of their mounts; mind you, the broncs weren't too keen, they didn't much care for the smell of blood. They'd have to get used to it; I wasn't about to pass up the chance of any bounty that was going begging.

My food pack was strapped to the dead men's packs and my stomach had about decided that eating was a thing of the past, so I figured that I'd get my prizes back to where Aggie was, out of sight in the timber. The last thing I needed was for someone to be riding up asking questions. Tying the two horses in line, I pulled the horse blanket out of the sand and tied it to the last horse so that it would drag along the ground, partly wiping out the tracks we were making. The wind would soon blow a dusting of soil over what was left.

Picking up the lead horse's reins, I walked it back to the stand of timber, mentally promising my stomach that once we got there it would receive my close attention.

26

The rest of the ride to Atlanta wasn't too bad at all. I was stopped by two white men who asked about the carcasses I was towing, but when I made it clear that I was a keen bounty hunter looking for more scalps, they quickly decided that they'd prefer to be elsewhere.

The town still seemed to be under military law. Blue-coated soldiers were everywhere, but it would be a long time before Atlanta would become the place it was. Hardly a solid building was left standing and raw timber shacks were growing like mushrooms on the damaged sites, replacing the imposing buildings that used to be there.

Half my mind was on Lily and the other half was on the high-smelling cadavers behind me; although I'd sheeted them down, passers-by were still eyeing me with deep suspicion. I spotted the church in the square where I'd left Lily the night I first met up with her. It was a kind of sheriff's office and barracks now, so I guided my bronc over to the hitching rail and tied my three horses to it, before heading for the double doors I remembered so well.

'Y'all wantin' somethin', bub?' asked a stumpy fella in a faded blue uniform with three stripes still on his arm. He was chewing a real big wad of eating tobacco.

'I'm looking for the town constable, friend,' I replied evenly, 'care to point me in the right direction?'

'That's me, bub. What kin I do fer yuh?' He stuck out a chubby hand. 'They call me Toby. What's your handle?'

Man! I tried real hard not to grin, but I couldn't help thinking of that old hound dog all covered in fox's shit back there on Lookout Mountain. 'Name's Joshua,' I managed to get out, without busting a gut. 'Bounty Hunter. I've got some cadavers outside I'd like y'all to take a look at.'

'Another one, huh? More bounty hunters around here than gophers on the prairie,' he muttered sourly. 'With half the population dead you'd think all the wanted men would have bin wiped out long ago, but seems there's still plenty to go around.'

'You want to take a look?'

'Not particularly, but it's my job, so let's get it done.' He spat a huge gob of brown liquid on the steps. 'Lift the sheets bub, and let's take a look-see.'

Up till then he'd been quite calm and peaceful; now he started choking and it took some slapping to get the chaw out of his gullet, and by the time he'd gotten rid of it he'd changed to a real blood red color.

'What the hell's gotten into you, mister?' I shouted. 'Don't y'all go dying on me now.'

Toby was still choking something awful as he pointed at the cadaver, so I reckoned he'd swallowed at least half the plug he'd been chewing.

'Man! Them's the ones who robbed the bank right here in Atlanta, just a few weeks ago,' he managed to gasp between coughs. 'Stole near on $3,000 in silver coin.' He began to drag me back up the steps. 'The major's gonna be real glad to meet you, young fella. Don't suppose you happened to find the money on 'em?'

Well, I thought about the $1,000 silver cartwheels in my pack, but I figured I'd earned that coin, so I played it real dumb as he bundled me into the major's office.

Major West didn't seem at all surprised that there was no news about the coin that had been stolen; he just gave me a bit of an old fashioned look as he shook my hand, and mumbled something about it being a stupid question.

'Dunno what's in their packs though, Major, I haven't had the time to sort through 'em yet,' I said, like a nice dumb black fella trying to be helpful.

The Major looked a lot more interested. 'You've got their packs and you haven't looked through 'em young fella? Why damn me let's just do that! Go fetch 'em in right now.'

Well, 'twixt you and me I knew exactly what was in them, but I let the good major rummage away, making my eyes look big and surprised at every find, just like a good black boy should. I knew all about the Le Mat, which was wrapped in an oiled cloth and snugged in the bottom of Clay's pack. But when the major found it, my face showed such amazement that the fellow took quite a time to explain its workings to me, and I listened with such attention that he patted my shoulder and told me what a clever fellow I was.

I'd heard it all before of course, because Mister Jesse owned one years ago, but what the hell! It kept him happy an' we black fellas is always willin' to learn. Yassah, Massa. One thing was for sure, the good major didn't find any coin in the bags, and you can bet a stack on that!

There were two 'Fliers' on the office wall, showing Clay and Tom with a reward of $500 on each. But I pretended not to notice them — until the good major offered me twenty dollars in confederate scrip by way of reward, telling me once again what a good fellow I was.

He hesitated as he saw my knowing grin and his handshake slowed a little.

'Something wrong, my good fellow?' he asked, glancing at the posters and back to my big grin.

'Why suh, I reckon you must'a misread the poster, is all, Major, them figures does surely read $500 each, just as surely as I used to be a top sergeant in the Glorious Ninth.'

Well, he coughed and spluttered some, but in the end, he said as how his eyes weren't too good these days. He opened the safe that stood in the corner of the room and shelled out a thousand dollars, at the same time gabbling on about how the Ninth was a regiment to be real proud of — just to cover his embarrassment — which fooled neither Toby nor me.

Still smiling, I thanked him most kindly and pocketed the money, collected the packs and strolled out. It was easy to smile; I had about as much coin as I could carry. More than I ever expected to own in my whole life: plus one rifle, two side arms and holsters, the Le Mat and a pepperbox, two broncs and all their gear. Man! This here bounty hunting was one profitable business and no mistake, and I still couldn't help grinning at the thought of old Toby and all that stale fox shit. What with one thing and another, it kind'a made my day.

I sold one horse and all its gear but kept the other one for Lily. The side-arms and rifle fetched next to nothing; seemed like everyone was selling off their ex-army pistols and rifles in exchange for food. I didn't get rid of the little pepperbox or the Le Mat. A man could never tell when a hideout gun, or a hard-hitting gun like the Le Mat, which carried nine .44 shots for the upper barrel, and a powerful smooth-bore firing a .60 gauge shotgun charge in the lower one, might come in handy.

The coin was on the heavy side so I stopped off at the new bank; a raw timber building built on the foundations of the old one, and exchanged most of the coin for Union paper money. I didn't take up the teller's kind offer to look after my money, although he tried to tell me how safe it would be. After all, Clay and Tom had already stolen their money once, so all in all I felt it would be safer with me, in a body belt I'd bought at the mercantile.

Then I was sidetracked for an hour by the most wonderful smell of meat cooking. Man! That was the biggest steak I'd ever seen in my whole life, and cooked so rare, it was just as likely to get off the plate and go back to grazing, if I hadn't kept it pinned down real good with my fork. Apple pie followed, and three cups of coffee, so strong a man could float a horseshoe on it, and a cigar to finish settled the whole thing down just fine.

Time I left, there wasn't a corner in me that wasn't filled to overflowing. My two horses were at the stables, also getting outside of a bag of oats and grain. The liveryman had orders to give 'em the best of everything, and a good currying to boot, while I wandered around what was left of Atlanta, asking questions about Lily.

Time I'd found her latest employer it was getting on towards sundown, and my 'good to be alive' feelings stopped right there. At first, the lady of the house refused to talk to me. It was one of the few houses that had not been burned to the ground and I was at the 'Tradesman's entrance'. The tearful black maid told me that a white man had called only yesterday asking for Lily, and that after a short conversation with the man, she had slipped on a light coat and walked down the road with him. Lily hadn't been seen since and Mistress Caroline was very angry about it.

Well, she wasn't the only one who was

angry; I had my dander up too, so I told the maid to tell her ladyship that I wanted to see her, or her man, right now! Maybe it was a bit high-handed, but it got me into the elegant sitting room, where her mistress was taking tea.

The woman stared at me for a few moments, letting me know without speaking, how dirty, and probably how smelly, I was, although it was not more than a couple of months or so since I'd had a bath. Maybe sleeping in stables or under the stars didn't help too much, but I'd had a real good face-wash only yesterday. Come to think of it, those cadavers had been smelling a bit on the ripe side, so pr'aps that didn't help any.

The tiny white nose twitched. 'Who did you say you were, er, young man?' She turned her head away and coughed politely as I moved closer to her, so I figured maybe she had a head cold.

'Joshua D, Ma'am, ex sergeant of the Ninth, and I'm looking for Miss Lily.'

She waved a little fan in front of her face; she seemed to have some trouble breathing, but I didn't figure it was that hot, so maybe it was the head cold. She coughed again. 'Why do you want to find Miss Lily?'

'Figure to take her away with me, Ma'am. Get married, buy a quarter section of land,

and do some farming.'

'Really? How nice! But you've come too late! A man came by only yesterday and Lily went off with him. Most inconsiderate of her I must say, servants are becoming much too independent these days, and I have so many things to do you see.'

'Can you give me some idea of what the man looked like, Ma'am? I asked your maid but she said all white people look the same to her.'

'What utter nonsense!' Mistress Caroline jumped to her feet in anger and stamped a tiny foot, making me jump back a pace just to keep out of her way. My sudden movement seemed to make her come over all faint again, because she waggled her fan so fast it set up a right old draft.

'Ridiculous girl,' she muttered. 'It's only black people who all look the same.' Then she seemed to remember I was still waiting. 'I didn't see him myself of course, but I do believe his name was McBain, or MacBade. Something like that; anyway, he claimed he was a friend, and that someone wanted to see her most urgently.'

I was already making for the door. 'Thank you most kindly Ma'am, but if the man's name was McBain I have to leave at once.'

'Oh, please do!' she replied, waving the fan

like air was going out of fashion or something; and when I took my last glance at her, as I shot out of the door, she was stretched out in her chair in what looked like a dead faint. So maybe the head cold was worse than I figured, but I had no time to stop and help. My big concern was for Lily.

Once outside, I headed for the livery stable and saddled up. The stable boy told me that a man answering my description of McBain had purchased a closed carriage from his boss and had tied a Palomino horse behind it. This at least gave me something definite to look for. It also gave me a chance of overtaking him, because a carriage could not travel as fast as a horseman with a re-mount. There weren't many ways a man could go in a carriage either. He would have to stick to main trails in or out of the city, so although darkness had closed in, the big old moon gave me plenty of light to ride around asking questions; and by the time I was ready to bed down, I'd covered most of the possibilities. Camping under the stars with a good cigar really helped my thinking. Whatever was happening to Lily right now was something I could do nothing about, so I had to plan carefully and get it right first time.

As usual, I was up at first light. After a quick breakfast I hit the saddle and began checking on the trails in and out of Atlanta, and although it was early there were plenty of folk astir; so I made it a point to question any wagon entering the city, and I finally got lucky. A Palomino is a distinctive horse, and one wagoner, bringing supplies from Columbus to Atlanta, remembered seeing one tied to the rear of a carriage heading towards La Grange.

'Seen it just yesterday,' grunted the wagoner, 'didn't seem to be in any hurry, right high-steppin' little team he had there. They were noonin' about ten miles back, last I saw of 'em.'

It had to be McBain! I thanked the man and offered him one of my remaining silver dollars for the information, but he just waved it away.

'Nice to have a jaw for a while,' was the way he put it, so I thanked him a second time and set Aggie on the trail, using that real long lope of his. The horse I was towing was a good, stout-chested roan mare. Maybe, if Lily was agreeable about farming, we could put Aggie and the roan together; they should produce some real good foals, if I was any judge.

I couldn't allow my mind to dwell on what was happening to Lily, so I tried to think of other things, and after a while my mind ranged back to Jesse Turnball. He must have been released from prison by this time. And while I'd been asking around in Atlanta about Lily, I'd also tried to find out about Jesse, but apart from the church that had been turned into a kind of barracks and law office, there was no place strong enough to have been used as a prison. So I figured that the most likely place Jesse would have been kept was Columbus.

The city had still been in the fight, even after Lee's surrender at Appomattox: Columbus was some forty or so miles beyond La Grange, set on the Chattahoochee river, according to the hand drawn maps Jesse Turnball had given me all that long time ago.

The city had been a Confederate stronghold in the war, with a big military force, amongst other things like making gunboats and such, so it seemed to make sense to me that if there was any news of Jesse at all, that's where I'd find it. After two hours of hard riding I swapped saddles and pushed on again. I was expecting to see the carriage in the distance, because we were covering the ground at a real fast lick. Mid-day came and went but still there was nothing out there.

I didn't bother to look for wheel tracks; the amount of traffic travelling the area had made the ground so hard that even looking was a waste of time, so I just had to make a guess and follow it through. Around mid-afternoon, a Conestoga towed by four powerful horses showed on the skyline, so maybe this was the good luck I'd been looking for.

By the time I'd reached it, the wagoner and his helper were preparing for their sun-downing. I called cautiously from the trail. And my 'Hello the camp,' was greeted with the snicking of rifles being cocked.

'Ride in slow and easy, hands behind the head,' one of the men called. 'Don't make any sudden moves now, 'cos we've got itchy trigger fingers.'

'Two hosses, one man,' I called back, 'don't get spooky on me fellas, some answers to a few questions is all I crave.'

Easing into the camp real slow I stayed in the saddle for what seemed a long time, before an old-timer sporting a spade beard, baggy pants and a leather bushman's jacket stepped out of the shadow of the wagon.

'Step down, mister,' he invited in a quivery voice, which was pitched kind'a high for a man. 'Sure sorry iffen we seem to be a mite careful, but there's many a hombre who'd like to invite themselves to these supplies, y'understand.'

'I'll just bet there are, mister,' I replied, dismounting. 'Name's Joshua D. Ex sergeant of the Ninth, pleased to meet you gents.'

'Union, huh?' This voice came from the deep shadows. 'Few months ago, y'all was the enemy, now we'm supposed to shake hands and be friends. That it?'

'Seems like.' My voice stayed even.

The man stepped into view and stuck out his hand. 'That goes for me. Can't think why the hell we had to go and shoot each other all to pieces in the first place. Was you a slave?'

The comment didn't have any malice in it and the handshake was firm, so I replied with a short 'Yep, was is right.'

'I kin see how that would rile a man. My handle's Wes and that's Virgil. Could y'all eat a bite of supper, Josh? You don't mind me callin' you Josh, huh?'

'Josh suits just fine, Wes, an' I'll be pleased to join y'all at the fire.'

The niceties were over, and before long the rich smell of Arbuckle filled the air; and, during a welcome supper of boiled sowbelly and vegetables, I told the two men about my search for the carriage.

At first, they shook their heads and I felt my spirits take a dive, like maybe I was on the wrong trail altogether. If they'd come all the way from Columbus and hadn't spotted the carriage, it must have turned off somewhere.

Then Virgil slapped his leg. 'We ain't

thinkin' straight, Wes. Remember we saw that one rider, an' what we thought was another fella all bundled up on that second hoss? I disremember who was ridin' what, but one of them hosses was a Palomino. D'you reckon they could have gotten rid of the carriage?'

'Like dumped it somewhere you mean?' asked Wes. 'Why would they dump a good carriage, and where? We'd have seen it.'

'Ne'mind where,' replied Virgil. 'There's plenty of small coulees a short ways off the main trail, and they'd move a lot faster on horseback. Yeah, I reckon that's what they did right enough. Two hosses, an' one a Palomino, is too big a coincidence, it's got to be them.' Virgil slapped his leg again in his excitement. 'You're on the right trail, Josh old son. Reckon they ain't too far ahead of you neither.'

I climbed to my feet and wiped my greasy hands on my pants-leg before shaking hands with the two men. 'Thank y'all most kindly for the supper, men, and I'm sorry to run out on you like this, but y'all understand, I just gotta ketch that jasper as soon as maybe, so I'll be riding through the night.'

Wes and Virgil urged me on; I had a feeling that, if they did not have the load of provisions to deliver, they'd have come with me. I learned something else also, that I had the natural ability to drop back into my old way of speaking when I needed to. It helped me to fit in with my companions; I'd had enough of being shown up in the past myself, so I sure didn't intend to make others feel out of place.

The moon was high and clear in the sky as I rejoined the trail and pushed Aggie into his usual lope. There was a fear in me that I might pass 'em in the night. But the urgency in my gut was pushing me on. The wagoners had told me that La Grange was a fairly small township, so finding McBain there might not be too difficult. But if he managed to get Lily to Columbus, it would be like trying to find a lone flea on a cow's back with my eyes closed. So to my way of figuring, it would be better to pass McBain on the road to La Grange and have to ride back over the trail. At least he would be out in the open so that I could deal with him.

★   ★   ★

My mind began to think of what McBain was doing to Lily all this time. I tried to blot it out by telling myself that McBain would get no satisfaction from hurting her unless I knew about it. He wanted to make me grovel in the dirt and he knew I'd be along, so I reckoned he'd be saving his pleasures until he had me hog-tied; it would really make his day to watch me squirm. This was my one hope. If I lost my head and made one mistake, he'd have me. McBain was a crafty, twisted snake, and I'd better be remembering it.

27

I was stiff, saddle sore by the time I rode into La Grange, and although it was early, the town was bustling. It seemed that every town I'd passed through was determined to get back to normal as soon as possible. There were plenty of ex-soldiers about; many still in the uniform of their choice, but although the town was in Georgia, the heart of the Confederacy, there were still more blue uniforms than gray around. The barber's hitching rail was a welcome sight; not that I needed a haircut but a good bath would be welcome just to lay the dust. It was also the best place to get information and the men who filled the tubs with hot water were usually the same color as me, so conversation would be easy.

A long soak helped to take the kinks out of my body, and time I'd finished, the water looked dirt brown, so maybe it hadn't been a head cold that had bothered that genteel white lady back in Atlanta after all.

The silver dollar I slipped to the water carrier made his eyes pop, and he just couldn't do enough to help me, but in the end I had to admit that the information was not what I wanted to hear. Fact was, he just couldn't remember the last Palomino he'd seen in La Grange. That left me with three choices. Either McBain had decided to by-pass La Grange altogether, and was heading for Columbus, or he hadn't gotten this far yet. So should I go forward or back? Or should I stay put for a while and hope McBain rode into the township? There was an easy feeling about the town, so I took my jaded mounts to the livery and ordered a good feed and rub down for them, while I fed my own face and re-stocked with supplies.

Having spent most of the day buying my goods, and asking questions about the Palomino and the riders without finding out anything worthwhile, I decided to spend the night in the stable with my horses. Maybe this wasn't such a good idea, seeing as how I'd had a bath and all, but what the hell! The stables were cheaper, and in spite of the war, white folks still weren't too keen on allowing blacks, or people of any other color for that matter, into their hotels. I reckon they thought the black would rub off or something, and here was I, as shining and clean as I'd ever been. It sure made a body wonder what happened to their brains.

At first light I was up and ready for the day.

I'd packed breakfast away long before the sun crept over the horizon, paid my livery bill, and was single-footing out of town, but I still hadn't made up my mind which way to jump.

La Grange seemed to be a stopping-over place for wagons carrying supplies from Columbus to Atlanta and points North. The burning policy the Union Army had carried out, and the confiscation of all foodstuffs for the troops, meant that there was a real shortage of goods everywhere. So, I spent some time with the wagons that had arrived overnight, asking the drivers if they'd seen anything of the two people I wanted to find; but I didn't get any luck from my inquiries, so it must mean that they hadn't gotten as far as La Grange.

I lit a cigar and stared over my back-trail, not knowing what to do for best. My task was damn near impossible; they could have turned off the trail anywhere if they had gotten rid of the carriage. My mind picked over the things I knew. There was nowhere between La Grange and where I'd camped with the two wagoners that would allow a carriage to leave the trail, except to run into a coulee; maybe for an overnight stay, or to dump the carriage. If it was for an overnight stay, then I'd meet them on my back-trail; if not, then I'd have to search every likely draw and coulee between here and where I'd met up with Virgil and Wes. It was one helluva task, but there was no other way. I was pretty certain that if McBain and Lily had been on the trail to Columbus, one of the wagoners would have seen them.

My cigar had burned to a stub. Grinding it out on my boot-heel, I gigged Aggie into action, and as I rode steadily away from La Grange, I checked over my guns. The Le Mat was in another holster on my left side, tied down good and tight, and the gutting knife was snugged down in the top of my new boots.

I'd changed my duds too. My uniform had been just about worn out, so I'd kitted myself out with a good heavy pair of levies and a bush jacket, a knee length duster coat and some new underwear. The pepperbox was in the bottom of one of the pockets of the duster, loaded and ready for use. I still had my Stetson, which was presently tilted over my eyes. At least Southerners wouldn't be staring at what they thought of as 'the hated uniform'. To them, being a black man was bad enough; the uniform only added fuel to the fire in their bellies.

Don't misunderstand me! I'm proud of being black, and I weren't no way ashamed of being a Union Soldier neither; fact is, I could do without the bother, so the less I was noticed the better. My one ambition was to find Lily and settle down on a small farm of my own. It didn't seem much to ask, and there was more money in my poke than I ever thought to see in the whole of my life. All I needed was Lily, and that quarter section of land; it seemed so close somehow, yet so far away.

The farther I rode from La Grange, the more certain I became that McBain had dumped the carriage, and had ridden off into the hills. The slow plod and search was getting to me, as I rode into box canyons, arroyos and coulees without success. The trouble was, they could have turned off on either side of the trail. The task looked hopeless, until I decided to stay on the main trail and look for any slight indentations in the soft soil on either side. The wind would have filled the marks in some, but hoof-marks would take just that little bit longer to be wiped out.

It was well past noon when I spotted a deep rut where a wheel had cut heavily into the soft soil as it pulled off the trail. Dismounting, I crouched over the mark, studying it for a long while. It wasn't deep, or wide enough for a heavy wagon. I moved forward like a hound dog on the scent of a bear, towing my two mounts behind me.

There didn't seem any place up ahead where a wagon could be hidden, just a few dips and humps in the ground, and if I'd been riding along at even a slow trot, I'd have missed the sign. McBain had done the same thing I'd done, the day my daddy had died. He'd driven the carriage behind a small hummock, and busted it to pieces.

I stared at the mess, a glow of excitement in me. Here in the shadow of the hummocks where the wind hadn't reached, the marks were clear to see. The marks of a woman's shoe, together with the heavier mark of an army boot where he'd hustled her to a horse. It meant that Lily was still alive. My thoughts about McBain wanting me to watch her pain seemed to be about right . . . unless he'd already satisfied his lust. The hoof-marks in the soil were partly filled, but not difficult to follow. I reckoned that in another few hours they'd have been wiped out, so at a reasonable guess I must be about four hours behind them.

Mounting up, I set as fast a pace as possible along the line of the tracks. They soon began to make a large curve. If they kept going in the same arc, they'd soon be heading to pass La Grange on the Southern side, making for either Columbus or Phoenix City. Maybe McBain was figuring that it would be better to hide out there than in Columbus itself.

The tracks were gradually becoming clearer as I rode, and by nightfall, there was hardly any loose soil in the tracks at all. My spirits lifted as I saw one set of tracks where the soil was still settling, it meant that I was getting real close.

Dismounting I began to follow on foot, but as the night closed in the tracks became more and more difficult to see, and twice I lost them completely. The moon was in its last quarter, so following them at night was out of the question. There was nothing else for it; I had to make a cold camp on the tracks. If a wind picked up in the night, they would be wiped out by morning.

Ground-hobbling the horses I settled back on my saddle; dragging the duster coat around me to keep out the night's chill, I lit a cigar and tried to calm my impatience with the smoke. It didn't work. My mind was thinking of all the things that could be happening to Lily, and my blood was running hot and cold in turns, as one thought chased another through my brain. I dassent try blundering about in the darkness in case they were close, yet a part of me wanted to be up and doing. Something. Anything! To take my mind off what might be happening. To stop my brain from churning, cavorting every which-way. Some time during the hours of darkness, sleep claimed me with dreams, restless and worrying; but in what seemed like moments I had forced myself into wakefulness, cursing myself for allowing sleep to claim me even for a moment while Lily was in trouble.

The night was still as black as the inside of a barn but it was the kind of blackness that warns country folk that dawn is not far away. I fished for a cigar, but the filthy taste in my mouth made me change my mind. I rummaged in my pack, and began to chew on a wedge of sourdough, washing it down with some two-day-old water. It would have been better with some Arbuckle to flavor it, but I'd managed on a lot less in my time.

As soon as the surrounding countryside began to take shape I was up and searching. The slight overnight wind had been kind to me: the tracks were still there, partly filled with dust, but easy to read, even from the back of a horse, so I saddled up and rode on. The trail was easy to follow; McBain had not tried to hide his tracks, so I could only suppose he considered that he'd done enough to confuse me. McBain knew I'd be along and he didn't want to lose me altogether. Just to delay me enough to get me mad, so's I'd make that one mistake. I lost the trail once; a herd of cattle had been driven across it, but by this time I was sure that he was heading for Phoenix City, rather than Columbus, so I cut straight across the cow tracks, and McBain's tracks were right there on the other side. Clear as could be.

Phoenix City was on the West Bank of the Chattahoochee River, opposite Columbus, so it made sense to go there first. He could always cross the bridge into Columbus if he wanted to lose himself, but he wouldn't want to do that until he'd had his fun time with me, and my woman If I had my man figured right, he'd want me to know where he was. So's he could lead me into a trap with Lily as the bait; but maybe, just maybe, he didn't know how close I was. Perhaps McBain was being just a little bit too clever for his own good. He'd always been one jump ahead of me in the past, so maybe it was my turn.

I stuck a cigar into the corner of my mouth, flicked a stinker into flame with my thumbnail and held the flame to the cigar, sucking in huge gulps of the fresh smoke. The harsh bite of the smoke felt good, it helped me to concentrate on what lay ahead. There was always one advantage McBain had; he was white, so if I caused any kind of trouble in the city I would come off second best. On the other hand, he couldn't stay in a crowded place too long. If Lily started to kick up ructions, being black would make no difference. Most men would help a female against a man.

My mind kept whirling around in circles, thinking and planning, hoping I was guessing right, and if that was so, I had some time to spare. I reined in close to a small stand of timber, lit a fire and set the skillet to cooking. The coffeepot was soon simmering in the hot coals and the welcome smell of Arbuckle lifted around me as I dropped a decent handful of coffee grounds into the water. A few slices of ham dropped into the pan, together with some beans and a few eggs, started my taste buds working overtime. Man! Did that taste good! But even while I was enjoying my meal, the plans and schemes were still spinning through my mind.

Three cups of Java later, with another of my cigars burning nicely, I pulled the hand-drawn maps out of my pocket. They were wrapped in an oilcloth, but they were looking the worse for wear by this time. Spreading them out on the floor, I traced my progress as far as Phoenix City.

By some sort of accident, I was heading straight down towards the Conecuh River, and the letter I'd promised to deliver for

Amos York all that time ago was with the maps. I took it out and read it a second time, Mistress Abigail was one poor unfortunate woman, and reading the letter left me feeling down somehow, so I went back to the maps. There was only a few small settlements between Phoenix and Mobile, with the Conecuh River flowing from the direction of Columbus towards Mobile, and maybe into the sea for all I knew. One thing was for sure, the York's farmstead would be ahead of me somewhere, and this was just the kind of area where McBain would want to take me if he could. So I'd give Phoenix a miss and make for the York farmstead in easy stages; maybe I'd steal the march on McBain at last.

I approached the Conecuh, close to a settlement called Troy, and rode about fifteen miles following the river toward Mobile; Troy wasn't on my maps, but Mobile was. It was the place I'd intended heading for, after I'd told Mistress Abigail York about her husband, but this was not something I was looking forward to. No sir! Which means that getting there was not so all fired urgent. So, I followed the meanderings of the river, stopping for a bite to eat at regular eating times, always watching my back-trail.

It was a sure bet that McBain was not too far behind me, but I was satisfied that Lily would not come to any harm. So, if possible, I'd like to get to the York farmstead and settle that business, so's I'd have a clear mind, when I met up with McBain. The man had haunted me for over three years and I intended to finish it right here.

On the third day I saw the farm, sitting close to the river in a little dell, which meant that the Yorks would have good water for the house without going too far for it. The fields were neat and tidy. If Mistress Abigail was the only one looking after the place then she was doing a real smart job of it, but what I had to do now might destroy her. I shrugged my shoulders, and rubbed a hand over the four-day-old beard. Guess I would look kind'a frightening to some little lady on her own, but there was no easy way to do this, so I'd best get it done.

The narrow dirt road led straight to the front door. A wisp of smoke was curling out of the stone chimney and although it was late in the year, flowers were growing in a wide border around the house, which was glistening in a new coat of whitewash. It sure was a place to be proud of, with neat laid out lawns and a long wire pen to one side, where chickens were clucking and scratching away, looking for bugs and such. Three barns were a short space from the house, and they also looked well cared for. Yes sir! It sure looked peaceful. For now!

Just for a second there was a flash of white in the doorway, and then it was gone. Almost as if I'd imagined it. I reined in at the stoop and started to swing my leg over, ready to dismount. There was a heavy double snick of a cocking rifle and I eased myself back into the saddle. Putting both my hands on the pommel, I waited.

'You want something mister?' It was a woman's voice but it didn't sound scared; fact is, I was more scared than she was, when I saw the hexagon shape of a Sharps .50 caliber Buffalo rifle-barrel poking around the door post. Man! This lady meant business. A hit from that thing, this close, would carry me fifty feet back up the path.

Managing to drag up some spit from somewhere, I swallowed, to ease the lump in my throat. 'Would y'all be Mistress Abigail York, Ma'am?'

'I would! What would you be wanting with me, young fella?'

'Rode a long ways to meet you, Ma'am, carrying a message from your husband; just like I promised him, the day he fell in battle.'

There was a quick intake of breath and the barrel of the rifle dropped a little. I'd figured that it was best to let her know her man was dead right off; maybe it was kind'a brutal, but there was no easy way.

'You said, 'When he fell'. Does that mean . . . ?'

She let the question hang there between us like a wall.

'Yes Ma'am it surely does.' My voice was low and sad for what I had to tell her.

'How do I know what you say is true, mister?'

I could hear the sob in her voice, although she tried real hard to hide it.

'The name's Joshua, Ma'am. Joshua D. I have some letters from him to give to you, but I'd be pleased iffen you'd point that rifle someplace else. Lady! You are just about scaring the shi– hell out of me with that thing.' I'd just about managed to change my manner of speech in time, or I thought so anyway, until she barked like a sergeant major. 'There's no need to blaspheme, Mister Joshua! I'd be obliged to read this letter, so please step down and come into my home if you will sir. But don't be touching those guns of yours. I don't want to have to shoot you, but I will if it's needed.'

And she would too! The tone of her voice said so, and I didn't doubt it for one cotton-picking minute.

I eased gratefully out of the saddle, tying

Aggie and the roan mare to the small hitching post, before stretching and bending my legs to ease out the kinks and stumping up to the doorway.

That big old Sharps poking into my brisket was turning my blood to lamp oil, but when I tried to ease it out of my way it didn't budge.

'Like y'all to take them guns out, one at a time, and put 'em on the floor, if you please, Mister Joshua,' she murmured; the sob was still in her voice but she wasn't about to give an inch.

'D'you mean before I come in, or after, Ma'am?'

'Iffen y'all don't do it before, there won't be any after . . . if you get my drift,' she replied.

I slid the pistols out real slow, and placed 'em on the stoop; I sure didn't want to give her any wrong ideas. No sir! But once I'd gotten rid of my pistols she seemed to lighten up a little, and my breath eased out in a sigh of relief as she took the rifle out of my breadbasket and put it in the corner of the room.

When my eyes managed to get used to the gloom I was shocked to see how tiny Mistress Abigail was, I'd take a bet she didn't weigh more than a hundred pounds soaking wet. How the hell she'd managed to lift that hulking great Sharps was a mystery. Neat and tidy as a new pin, Mistress Abigail was, with her arms folded across her breasts and with her graying head tilted to one side, like an inquisitive bird; she waited for me to do the talking.

When I just stared, the little lady decided she just couldn't wait any longer.

'You said you had a letter for me from my man. That the truth, Mister Joshua?'

'Yes-um,' I replied, 'but it ain't good news, and that's a pure fact.'

She waited patiently while I fished the roll of maps from the inside of my coat and unrolled them. The bundle of papers was inside, and I handed the pile to her without saying a thing.

Mistress Abigail was trembling so bad that she could hardly stand. So I put my hand under her elbow and helped her to the rocker, close to the fire, and when she was comfortable I told her, kind'a quiet like, that I'd be outside if she needed me, and backed off. This was her time to be alone with her man, aye and her boy too. She didn't need an outsider to witness her grief, so I tiptoed away, collecting my guns from the stoop as I passed.

The peaceful scene of chickens scraping for grubs, and my two horses standing, hip-shot, in the hot sunshine, could not tell the story of what was going on in that neat little house, as Mistress Abigail was reading her man's last words. Life was a bitch, I thought roughly, as I bit the end off of a cigar and lit it with a stinker struck on the seat of my pants, and felt the harsh but soothing bite of the smoke on my throat and lungs as I sucked it deep, trying to focus my mind on Lily and that damned madman McBain; if my calculations were correct I'd be expecting them to be coming this way in a few days . . .

My ponderings were cut short by a high-pitched, keening cry from the house . . . Abigail had hit the bad bits! There was nothing I could do to ease the pain of her burden, and unless she called me, fighting it was her business. The smoke tasted sour in my guts now, so dropping the cigar to the ground, I mashed it into the dirt with my boot to ease my helpless anger.

Aggie blew softly through his nose and the roan answered him. They couldn't be bothered with other people's burdens. I strolled over to them and began fondling their ears, muttering to them, trying somehow to make the animals understand what was going on here, but knowing it was just a way to waste time until the little lady inside managed to stifle her grief. It was going to be a hard battle, but she'd make it somehow, she was that kind of woman.

An hour passed, maybe two, as my mind kept trying to sidetrack what was happening in the house, and I was still lounging on the hitching rail when the front door creaked open. There was a thought in my mind, that although Amos York had asked Abigail not to blame me for her man's death, maybe she weren't quite so understanding. That big old Sharps came to mind and my head swiveled toward the creaking door as fear bit into my stomach.

The little lady was leaning against the doorframe, her hands clasped in front of her as she tried to regain her composure. 'I'm real sorry to have kept you waiting so long, Mister Joshua,' she murmured, her voice almost breaking up under the strain. 'I'm sorry, too, that I treated you so harshly when you had traveled so far to bring me my letter.'

I pulled my Stetson from my head as I walked humbly towards her. This lady deserved all the respect I could give. 'Please Ma'am, don't be troubling yourself,' I said, as that Goddamned lump came into my throat yet again. 'I'm just so sorry to bring a fine lady, like yourself, such bad news.'

'Come in, come in,' she replied with a sad smile, 'most people would not have bothered to take such trouble.'

'But I promised him Ma'am.'

'You promised him? You mean you actually spoke to my husband? How could that be?'

I took her arm and guided her back into the house. Sitting her back in the rocker, I knelt beside it. 'Y'see Ma'am. It was like this. The battle was roaring around us and there stood your man. Right in front of me. H-he dived right on to my bayonet. There was nothing I could do! Although to be honest, we'd have done our darndest to kill each other anyway. We were on opposite sides you see.'

She patted my shoulder. It seemed silly somehow, this tiny woman patting my shoulder to stop me from worrying.

'Please Mister Joshua, don't fret so,' she said quietly. 'I understand that you were enemies, but he actually spoke to you? Could you please tell me exactly what my man said?'

'Yes'm. He asked me if I'd do my best to deliver his letters to you, asked me to read them too, so's I'd understand.'

'And you did — read them I mean?'

'Yes'm. He said to read it so I did. Was that all right?'

'Yes yes, of course it was. But did he say

anything about me, or our son? Please tell me.'

'Yes'm. He said to tell y'all how sorry he was that it had to end this way. That he loved you and your son very much, and how he knew you'd look after the farm right well, no matter what.'

Okay! So, it weren't exactly true. So, who's to know? The look on that lady's face made it worthwhile, and it's one of the good things I've done in my lousy life, so far. The other one was still to come. The day I'd marry my Lily, if we ever managed to get around to it. Goddamn! I just wish I knew her last name. I never did find out about that.

I decided to sleep in one of the barns with my two horses; it didn't seem proper to sleep in the house with a woman there on her own, although Mistress Abigail seemed at ease with the notion. Lightning flickered in the distance as I went into the barn. Then the rain began crashing on the tin roof, making so much noise that trying to talk to my horses was a waste of time . . .

28

The rain was still hammering down at dawn, when my stomach decided I'd had enough sleep for one night and it was time for me to be moving. A good mug of coffee would just about hit the spot, I thought, taking the pepperbox from my duster coat pocket and slipping it into the folds of my sleeping blanket, before rolling the blanket into a tight bundle, and tying it with its two rawhide thongs.

It didn't do to leave a loaded gun in a pocket when the coat might be hanging from a peg, where anyone could knock into it and cause it to fire. Most pocket pistols were unreliable, and a pepperbox was worse than most, so I figured that wrapped in the blanket was the best place to keep it, for the time being. Maybe Abigail was up and about, but I doubted it; the news I'd given her yesterday was enough to floor a woman twice her size.

Easing the door open against the wind and rain, I stared through the darkness towards the house. There was a light burning in the kitchen. This woman had to be made of pure steel. My stomach was complaining as usual, so I strapped the two guns around me and put on the duster coat. Then I pulled the Stetson well down, tight over my forehead, before venturing out into the wildness of the early morning. Man! Was that wild! The wind tried everything it knew to rip the coat from my body and the hat from my head; I had to lean hard into it just to make headway. What had been dust under my feet yesterday was now a morass of thick, clinging mud. Maybe I should have stayed in the barn, but my grumbling stomach had another tale to tell.

Kicking as much of the mud off my boots as possible before stepping up onto the stoop, I banged on the door with my clenched fist, so's to make Abigail hear above the din of the storm. Maybe she couldn't hear me, or perhaps it was the other way around, and she wasn't shouting loud enough for me to hear her reply, so I twisted the latch and opened the door. The light was burning bright in the kitchen so I stepped inside and eased off my muddy boots. Unlimbering my gun-belts, I placed them beside my boots and called a second time, as I padded towards the kitchen.

Maybe it was because there had been no answer to my call, or perhaps it was because my stockinged feet made very little sound on the board floor, making every other sound seem louder than usual. But a creak of a floorboard behind me set the hairs on the back of my neck tingling. I crouched and started to turn. The blow that was meant for my head skidded off my headgear and slammed into my shoulder, sending a numbing shock down the full length of my left arm. I managed to parry the second blow, taking the sting out of it with my other arm while my numb and useless left one hung at my side. McBain cursed his frustration as he swung the clubbed pistol a third time, and although I rolled desperately to get away from it, the gun bounced off my useless shoulder again, sending waves of pain clear down to my fingertips. Scrabbling away from him, and making a crouching run into the kitchen, I caught a brief glimpse of Abigail, tied to the rocking chair, with Lily beside her, also tied.

Apart from my legs, my body was useless! Even if I'd had a pistol in my hand, I would have been unable to use it. I had to get away somehow, and my mind searched for a way out of my trouble while I was still scrabbling along, with McBain cursing behind me as he tried, yet again, to club me with his pistol. The big kitchen window was in front of me! It was the only way. I charged forward and catapulted myself toward it, forcing my dead arms up to shield my face, as I crashed through in a shower of broken glass and timber, onto the wooden stoop outside, before rolling off into the mud below.

It was still dark, and McBain, blinded by the light in the kitchen, could not see me. In spite of the rain, I could hear his curses fading as he charged back toward the front door. I'd gained a little time, but that was all; he'd be out in moments.

On the heels of the thought, the front door burst open. His silhouette was outlined in the light of the doorway for a moment, before he began a mad dash towards the barns.

We both knew why! My rifle was in one of the barns! My weary body didn't want to move but it had to. Stockinged feet slapping and slipping in the cold mud, I pushed forward, but McBain had all the advantages. He could blunder along safe in the knowledge that my pistols were in the house, whereas he could start shooting at the slightest sound. Only the hammering rain was helping me, and even that had its disadvantages. Once again, Lady Luck deserted me; there were three barns, but McBain chose the right one first time. Maybe the horses had given it away. I was just yards away from the barn when the door slammed open and I heard McBain's yell of triumph telling me he'd found my rifle.

Cursing my stupidity, I began to run back

towards the farmhouse. I should have stayed there! My pistols were just inside the front door. I should have remembered, but my mind had been too scrambled.

Moments later McBain came charging out of the barn. He must have seen me framed in the light coming from the farmhouse. He fired my rifle and a buzz of displaced air warned me of how close he had come to tagging me, so I had to forget my pistols. He'd get me for sure if I stopped in the light of the doorway.

Cutting around the side of the farmhouse to put myself out of sight, I stumbled over the chopping block, damn near breaking my toes. My curses stopped. Maybe, just maybe there was some weapon here I could use. There was no axe in the chopping block so I scrabbled around in the mud for a block of wood or branch. Anything that would make me less helpless. My toe stabbed into something, making me curse with the pain of it. I felt around my foot and found the long flat blade of an old machete. The morning was lightening up a bit now, enough for me to vaguely see the blade. It was a big old blade, about 24 inches long, and though it was rusted, a touch of my thumb on the cutting edge drew blood, letting me know just how sharp it still was. The broken wooden handle didn't matter a damn, the wide metal tang that still held the remaining part of the wooden handle was plenty good enough. I had a weapon! But I'd have to get real close to use it.

A second shot slapped into the chopping block and I scrabbled away again, keeping the walls of the house between McBain and myself. I was still carrying the machete. Maybe it wasn't much of a weapon against guns, but it was better than nothing; and the rain was helping me a little, because although the day was moving along, it was almost impossible to see, even a short distance through the continuous downpour.

Another bullet chopped a piece of stone out of the farmhouse wall close to me, making me dash in a crouching run for the next corner, but this couldn't go on. McBain wasn't thinking too clearly either, but it was only a matter of time before he realized that all he had to do was to threaten to shoot Lily and Abigail, and he'd have me. I had to get my scrambled brain together before McBain started thinking things out!

My mind searched frantically for some ideas. McBain could pop up anywhere, so I had to hide. Someplace where he'd have to come close before he spotted me. The back of the house was the only place I was really safe;

McBain could watch the front and the two sides. He wouldn't leave the front unguarded; he knew I'd make a dash for my guns just inside the front door if I was given half a chance.

I'd noticed that McBain was staying on the raised stoop running along the front of the house; he was out of the rain, and by moving along the front, from one side to the other, he could watch each of the two sides in turn.

From my place at the far corner of the house, I noticed the way the hand holding the pistol slowly sneaked around the front corner, pointing towards the rear, before he poked his head around for a quick look. He knew I was back there and all he had to do was wait, but it wouldn't be long before he realized he could scoop up my guns, and use his captives to bring me in.

Waiting until he had taken his look in my direction, I ran down the side of the farmhouse, my stockinged feet hardly making a sound over the noise of the storm. There was a four by four timber post which made the corner of the building and I crouched beside it, waiting for the hand holding the pistol to come sneaking around. It seemed a long wait, and I was beginning to get edgy by the time the barrel eased around the corner, just above my head, then I swung the machete, putting as much power into the swing as my injured shoulder could manage.

McBain's scream was high-pitched and awful, like a woman's, rather than a man's bellow of pain. The hand, still holding the pistol, fell beside me as the gun exploded, and a big gob of blood that dropped from the severed hand flopped into my face. I heard my rifle clatter to the floor of the stoop as McBain gave out with another scream.

Wiping the blood from my eyes with the sleeve of my coat I charged around the corner, the machete raised, ready to take his head off if that was what I had to do. McBain was on his knees, sobbing like a baby, his right hand holding the stump of his left, attempting to stop the blood pumping from his wrist. He was wasting his time, the blood pumped anyway. I swung the machete, intending to finish what I'd started. The war had hardened me; many a good man had died through being squeamish and I wasn't about to make that mistake.

Like most bullies, McBain started begging for his life. Almost gabbling, in his desperate pleas, for something he would never even think about if it was me holding my wrist! He'd just give that insane laugh of his, and the axe would fall. He'd really enjoy doing it, too. This man had given me almost three years of trouble. He had killed his own comrades to have his way. Even one small boy I knew of, and God knows how many others had suffered his perversion.

Well, I wouldn't enjoy such a thing, but I'd do it anyway, for them! I swung the old, rusty machete with all my strength and his babbling pleas suddenly stopped . . . forever!

He'd almost had me, and I was shaking from head to foot, partly from the cold, but that wasn't all. No sir! I'd always known that one slip could be my downfall, yet I'd almost let it happen. My stomach rolled a little as I stared down at the body on the stoop; the head had rolled into the mud below, but my experiences had hardened me to such sights. My hands, face and duster coat was covered with McBain's blood, so I stepped into the pouring rain; the whole thing had been a messy business and I couldn't walk into Mistress Abigail's kitchen looking like a leftover from a slaughterhouse.

In the brief moment I'd seen the women, in my mad dash through the kitchen, I'd realized that they were both tied and gagged. They'd be wondering what the hell was going on, but it would be better for them to wait until I'd cleaned up a little, and the pouring rain soon washed most of the blood off me. My socks had no bottoms left in 'em, but hell, a man couldn't have everything. I'd beaten a madman against all the odds and I felt good about it. Maybe that was wrong, but it still felt good to me, and in my book, that's what counted.

I put one foot against the body and rolled it off the stoop, to give the rain a chance to clean it up a little. I'd bury it later, once the rain let up, but for now it could stay where it was. My feet were covered with mud and blood so I stuck them out into the rain, one after the other, until they were washed clean. It wouldn't do to march all that muck into Mistress Abigail's nice clean home.

I strapped my guns around my waist as soon as I entered the house. I'd never make the mistake of leaving them off again, and you can bet a stack on that!

The two women had been struggling to get free while McBain had been out chasing me. Lily had managed to tip her chair over and had broken it and she was about ready to get up as I walked in. Man! She flew at me like a tigress, ready to tear my eyes out. She skidded to a stop when she saw it was me, and put her hands on her hips while she inspected me.

I grinned. It was a mistake!

'Y'all think it's funny? All this trouble I bin through, is funny!'

'No Ma'am, I don't think it's funny at all!'

I told her, but the smudges of brown streaking her face and the big blob of whitewash on her nose were funny, and I had one helluva job holding back a chuckle.

'I look a mess, huh?' she asked, trying to preen in front of me.

'Now you mention it,' I murmured.

'You should talk!' she flared back at me. 'Man! Y'all look like somethin' the dog buried about six weeks ago. Why don't you be a gentleman and untie the little lady?'

'Yes'm,' I said, dutifully slipping my knife from its sheath on the gunbelt and cutting the ropes.

Abigail threw the ropes aside and jumped to her feet, her anger boiling to the surface. 'Where is that awful man, Mister Joshua? He deserves a good whipping, bursting into my home and tying up two ladies like that, and then having the gall to eat my good food into the bargain. He'll come to no good, I'll be bound.'

'He's dead, Ma'am. Out by your front stoop.'

'How did he die?' asked Lily, curiously. 'Bullet?'

'Does it matter?' I asked quietly, longing to wrap my arms around her. 'He didn't hurt you did he, Lily? I mean . . . '

'He did not!' she replied, her voice high

with anger, as if the whole thing would be impossible without her consent, and although I'd seen it happen to others I wasn't about to argue with her. Like I said, I'm not exactly stupid.

'I think it's about time we fed this man of yours,' interrupted Abigail, rolling up her sleeves. 'He's saved us both and that monster is dead, yet here we are, arguing. You do feel like some breakfast don't you, Joshua?'

'Of course he does,' scoffed Lily. 'From what I know of him he's always hungry, and who said he was my man anyway?'

'I did,' replied Abigail, with a knowing wink at me, as the pots began clattering under her busy hands.

Lily still glared at me with her hands still on her hips, so I gave her a lop-sided grin and wiped some of the whitewash off her nose with a rather dirty forefinger.

'You heard the lady,' I grinned, taking off my duster coat and dropping it on the floor. 'I'm a hero, so get me some breakfast. I rather fancy having two women waiting on me.'

I reckoned Lily was going to say something unladylike so I touched my lips and pointed at Abigail's back, shaking my head and silently tuttutting, as I sprawled into one of the kitchen chairs which were set around a well-scrubbed deal table.

Lily turned away from me without a word, but I swear there was steam coming out of her earholes. This woman of mine sure had one hell of a temper and no mistake. A hot temper must work wonders, because in next to no time at all, the smell of Arbuckle, together with fried ham and eggs, was filling the kitchen, and when I'd put that away, there was hot pancakes covered with molasses. Man! I was more than ready for the first cigar of the day after that feast.

As I smoked, I watched Lily's attempts to wash the dirt off her face before she came and sat down beside me. The anger in her had gone and she was fluttering her eyes at me in a way that made me feel real good inside. Fact was, I became so interested in what I was seeing, that the smoke went down the wrong way and damn near choked me.

'Rain's let up, Josh, d'you think you might take that cadaver off somewhere and bury it?' asked Abigail, with a sly smile.

It stopped my choking and brought me back down to earth with a bang. 'Yes'm,' I muttered, as my face started to burn and I stood up to cover the embarrassment of my thoughts, almost kicking the chair over in my hurry. My clumsiness brought a laugh from Lily, a high tinkling laugh that set my pulses racing as her long eyelashes flickered up and down over those sloe-black eyes. Make no mistake about it, she knew just what those eyes were doing to me and so did Abigail, so I made my excuses and ducked out of there real smart. I knew when the dice was loaded against me.

The rain had gone and the sky was as blue as could be, but the mud was still thick on the ground. There were some digging tools in one of the barns where the Palomino and the Bay mare were tied. It was a different barn to the one I'd used, which explained why McBain had not discovered me when they arrived.

Abigail had already told me that McBain and Lily had arrived at the height of the storm, which was why she'd let them in. 'Soaked to the skin,' she'd said, and because there was a woman present she'd let her guard down, but, by sheer luck, she hadn't mentioned me being in one of the barns.

I saddled the Palomino, collected the tools, and rode back to where McBain was lying. Flipping the coiled lariat I'd found on the saddle, around McBain's feet, I tied the other end to the pommel ready to drag the cadaver away but Abigail didn't seem to like my method of toting the body.

'Couldn't you just lift it on to a horse, Josh? It looks so undignified, towing him like that,' she said, a bit shyly.

'He don't know and I don't care, Ma'am,' I replied gruffly. 'He never was any good and he died the way he lived. Wouldn't even bury him iffen I had my way, but I won't leave him above ground to bring the carrion to your door.'

Abigail visibly winced as I picked up McBain's head by his thinning hair and pushed it between the dead man's legs, to keep it in place while I towed him away.

'You're a hard man Joshua D,' Abigail murmured, as I collected the tools, mounted and turned the horse towards the fields.

'You have to be with people like McBain, Ma'am,' I replied, kicking the Palomino into motion. 'This won't take long.'

I noticed that Lily didn't come out onto the stoop, but I could see her peering past the chintz curtains. It surprised me that she was so squeamish, but maybe it was a good thing. Lily was young, maybe three or so years younger than me, so it would be good if she didn't have to see the things I'd seen in my short life. Like I said, the burying didn't take long because I didn't dig very deep, just enough to keep the varmints away. Then I lit one of my few remaining cigars, mounted, and ambled back towards the farm.

Things were gradually coming together, I

thought with quiet satisfaction, the warmth of the sun and the slow pace giving me a dreamy feeling of peace. Until now, my life had seemed to be travelling in a full circle. The frantic run from my home near Winston, and Salem, in North Carolina, and clear up to the Virginia Borders around Parkesburg, a city at the mouth of the Little Kanawha river, where Mister Jesse did some of his spying stuff; across the bottom of Ohio, and through Kentucky to Nashville.

The names flitted through my memory. Chattanooga: Chickamauga: Atlanta and Savannah: Columbia in South Carolina, and back to where I started. Then clear up to Richmond, but it hadn't ended there. Somewhere along the line I learned to speak decent American. Found myself a lovely girl, and traveled all the way back again, until I passed Atlanta for the second time; a second circle, but from there to the Conecuh I'd broken away from the circles, and from here on I had to find my own way. No more hand drawn maps, like those kindly given to me by Mister Jesse. I was breaking new ground at last. There was a long haul in front of me and I didn't rightly know just where I'd end up. But one thing was for sure. I wanted my quarter section of land and I wanted Lily. Goddamn! But I'd have to ask that woman her other name. If a woman's gonna have a man's children he had to know her last name, didn't he?

The two women were waiting for me on the stoop as I dismounted. It was easy to see that they'd both washed and scrubbed all the dirt off themselves, and changed their clothes to boot, though where Lily managed to find different clothes was a mystery to me.

The stoop had been scrubbed clean of blood also. It looked so white I thought that perhaps I should take off my boots, just to step on it. 'Well now, ladies,' I grinned, 'y'all look so pretty and clean, it kind'a makes me wonder how the he- hum, you managed it.' I'd already seen that frown on Abigail's face, so I managed to change my manner of speech just in time.

'You take him out to the shower box and show him how it's done, Lily,' Abigail replied with a kind'a crafty grin. 'I'll get the coffee pot simmering.'

'Yeah. Right, Abigail,' Lily said, a mischievous grin on her face. She crooked her finger at me. 'Follow me, Joshua D,' she murmured. 'It's clean-up time for you also.' So I followed her — which maybe wasn't quite sensible — and Lily led me to this tall, square box with a small door in it, and a set of wooden steps at the side, with a big platform near the top

'In you go,' Lily told me, with a little laugh. 'Pass me out those filthy clothes through the little hatch on the side and get soaped up. You're having a bath, Josh. I've already fetched the clean duds from your saddlebags.'

I started to argue. It was a waste of time. Before I was aware of what was happening she'd bundled me into this box thing and dropped the bar latch on the outside.

Inside there was a big square tin tray, about a foot deep, filled with hot water and a big bar of lye soap on one of the ledges.

Well, this was fine by me. I stepped in and began soaping up, but twelve inches of water was hardly enough to soak myself in. Okay for those little females, I thought, but this water was going to be like mud before I'd finished.

A shadow fell across me from above. Startled, I looked up in time to see Lily's laughing face staring down at my nakedness. I opened my mouth to shout . . . in time to receive a big pail of ice-cold water. Man! No wonder there weren't much water in the pan. My yell damn near drowned me, as more water hit me in the face. I'd just about managed to save myself by coughing and spluttering when a third and fourth pailful hit me. Cold! Man, I'd never been so God-damned cold in my whole life — well almost never — and God alone knows where my manhood went with all that ice-cold water pouring over me.

I'd just about had all I could take, when Lily shouted, 'Hey, catch!' and a big fluffy towel floated down towards me. Was I glad to see that! At least I could cover my manhood, not that there was anything to see by this time, but getting the towel must have meant that the cold water treatment had finished, thank God!

'Hey, Lily!' I shouted, 'D'you mind telling me your last name?'

'Why d'you want to know?'

'You've just seen me jay-bird naked, don't you think I'm entitled to know your last name?'

'No.'

'Is it that bad?'

'You'd only laugh.'

'Me? Why would I do such a thing, Lily?' I wanted to know even more than ever now.

'Promise you won't.'

'I promise; come on Lily, what is it, don't be shy. I won't laugh. Honest!'

'If you laugh I'll brain you . . . it's Pond.'

'POND! Lily P-POND!' I was doing my

best, I really was. 'You mean someone called you L-LILY P-P-P-POND?' I began to splutter.

'You just dare, damn you. What about yours? Joshua D. What the hell kind of name is that for a man anyway?'

My spluttering turned to a small laugh at first, but it just grew and grew. The more I thought about it, the dafter it seemed.

'Damn you Joshua D,' she screamed. 'I knew you'd laugh. I just knew! So, laugh at this! You mangy black skunk,' she howled, as she tipped another full pail of water over me, and threw the pail after it.

The damned thing fetched me a real crack over the head, but what made me madder than hell was that I was wet again, and the towel too. But I was still laughing like crazy. Well! I mean. LILY POND! If that isn't worth a good belly laugh, what is? I hadn't had such a good laugh in a coon's age but then, my life so far hadn't exactly been funny. What with one thing and another, laughing had not been my main pastime that was for sure.

It had gone quiet up there on the platform and I was beginning to feel the cold cutting into me. Calling to Lily was getting me nowhere, she was so Goddamned mad that she'd probably walked off and left me. So, I tried the door. She'd removed the bar and the door creaked on its leather hinges as I cautiously eased it open. My clothes were piled on a rock in the middle of the field. There was no sign of Lily, and believe me, I looked around very carefully before starting to run for my clothes.

The door slammed shut behind me, and I heard a high-pitched screech of laughter. Too late! I realized I should have wrapped the wet towel around me. Lily was leaning against the door, having a real good laugh at my nakedness, so I ran like hell for my clothes; and to make matters worse, Abigail came out of the farmhouse to see what all the noise was about.

Hell! Have you ever tried hopping around, naked, on one foot, trying to get into a pair of Long Johns with two women staring at you and laughing fit to bust? Long Johns ain't the easiest things to get into at the best of times, but with two women watching! Why, I was so embarrassed that I even tried to get both legs down the same Goddamned hole, which took even more time to sort out. Man! It was several days before I could look those two women square in the eye, without 'em laughing their stupid socks off, and me going as red as a black man ever could.

Believe me, women can be real cruel at times, but I vowed to get my own back on Lily one of these days. It might take a while, but I'd get there.

29

Ten days passed and I was feeling easier in my mind all the time, working around the farm, repairing the window I'd busted, and generally doing chores that were too heavy for Abigail. My horse remuda had increased to four now, with the addition of McBain's two horses. I'd offered them to Abigail, but she was afraid to keep them in case she was accused of horse stealing. Carpet-baggers didn't need much of an excuse to kick a lone woman off her farm.

Abigail hinted that we could stay right there, but I needed to have my own land, much farther away from North-South troubles. Somewhere in the deep West perhaps, where the prejudices of the war might not be so strong; and anyway, I had a feeling that Matthew would be on my trail once he discovered what had happened to his brother. Right or wrong just wouldn't come into it; he'd made that plain to me. 'Next time we'd be enemies,' he'd said, and I believed him.

Two more days slipped by before I began to get the feeling that something was wrong.

Nothing special. Just a nagging feeling that I was being watched. Someone out there was keeping an eye on me. The feeling of unease began to deepen when I found two sets of horse prints in some dried mud, on the outer rim of the North Pasture, and it had me staring over my back-trail. The prints must have been made after the big storm twelve days ago, but before the sun had dried out the ground. Yet no one had called at the farmstead, and we'd not seen anyone passing near the spread. The land was reasonably flat, so we could see a fair distance, and someone passing would have been enough of an occasion to be noticed.

That night we had another storm, a real hell-raiser. I was up at dawn as usual, but this time I didn't wait for food, not even a cup of Arbuckle. My horse was already saddled, and before the sun began to lighten the land, I was pushing Aggie towards the North Pasture at a steady lope. There was a small wooded section of about twelve acres on the extreme edge of the North Pasture, close to where I'd seen the prints, and I figured to get into cover there before anyone else was around. If there were any riders, I'd be sure to see 'em

I hadn't said anything to Abigail or Lily about my suspicions in case they started to worry. Maybe I was getting a thing about being followed by Matthew and some of his men. I'd been laughed at enough lately and I didn't figure to give those two women something else to laugh at.

Crouching in the brush close to the edge of the woods I watched and waited. A smoke would be nice, but I was fresh out of cigars. One of the reasons for hanging on at the farm was in the hope that a supply wagon would be coming through from Mobile, heading for Atlanta. Abigail had told me that she'd often managed to buy from or do a deal with, a wagoner, for supplies in exchange for livestock or cash. Well, I had two horses to trade, or I could pay cash, it made no never-mind to me either way.

I wanted to get a real stock of supplies now that Lily had agreed to come with me, because living off the land would be a hoss of a different color with a woman siding me. Bet she'd even want soap and such; a carriage too I shouldn't wonder. Maybe even a bath! Women were funny that way.

Morning wore into afternoon, but I'd seen nothing of any other riders; and searching through the stand of timber would take some doing, so I remounted and jogged back to the house. Yet the moment I rode out into the open fields, there was this feeling of being watched. D'you know the feeling? It's like an itch in the small of a man's back that he just can't scratch.

The women wanted to know where I'd been, but to my surprise they didn't laugh and poke fun when I told 'em. They just stared off towards the timbered area, just as if they could see what I couldn't.

Next day I made the same run ... and found the hoof-prints again. I knew they were the same prints because one of the shoes had a V-shaped nick in it. There'd probably been a fault in the casting and the piece had fallen out as the shoe had worn down. If it wasn't changed soon, the horse would be limping, and that could be to my advantage

Two horses didn't always mean two people, but from the depth of the imprints, I'd say that both horses were carrying riders. Was it Matthew Franklyn and one of his men? Or another two more bounty hunters, hoping to cash in on a reward? Now I was more determined than ever to move on. There were at least two men out there, maybe more, and they didn't seem to be going anywhere.

Abigail could be in real trouble if they were carpet-baggers looking for a reason to take over her farm. I could become that reason!

Waiting can get a man down, but I was prepared to wait another three days in the hope that a supply wagon would be coming by, but Abigail reckoned we could be making a mistake by hanging around. She argued that, as she had plenty of supplies, she could put together enough to last Lily and me three or four days if we were careful, and we'd be sure to meet a wagon out of Mobile in that time. Fact is, by my calculations, and by what Abigail had told me, with any luck we could be in Mobile in four days.

We decided to set off as soon as it was full dark; by making use of the four horses, we could put a lot of space between our followers and us by morning. Saying goodbye to Abigail was a tearful business for Lily. The two women had become real good friends in the short time they were together, while I was only interested in moving out as soon as possible. I'd said goodbye too often in my short life to feel anything one way or another. But looking back at the farm as we rode away made me fearful about what would happen to that tiny lonely lady. Robbed of both husband and son, by a war that was proving to be not much more than a useless waste of life, because things hadn't changed worth a damn. Not yet, anyway.

I was riding Aggie and Lily was riding the Palomino, the packs were strapped to the other two horses, and after a slow easy ride away from the farm, we picked up the pace to a long easy lope. Lily was handling her mount surprisingly well and woman-like, she noticed I was watching her.

'What's the matter, Sojer boy! Did y'all think I was gonna get on this nag the wrong way around or somethin'?'

Man! Could she be sarcastic! I just showed her my teeth in a wide smile and told her how grateful she ought to be, to have such a handsome fella looking after her, and that if she didn't watch herself I might just have to give her a good spanking. Well, I didn't listen to her reply, which was probably just as well. I might have learned a few cusswords I hadn't heard before . . . but I doubt it.

We'd traveled a long way; yet again, I felt the hair on the back of my neck lifting. Someone was out there, and in spite of our leaving after dark, we hadn't fooled 'em. Lily recognized my concern, but she kept her voice even and sarcastic as she lifted her mount into a faster pace to keep up with me. This woman was one quick learner. I'd have to find out if she could use a pistol as well as she could ride, as soon as we could spare the time.

I pointed ahead, silently urging her to go on in front of me. I passed the lead reins of the other two horses to her and began to drop back while Lily eased ahead; still back-chatting, as if she hadn't a care in the world. I pulled Aggie to a halt and slipped out of the saddle. Ground-hitching the horse I moved away from it and dropped onto my stomach, to see if anyone else was out there, outlined against the lighter shade of the skyline.

I lay close to the ground for a long time, my eyes scanning backwards and forwards. But there was nothing to see. Whoever was out there was good, very good. They'd anticipated my every move. They could even have slipped around me and be close to Lily by this time. That thought sent a cold knot of fear into my gut looking after myself was one thing, but now I had someone else to worry about, and that worry was nagging at me as the minutes dragged by. Half my mind was telling me to stay right where I was, while the other half was urging me to go racing after Lily. Lily won! I slid quickly into the saddle, feeding steel to Aggie as he stretched into a gallop.

I was sure that Lily would keep a straight course, but as the miles flew by under Aggie's racing feet the knot of worry in my gut grew and grew. Ten minutes stretched into thirty, and still there was no sign of Lily. Then I saw a lone horse, ground-hitched on a little knoll ahead. My first reaction was of relief, but it was quickly replaced by fear. Why would she put a horse out in the open like that? Skyline'd, making it easy to see? If it was a trail marker for me, it would also be a marker for the people who were following us. I dismounted on the run, expecting the sound of a shot and the tug of a bullet at any moment. This was a trap and I'd almost ridden right into it like a greenhorn kid. My worry for Lily had made me careless!

Easing myself through the grass like a snake, I worked my way slowly around the little knoll, still expecting trouble. I found nothing. The horse was munching contentedly at the grass, but was not moving around at all, and while most horses will stay ground-hitched for a short while, they soon get restless and begin to move around a little. It told me that the horse was tied to that spot. Someone had meant me to find it. Made bold by my own reasoning, I slowly eased myself erect. Almost at once, the horse turned its head to look in my direction, watching my slow approach with interest.

I heard the flat crack of a rifle; seconds after the bullet smacked into my left shoulder, it felt like the kick of a mule and the pain turned my arm numb. A following shot flipped the Stetson from my head in a very near miss; and, as I dived to the ground, I managed to stifle the cry of agony as the pain lanced through my body when my damaged shoulder hit the hard earth.

Allowing my body to roll down the slope towards Aggie without crying out was no mean task. Each time my weight pressed the injured shoulder into the ground, I felt a sickness in me and my mind tried to blanket me into darkness, but I weren't gonna let it happen. I had to keep dragging myself out of it, to control my roll down the slope, so that whoever was out there would believe they'd been lucky enough to kill me.

I hadn't fooled them! There was another sharp crack and my horse fell to the ground, like a sack of grain dropped from the side of a wagon. They'd lost sight of me in the darkness as I slid and rolled toward my horse until I was stopped by the bulk of its body. Aggie lay without moving, as dead as he'd ever be, and a part of me cursed the mindless bastards who could shoot a dumb animal for no better reason than to put me afoot, while another part of me cried for the loss of a good friend and companion.

Aggie was lying on his left side with the Henry rifle in its boot on the right. So maybe some luck was with me because at least the rifle was not jammed under Aggie's body. Pain dragged at me as I reached for the rifle and eased it out of the saddle boot, but I managed it OK, tucking the rifle under my damaged arm. I levered a cartridge into the chamber and lay beside the horse, waiting for someone to show themselves.

Even in death, Aggie was giving me one last service; protecting me from the bullets of my enemies. It was hard to explain my feelings as I lay there waiting for something to happen. Something that would show me where my enemies were. The agony in my shoulder built a useless anger in me, pinned down in one position, when everything in me was screaming for action and revenge. Yet, at the same time, hoping that my stillness and silence would tempt whoever was out there to come close enough for me to line my sights on him.

A full hour ticked off in my mind between bouts of dizziness, and I had about decided that whoever had been out there was gone, when another sharp crack had me ducking for cover. On the heels of the shot, there was a squeal of pain behind me. Twisting my head, I watched that other horse, up there on the knoll, collapse in a heap and lay without moving.

Despair struck at my gut. I was afoot for sure now. Wounded, God alone knew how badly, and come morning they'd have me out in the open, with only Aggie's body for protection. It could be only a matter of time. My stubbornness kicked in about then; I wasn't about to lay down and die so it was 'Spit or close the window time,' and I'd go down fighting, not hiding behind a dead horse. I remembered Lookout Mountain. Things had seemed impossible then, but giving up was not in me and I wasn't about to change now. Lily was out there somewhere. If Matthew was with her, I was pretty sure she wouldn't come to any real harm, but if they were bounty hunters, then the quicker I got myself out of this mess the better. Feeling sorry for myself would only keep me pinned here until a bullet cut me down, and I was getting real sick of people interfering in my life.

With this new feeling in me, I settled back and wiped out the anger, giving my buzzing head time to settle down, to search for a way out of the mess I was in, by trying to remember the area I'd ridden through and places where I could hide.

There was a small amount of food in the pack tied to my saddle, and some ammunition for the guns, tied into my bedroll. The money I'd earned was still strapped around my waist, but that wouldn't buy me a horse or food way out here. In fact, it was one of those times when all the money in the

Goddamned world wouldn't make one bit of difference to the here and now.

My shoulder was numb and the arm almost useless, so, using my good hand, I cut my pack and bedroll from the saddle and used the cords to make shoulder straps. Making the injured arm work enough to help with the tying, and slipping the loops over my shoulders, made me sweat some, but I got it done, and it left my hands and arms free to carry the rifle. It would also help me when I started to belly-crawl away from Aggie, back towards the knoll.

I wasn't looking forward to using my injured arm to crawl back across the ground I'd so recently rolled over at all, but it had to be done, so I took a deep breath, set my mind to it and started to crawl. It took a lot of effort and plenty of sweat to get back to the bottom of that little hill, but I hadn't drawn any rifle fire, so maybe my caution was worth the effort. I eased far enough around the hill so that my movements could not be seen by whoever was waiting out yonder for me with a loaded rifle. Now that the hill was protecting me, I started a crouching run towards the timberline.

We'd stayed close to the Conecuh River since leaving Abigail's farm, only cutting across country to keep in a straight line instead of following the river's meandering path, and it also kept us out of the timbered area. But half a mile or so is a long way in darkness, and I was beginning to believe that my sense of direction was out of kilter until I saw the dark shadows of the trees, outlined against the brightening sky.

Man! Was I grateful to get into the trees. I straightened up to ease my aching back. Resting was out of the question; I needed a hole to hide in real fast! It wouldn't take those fellas long to figure out my moves. So far they'd been one step ahead of me all the way, and I weren't at all sure that they hadn't already done their figuring, because whoever was in charge was one smart son-of-a-bitch, and no mistake.

My enemies had cut me down in one night from a man with four mounts, a woman, and plenty of grub, to a man afoot, wounded, desperate with worry about his woman, with little food and almost no chance at all ... 'almost!' was the word! Because I was gonna prove to one sly son-of-a-bitch that, wounded shoulder or not, he wasn't the only smart-ass around.

A volley of rifle shots cut into the trees. The smartass had done his figuring and I was about to reply, aiming at the flashes; but it only took me about three seconds to realize that they didn't know where I was hiding, and they were waiting for my shots, so that they could pin me down. I grinned in the darkness; they'd have to get smarter than that to catch me out now.

As I started moving into deep timber, it began to rain. In no time at all it was falling in torrents, and I was wishing that I still had my Stetson as I hurried toward the river, cutting deeper and deeper into the forest, looking for a hiding-place in the trees or rocky outcrops. I pushed aside a big trailing bush that was growing out of the sloping rock-face and there was my answer. A narrow cut in the rock that led into a small dry cave.

If I'd had the time, I'd have said a little prayer to the white man's God. But time was not on my side. So, dumping the gear on a ledge, I went back out into the storm to make sure there were no tell-tale footprints to give me away, before returning into the cave to sort out my wound, and to see what food I had in the saddlebags. The dizziness had left me now, so I peeled off the duster coat and jacket with considerable care. But my poking around the shoulder had only irritated the wound and it set to bleeding again. Still, it was worth the pain, because from what I could feel, there was nothing broken. So I kicked off my right boot, rolled up my pants and, using the gutting knife, I cut off the bottom half of one leg of my Long Johns.

People say Long Johns are a pesky nuisance but they sure do make a good bandage. I bound the piece of cloth tightly around the wound, over the top of my shirt, tying it off as best I could in the darkness of the cave. It began to feel better right off and I gave a grunt of satisfaction as the pain eased, helping to build my determination to fight. Pulling on the jacket gave even more padding to the wound, so I decided to sort out the supplies, while my spirits was being boosted by the easing of the pain.

The food in my saddlebags wouldn't keep a cottontail alive for long; some hardtack, molasses, salt, and a bottle of stinkers, together with three lumps of sourdough bread, and that was it. So, food was going to be a problem. There was plenty of meat on the hoof out there, but with men hunting me, catching and cooking it was going to be a hoss of a different color. One thing I was sure of. They weren't gonna beat me. Come hell or high water.

The duster coat had saved me from the worst of the storm, although it was pretty well soaked through. If I'd had my Stetson most of the storm would have missed my body, but water had been running through my hair and down my neck, soaking the long johns, clear down to my waist. I hung the duster coat over a rock outcrop, sure that it would dry within a few hours.

To take my mind off things I fished a chunk of the sourdough out of my pack, chewed like hell, and pretended I was enjoying it . . . I was a liar! My mind kept taking me back to Abigail's farm and all that good chowder. Life sure is a bitch! I thought, as my teeth ground into the sourdough.

Eventually I untied my bedroll; the blanket was wrapped in a slicker, so it had been protected from the rain. Spreading the blanket out on the smoothest part of the rocky ground, and wrapping it around myself, I tried to rest. But sleep didn't come easily; the damp chilly air and the steady throb of my shoulder did nothing to help, and all the while my mind kept churning away, wondering what was happening to Lily.

The rain was still hammering down when I awoke, so I sat there feeling like pure hell, just staring at nothing, until it was light enough to check that my weapons were in good working condition after rolling down the slope. And having done that chore, I figgered that it was time to take a look around. I'd had breakfast for supper, if you get my meaning, and I had no water to make coffee — if I'd had some coffee in the first place — if I dared to light a fire. That sure is an awful lot of 'ifs'.

Shrugging into my duster coat, which had dried out real well in the cave, I walked to the opening and eased aside the screen of bushes. There was a runnel of water gushing down the side of the rock's surface so I hurried back into the cave for my coffeepot. It was brackish but drinkable, and I couldn't afford to be choosy. There were even some bits in it that could have been termites or weevils. But like I said, I couldn't be too fussy, and it did help to fill a hole in my gut. I filled the pot a second time and carried it back into the cave. At least now I'd have some water, even if it stopped raining before I got back.

Searching through the close-packed trees and bushes was pretty much a waste of time, unless I got really lucky, but the same applied to my hunters. All I had to do was to make sure there was no sign for them to follow, which ain't quite as easy as it sounds, but Mister Jesse had taught me well when we were spying together and I hadn't forgotten a damned thing. Mid-afternoon, or thereabouts — it was difficult to tell in the misty darkness of the trees and the pouring rain — Lady Luck smiled on me in the shape of a cottontail caught in a wire snare. It was still warm when I eased the snare from around its neck. My enemies had provided me with dinner. Maybe I wouldn't be able to cook it, but a man can't be expecting everything.

I was tempted to take the snare, but that would only lead them to me, so I spread the wire open and set it in the grass. With any luck, they'd think nothing worthwhile had passed that way. It told me one thing for certain. They weren't too far away. A man didn't set snares to catch food and then move so far away they'd have a job finding the place a second time, so I spent a long time making sure that I left no sign around my small cave. Now, I knew roughly where they were, but provided I was very careful, they could not know my hideaway, and the way those bushes hung down over the opening, it sure would take some finding.

30

By the time I got back to the cave I was feeling kind'a woozy. As if the floor was about to rise up and slap me in the face. So I put the cottontail on the ground, intending to skin and clean it, once my eyes adjusted to the darkness of the cave; but just getting out of the slicker drained the last of my strength and I sank down on to the blanket with a groan of pain.

When I awoke it was full dark; one minute I was sweating like a bull on heat and then the shivering would start. The shoulder was throbbing away and the pain had worked all the way up into my neck, which was also throbbing like hell. I tried to sit up when I heard voices, but everything slipped out of kilter, and the next time my eyes opened, it was to see daylight glinting between the bushes as the slight wind kept brushing the trailing branches aside.

There was a rustling noise and something moved close to my hand. The pain had eased a little, and I managed to turn my head enough to see a large rat having a go at my cottontail. Somehow, during my sleep, my good hand had gotten tangled in the straps of the food pack. Well, no Goddamned rat was gonna pinch my cottontail! I swung the pack with all the force I could muster and caught it fair and square. It wasn't dead, but believe me, it couldn't get away fast enough, falling and tumbling over itself in its haste. Whether the pain it gave me was worth it is another matter, but at least I knew that I was able to strike back at something!

My stomach was beginning to think my throat was on furlough, and trying to stand was a waste of time also, because my legs would hardly hold me, and I had no real idea of just how long I'd been out of things. Even sitting up with my back against a boulder was quite a chore, but now I could reach my coffeepot. The water probably had more weevils and other swimming insects in it than I'd like to imagine, but food was food, so I swallowed half of it in one long gulp. It tasted like the most wonderful drink in the world, weevils and all!

The thought made me remember the molasses and the other pieces of sourdough bread in my pack. I was so weak that I could hardly open the jar of molasses, but oh Man! Was that good! And the sourdough went down a treat too. Then came the hardtack. The strength was building in me minute by minute, so when I'd eaten enough I eased my tired body back into a comfortable position and slept.

When next I opened my eyes it was full dark and I was feeling much better . . . until my worry for Lily came back. There was nothing to tell me how long I'd been out, except the smell from the cottontail. It was so high that it was about ready to fly, but I'd eaten worse, so I gutted and skinned it, which was some job in the darkness of the cave. The meat didn't smell too bad, and in the darkness a man could hardly tell whether it was cooked or not, so I just ate the legs, and probably some odd bits of fur, with my last piece of sourdough bread.

My stomach rumbled a few times when I thought about it being raw, but what the hell, animals did it all the time and they seemed to do all right. The last of the water washed it down, though by this time it was also beginning to stink a little, and the amount of wild life in it was making it kind'a soupy, so I ate some more of the molasses and that did the trick OK.

My resolve was beginning to build again. Standing was a bit of a chore to start with but my body soon settled down to what I had to do; so, throwing the remains of the cottontail into the far corner of the cave, I slipped into my duster coat. The comforting feel of the pepperbox in my right hand pocket reminded me to check my pistol and Bowie. I was leaving the Le Mat, the gutting knife, and my rifle behind, just in case I needed a fast back-up in the cave. My shoulder and arm was not giving me too much trouble, but I wouldn't be able to shoot a pistol or rifle with it, nor wield a knife neither.

I was doing what Mister Jesse always said to do. 'Travel light and travel fast. Don't carry things you don't need, they can only get in the way'. If it was good enough for him, then it would do me fine. I eased the bushes aside and stared into the darkness for a long time. The moon was still in its first quarter, and beneath the trees, it was almost black. It would be a tough chore to make sure that my footprints didn't show come daylight, but I had to take some chances.

My movements were slow and careful, checking every footstep possible, so's not to leave any prints. In my weakened state, I'd stand no chance in a fight, and I could hardly walk, much less run; only my stubborn will was keeping me going. There was a chuckle of water over stones to my right and I was longing for a decent drink. The temptation was too great to resist.

It took me a long time getting there.

435

Staying close to the ground, watching for small twigs or rotten branches that could crack with the sound of a pistol shot in the stillness of the night; and my enemies could be so close, even around the next bend in the trail I was following. Suddenly I was there, beside the smallest stream. It was only there because of the heavy rain and it would be gone by tomorrow. I crouched over the water for a long time, like a hunted animal, waiting for trouble to find me, my eyes searching the undergrowth until they were heavy with strain of it. Yet all the while, aching, longing, to bury my face in the cool water. My mouth tasted of iron from the cottontail's blood, and my lips were cracked and sore where the blood had dried on them, and my stomach kept heaving at the thoughts of my last meal.

Forgetting my injured shoulder for a moment, I eased forward, taking my weight on my hands. The pain hit me like a bolt of lightning, almost dragging a scream of pain from my sore mouth as I fell forward into the water. I lay there, gasping with the pain of it, my eyes searching frantically for any sudden movements. Nothing happened, and soon the night noises started again.

It's hard to tell about that wonderful feeling as the cold water washed over my lips and face. I rinsed my stinking mouth and spat several times, to get rid of the iron taste, before drinking my fill. It was sweet, clean and icy cold. No drink on earth could ever taste so good. I lay there enjoying the feel of it for about twenty minutes before carefully easing myself upright. I felt good, but now it was time to start hunting for my woman, because that's where my enemies would be. Holding her, coaxing me to try to get her back.

The first signs of dawn was beginning to lighten the darkness of the forest, as I made my way back to where I'd found the cottontail in the snare. It seemed sensible to start there, since I knew for sure my pursuers had already visited the place once, and they would be bound to go there again, to see if the snare had caught something. The snare was gone, but they'd not taken any trouble to cover their tracks. Either they were not worried about the chances of one lone man finding them, or perhaps they hoped I would!

My quick eye-search of the area showed three sets of boot-tracks, not just two, as I'd thought. Three men, well-provisioned, against one who was afoot and wounded must seem good odds to them, so maybe they were getting a mite careless. It would make a nice change. So far Lady Luck hadn't quite deserted me, what with the cave, the cottontail and the water, but I'd be obliged if she gave it a little more effort; like maybe getting one of 'em to break a leg, or maybe something more fatal.

My musings did not hold me back or cut down on my caution. They could afford a few mistakes. I couldn't afford one! The trail was easy to follow and told its own story. Here one of the men stumbled over a tree root, here a snare had been set and had since been removed. A stub of a cigar stamped into the soft earth set my urges going. It was something I should never have started, but my tongue flicked over my lips at the thought of a good cigar between them, while my eyes searched both sides and ahead.

An hour passed as I made my slow way through the forest, expecting at any time to hear the spiteful crack of a rifle or pistol. The noise of the birds singing high up in the trees served to cover any small noises on the forest floor, noises I needed to be able to hear. Ahead of me was a big clearing. I moved to the very edge of it, my eyes roving backwards and forwards. A huge jumble of rocks in the far corner caught my eye. There was a big slab of overhanging rock above the pile, so I slipped through the trees around the clearing; and once I got up close, I could see where the horses had stood, in a small coulee behind the rock pile, while the overhang had provided some sort of shelter from the rain for my enemies.

I could see footprints everywhere, without moving into the clearing, and it was easy to see that the men had spent some time here. My heart gave a lurch of pleasure as I noticed a small boot mark. Lily had been here, and was still able to move around! Easing past the rocks I moved into the forest again and followed the hoof-prints of five horses, four being ridden, while the fifth must have been carrying the men's gear; that hoss had thrown a shoe and was limping slightly. That damaged shoe must have finally worked loose, because none of the marks showed a shoe with a nick out of it.

It took me some time to figure out that we were moving in a big circle. They hadn't given up on me, they were just casting around looking for my spoor, because every once in a while one or the other would dismount and do some searching.

A hoof-mark, still filling with water, warned me that I was closer to them than I thought. Maybe I could take out the next one that dismounted to look for my prints in the soft soil; so, slipping deeper into the trees, I began moving faster, hoping that I could maybe pass 'em, but I didn't even get close. My shoulder had been aching for some time, a dull throb that seemed to be pounding into my skull, and in my hurry, I didn't see the small slippery hollow. My foot sank into it and threw me forward, smashing my injured shoulder into a low, but heavy, branch.

God! The pain! It felt as if somebody had shoved a red-hot poker into the bullet hole as the agony of it screamed into my brain. My mind refused to accept the pain, and I collapsed right there . . .

I seemed to be in an icy cold river. The water was washing over me, causing me to shake and tremble. My head dipped beneath the surface and I came out of my faint, choking and spluttering. It was raining, real heavy, and my face had been resting in a hollow, which was filled with water from the downpour. Choking and spluttering I lifted my head clear of the pool, which had started to drown me, and rolled to one side. It was pitch dark and I was soaked to the skin. The cold had eaten into my bones making me tremble and shake like a leaf in the wind. There were no human sounds around me, which meant that my carelessness had cost me my quarry and I was back where I'd started. It would be useless to try to find tracks in this awful weather, even if I could find the will to try.

Returning to my cave was not going to be a problem. The men had been travelling in a large circle while they were searching for me and my cave was only a short distance away. In fact, if I had stayed in my cave and waited they would most probably have passed by. Still shivering, and with my spirits in my boots, I staggered to my hiding-place and almost fell inside. Crawling to my blanket, I rolled into it and tried to sleep. Between bouts of shivering, when nothing I could do made my body warm, and other bouts of heat when the sweat poured from my body and my groans sound deep and hollow around the cave, I must have slept a little. Because when I finally roused myself, bleary-eyed and aching all over, sunlight was glinting through the bushes that guarded the cave from prying eyes, and I could hear the birds twittering and singing outside.

My shoulder was throbbing like hell, and I felt as weak as a newborn babe, but to my surprise I was still alive ... and hungry! Without being too hopeful I pulled the pack towards me and searched through it with my good hand. I found a few strips of jerky and the empty molasses jar, but that was all. It was better than nothing so I just lay there, chewed the jerky and swallowed. It was hell on the throat without a drink of water to wash it down, but it was better than thinking about the rest of that cottontail somewhere in the far corner of the cave. I knew it was still there by the smell.

Like I said, the molasses jar was empty but there was still a small amount clinging to the sides. I ran a dirty finger around the inside of the jar until it was so clean it didn't need washing. Then I lay back and rested my weary body. I was too tired and weak to wonder what I was going to do next, but one thing was for sure, I'd do something! Lily was my woman, and those men weren't about to stop me finding her. I'd walk over their dead bodies if I had to and to hell with what happened after.

Dozing off to sleep seemed to be getting a habit with me, because a woman's voice, raised in anger jerked me out of my slumbers. It was getting dark in the cave, so I guessed the day had slipped away without my knowing it. Getting to my feet was pure hell, and my shoulder had swollen so badly that the whole of my arm was one mass of pain, and the coat was as tight as a second skin.

Stifling a groan, I padded to the opening, eased aside the curtain of bushes and stared out into the early dusk. I realized that the plod of hooves fading on the trail was giving me a second chance! I snatched the Le Mat from the ledge of rock, pushed aside the bushes and began to hurry after them. I had no clear plan in mind, but my strength was running out fast and there was no food to build it up again, so I had to do something to level the odds. Now!

As I moved along, the ache in my limbs began to ease. I was holding the Le Mat in my good right hand; the hammer had already been set to fire the recessed center nipple, which would fire the big lower smoothbore, loaded with a full charge of buckshot. This time I moved with more care as I caught up with, and passed, the slow moving horses. I wanted to be as close as possible, but after firing the heavy gun I had to be able to escape.

In the short time left to me, there was no real place to hide, or time to plan. So I crouched beside the bole of a large tree and waited in the deep shadow of the forest for them to come to me. I could see from the silhouettes that Lily was in front, with one of the men riding close beside her. A second man rode just behind them towing the packhorse, which was limping badly.

It was no use. They were all too close to Lily. The Le Mat would spread the buckshot too wide over the distance, and my woman could be torn to pieces by it. But at that moment, the third man, who was riding slightly behind the others, pulled his mount to a halt and stared back down the trail, as if he had heard something that made him curious.

Satisfied, he seemed to shrug his shoulders and set spurs to his mount in order to catch up with the others. It was my chance! I laid the barrel of the gun in a V notch on the tree and waited. He was still a few yards behind the others as he rode into my sights and the report of the gun was like the almighty crack of a thunderbolt! It swept the man from the saddle as if a giant hand had smashed into him. The horse reared, and squealed in pain as some of the buckshot cut into its hide. Then it charged into the other horses, kicking and squealing.

I had a quick glimpse of Lily taking advantage of the mayhem as she screamed and kicked her horse into a gallop, but the man beside her was only moments behind Lily as he chased her out of my sight.

The force of the explosion spun the gun out of my hand, and before I could draw my other pistol the last man had released the packhorse and was charging toward me, firing his own pistol as fast as he could cock the hammer and pull the trigger.

Huge wooden splinters began to hum

around me as the bullets slashed into the tree, and I was forced to duck and run for my life. The thunder of the horse's hooves were loud in my ears as I twisted backwards and forwards through the trees, while the crash of undergrowth came ever nearer, and bullets continued to whine around me, or slap into trees as I passed. The firing stopped while the man must have drawn a second pistol and more bullets began to seek me out. Keeping my mind on the firing, I counted six shots; both his guns were empty and there was no time for him to reload. The breath was rasping in my throat as my tortured lungs desperately tried to pump air into my weakened body. I was near spent and the horse was still charging toward me as I managed to slip behind two trees, which were growing together.

Screaming pain shot through my shoulder as I used it against the trees to turn my body towards the rider. The Colt flowed into my hand, hammer coming back to full cock in a fluid easy movement as I raised it. But the horseman guessed my plan and had already turned his mount into the trees opposite, dodging between them like a madman as my bullets tried to cut him down.

My shots came close! The squeal of pain from his mount told me just how near I'd come to nailing the bastard; but then he was gone, and the forest became silent once more, except for the rasping of my tortured lungs and the throbbing, thumping pain in my head and shoulder.

In spite of the pain, my brain was still ticking over. I remembered the packhorse. It was lame so it was no use as a riding animal, but it carried the food! I forced my shaking legs to carry me back to where the pack animal was still standing, hip-shot, favoring its injured leg. I didn't look to see if anyone was close, and danger was beyond my understanding right then, as I slipped my pistol away and drew the Bowie knife.

There were three large packs, and one smaller one tied to the saddle. I cut all the ropes and allowed them to fall to the ground. My weakness would not allow me to lift any of the large packs, and even the smaller one sent waves of pain through me, but by crouching beside it I managed to get the strap over my good shoulder and stand upright.

In the background of my mind, I could hear Lily screaming and shouting farther down the trail. There was a noise that sounded like a slap and a mannish growl, followed by a heavy blow. I had to control my useless anger and force my mind to think of escape. My knife sliced through the saddle straps and I slapped the horse on the rump, sending it galloping down the trail towards the noises I'd been hearing, hoping to cause even more problems for my enemies, before leaving the trail and fading back into the forest.

My mind was seething with anger at the sound of the heavy blow I'd heard. The fact that Lily was no longer shouting made me sure that someone had hurt her, but there was nothing I could do! I'd have to be specially careful now. I could hardly stagger along carrying the pack, and the pain in my arm and shoulder was making me careless about tracks. But I couldn't afford to be careless, not even for a minute, or they'd track me to my cave. So, I forced my wandering mind back to watching for mistakes.

The two men would be surer than ever now, that I was hiding close by. Maybe they wouldn't know how weak I was, but they'd be able to make a damned good guess; and as I backed into my cave, my mind searched anxiously for anything I might have done wrong. My eyes, aching from the continuous pain, stared at the ground, looking for any telltale sign that might give me away. But I could see nothing to cause a problem, so I lowered myself onto the blanket, removed the pack from my shoulder and slumped against it, allowing the aching bones to relax, and the breath rasping in my throat to ease.

I had no idea what was in the pack, but I hoped it held something to eat. My taste buds began to drool at the thought of it, but with my luck, I'd probably stolen a tent or something just as useless. My stomach couldn't wait any longer, so I wriggled back to the cave wall, dragging the pack with me, and began searching through it.

A bag of Arbuckle. Man! Could I drink some of that! My mouth watered at the thought. A pack of hard tack was next. Unwrapping it I stuffed a piece in my mouth, and began to chew, while I dug deeper. Some sowbelly and beans was next; maybe I'd chance lighting a small fire in the cave, and it was a risk, but man oh man! The very thought of sowbelly and beans, with a good hot can of Arbuckle, damn near made me start dribbling.

There were four eggs in a small square box at the bottom of the pack; they slipped down my gullet one after the other. Slick as silk they were, and when I'd finished, a second piece of jerky followed 'em down. I was feeling better by the minute.

I gave up searching about then and eased my way back on to the blanket. Things seemed to be moving in my favor at last, I thought, as drowsiness began to sweep over me and I pulled the blanket close to keep out the damp cold of the night. Maybe it was the food pushing a new determination into my body, or maybe my shoulder was getting better. Whatever it was, I knew that, come hell or high water, I'd be after those two men come sun-up; and with those good thoughts, my mind eased as sleep dragged me down into a deep satisfying emptiness . . .

31

I came awake with the feeling that something was different! The bird noises were missing, and there were no animal noises either. My body felt rested for the first time since I'd been shot. I was tense and alert and looking for trouble as my hand slipped the Army Colt from its holster, thumb easing back the hammer as I reloaded. My eyes, used to the darkness of the cave, were flickering around, searching for something, anything, that had caused me to wake up so suddenly, but there was nothing.

Breath gusted from my mouth. I hadn't realized I'd been holding it, waiting for something to happen. Still not completely satisfied, I slowly stood up and eased towards the cave opening, the pistol in my good hand still cocked and ready to fire, as I stood just inside the screen of bushes. It was still dark outside as I pushed the bushes aside, and my body relaxed. A thick blanket of fog had settled in overnight, deadening all sound, and that was the reason for my anxiety. The normal forest noises were missing and that had pulled me out of my sleep.

Easing the hammer of my Colt, I slid it back into the holster. My taste buds were acting up at the thought of a good hot breakfast. With the heavy fog around, now was as good a time as any to take a chance on filling my stomach with some good tasty food; so, slipping out into the chill morning air, I fished around under some close-knit bushes, and raked up some small dry twigs and leaves. Past experience had taught me that even the heaviest rain would not get through a really dense bush close to the trunk.

My shoulder was not giving me too much trouble this morning, but I had to be careful not to get the arm raked by thorny bushes, and a man also had to be real careful where he put his hands. Some of the rocky places under bushes, where rattlesnakes like to hide from the cold, can be kind'a nasty; but, in next to no time at all, I had a cheerful, smoke-free fire burning at the back of the cave. I'd found the skillet in my own pack, and had filled my coffee pot with water from a tiny gully that had been filled by the run-off down the rocks at the side of the cave.

The heavy storms meant that the water was fresh and clean. Not that it mattered much to me either way, I thought, as I threw a good handful of Arbuckle into the boiling water, and enjoyed the beautiful smell of the coffee mixing with the smells coming from the skillet. I kept a wary eye on the cave opening while I was eating my chowder, and I made real sure the fire was out as soon as the meal was cooked, you can bet a stack on that. The last thing I needed was those two men catching me feeding my face.

Slipping on the duster coat to help keep out the cold, I eased aside the screen of bushes, and moved cautiously out into the fog. If anything, it was thicker now than it had been at first light. It was like a heavy blanket, deadening all sounds, which was maybe to my benefit because I knew where I wanted to go. Back to where the packhorse had been, if they'd left any trail at all that's where I'd find it. Just don't get lost in this Goddamned fog, I told myself, moving slowly forward into the thick mist.

Man! It was thick! The water was soon running down my duster coat like rain, as huge drops of moisture fell from the trees. I was just beginning to figure that I'd missed my way when I almost fell over the fella I'd shot. He was lying on his face. His two partners hadn't even bothered to bury him.

Trying my best to see into the fog, I turned the body over. The man was a stranger to me so I figured him for a bounty hunter and did a quick search. Maybe they hadn't bothered to bury the fella, but they sure-God didn't leave anything on him. My search came up empty.

Knowing I was in the right place gave me the confidence to move on down the trail, keeping my eyes as close as possible to the ground, looking for sign. I was right! They hadn't even tried to wipe out the sign. Hoof-marks and boot marks were all around the spot where I'd stolen the food pack. Casting around the area, I saw that they'd moved on down the trail, towards where I'd heard Lily shouting and cussing.

One set of tracks overlapped the other, and one horse had a limp. My mind was fixed on reading the signs as I moved slowly forward into the fog. Here the back two horses had met with those in front. A bit further on I could see where Lily had tried to get away from them by leaping from her horse. The small marks made by her shoes as she dug her toes into the soft earth; I could almost see her in my mind, powering away from the men in a mad dash for freedom.

One man's footmark was there also. The anger built in me when I saw where Lily had fallen, or was hit, or pushed to the ground. There were drag marks, where small stubborn heels had dug into the earth, still fighting to the last, before the horse tracks started off again every sense I had was concentrated on the hoof-marks. I half-noticed that the fog was gradually turning into mist as the rising sun was burning off the dampness in the air, but I ignored it.

The ground was rockier now, and the sign was getting harder to find as I turned into the beginnings of a long brush-choked canyon. But like a hound on the scent of a bear, every nerve was stretched, desperately wanting to find the end of the trail and get these men off my back once and for all. I was still carrying the pistol in my good hand, longing for the time when I could get those men in my sights as I moved around bushes and boulders, following tracks which were getting harder to find.

Then they petered out altogether! My brain screamed a warning as I scanned the trail ahead, searching for danger in the mist-covered gully. The bushes were closer here, almost closing the trail off completely. Changing the pistol to my left hand, so that I could push the bushes aside with my good arm, I moved slowly forward, every nerve tingling, waiting for something to happen as the branches snapped back across the trail behind me. I breathed a sigh of relief. There were the tracks, still ahead of me. A horse could push through these bushes easily, but on foot, it was tough going, so maybe I was worrying over nothing.

The duster coat was a big help, protecting me from the slap and scratch of branches and thorns as I eased farther into the canyon. The mist and fog was getting thicker the deeper I went into this cold, shaded hollow, but I figured it helped to cover my movements, just in case one of the two men I followed were watching their back-trail.

I stopped again as the warning signals flashed in my mind. One of the horses had turned away from the trail while the other three went straight ahead! My eyes started searching around me, but I could see nothing in the mist, which was weaving like smoke in the bushes. Pushing another branch aside with my good arm, I stepped into a small clearing. The warning screamed through my body as I heard a rustling behind me!

I started to turn, the pistol still in my injured hand. Every nerve in my body tried to force the gun towards the noise, but it was hopeless, and before I could take the pistol in my good hand, something heavy and solid slammed into my wounded shoulder.

Man! Nothing! No words in this whole Goddamned world could ever describe the pain that shot through my body. I could feel my eyes bugging out of their sockets. My mouth opened to scream but no sound came out. Then I was trying to suck air into starved lungs, as my mind slipped out of kilter and I collapsed in a heap. Through red-rimmed eyes, hazed with the pain, I stared up at the wavering figure of the man standing over me, with a thick branch in one hand and a gun in the other.

As the wavering slowly came to a stop, I recognized Matthew Franklyn. Everything I had was forcing me to concentrate on the man standing over me. He looked like something out of a nightmare with the mist weaving around him, holding the thick branch and staring down, the hatred burning into me.

'You killed Luke, damn your eyes, and I let you go free,' he growled, the bitter anger of his voice spilling over me.

I tried to answer him but only a kind'a gobbling noise came from my throat as the pain washed through my body again and again.

He touched my wounded shoulder with the log, setting fresh waves of pain crashing over me.

'I'm gonna kill you a little bit at a time, you son-of-a-bitch,' he snarled. Then he raised his head, and shouted to that other man farther along the trail. 'I've got the bastard and I'm gonna kill him. If you want to earn the reward I promised, you'd better kill his woman before I get to her. Otherwise, you're on a hiding to nothing, fella, d'you understand me?'

I heard a reply, muffled by the mist. The pain was beginning to lose its bite a little; it was Lily Matthew was ordering to be killed! That thought did more to clear my brain than anything else; it was like being douched in ice-cold water, freezing the thought of pain out of my mind.

The nerves in my good hand seemed to be working; it was close to the pocket of my duster coat. Matthew still had his head raised, staring up the trail, head cocked, as if he was listening to what was happening up there. Slipping my right hand slowly into the pocket, I gripped the pepperbox. It was my only chance!

The mist was helping to cover my movements and Matthew had grown careless. He was standing over me, his legs straddling my body. To his way of thinking, I was almost unconscious, badly wounded and unarmed.

Hell! With a thick branch in one hand and a pistol in the other, he had every right to get careless . . . Almost!

The pepperbox fitted into my big hand real

nice as it slid from the pocket. I'd only get one chance, so the bullet would have to go where it would cause the most damage; and there was Matthew, towering over me with his legs wide open.

Just one chance; because, if I missed, there might not be a time for a second.

I pulled the trigger . . . Nothing happened!

Matthew stared down at me. I could see fear and horror spreading over his face when he realized where I was pointing my little gun, and it was as if the thought froze his whole body for a few vital seconds.

Desperately, I pulled the trigger a second and third time. The explosion on the third pull reflected my own terror, and I went on pulling that damned trigger until the pistol was empty, although I knew Matthew was no longer standing over me. I had seen his groin burst open, as two bullets ploughed into his manhood, and I'd felt the heat of his blood splash my face as it poured over me, before the other bullets threw him backwards into the bushes.

There was the sound of a shot, followed by a woman's scream from somewhere ahead; it straightened out my senses. I pushed myself up on trembling legs and started to run through the mist that was curling around the trees and bushes. It seemed like I was running waist-deep through molasses. Trees flashed past me yet I did not seem to be moving. There was a scream in my throat, a long, drawn-out Noooo! But there was no sound coming from my mouth, only an aching, gut-wrenching sob.

I had no gun! My hand dropped to the Bowie, my only weapon, as I ran; the mist seemed to weave away and I saw Lily dash from one large boulder towards another. A second shot made her duck into cover, and, just for a moment, I saw the heavy dark bulk of a man. My trembling was gone as I powered toward him. Yet, I was not closing the gap fast enough.

Lily broke from cover. The man paused, took deliberate aim, and fired. I was only a few yards from the man, but I was too late!

Suddenly Lily was slapped to the ground!

My scream came out then, in a mighty roar of anger and despair against people, color, and life itself, as I drove the Bowie, right up to the hilt, into the man's kidney. In my crazy madness I pulled the knife out and put all my strength behind a second mad thrust into his other kidney. The man was still falling, with my knife in him, as I charged towards the body of my woman, great sobs welling in my throat.

Ignoring the pain in my shoulder, I threw

myself down beside her and cupped her body close to mine with my good arm, as the tears ran from me and dripped over her face.

I felt her move! By God, she moved! Yet there was so much blood running down her face! Her eyes flickered open, and in my excitement, I began calling her name.

She stared at me for a few seconds, her eyes blank. Then they cleared and she threw her arms around my neck, pushed her face against mine, and I could feel her tears against my face.

'By God, Joshua,' she muttered into my ear, 'you were so long comin', I just never thought you'd ever make it, man.'

'Baby I'd never give up on you. Never in a lifetime,' I muttered.

'An' you'd damn-well better not either, Joshua D,' she whispered. 'If I'm gonna be carryin' your babies I'm gonna be dependin' on you, mister, so don't you forget it.'

'I sure won't,' I agreed, feeling a happiness I'd never felt in my whole life, welling up inside me.

When I looked at the wound on Lily's head, I could see that the bullet had clipped along the side of her skull and the top of her ear was missing. She'd have one hell of a headache when the numbness wore off, but apart from that, she seemed to be OK.

A scrabble of movement behind me sent a cold shudder along my spine as I spun quickly around. The man should have been dead, but there he was, pulling himself into a sitting position against the bole of a tree. The man had almost killed Lily; he'd tried hard enough.

She started to get panicky as I climbed to my feet, but I patted her hand and told her there was something I had to do; I didn't tell her what, but the man would not be walking out of this canyon . . . ever!

As I moved toward him, I realized that there was something very familiar about the man, and when he tilted his head to one side I saw the pointy beard and the waxed pointed moustaches! 'Mister Jesse!' The words were torn from me.

'That you, Josh? Can't see too well old son, everything's kind'a blurred.'

I was already kneeling beside him. 'Hell, Mister Jesse, I done stabbed y'all.' My old way of speaking had slipped back without me thinking about it, in my concern. This man had taught me everything I knew. He was the only man who'd ever shown me any real kindness in my life.

'Where'd y'all come from, Mister Jesse?'

'I don't know, son. Last thing I seem to

461

remember was being in a confederate jail. Some place near Mobile. Is the war over, boy?' His eyes kept misting over. 'They tortured me real bad, Josh. Thought I was going mad there, for a while.'

He seemed to drift away for a short time, and when he looked at me again, I could see the madness in his eyes.

'You can damn well torture me all you want, you bastard,' he snarled. 'You'll get no information out of me, I'll break out of here, you'll see. Young Josh will be coming for me like he did in Virginia, fooled the lot of you that time, didn't he?' Then he started laughing, high and screechy, like a woman would laugh.

Lily came over and crouched by my side.

'He goes like this all the time, Josh,' she muttered. 'It's kind'a scary, huh? Reckon the old boy's mad clear through.'

'Maybe. But this is the guy I was telling you about in Atlanta. The man who saved my life, he taught me everything,' I replied.

'I know. He told me about it whenever he came out of the madness, but he soon slips into it again, then he changes into a different person. Scares the hell out of me. Man! He's fearsome then.'

'Josh?' The voice was very faint, so I leaned closer and he grabbed my coat. 'Listen, Josh, there's a guy after you. Don't let him catch you, boy, he's a nasty bastard. Said you killed his brother.'

'He's dead, Mister Jesse, and what's worse, I've stabbed you, too.'

The eyes cleared again, and the voice came over clear and strong. 'I know, Josh, and I'm glad you did. Don't cry for me, son, just be pleased that you helped me to die. I don't want the madness that's in me, you did me one big favor, fella.' His eyes closed and he seemed to be sinking, then he roused himself again.

'Just bury me here, Josh, there's a good fella.' He grabbed my coat again.

'Write about it, son,' he muttered, so quietly I could hardly hear him. 'Tell 'em all how useless war is. For God's sake don't let it ever happen again, Josh. Promise me you'll try, man.'

I was shocked. Me! Write about the war?

He shook my coat. 'You'll try, Josh. Promise?'

'Why, y-yes sir, Mister Jesse,' I muttered. 'If that's what y'all think I should do then I'll surely give it a try.'

His hand slipped from my coat and his head slumped forward. Blood flooded from his mouth. Mister Jesse had gone to his maker.

I sat back on my heels and tears ran down my face as I cried like a baby, unashamed of my tears in the loss of my good friend Mister Jesse.

Epilogue

I managed to get Lily and Mister Jesse back to the cave, using the horses belonging to Matthew.

Lily and I stayed there for four days, to build up our strength, and before we left, I laid Mister Jesse out on the floor and wrapped him in his own coaching coat. I knew, somehow, that it was the way he'd want it. Then I sorted out a pile of rocks and filled the narrow opening right to the top to keep out the animals.

We rode a long way, Lily and me, before we settled on our quarter section. Maybe we hadn't met with the preacher yet, but I'll tell a man, we're as married as anybody could be, and just to prove it, there's a squalling noise coming from the front yard. Guess that fool kid of ours has fallen down in the dirt again. You'd think he'd learn; but as many times as Lily scrubs him clean, that damned whippersnapper of ours comes back as black as can be — and that ain't supposed to be funny neither!

Mister Jesse would be real proud of me, with my quarter section, my good wife and young Jesse. Yep, that's what we called that boy of ours, right enough.

Everything seems peaceful just now, but I reckon Mister Jesse was right about wars being a waste of time. The differences between the Blue and the Gray is still there, and now Homesteaders like me and Lily are being called Nesters.

I hear tell that masked men wiped out a whole nester family only the other week, and their place burned to the ground.

I don't reckon it'll ever end till Hell freezes over. Still, I promised Mister Jesse I'd write it all down. It sure took some doing, but now, by God, I've got it done.

Yesterday I saw four mounted men on the hill yonder. Couldn't see who they were because the sun was in my eyes, but my next job is to clean up that good old Henry rifle of mine. Just in case!

We do hope that you have enjoyed reading this large print book.

Did you know that all of our titles are available for purchase?

We publish a wide range of high quality large print books including:
Romances, Mysteries, Classics
General Fiction
Non Fiction and Westerns

Special interest titles available in large print are:
The Little Oxford Dictionary
Music Book
Song Book
Hymn Book
Service Book

Also available from us courtesy of Oxford University Press:
Young Readers' Dictionary
(large print edition)
Young Readers' Thesaurus
(large print edition)

For further information or a free brochure, please contact us at:
Ulverscroft Large Print Books Ltd.,
The Green, Bradgate Road, Anstey,
Leicester, LE7 7FU, England.
Tel: (00 44) 0116 236 4325
Fax: (00 44) 0116 234 0205

THE ARTIST OF EIKANDO

Linda Lee Welch

Junko Bayliss is a potter, famous for her exquisite designs. From the outside, she is seen as a successful, independent artist, but from the inside, Junko knows that her personal life is a mess. When her elegant but emotionally cold parents die only a few minutes apart, Junko is left to ponder the question marks that always hovered over her parents' lives, and their strange behaviour towards their only child. When her Aunt Helen hints at a mystery — something shocking that happened to Diane and Peter Bayliss during the Second World War — Junko decides to visit Japan, where her parents met, and hunt out their story . . .